I0596961

GRIM AND PROPER

A HOPE SPRINGS MYSTERY

Shana Hellman

Hammett Lane   San Diego

Copyright © 2016 by Shana Hellman

All rights reserved. No part of this publication may be reproduced, distributed or transmitted in any form or by any means, without prior written permission.

Hammett Lane
330 J St, Suite 302
San Diego, CA 92101
www.hammettlane.com

Publisher's Note: This is a work of fiction. Names, characters, places, and incidents are a product of the author's imagination. Locales and public names are sometimes used for atmospheric purposes. Any resemblance to actual people, living or dead, or to businesses, companies, events, institutions, or locales is completely coincidental.

Book Layout © 2015 BookDesignTemplates.com

Grim and Proper/ Shana Hellman. -- 1st ed.
ISBN 978-0-9974417-1-0

To my extraordinary family—you are my heart and soul.
To Cathy, whose friendship has been one of my greatest blessings,
and who has given me endless support through the years.
To Diana, who understands me like no one else.
And to Lorraine and Cary, who listen with their hearts, and are
bright lights in this world.
Thank you all for everything.

CONTENTS

Chapter One

"I see...death."

My breathing stopped at the woman's words. What? Was everything I had been told before true? Panic suddenly set in, and I could feel my breakfast moving up the walls of my stomach and into my throat.

Her dark eyes gazed straight into mine, aloof and unblinking. Squat, ring-less fingers hovered an inch above the tablecloth, moving slightly, tracing unknown patterns in the air.

The words started to pound through my head and my heart started to flit around in my chest. It couldn't be true. It just couldn't. Why wouldn't death just leave me alone?

This fear had followed me for years. But it hadn't beaten me completely yet, and I wasn't going to let it beat me now. I was determined not to make the obituaries this year.

"What? Is that my whole fortune?" I looked at her in dismay, hoping to confirm that I had misheard or there was more information forthcoming. I must have misheard. "Don't I get long life, undying love, a massive fortune? What about a little happiness? Anything good at all?"

"Death," she repeated, her nostrils flaring as she spit out the word.

Vague unease crept past my defenses...this was too similar to that other time, that other prediction. Death was stalking me! If it was true, and they were both right, I now had less than a year to live. Something terrible really was going to happen to me.

"Death will find you," the woman had said so long ago. And now it was happening all over again. A bubble of fear stuck in my throat and I began to repeatedly mumble, "Think happy, be happy" in a low hum, reassuring myself that as long as I could still speak, I could still breathe.

"Quiet. I'm not done." She took a monumentally deep breath and closed her eyes, rubbing her sweaty palms along the smooth surface of the crystal. "Here it comes again. Wait, wait...I have it now. Death...Death will be your friend. He hovers close to you, waiting to pounce."

It took a few moments for the words to penetrate, so intent was I on her expression. I felt I was watching a bad "B" movie, and for several seconds I was completely under her spell. And then I heard her— truly heard her. 'Waiting to pounce?' What was that? Give me a break. No one really talked like that. A little of the fear dissipated. She was nothing but a con, a fake. This woman simply watched way too much daytime television. As a matter of fact, I think I might have even seen her on Jerry Springer once—yes, even I occasionally watched that train wreck of a TV show though I would never have admitted it in public. I wanted to push myself out of the chair and storm out, like a tempestuous heroine in a romance novel, but that part of me fixated on my own death kept me from moving. What if she was right?

"What exactly does that mean? Death hovers close to me, waiting to pounce? Am I going to die? Should I be extra careful crossing the street? Go see a doctor? What?"

The fortune teller shrugged her shoulders. "The crystal ball tells me only one thing." She paused for dramatic effect. "Death will be your friend." Her voice bellowed out the last few words, and the flimsy card table rattled slightly as my knees jumped in response.

The hell it will be! I consider cheesecake more of a friend, and we only socialize a couple of times a year. Death by chocolate was one thing, becoming friends with the grim reaper was another. I was not going to give in to fear again.

Since I could find no appropriate PG verbal response, I decided to settle for righteous outrage. I had seen my mother use this tactic often enough. Heaven knew it always worked wonders on me. "You can not be serious." I even raised an eyebrow—or at least I tried and thought it might have partially succeeded.

She clicked her tongue and tossed her hand into the air, as if throwing my disbelief somewhere in the distance behind her. "I am paid to tell you what I see. I am not paid to tell you what you want to hear."

I didn't agree with that. A good fortune was exactly what she was being paid to tell me. That was what everyone paid psychics for—to hear that their lives were going to turn out just as they hoped. If people wanted to hear the depressing truth they would study Nietzsche or watch the ten o'clock news. Like most people, I preferred to meander along in the belief that my life (or what remained of it according to this fortune teller) was going to be happy, and that good people had good things coming to them. I had spent the last ten years trying to believe that I was due for some good fortune, and I did not want any illusions shattered--especially today. And especially not by some crackpot wearing a bad gypsy costume and smiling at me like a plump Mata Hari. I needed a good reading this time. I needed to know the old reading was wrong. I needed to hear that I would be fine and live a long and productive life well into my nineties.

"But that can't be it. 'Death is your friend' isn't a proper reading. That's only four words for goodness sakes," I stammered.

"Oh, and you wrote the handbook on psychic predictions?" I think she actually looked pleased at my discomfiture.

"Of course not, but everyone knows that you get more than that. A fortune cookie would give me more information than that, and include lottery numbers."

"But not accurate information. And as for lottery numbers, that is just pure luck. My gift tells me you will never have that kind of luck." She gave me a sly, triumphant look, and I felt a wave of revulsion go through me. This woman was obviously used to conning customers. I was just another patsy, and what was worse, a willing one.

A sudden desire to walk out and slam the door possessed me. But I was more dignified than that, and unfortunately too old for tantrums. I just couldn't be that rude, no matter how badly I tried, literally. Clinically, it just didn't seem possible for me. Even if I could overcome my OPD (Obsessive Politeness Disorder—honed into me by my mother while still in the womb I suspect), there wasn't a door to slam, just a flimsy tent flap hanging on a curtain rod.

The thought of that curtain rod brought my surroundings into sharp focus, and with it, reality. The psychic's tent wasn't special, it was just an average plastic creation, dirty at the edges from the fingerprints of numerous visitors. I had seen enough of these tents at weddings and garden parties. Cleaner ones, of course. And now that I thought about it, her tablecloth was checkered, just like the kind my mother would put on a picnic table when I was little. It was really very commonplace. She was just a middle-aged woman earning a living off of people's desire to know what was going to happen. Like most people, when I was younger I thought I wanted to know my future. Now I wasn't so sure.

"If that's the whole prediction, then I'll go." My absolute need for common courtesy forced a stiff "Thank you, Ma'am," from my lips. I stood up and automatically smoothed out non-existent wrinkles from my dress.

The fortune teller stood up with me, holding out her chubby hand. Even though I tried to pretend I didn't see it, my hand still somehow met hers, and I grasped her sweaty palm. I envisioned her sneezing into her hand and not cleaning it, and jerked my hand back abruptly. And then I was embarrassed at my rudeness and blushed a little in shame.

I could feel her calculating eyes boring into mine, weighing what she was going to say next. "Now, don't be alarmed. I didn't say you were going to die, did I? That is just one possibility. Your fortune can be interpreted in several ways. Maybe you will be lucky and someone close to you will die. Do you have any sick relatives?" That didn't seem very lucky to me.

"No?" she prodded. "Oh well. A career change? Are you applying for a job at a funeral parlor? No?" I shook my head and she smiled sympathetically at me. "Don't give up hope. Maybe it will be a quick and painless death." She winked at me and laughed a little, though I didn't find anything humorous about it.

I had no idea what to say. My mother would know what to say to that. My mother always knew what to say. I just stared at the woman, looking like a supreme idiot.

"I hope you have a nice birthday," she said, all dramatics now finished. "That's twenty dollars, please."

I reluctantly handed over the cash and she thanked me, but only after holding the bill up to the light for an insultingly long time. Then she proceeded to check her face in a small mirror that was hooked on the back of her chair, and ran her tongue over her teeth. I noticed an abundance of yellow stains and quite a bit of overlap. She was a walking poster for teeth whitening and dental hygiene.

I was dismissed, so I muttered my thanks and stepped outside into the sunlight, hoping I wasn't damning myself to death by skin cancer.

Chapter Two

Courtesy has two meanings: something done out of politeness, and something given free of charge. Unfortunately, the first kind of courtesy is rarely free of charge. The cost comes from tedious discussions about honeymoons that don't interest you since you weren't there, baby photos of a child you are not related to and will never meet, and complaints of illnesses that are so detailed they are likely to create hypochondriacs out of all who hear them. And there is nothing more insensitive than a coworker who takes advantage of those long-suffering people (that would be me) polite enough to ask questions out of simple courtesy.

That's not to say that on a rare occasion I haven't been highly amused by anecdotes about a ski trip laden with disaster or found myself interested in hearing about an illness that I realized a friend of mine was also suffering from. But again, those occasions are usually very, very rare.

However, I was raised to have good manners, and having realized at an early age that politeness offers other people tiny slices of happiness, I almost always find myself compelled to exert my energies in this direction. Someone once told me this compulsion (my OPD) isn't because I am a particularly nice person, but because it gives me a sense of control (it was probably my mother who said it). And yet, there are times when I am unbearably bored by my coworkers' gifts of gab. This is one of the problems with writing a column about etiquette. I can make the column humorous, sarcastic, and, on occasion, even informational, but that doesn't change what it is really about—how to go through life offending as few people as possible. Because of this, people expect me to ask questions about their everyday lives as soon as I see them, and then they take it for granted that I will listen expectantly while they drone on about their weekend or their son losing his first tooth and how they were terrified for a whole minute that he had accidentally swallowed it. And I do exactly as they expect. I smile and nod and generally make them feel good. And most of the time it's worth it.

Sometimes it's not.

So when I stepped off the sidewalk on Broad Street and walked into the cluttered offices of The Pennsylvania Standard Press, and was immediately accosted by Veronica Sorenson, the newest secretarial assistant for the Entertainment and Lifestyle sections of the paper, I knew I was in for a really long conversation—the kind that you nod and grunt at the appropriate times, while actually thinking about a polite way of excusing yourself.

Veronica, who was young and eager to please, had quickly become popular with the writers because she was willing to do extra research and make lots of tiring calls to confirm phone numbers, addresses, and the spelling of unusual names. And she didn't complain. However, she talked a lot. I mean a lot. More than anyone I have ever met. And it was usually non-stop.

Today it began like this: "Hey, Hope. Did you have a good weekend? I did. I went down to the beach with my boyfriend. He thought it would be too cold, but it was fine. I told him that it was quite warm for early May and the beach wouldn't be so bad. And I was right. The drive was pretty tiresome though," she went on, "but it was worth it. We would have gotten there faster if I had driven, but he wouldn't let me. I don't know why. I'm a better driver than he is. Men! I don't understand them."

At this point she paused for air, and it was as if I could see her sucking all the oxygen away from the people moving rapidly past her.

I moved to her right to pick up my mail from behind a large desk holding an equally large man, and she scooted along next to me, eager to tell someone about her exciting plans. "Don't move, Tom. Hope needs to get her mail." She gestured to him to remain seated. "No, no, you're fine. Just don't move or roll your chair back. Just keep working." Another gulp of air was sucked out of the room, ostensibly limiting Tom's breathing. He just looked up at her, grunted, and went back to what he had been doing. "As I was saying, Hope, we almost crashed when some trucker pulled in front of us. I guess we were in his blind spot. But we made it to the beach in one piece and had a really great clam bake. A couple of my friends came along, too. They went down in a separate car though, thank God. And then we stayed the night there. Not on the beach, since I think that's illegal. My parents have a house along the shore and let me use it when they aren't there, which is pretty nice of them, except that they let my sister use it too, and she is always there. I don't know if you have a sister, but they can be real pains in the ass. Excuse my bad language."

For some reason people always feel obliged to apologize to me for bad language and spotted clothing. My mom says it's because I have a genteel air; my friend Jilly says it's because I give off a conservative vibe. I'd prefer refined, tasteful, or even practical. I'm definitely not perfect, and while I do try to watch my language (my mother having been somewhat successful in drilling decent English into my head), I have my share of verbal obscenities, spotted blouses, and damp, crumpled hand towels. And I like a good party as much as the next person. To put it bluntly, no convent would take me.

Veronica continued along in the same vein, describing every little detail of her experience at the beach and throwing in some examples of atrocities her sister had committed, as well as a few apt expressions, for which she then rapidly apologized.

We had simultaneously made our way to the second floor, where the Entertainment and Lifestyles section hobnobbed alongside the copyeditors. Or so we liked to think. In actuality, I was required to share a large work desk with three other employees: the weekly book reviewer; the weekly fashion columnist; and the daily crossword/games editor. We all "worked from home" and for the most part were glad of it.

Before reaching my desk, Veronica changed subjects, raised her voice to be heard over any nearby babble, and began inquiring into the protocol of office birthdays. "Hope, I'm so glad you came in today. It's Alice's birthday. You know, Alice from the Editorial Staff." She made them sound like royalty the way she over-hyphenated the words. "And we wanted to know if we were required to get her a small gift." She made a hand gesture that seemed to include the few stragglers milling around the office, but no one seemed to really be paying attention. "The Editorial Staff has pitched in to buy her a gift certificate to a restaurant, but no one else thought of doing anything."

Since being forced to spend money on someone you barely know is of great importance to most people, the few people who were within earshot suddenly snapped to attention.

"No. Etiquette does not require that you do so." This is one of my favorite things to say, simply because it sounds terribly impressive--as if I were a lady from a hundred years ago wearing a corset and a stiff gown, wagging a fan about and raising my eyebrows at all manner of innocuous things. But, according to my mother, I was not a lady in that very traditional sense. My mother insisted it was a quality one was born with, and which I most definitely lacked. So my mother finally gave into her lifelong despair of ever making me that kind of lady, and simply taught me the conventions of etiquette.

Several people looked relieved at having been able to save a few bucks. "Actually, the newspaper has a small fund set aside to buy employees flowers on their birthday, and they claim it's from the entire staff. You're covered."

Veronica threw in an amazed, "Really? Everyone? How do you know? Is it in the employee handbook?"

I never actually read the employee handbook. I'm not sure anyone actually employed at the paper had ever read it. As far as I could tell, it was simply for figuring out how to locate the fire extinguishers and the nearest escape routes (which are always blocked by broken copy machines anyway). "No. I asked about birthdays shortly after I started working here." When I first got the job as the etiquette columnist I was so gung-ho and eager to impress that I thought it would look bad if I forgot a co-worker's birthday. And I baked for every holiday—for everyone. And wrote thank you notes for everything anyone did. That got old really fast.

You can't remember everybody's birthday. And so the beauty of monthly office birthday parties.

"Thank God. I'm broke this month and I am not spending any money on that stupid cow if I don't have to," piped in a voice I immediately recognized.

Sally Jordan, the crossword/games editor, simply by her frequent presence at our desk, had become a friend of mine, and we greeted each other enthusiastically. She nodded at Veronica with a little less enthusiasm, apparently having already been forced to listen to version one of the beach escapade. "Why would you spend money on a gift for someone you barely know? And don't even like. It's the stupidest thing I ever heard."

I secretly agreed with Sally, though I wouldn't admit it in front of the others. I headed to the far end of the room, where an attractive row of narrow, but tall, windows looked onto Broad Street. I sat down at one side of the massive desk and relieved myself of my purse and mail by throwing it in a heap at my elbow. Sally, noticing this and smirking at me, finally interrupted Veronica, who had followed us and started to discuss whether or not the sports editor had acquired a hicky on his neck, or if he was simply suffering some skin disease.

"Really, Veronica, no one wants to hear about that! Can't you talk about something more pleasant—like people starving in Nigeria?" Sally demanded.

"I thought it was Ethiopia," was Veronica's only response, and Sally gave her a look of disgust before turning her attention back to me.

"Hey, Hope, do you think you could do me a huge favor? My family is going out of town in a few weeks and I agreed to housesit. The only problem is that I also promised to go to D.C. with my fiancée that weekend. His college roommate is getting married and we've known about it for ages. I just forgot that it was on *that* particular weekend. Can you please help me out? You don't really have to do much, just go over on Saturday afternoon and walk my parents' dog. Oh, and feed him too. No scooping poop or anything like that. And he's a schnauzer, so you don't have to worry about him being unfriendly. You've met him before, right? At the barbeque I threw last month?"

"The grayish-black one with the white stomach?"   My

mind was actually saying, 'The one that peed on my purse? The one that I consigned to hell several times?'

I would have preferred to pretend I had never met the dog, because the incident still caused my coworkers to snicker whenever it was brought up. I wondered if I should write a column listing all the reasons one should never put one's purse on the floor.

"Yeah. He's a sweetie, isn't he?" Sally gave me a pleading look. She knew I hated that dog. "Please say you can do it. I've tried everyone else I know already." Dramatics coming from Sally were a big deal, so I considered helping her out. But then she added, "You're my last hope. Hehe. Get it? Hope--like your name."

I just stared at her.

"Not funny, right? And everyone says it?" Her cheeks took on a slightly redder hue and she bit her lip. "I'm desperate here."

I sighed and gave her a wan smile and she perked up a little, and started to do some sort of dance moves. She looked like she was doing the funky chicken and the robot in one.

"Sorry. It won't ever ask you to pet sit again. But I really am in a bind."

I nodded. "Okay. It shouldn't really take too long and they don't live that far from my parents. Are you sure that's all I have to do? Just walk him and feed him?" I really hoped he wouldn't tear the house apart and leave large piles of gifts inside for his owners, making me look like a crappy dog sitter.

"Yeah. Like I said, it shouldn't be a big deal."

Right. Those words usually indicated the exact opposite. It probably was a big deal and I was in for it.

"Why couldn't you find anyone else to do it? Like your parents' neighbors? Surely not everyone is going out of town?" Maybe I could still get out of it.

"No. It's not that. It's just that Weasel goes crazy if he sees other dogs around. He's an absolute chicken. He panics and then runs and hides. But don't worry, it never takes too long to find him. And most of the neighbors just didn't want to have to walk their dogs and then go walk another dog." She sounded like she couldn't understand how anyone could not want to walk dogs more than once a day.

"Well, exercise is good for me. I haven't gotten enough walking in lately." This was yet another instance of mind and mouth functioning on different levels. My mouth agreed while my mind was still looking for a plausible excuse to get out of it. I briefly contemplated arguing that my cat would object to me smelling like a dog, but that was about as paltry an excuse as they come.

"Thank you so much. You're the best. I'll tell you what, I'll take you to lunch today as a thank you." This was pretty effusive for Sally, so I felt a little less put-upon.

"I can't today. I'm having lunch with my mother. I'm only here to drop off my work for the week and pick up my mail."

Once a week my mother and I have lunch together so that she can quiz me on my love life and I can learn the virtue of forbearance. It's not that my mother and I have an antagonistic relationship. We don't. She is simply stuck in a time warp, wondering why I have only partially conformed to her standards and am still single. And when I am with her I am stuck in the fifth grade, wanting my mother to be pleased with me. I'm not willing to bat my eyelashes at men, cast them shy glances, and continually drop my purse to get their attention, and she isn't willing to let the subject go. One of us would have to cave eventually, and I was determined that it not be me.

But if I intended to go over my work with my editor in time to make it to lunch with my mother, I would actually have to start the process. "Is Ari in his office?"

"Yeah, but he's got Eugene with him. When I walked by I could hear them chortling over some stupid joke or other. They are probably in there smoking cigars and reminiscing about how good it would be if they old boys club still ruled the world," Sally said. She wasn't particularly fond of some of the decisions Ari had made lately and had been pretty vocal about them to anyone who would listen.

I frowned. "I can't wait all day. It *would* be Eugene in there. I just hope he decides to go unfairly criticize some restaurant in the next few minutes."

Eugene Schreier was the food and wine critic, though he preferred his colleagues to refer to him as the 'in-house gourmand'. When my best friend, Jillian, opened a restaurant called The Bon Vivant several years ago, Eugene, in a fit of snobbery (the hostess, not knowing who he was, did not seat him right away), gave it a slightly-less-than-mediocre review. The clientele seemed to disagree with him, though, and still does, because Jilly does a good business. But the review still rankles with me, if not with Jilly, and I have never really forgiven Eugene for his contemptuous attitude.

"Don't get your hopes up. He brought his own lunch today. Well, he brought *a* lunch. It's from some fancy-schmancy place in Manayunk. I think he must be friends with the owner because I wouldn't think a place like that did take-out." Sally felt uncomfortable in fancy restaurants, and had a pretty limited palate, so she had never found much in common with Eugene and mostly ignored him.

I, on the other hand, would eat my way around the planet if I could. Normally a person like Eugene, who appreciated good food, would be someone I would enjoy conversing with, but Eugene has that rare ability to get on my nerves *and* make me lose my temper. There are plenty of people that can annoy me, but few can rouse me to extreme emotions. There was just something about Eugene that got under my skin. His attitude, maybe. His slightly smarmy appearance. His overly-refined speech. Or maybe just the fact that he didn't like me and I knew it.

I wasn't about to go interrupt Ari and Eugene, so I turned my attention back to Veronica, who had lapsed into a surprising silence. She was alternating between picking cat hair off of her sweater and casting quick glances at her empty desk.

"Veronica, what is the easiest way to look up a genealogy?" I asked, wondering all the while what was so fascinating about the empty desk.

She blinked at me. "What? Why? Are you trying to research your ancestors? They have services for that. My mom had one done for my whole family. She didn't bother with my father's side though."

"Your mom would probably hit it off really well with mine," I said, wondering if Veronica was anything liker her mom. It didn't sound like it. "My mom did a genealogy of our family, too, but it included my dad's side. She said that was the only way he would pay for it."

Sally snorted at that, but didn't say anything. Veronica just nodded empathetically.

"I actually need to find out about the family of a client. It's for a ridiculously detailed wedding announcement." I sighed. I hated writing those kind of things.

"Whose?" Veronica asked.

"Colby Raines and Evan Whittington. Colby's mother wants a large spread in the social column. She probably thinks it will help her husband's political career. He's running for the governor's office."

Sally knew the names and looked unconvinced. She snorted. "Maybe, but most likely she wants to tout her self-importance to all the morons that read the social column." She quickly lowered her voice in case others might hear her deprecatory remarks about the social column. "And I've heard some of those speeches her husband has given. Talk about middling. He never seems to take a stance on anything. It seems to me that the whole family is a bunch of good-for-nothings that society could do without." Sally gave a "So there!" nod and went back to what she had been doing.

Veronica was still focused on the part of the conversation that involved weddings, her most favored topic recently. "I didn't realize writing a wedding announcement was part of your job. Is it for the event planning you've been doing? Couldn't you just give the information to the social columnist and have her do it?" she asked.

"Usually, but I specifically agreed to do it. And if I hadn't agreed, I would probably hear from the bride's mother for the rest of my life about how I didn't do it and handed it over to some stranger."

My expression clearly showed my disgust for Susan

Raines, the mother of the bride, and my increasing disgust for myself. Note to self: Pride does not goeth before a fall. It riseth up unexpectedly and then trips you until you fall. A monetary need to take on work doing event planning was quickly bringing down my self-worth and I hated it.

"Close to the family, are you?" Sally said sarcastically.

She was laughing at me, the ingrate!

"No. I've known them for about fifteen years, but we are *definitely* not close." I slowly and deliberately moved my head from side to side to emphasize the point.

"*Those* kind of friends. I see. Maybe I can help you," Veronica said enthusiastically. "I have some extra time on my hands right now. And I have done this kind of thing lots of times before." Veronica looked like a puppy given a bone. It was really rather endearing.

"Veronica, you're a life saver. I wasn't even sure how I was going to go about it. But don't do it if you don't have time. I can do it, you know. I don't want you to be put out."

"No, it's fine. Unlike you, my boss is on vacation until the end of the month. I really do have some spare time. I just need as many details as you can give me."

I launched into a slightly incomprehensible history of the Raines and Whittingtons as far as I knew, while Veronica copiously took notes and Sally watched with a look somewhere between amusement and fascinated horror.

After several minutes had passed in this fashion, the door to Ari's office opened slightly, and then stopped, a hand on the inside knob pausing to respond to a low-voiced question. Veronica practically ran to her desk, sliding into her chair and setting her hands instantly upon her keyboard, and Sally shuffled the papers on her desk, hoping the noise would make her appear busy.

When the door finally opened enough for a body to step through, a slightly balding man in his late forties stepped through. He was of average height, slightly chubby, though this fact was only noticeable in his hands and cheeks, and his most distinguishing feature was a hawk shaped nose. He was wearing a suit and tie, with a handkerchief neatly folded in his front pocket, and his shoes were thoroughly polished. By and large he was a decent looking man, possessing quick, intelligent eyes, and a ready smile. But the smile was seldom directed at people, being saved primarily for the dog at his side: a medium-sized poodle mix named Jezebel. No one had yet figured out what breed contributed to the 'mix' in Jezebel's ancestry, and Eugene wasn't telling.

In his left hand he held a small brown bag with paper handles, as well as a thick, plastic bag with indistinguishable red lettering on one side. A pleasant odor was streaming from the plastic bag, and I assumed it was Eugene's special lunch.

It was such a silly thing for him to be proud of. What you ate didn't make you a better person. And suddenly I was annoyed with Eugene and then annoyed with myself for being annoyed.

With his hand now resting on the outer doorknob, Eugene surveyed the assembled employees but didn't approach anyone.

He probably doesn't have anyone to talk to. How sad! A stab of pity surged briefly through my heart before I squashed it.

It's his fault, my personal little devil said. He could try to be nicer.

I briefly wondered if my prejudice was getting in the way of my judgment, but as Eugene's eyes lit upon me, and he quickly glanced away before returning his gaze to me, I knew that it was not one-sided. The only thing I had ever really liked about Eugene was the fact that occasionally he behaved as if I didn't exist, ignoring me completely. I won't pretend that I didn't hear him making snide remarks about my column several times a month, but since the comments were usually both humorous and accurate, I felt that I wasn't really justified in taking offense. If you can't laugh at yourself, you have no right to laugh at the foibles of others, and there are times when I find my column, even my life, completely ridiculous.

But I still couldn't like Eugene.

"I guess I had better get in there now, before someone else beats me to it." I made a quick survey of the room, trying to divine whether or not one of my coworkers intended to beat me to the office.

"True. But watch out for Eugene. I know he usually ignores you, but he looks like he's still in a fighting mood. I forgot to tell you earlier, but he's on the war path," Sally said.

"He's always on the war path. What happened this time? Did he leave his pooper-scooper at home again? Because if he did, he's out of luck. I don't have any extra plastic bags or handy wipes."

Sally shook her head, though whether in negative or bemused exasperation was not clear. "I don't know why the management lets him bring a mangy dog into a business office. Eugene's not blind. He doesn't need a seeing eye dog."

"I like his dog. She's the best thing about him. I bet she could write his reviews just as well as he does."

"Be nice, Hope. This isn't like you. Eugene's not so bad. At least most of the time he isn't." Sally's obviously didn't believe that, and she was rolling her eyes and giving me a rueful smile as she said it. "Since you asked," she turned to make sure Eugene was still far enough away that our conversation was private, "he's been in a foul mood all morning. Remember that lunch I told you about. Well, he left it in the refrigerator in the employee lounge. Without his name on it. Of all the dumb things to do! And when someone ate part of it he went ballistic. He insulted just about everyone on the floor, demanding the perpetrator be denounced. I would have laughed so hard if I hadn't been one of the people he accused."

I contemplated this information. I hadn't been here so he couldn't accuse me, but still...

"Maybe I can walk around him. I can pretend that I want to speak to someone on the other side of the room and do a circle."

"Uh-oh. Too late now. Here he comes."

Sally was quite right. Eugene was striding purposefully toward us, a small grimace on his face. Jezebel followed at a more sedate pace, keeping directly behind the lunch bag, obviously hoping to catch any chance droppings without her master knowing.

"I've been waiting all morning for you to show up, Hope. It's nearly lunch time." He raised an eyebrow at me.

I can't believe he's scolding me for my tardiness!

"I had things to do. Ari doesn't care when I come in." Why was I justifying myself to him?

"I wanted to give you this." He dropped the brown bag on the desk in front of me. "Since I used your last ones, I bought you some new wet wipes."

I was looking both pleased and surprised, but the pleasure faded abruptly when Eugene put on an ironical smile. "That is what a well-mannered person does, isn't it? I would hate for you to publicly denounce me as a loutish boor."

As if I ever actually said something like that. Actually, I wish I could remember to say things like that. "I'm sure you could never be loutish, Eugene."

Sally snickered, but Eugene's face remained perfectly still. He bent slightly to pet Jezebel, who sidled next to him, and then straightened, a look of delight in her eyes. I could see Eugene prepare to launch a verbal attack that would undoubtedly flatten me, but before his mouth could even open, someone on the far side of the room called out to him. "Eugene, come over here and help us settle an argument, will you?"

"Excuse me, ladies, but I am needed elsewhere. Jezebel, come." His shoes clicked as he turned and strode away, Jezebel tagging behind him, her nose nearly touching the bag.

"It was nice of him to buy you those wipes. It was the right thing to do."

I looked down at the bag in front of me. "I know. And he even bought the same brand. I guess that's pretty thoughtful. But still..."

"He just likes making fun of you because he knows you are too smart to take this life as seriously as the rest of this crew--and because you can call him on his pretentiousness. You're not exactly an easy target. Look at how he ignores Veronica as if she were not worth his time. I bet he thinks she can't even recite the alphabet." Sally looked like she also didn't think Veronica could recite the alphabet.

"But if he actually spent time talking to her—"

"Forget it, Hope. He won't. Give over on the guilt. He insulted you first. And don't pretend that insulting him back didn't give you at least a small amount of pleasure. Your guilt complex is worse than mine. Not that that's saying much." She shook her head again. "I am so glad your mother didn't raise me."

"I bet you are. You never would have made it out of the house in those blue jeans. She hated the day I left high school because not only was I out of her daily scrutiny, but I no longer had to wear a uniform. I went crazy and bought so many pairs of blue jeans I thought she would have an apoplexy." I sighed gleefully. "Ah, the good times."

"And yet you continue to have lunch with her?" Sally was the sort of person who cut family ties as soon as they began to choke. I didn't have the heart to do that. I was more likely to offer up my neck instead.

"She is my mother. And she does love me, despite my gross failure at finding a husband at an early age. Besides, she usually pays."

Sally laughed. "It all becomes clear."

"And on that note, I had better see Ari. Otherwise I will be late. And if that is the case, she will probably make *me* pay."

I expected the conversation with my editor to be over in a few minutes, but he was in a garrulous mood. By the time I did escape, I had promised to write several extra columns on pre-decided topics, had explained for the umpteenth time why scratching anywhere below the waist was inappropriate in public, and had explained to him exactly why his wife was correct in insisting that when a person says, "We must do this more often," he or she really means that he had a good time despite prior misgivings, and would not mind doing it again as long as it was next year, and not next week. Ari didn't understand women and for some inexplicable reason felt comfortable asking me to explain to him just about everything his wife said to him.

The time was considerably advanced when I practically threw myself out the door of my boss' office, scooped up my belongings, and dodged several staff members who were carefully balancing a birthday cake and a trio of pink balloons.

I was far too conscious of the exact amount of time it would take me to get to the restaurant where I was meeting my mother, when Veronica came bouncing up to me. "I heard you telling Sally where you were having lunch today, and I remembered that I ate there a few months ago. As if I could forget it. I'm pretty sure I got food poisoning from the food there. It could have been what I had for breakfast that day, but I don't think so. I don't usually eat much for breakfast. But I remember that lunch I had the Caesar salad with shrimp. You don't forget something like that when it makes you sick as a dog. When I was eating it I thought it was pretty good, though. But I guess you can't always tell if something has gone bad. My boyfriend had the spinach salad and he was fine. So it was probably the shrimp. The spinach salad had bacon, I think, not shrimp, which was probably why he was okay."

I should tell her I'm going to be late if I don't leave now, I thought. Before she catches her breath again.

But Veronica seemed to catch her breath quicker than the average human. "It was the most horrible thing ever. At first I just got some cramps, kind of like period cramps, and then I got diarrhea..."

I tuned her out at this point, wondering what made her think I wanted a list and description of her ordeal. Some things were definitely left better unsaid, and food poisoning came second only to the reasons why your boyfriend was dumping you.

To my ears, the ticking of my watch began to grow deafening, reminding me with every loud tick that I was going to be late, and with every loud tock that I was probably going to have a parking ticket from an expired, over-priced meter.

I had never envisioned Eugene in the light of a savior, but as he walked up to Veronica and I, hope sprang to life in my breast. Here was a way of tactfully ending this conversation and thereby making my appointment on time. "Eugene, Veronica has just been telling me about an incident of food poisoning at one of our local restaurants."

Eugene raised an eyebrow in that wondrous way that

said, "You wish me to speak to you about such a trivial subject? En garde, you fool. I will vanquish you for such impudence." Luckily for me, the eyebrow was directed at Veronica.

"Is that so?" He politely set his lunch, which he had been delicately carrying under his arm, down on the table, and pulled Jezebel out of the walkway.

"Yes. She should tell you all about it, just in case you want to do a follow-up review of the place." I've done it! I can wave goodbye and walk down those stairs, minus feelings of guilt for deserting Veronica.

"It wasn't your friend Jillian's restaurant was it? I've been thinking of going back there and seeing what makes it so popular." He pretended to look thoughtful. "I wonder if the menu has changed since I was there last. It could only be an improvement."

That was too much! I moved a step closer to Eugene, ignoring the fact that I was only inches from Jezebel's tail, and looked him over with my haughtiest glare (the one my mother taught me). Two could play at this game. "It's fortunate that you have found a job that requires very little brain power. If only the rest of us could make a living off of our taste buds. Superior taste buds, in your case, or course." My smile dripped hauteur.

"I'm not sure you would enjoy it, Hope. You already eat alone so often, doing it even more frequently might make you feel even more despair, as if your life was slowly wasting away. It wouldn't be good for your mental state." He returned the smile.

"You would know about that, Eugene, and could advise me best on the matter." Now neither of us was smiling.

"Uh, excuse me, Mr. Schreier? If you want me to tell you about the restaurant, I will. It was a couple of months ago, but you never know." I should hug Veronica for stepping so bravely into the foray, but that would probably make me even later.

Eugene seemed as anxious to depart as I did. "Unfortunately, young lady, I do not have time now." It was quite obvious Eugene wasn't even attempting to be either fatherly or a gentleman, but had merely forgotten Veronica's name. "Hope will have to be your audience. She loves hearing about those kinds of things." He gave me a smug smile, urged Jezebel forward, and walked nonchalantly down the stairs.

"But Hope's already heard most of it," Veronica called after him.

"Tell her again," came the low response. And Eugene disappeared from view, leaving me muttering to myself, and Veronica looking as if she just might tell me again.

I wasn't about to stay and hear the story repeated, so I uttered a hurried goodbye and started toward the first step.

"Oh, wait. Hope, he's forgotten his lunch. Someone should try to get him before he leaves the building." She gave me a simpering look. "You're on your way out as it is. And I, well, um, I'm needed here." She picked up her phone and popped open the numbers screen.

The coward.

"Fine. But when I'm late for lunch with my mother, I'm blaming it on you. And don't think she won't hunt you down."

Veronica laughed, but I wasn't in much of a laughing mood. The two most important events for a child to be on time for are birth and meals. The former event loses importance over time, while the latter grows in proportion with the ability to use utensils. Mothers almost always appreciate their children being a little early to both. Therefore, when you are tardy for a meal, make a special effort to remind your mother how well she taught you in regards to utensils. While only a small consolation, it could mean the difference between receiving nothing for your birthday or receiving a pair of argyle socks instead. And I knew that if I didn't suck up to my mother I wouldn't even merit the socks. And if I were prone to cursing, I would have done so now. I was definitely going to be late, something my mother considered as great a sin as adultery or murder. And whatever the eight other commandments were.

The image of my mother in biblical robes and standing atop a mountain holding stone tablets popped into my head. Damn! Yes, god-like image of my mom, I have indeed cursed.

I'm going to have to sit through the uncomfortable scene of my mother looking at her watch as soon as she sees me, shaking her head sadly, and mumbling quietly that she had failed as a mother (we have replayed this scene enough times that I could tell you the exact angle at which she will tilt her head and the exact wording of her forlorn speech). Life was not fair. And it was all on Eugene.

Still hoping to avoid such an incident (and maybe be only a few minutes late), I picked up the plastic bag and hurried down the stairs--at a pace that was still moderately safe and whilst holding the railing, as I was not about to tempt fate or death or anything today. I nearly collided with Tom at the bottom step. He would have jumped out of the way, but he was slow and I side-stepped past him, heading straight for the front doors. Eugene always parked in the parking garage next to the alley, and I was determined to catch him before he got to the stairwell. I had no desire to wander through a dark parking garage, trying to avoid puddles that looked like oil but smelled like urine.

The bright sun reflecting off the pavement blinded me for a moment, and it was several seconds before my vision cleared enough for me to turn towards the corner of the building, and the bleak alley that bordered it. Eugene was turning the corner, Jezebel dawdling behind him trying to sniff the rusty, empty newspaper stand that inconvenienced so many pedestrians.

I hurried in that direction, bumping two middle-aged women wearing identical glasses and a businessman who started to grumble and examine his scuffed shoes. Eugene was half-way across the street, heading straight for the bright orange door that proclaimed itself as the doorway of level one, when I called out to him.

"Eugene, hold on." I called over to him. My car was in the opposite direction and every step was making me later and later to lunch.

Eugene looked back at me, as if he half-expected that I had a grenade with his name on it. My pacifist instincts were instantly offended.

"You forgot your lunch," I said rather stiffly.

"What? Oh. Thanks, Hope. I probably would have remembered before I got into the car though." He started walking toward my outstretched hand, Jezebel excited at the prospect of sniffing a large and malodorous puddle in the middle of the street.

So much for gratitude! Of course he would have remembered. Heaven forbid Eugene forget anything-- even something as trivial as food!

But I held my peace, not wanting to enter into a conversation, simply wanting to get to my car before the meter maid did.

I wasn't about to step into the filthy alley unless absolutely necessary, so I stopped at the edge of the sidewalk, my toes nearly even with the drop. I relaxed my arm slightly, letting the bag dangle loosely, and waited for Eugene to come fetch it.

Eugene was trying to yank Jezebel away from the puddle, and I looked toward Broad Street to see if there was any abhorrent meter maid just waiting to pounce on my car.

With my head turned, I didn't instantly see the flash of sunlight off of metal or the sudden advent of color in the murky alley. But I did turn in time to see the sudden surprise on Eugene's face, which quickly turned to terror. I screamed a warning to Eugene just as a loud thud echoed through the narrow lane. A car whirred past, the tires squealing as they left dark imprints on the concrete. And there was Eugene, crumpled and bleeding on the ground, as still as a corpse.

Even as I could hear the car speed away, narrowly cutting the corner, the reality of the situation eluded me. It wasn't until I noticed that Eugene's trousers were torn at the knees and his handkerchief was dangling out of place, that I comprehended what had happened. Some maniac had just hit Eugene.

I stood there, my feet glued to the sidewalk, all thoughts frozen in my mind. A small crowd of onlookers was quickly gathering, though few dared to step into the street. I could hear loud voices yelling for someone to call 911, while other voices were screaming in horror, and at some point I thought I heard an ambulance approaching from a distance though I knew there hadn't really been time for that. I thought one of the voices screaming was mine, but no, my screams were silent though equally ghastly. Several mothers spirited away their children, and businessmen were streaming from nearby office buildings, eager to see what the commotion was about.

And then there was a slight movement, and to my surprise Eugene turned his head in my direction. His eyes seemed unfocused and his movements were spasmodic as he raised himself to his elbows. When his vision finally cleared he looked up at me and glared, while I stood there, stock-still on the sidewalk, gazing back at him in alarm and surprise. Eugene looked in the direction of the disappearing car. "Did anyone see that? I think that bastard deliberately hit me! Did anyone get a plate number. I am definitely suing."

I'm dreaming, I repeated over and over to myself. This cannot be happening. Eugene is not rolling his eyes at me in disgust. He isn't craning his neck to see where the offending vehicle had disappeared. It's not possible! It can't be possible.

My mouth was practically on the sidewalk. My breathing had stopped. I just couldn't believe what I was seeing.

Eugene stood up, dusted himself off, and bent down to check Jezebel, who had also risen and was shaking pieces of gravel from her previously exquisite fur coat. There was no blood on either or them. I couldn't even see a rip in Eugene's clothing. But something was even more alarmingly wrong. There were now two of Eugene and two of Jezebel: one pair lying inert and bloody on the pavement, the other pair suddenly staring aghast at their mangled bodies. There could be no mistaking what I saw.

But there must be a mistake, I told myself. You're in shock. You're seeing things. People can't be in two places at once. If you close your eyes for a moment, and then open them again, the illusion will have vanished. It has to!

I obeyed my mind, closed my eyes, kept them closed for several seconds, and then opened them. Eugene was still standing there, looking down at his body in silent terror.

He then looked around at the crowd, at the men checking his pulse, at the lady on the cell phone rapidly talking to someone in an urgent tone, at the children trying to peak at the scene while their parents ineffectually shielded them. He waved his hands in front of the newly arrived paramedic's face. "Hey, buddy. What's going on? Was somebody else hit?"

No answer.

"Excuse me, sir, but who is that? He looks so much like..." Eugene bent down to peer at the body. "It can't be," I heard him say. He stood up and looked again at the crowd. He waved at several of them in turn. And still no one noticed him.

And then he looked at me. Of the entire crowd, I was the only one looking at him—at the ambulatory him, that is.

I could see him and suddenly he knew it. His eyes widened. Those dark eyes, now scared and confused, normally intelligent and quizzing, were turned questioningly to mine. He opened his mouth to speak, but before any words came out a paramedic rushed up and ran right through him. I flinched, as if the assault had been on my own person, and Eugene gave a loud gasp, almost a scream.

I shook my head, surprised at the tricks my mind was playing on me.

No, no, no! That man couldn't walk through Eugene because Eugene is still on the ground. None of this is possible! That noise you heard was nothing. You probably made that sound yourself. That had to be the answer.

The only problem was that the Eugene who wasn't supposed to be there still was, and he was watching me intently, a stunned expression on his face. I shook my head again, trying to will the vision out of my mind, but it would not leave.

"Hope? Can you see me?" The vision's voice was tremulous, and I leapt back, not knowing how to respond, or even if I should.

What do I do? Oh God! He-it can't be speaking to me. Now I know I'm crazy. Or maybe I'm in a state of shock. I just need a shot of valium. This other Eugene isn't real. He can't be real.

It occurred to me that if I told myself this long enough it would be true.

He saw my movement, my consternation, and drew

back. The dog at his side barked at me, and then stared back at him, pleased with herself. She licked his hand, and then was still, her tongue lolling, waiting for her master's instructions.

By this time the police and ambulance had arrived, and the number of uniformed men was growing at an alarming rate. The man leaning down by the body was shaking his head. I could hear him tell the police officers that it was too late--the victim was dead.

I choked on the air, which suddenly smelled of death and grime, and put my hand to my mouth. I was going to be sick, the vile rising in my throat was a clear indicator of that. And I knew I wasn't dreaming.

I had to know for certain if my vision was real. I looked back at where the specter of Eugene (I didn't know how else to think of it) had stood. He was gone.

Relief coursed through me, so much so that I felt dizzy with it. But it was short lived. I felt a strange compulsion to turn to the right, and there he was, half hiding behind the building on the corner. He was watching the proceedings with as much absorption as I was now watching him. Perhaps he felt my stare, because he looked at me suddenly, and a frown formed between his eyes. And then he turned and ran, Jezebel following at his heels. His distinctive swagger was apparent even in his haste. And with that thought came a sense of finality. The food dropped from my fingers and landed with a dull splat on the dark cement at my feet.

I became numb, shock turning my mind into a blank. An officer approached me and asked me if I had known the gentleman, and I nodded bleakly. And then the questions started.

Chapter Three

"Where do you keep your sugar tongs?"

Sugar tongs? What could she possibly want with sugar tongs? "I don't own any sugar tongs, Mom."

"You don't? How do you serve the cubes from your sugar bowl?" She sounded slightly confused. I supposed it hadn't occurred to her that very few people used sugar cubes these days.

I sighed. Some things never changed. "I'm too cheap to buy sugar cubes and regular sugar. You'll have to use a teaspoon." That's right, Mom. I don't even own the proper spoon for serving sugar. Maybe defiance wasn't the best mechanism for shock, but right now it was all I had.

"Oh well. Never mind. I'll make do." I could almost hear my mother's voice adding a quip about primitive living. She was probably shaking her head and worriedly searching my cabinets and refrigerator to make sure I was eating balanced meals.

My mother has always believed the old maxim that tea is a necessary comfort in any crisis, so I wasn't surprised to see her walk out of my kitchen carefully balancing a tea tray in one hand and a fresh box of Kleenex in the other. It would have made sense to place the Kleenex on the tray as well, but subconsciously my mother probably didn't want to spoil the effect. She should have looked closer at the tray though, since not one piece of the set seemed to match, and a box of Kleenex could only have added a touch of elegance.

The Kleenex was good thinking, though. I surveyed the already used box that was sitting on the coffee table in front of me, and quickly swept the used pieces into a small trash bin my mother had brought over.

"Drink your tea. It will make you feel better. I made your favorite—chamomile. And then I added a little milk and honey." Not my favorite--hers. I preferred Earl Grey, but according to The Sylvia Pearson School ('For Young Ladies' had been removed from the school name a decade before I attended, but it was still implied in every aspect of the education provided) of which my mother was headmistress, Earl Grey was a tea that was usually reserved for mixed company only.

"Remind me to give you your grandmother's tea set. I can't think why I haven't done so before. Is this what you use when you have guests over?"

"I almost never have guests over. Except close friends, and they usually don't care. I prefer to spend my money on other things like water and electricity. That sort of thing."

"Well at least you dress well. You get that from me." Implying, of course, that every bad habit I have acquired over the years was the fault of my father. Since my mother adored my father, and he was hardly trailer trash, she probably meant no offense to him. Maybe she really blamed all bad habits on television and video games.

"Go on, drink up. It will help settle your nerves." She was taking dainty sips, while eying me with concern. "Are you feeling any better?"

"I don't know. I can hardly think. I've never seen anyone die before. I mean I saw Grandpa at his funeral, but he was already dead," and after a second I added, "and wearing corduroy and polka dots."

In my opinion, corduroy on corpses lessened the finality of the scene. How could it not? Who would want to be buried in corduroy? Wearing it to your own funeral indicated that even in death you still had a sense of fun. And a polka dot handkerchief added to the surreal feeling that perhaps the whole death had been a joke, and the deceased intended to jump out and yell 'boo' at the mourners. Of course my grandfather didn't jump out and yell, and Eugene hadn't been wearing corduroy, but a very nice, dark suit. It was, I realized, entirely appropriate for death.

My mother must have agreed because she moved to sit next to me and put her arm around me. "But that's different. He looked peaceful, although slightly ridiculous. And he didn't die a painful death. It's not surprising you're so upset."

I complain about my mother a lot. Who doesn't complain about their mother? But I hope I'm still pretty fair-minded. The two things about my mother that I won't deny are that deep down she is genuinely nice, despite her obsession with the proper appearance of things (something she inherited from her own mother), and that she knows instinctively when someone needs help. That isn't to say that she always says or does the right thing, but she tries her best.

"I know. I guess I'm still in shock. And then I thought I was seeing things. And that only made it worse." I remembered Eugene getting up and running away. I shuddered.

"What do you mean, honey? Did the image keep replaying in your mind? They say that happens."

"No, not that. I thought I saw..." I hesitated. Did I really want to tell her about my moments of insanity? She would undoubtedly say that I needed a long stay in a sanitarium, or even worse--her house.

Luckily I was not required to finish my sentence as the doorbell rang. I always jumped at the doorbell, it having a particularly loud ring that echoed throughout the small apartment. My mother didn't jump or spill her tea, but I could feel her leg twitch next to mine.

"Are you expecting anyone?" My mother sounded both curious and hopeful. I could see her mind checking off the possibilities: man—hopefully; friend--quite possibly; solicitor—perhaps; pizza delivery--most likely.

My cat, who had hidden under my bed the moment my mother entered the apartment, made a brief foray into the living room at the sound, probably in hopes it was a pizza delivery, but upon seeing my mother, gave a shrieking meow, and raced back to his hiding spot.

"I called Jilly. Maybe it's her."

"Oh. In that case I'll get the door. You just stay here and relax."

It was indeed my oldest and dearest friend Jilly, and she was carrying a box of pizza and an extra box of Kleenex. This foresight was why we were such good friends. How could my mother imagine that tea would be more of a comfort than pizza? If Jilly had added a few éclairs I might even have been able to convince myself that Eugene was probably in heaven having a grand old time. But then again, perhaps not.

"Hi, Mrs. S. I knew I'd find you here. I wouldn't have expected any less of you." Jilly beamed at her and leaned forward for a kiss on the cheek.

There was not a soul on the planet that would dare call my mother 'Mrs. S.' except Jilly. But Jilly had always been a favorite with my mom. I wasn't sure if this was due to Jilly's outrageous flattery, or to the fact that her mom died when Jilly was only thirteen, leaving her in the care of a kind but obtuse father. Not having a mother was the greatest cause for pity in the world according to my mother. I could think of worse; for instance, getting a fatal and painful disease or being forced into prostitution while subsisting solely on sardines. But then, I had a mother who made sure those things never happened to me.

"It's so good to see you, Jilly. You're looking a little tired, though." My mother eyed the pizza box warily, as if the pizza's calories were visible little monsters jumping out of the box enabling her to count them. "I don't know how you and Hope stay so thin."

Jilly winked at me while my mother was still contemplating the pizza. "You're a fine one to talk. As if your figure wasn't perfect."

My mother gave Jilly the smile that she reserved for special occasions, like when the president visited. "You're so sweet. But I know you are telling a fib."

She escorted Jilly to the sofa, from which I still hadn't budged, and offered to fetch a cup from the kitchen so that Jilly could enjoy the tea as well. Jilly offered to get her own cup and came back a minute later holding a coffee mug. My mother looked at it with a pained expression, but kept silent, and Jilly winked at me again.

"How are you holding up, Hope? I still can't believe it. What a horrible thing to see happen." Jilly hadn't been overly fond of Eugene, but she still knew him, and I thought she was probably visualizing the scene in her mind. Her imagination was pretty vivid.

My mom headed for the kitchen to retrieve some plates and silverware (all of which matched I was proud to note). "So sad to be killed unnecessarily. I didn't know the man, but still 'any man's death diminishes me.'" My mom peeked through the doorway and gave the two of us a pointed look, and I realized that she expected at least one of us to come up with the author. I suspected that if I didn't think up the author I wouldn't hear the end of it. Ever. And my mom would probably write the damn quote on my next ten birthday cards as penance. But I was too tired to rack my brain for the answer. And honestly, I couldn't believe she was quizzing me at a time like this.

Luckily, Jilly sensed my mood. "I know this one, Mrs. S. Just give me a minute." Jilly's eyes scrunched together a little, and her shoulders tightened, her body curving inward. It was her thinking stance and always made her look like a little girl who was just told she wasn't allowed to join the grown-ups and couldn't figure out why. And then she sighed, straightened up and winked at me. She discreetly pulled out her cell phone, rapidly typing in the quote.

A moment later, she broke into a smile, and called into the kitchen. "'John Donne, Mrs. S. As if I could forget such a great man. You read that poem at our graduation. Not that I remember all of it." Or any of it probably. God knows I didn't.

My mother came back into the room, looking inordinately pleased with herself for having made such a positive and educational impact on Jilly's life, and I suspected that this year's graduates from The Sylvia Pearson School (For Young Ladies In Need of Manners and Morals) would be condemned to hearing Mr. Donne's views on life, death, and how to succeed in every social situation.

"Very good, Jilly. I thought of that particular sermon because you two are so sensitive. Every time someone dies or a crime is committed you both want to cry, even if you didn't know the person. I know that you can hardly stand watching the news anymore, Hope. That's not so surprising since they don't seem to report anything pleasant. It's painful to watch the world slowly fall apart." She looked slightly despondent, but then shook her head and cleared away any negative thoughts, her mind back on what she could do to make Jilly and I comfortable. Her answer was to clean.

"You don't have to do that, Mom. I can do it later. Why don't you come sit with us and have some pizza?"

"No, thank you. I can't stay too much longer or your father will be wondering if he shouldn't have come as well. Aunt Maude is supposed to call tonight, and I insisted that one of us had to be home to talk to her. I just want to see if there is anything in here I can tidy up for you. It is so much easier to relax when your home is clean. Oh, and that peanut cat of yours is now hiding under the table. Do you want me to move him to your bedroom?"

"No, leave him. And he's not a 'peanut cat'. His name is Nutter Butter, as you well know. And as long as he isn't on the table, it's fine. He's just scared of guests." Or in this case, just my mother. I was surprised he had left the security of the bedroom, but pizza was a big draw for him. "He'll probably come out from under the table eventually and try to steal some of Jilly's pizza."

My mother's face scrunched up briefly and I could tell she was horrified at the very thought of it. She coughed lightly into her hand and nodded, smiling in that condescending way she occasionally did. I expected my Christmas gift this year was now going to be a book on how to properly train a cat.

I really, really loved that cat at times like these.

"I'm going to be horribly rude, Mrs. S., and ask Hope for all the gory details." Jilly barked out, seeing the warning signs flashing brightly on my mom's face.

"You go right ahead, Jillian. Your father won't hear any tales from me." If my mother had been standing next to Jilly, rather than cleaning up my perfectly neat kitchen, she probably would have patted Jilly's head and bestowed upon her an indulgent smile and a piece of candy.

Jilly gave a small smile. I knew exactly what she was thinking. My mom hadn't been overly fond of Jilly's dad since he got roaring drunk at Jilly's husband Martin's bachelor party and thus showed up to Jilly's wedding so hung-over he could barely walk. In his defense, it was the first time he had gotten drunk since Jilly's mom had died. In my mother's defense, it was the first time in her life she had to go to a wedding wearing shoes that didn't coordinate with her dress because the bride's father had been sick all over her favorite pair. Luckily, the ceremony had been held on a lush lawn that was only a five-minute drive from my parents' house, and she was able to quickly go home before the reception. My mother probably would not have been able to show her face in public if she had been shoeless at a church.

"Come on, Hope. Tell me everything," Jilly prodded. "There's something else bothering you besides watching a colleague be hit by a car. Not that that isn't a horrible thing to happen. I can picture it now. Blood everywhere and people screaming." Jilly shuddered at the image she had conjured up.

"That isn't quite how it went. I mean there was blood and screaming, but not too much of it. Eugene didn't bleed too much." No, instead he got up and walked away while his other self lay there dead. I couldn't say that, though. "And I think I might have screamed, and maybe a few other people. I don't really remember. It happened so fast, and then everything after that was...a blur." Well, it was. So maybe I could remember a little more than that. This was a lie of omission, which everyone knows isn't really a lie at all.

"I know that isn't all. You have a guilty look on your face. Did you vomit and are embarrassed?" Jilly poked at my side. I hated vomiting and she knew it.

"No. But, I can't help thinking that if it hadn't been for me, he wouldn't have died." Where did that come from? Was I really partly responsible? Had my subconscious been aware of this the whole time?

"What? Why ever would you think that? That's the most ridiculous thing I've ever heard." Jilly was outraged and that made me feel a little better.

"Don't say that until I've told you why. Then maybe you'll think it was my fault, too."

"I doubt that, but go on. I am curious how you have

somehow managed to pin this on yourself."

I wasn't sure where to start. "I guess I think I might be partially responsible because I was the reason he was standing in the middle of the street. I was returning his lunch to him, but I didn't want to step into the alley, so I made him come get it from me. And then he was hit. And the dog." Suddenly I started crying again, small sobs that nevertheless sounded like hiccups coming from a large frog. "And I was so concerned about a stupid parking ticket that I wasn't paying attention. I didn't warn him in time. And—and I didn't even get that parking ticket!" I choked on a sob, and reached for more Kleenex.

Jillian interrupted me, shoving a Kleenex at my face until I took it. "Come on, Hope. This is ridiculous. First of all, you couldn't have known that some maniac would run down an innocent person and keep driving. You're not psychic. And as for making Eugene cross the street, well, I can't imagine anyone making him do anything he didn't want to. If you had his lunch he probably didn't want you holding it any longer than was necessary. And as for warning him, I think that if you tried that was enough. If you hadn't tried to warn him I might think you didn't do enough, but you did. What do you think you could have done that would have made a difference?"

When I would have spoken, she waved me off, continuing in a rather authoritative voice that was similar to the one my mother used on recalcitrant children. "And don't go on about crossing the street yourself, because I can see you want to bring that up again. That is so dumb it makes me angry. If you had, you would be in the mortuary, and I would be bringing Kleenex to your mother and wondering if she was going to start taking me to task every time I used the wrong fork. And I wouldn't have you there to comfort me when she decided that she should stop by at my house every week just to make sure I was folding my laundry properly. That would have made me cry harder than you can imagine. No, I'm not kidding. I am perfectly serious." Jilly forced a stern look on her face, and I was again reminded of my mother.

I looked at her, and for an instant I wanted to laugh. But then I remembered that Eugene was dead, and despite what she said, I might have been able to do something. And then there was that whole business about seeing him rise from the dead. What would people make of that?

My mother walked into the room, removing the apron she had borrowed, and sitting down next to me. "She's been crying again, Jilly."

"Yes, ma'am. I'm sorry. But it is the stupidest thing I ever heard. Hope actually thinks she was partly responsible for Eugene's death." Jilly was giving me a look of scorn, which was shared by my mother, though to a lesser extent.

Guilt was not an acceptable emotion according to my mother. At least not for her. If you tried your best, there was no reason to feel guilty; if you were always unfailingly polite, there was no need to feel guilt. My mother truly believed that ladies who graduate from The Sylvia Pearson School (For Young Ladies Who Desire Social Acceptance Rather Than Scientific Aptitude) never feel guilt because they never do anything that would cause that emotion.

"Hope, the only person responsible for this man's death was the driver of that car. He could have stopped. Even if it was too late for him to have stopped before hitting the man, he should definitely have stopped after. You have nothing to feel guilty about. You just have to believe that it was your friend's time to die. There is a plan, even if we don't know what it is."

A plan? What plan? The Make Hope Springs Cry with Guilt, Horror, and Shock plan? The Eugene Schreier Gets to Suffer a Painful and Unnecessary Death plan? Maybe it's the Life is Just a Series of Random and Disturbing Acts plan? No matter the nature of the plan, it was not going to reassure me.

"Maybe your mom is right, Hope. Maybe all of this happened for a reason." She gave me a lopsided smile and whispered low enough that my mother couldn't make out her words. "Maybe it's a sign that you should give up writing nonsensical columns about manners no one takes seriously anymore, except maybe your mother and her socialite buddies. You might be one of the politest people I know, but I don't even think you really care so much about all that. You just write all that stuff because you already know it and can't think what else you want to do with your life. Maybe this is a wake-up call, showing you what is really important in life."

"What was that, Jilly?"

"I was just telling Hope that she should learn from your example and make the most out of every situation, good or bad." She gave my mom an outrageously angelic smile.

Jilly believed that telling white lies was the pinnacle of politeness. Everything else was just form and consequence leading up to those inevitable lies. This was why she never felt guilty about uttering them. To Jilly, white lies are a form of politeness, and like most things courteous, they make people happy. It was the one thing she learned from The Sylvia Pearson School (For Young Ladies Who Want to Make a Monetarily Advantageous Marriage). I learned it almost as well as she, though I could never quite remember how to avoid the guilt.

"Maybe you're supposed to take up serious writing about the evident callousness in the world and win a Nobel Prize." Jilly continued, a flippant gleam in her eyes, but a serious note in her voice.

"Or maybe I'm supposed to have a religious conversion and become a missionary?" They didn't smile at my quip, but then again neither did I. "Okay, okay. I know this stuff happens everyday and people use these lessons to their advantage, although I can't imagine how. And I know I have to move on, but it's hard to forget those images. Geez, you could give me at least twenty-four hours before expecting me to forget the whole thing. Except for its character-building value," I added a little peevishly.

"Don't forget about it. Remembering isn't the problem. It's getting fixated on it that's the problem. Just move on. That's all you can do." Jilly sounded like she knew what she was talking about, and I guess she did. She'd watched her mother die in a car accident and had survived. I watched someone I wasn't close to die, and I was falling apart. If only I hadn't seen...

You saw nothing, I told myself again. Nothing.

And I kept telling myself that over and over again. By the time my mother and Jilly had left I was convinced that this nagging feeling of guilt had caused me to see things that weren't there. It was almost calming. Almost, but not quite.

Chapter Four

Nutter Butter's slightly overweight (okay, seriously fat) checkered tabby body lay curled in a ball on my feet, making movement nearly impossible. I didn't care much, though, since movement wasn't integral to lying awake, staring at the ceiling, and making shapes out of the shadows. Probably not a healthy pastime after having witnessed an accident, but I didn't seem to have much choice at the moment.

The shadow to my far right, nudged in the corner, kept becoming a faceless man dressed in a long robe, and the shadow directly above me was looking eerily like a wolf or vicious dog. Fortunately, the shadow to my left looked like nothing more than a very dark Stay-Puff Marshmallow Man. As long as I pretended to never have seen "Ghost Busters", I could look at him indefinitely. And maybe I would eventually fall asleep to images of S'mores or peanut butter and marshmallow sandwiches. That had to be better than images of men being run down by speeding cars.

But marshmallow sandwiches were not to be in my future.

Get to sleep, you idiot! You have to go to work tomorrow, I reminded myself for the hundredth time. I wanted to sleep, yet every time I allowed myself to drift off panic would suddenly set it.

I'm the type of person for whom lack of sleep not only makes me feel very ill, but also makes me highly imaginative. Every creak in the building, scraping shoes of pedestrians on the street, and clinks from the raccoon going through garbage can in the alley was intensified until there was a cacophony of noise outside. My heart shuddered nervously in response to every sound, until I was certain I was going to make myself sick. An irrational cowardice was slowly taking over my body, and I felt ashamed, though no less nervous.

But I was determined to shut down any crazy fears that might surface and remain calm and rational. And so when I first heard the voice, I was certain it was nothing more than my imagination. Definitely my overactive imagination.

"Hope? Hope?" It was a man's voice, scratchy from nerves.

Ah, I thought drowsily, it must be a man praying to God, hoping God will grant him sleep too.

"Hope? Are you awake? I hope you can hear me because I need to talk to you."

Nope. Not someone praying to God. Some crazy person outside my window, asking me if I'm awake at two a.m.

"What?" My mind screamed. I felt someone moving on the bed. My body instinctively flinched, the upward half shooting into the air with a vicious tug on my muscles, the lower half stretched taut because it was held in place by an unnatural weight—Nutter Butter.

Ouch! That hurt!

I flicked on the light, hoping to scare away any burglars, and reached for the phone.

"Oh, good. You're awake. We need to talk. Can I come in?" That voice again, sounding desperate. I was pretty sure it wasn't Nutter Butter talking to me, I mean I'm not so crazy as to think that, but I double checked anyway. Nope, not him. He was still prostrate on the bed, alternating between snoring and giving me the evil eye.

"Whoever you are, go away. I'm armed." I hoped I sounded confident because I didn't feel equipped to search for a weapon and then use it. I wasn't sure I even had anything that could be used as a weapon. "I'm going to call the police."

"No, Hope, wait. It's me. Eugene." The words didn't filter into my consciousness so well as the tone of the voice. It was so familiar. But I still wasn't about to open the door at this hour—nobody showed up this late unless they had bad intentions.

The voice was pleading now. Good. Pleading was good.

This showed I had the upper hand. I needed the upper hand to deal with a burglar, or, heaven forbid, a murderer.

That's a scary thought. What a day! Now I'm going to be murdered in my bed. Great! The perfect ending to a rotten day!

I reached for the phone, hoping it was charged.

Slowly, my befuddled brain recalled the interloper's words.

How does this criminal know my name? Did he say he was Eugene?

Oh no. It wasn't bad enough that I was seeing things this morning, now I'm hearing things too. Just ignore him, I thought, and he'll go away.

"Hope? I know you're awake because your light is on," the voice chimed in.

I quickly switched off the light.

"Hope! It's me. Eugene. Eugene Schreier. I know you can hear me. Would you please let me in?" He sounded annoyed now.

That was bad. Or was it? If it's all in my mind, it doesn't really matter, does it? Because it isn't real.

But if it isn't my mind, then what? I didn't think I was on Candid Camera. Was I really hearing a dead man?

"Hope. Would you at least go to the front door? You can look at me through the eyehole. I'm pretty sure you'll be able to see me." He was pleading again.

No way! I was not about to give in to my guilt-ridden mind, overly creative mind to find what— a criminal or ghost? Neither appealed to me.

"It really is me. I know you think I'm dead, and I guess I am, but it is still I—I mean me—no, I. I must be a ghost. Would a criminal care so much about his grammar?"

Of course he was a ghost. (If the voice was real, that is). The thought that I should speak to him to verify his identity came to me, but I quickly tossed it aside.

"I know you could see and hear me in the alley today after the accident. You are the only one to see me so far. I need to talk to you. I don't know where else to go."

I still clutched the telephone in my hand and realized I

was gripping it so hard my knuckles were white. I dropped it on the bed, staring at my fingers.

Am I crazy? I probably am. The shock of today was too much for my mind and it has finally collapsed. I'm going to end up in a facility with my hair left un-brushed, wearing nothing but a granny nightgown and sketching bad art with crayons. A very unpleasant prospect, indeed.

"Just go open your front door. I could come in anyway. I've learned I can walk through anything. I'm just trying to be thoughtful. If you don't open the door, I'll just walk right through the wall." Now he sounded smug. And smug was bad.

"Don't you dare walk through my wall. What kind of a ghost are you? Were you raised in a barn? Don't you have any manners?" Oh my God, did I just say that? I am now officially my mother. "I mean, if you are a ghost and not my imagination, you could have the decency to wait until I'm ready. I'm not dressed or anything."

"I don't care about that. You're too scrawny for me, anyway. I prefer women with a larger bosom and a bit taller, Pip-Squeak. And to think of it, I'm dead so I doubt that kind of thing matters." He sounded annoyingly like Eugene. "And if you open the door, I won't walk through the wall. I promise."

"I don't know. Eugene never kept his promises. And I could be sitting here talking to you through my bedroom window, but in reality actually talking to myself. As a matter of fact, that's what is probably happening right now. It's my guilt overpowering my reason. And did you just call me Pip-Squeak? You're not much that much taller than me, you hypocrite. And my chest size is just fine." I shook my head. Why did I have to throw that in?

"I'm not a hypocrite, Pip-Squeak. Yeah, I said it again... And you're not talking to yourself. You're talking to me. Isn't that obvious?" He paused, as if searching for any means to convince me that he was indeed a ghost. "Would your mind create such an honest ghost?"

"An honest ghost? If by 'honest', you mean rude, probably not." I thought about it for a second. I still wasn't giving in, especially after he insulted me. "But maybe my mind is clever enough to think up an accurate version of Eugene. The Eugene I knew. He wasn't exactly the nicest person on the planet."

He gave a loud sigh. "Oh, please. This is ridiculous. Come on, Hope. You're being an utter idiot. What do I have to do to convince you?"

I didn't respond, and he couldn't seem to think of anything, so he did what he had threatened, and walked right through the wall and into my bedroom.

And it was Eugene, looking exactly as I had seen him rise after the accident—immaculately dressed and with Jezebel at his heels. I screamed, trying to throw myself out of bed and get to the far side of the room. But I had forgotten about Nutter Butter, who was weighing down the lower half of my body.

Before I knew it the cat was flying through the air towards the window, and I was headed in the opposite direction. It wasn't a graceful fall. I landed hard on the floor, dragging half the bedding with me.

Nutter Butter wasn't so lucky either. He landed at the edge of the bed, right in front of Jezebel face. Nutter Butter, sensing an invisible, yet threatening presence, looked around in alarm, his fur on edge. He swiped the air with his right paw, sending it directly through the ghost dog's nose. That was enough incentive for Jezebel. She had found a playmate, albeit an unwilling one. With a low bark and wag of the tail, she put her paws on the edge of the bed and barked right in Nutter Butter's face. The cat, somehow attuned to the presence of the ghost dog, and realizing he had a new nemesis, jumped back in terror, running in circles atop the bed before flying off it to seek sanctuary under the kitchen table. Jezebel gave chase, and I could hear the cat hissing and meowing, still not knowing exactly where the enemy was.

And that was when Eugene started to laugh. And laugh. And laugh. And laugh. "You look so ridiculous, Hope. Just like that dumb cat of yours. If only you could see the look on your face." He started pointing with one hand and trying to cover his mouth with the other.

I could well imagine the look on my face. "It's not funny. And my cat isn't dumb. Certainly no dumber than a ghost dog chasing a living cat." I glared at him full force, but he continued to laugh. I tried to save what was left of my dignity by disentangling my body from the sheets so that I could get off the floor. All I ended up doing was sending the sheets flying into my face, mussing my hair and making my mood even darker.

Nutter Butter came tearing back into the bedroom, having found the kitchen no safer, and tried to hide under the sheet I was trying to ball up and throw back onto the bed. "Go away, Nutter Butter," I barked out. But he didn't listen, hiding himself behind my body when the sheet was taken from him.

By the time I was standing again, Eugene had admonished Jezebel and had her sitting like an angel at his side, perfectly oblivious to the fact that my cat was now regarding a point slightly to Jezebel's right in absolute terror.

"I did warn you. I told you to let me in the front door. That way you could have put on a bathrobe and brushed your hair first." He still sounded smug.

I looked down at my t-shirt and cringed inwardly. It was the one advertising the chicken joint down the street, boldly claiming to have "the best breasts and shanks in town". But I had my pride, and it wasn't going to let me grab a bathrobe. I would stay exactly as I was, or be damned. After all, Eugene was the interloper here. The fact that I then automatically brushed down my hair with my fingers and smoothed my shirt was nothing more than a habit.

Eugene looked like he was about to make a crack about my t-shirt, so I decided to get down to business and demand to know what it was he wanted.

"I want to know what happened to me, Hope? I have to know why I'm here."

"You were hit by a car, Eugene." Don't ghosts have memories? I hoped my mind wasn't going off its rocker just to have me make inane conversation with a person who had been relatively intelligent when he was alive.

"I know that, you moron. Why am I a ghost? How come I haven't headed off to heaven or something?"

I looked at him quizzically. How could I know something like that? Maybe God was getting picky. Maybe he needed to Google it to find out. Could ghosts surf the Internet? Great! I'll end up stuck doing his work. Isn't that just like Eugene! I'll be forced to check out books or visit paranormal experts, or even phone a hotline, I suppose.

No, wait! What am I doing? Why are you even thinking like this? He's not really here. Just ignore him, Hope. He isn't real, and if you ignore him long enough, he will go away.

I wasn't sure that Eugene was really going to follow my line of thinking, so I decided to say it aloud. "You are not real. You are a figment of my mind. I am just going to ignore you, so you might as well go away now."

Eugene just laughed. When I turned my back and tried to climb back into bed, warily glancing over my shoulder, he stopped laughing. "You can't be serious, Shorty. You see me, you hear me, and you were carrying on a conversation with me. And now you are saying it's all in your mind and you are going to ignore me. It won't work. I'm a ghost. And I'm not leaving until I have the answers I came for."

I climbed into bed and pulled the blankets tight around me, the sheet still crumpled in a ball at the end of the bed. "I'm going to sleep now." I wasn't sure if I was telling Eugene or myself, but I felt it needed to be said. "When I wake up, you will not be here."

"That's what you think. I told you I'm not leaving until we've talked. You might as well just get it over with," he snapped.

I was not going to give in to his demands, and so, I shut my eyes. The light was still burning brightly, causing multi-colored shapes to appear under my lids, and the shapes kept forming Eugene's head. I am NOT going to open my eyes, I told myself.

I opened my eyes.

He was still there, standing at the edge of the bed, looking at me with an expression of disgust and impatience on his face. It was such a common expression for Eugene that I suddenly wanted to cry.

I shut my eyes again, this time determined to keep them that way.

"Fine. Be this way. It won't do you any good. I'll leave you to sleep, but I'm not leaving the apartment. I'll just wait in the living room until you are ready to talk." He paused, and then added dryly, "See you in the morning, Pip-Squeak."

I waited a few minutes before opening my eyes again. I tilted my head slightly and looked around my bedroom. It was clear. There was no Eugene, no Jezebel, and no insanity. And in the morning, I told myself, everything would be back to normal.

Exhaustion set in about an hour after I first shut my eyes, and I fell asleep to my mind chanting, 'You are not crazy. You are just in shock. You are not crazy. You are just in shock. You are not crazy. You are just...'

Unfortunately, if anyone controls the future, it is probably a grandiose being with a booming voice, a caustic sense of humor, and an affection for French existentialist playwrights. He (or she) undoubtedly likes to play with humans the way the neighbor boy plays with his slingshot—ready, aim, fire, and then run away while the victim exclaims, "Ouch, that hurts!"

In this fashion, morning came far more rapidly than good taste would dictate, leaving me drowsy and sullen--a ruthless combination.

When someone says he or she is not a morning person, it is probably because instead of waking up to bright sunlight streaming through the windows, illuminating a peaceful scene of rabbits running through a forest and the smell of brewing coffee in the kitchen, he or she wakes up to find that the alarm clock has suffered a fatal mishap, the sky is pouring out its misery, and there is a ghost sitting in the aforementioned kitchen. And the ghost is not brewing coffee or making scones, or doing any of those pleasant culinary endeavors, but is instead trying to open the kitchen drawers so that he could inspect the silverware for water spots.

Chapter Five

I woke to the sound of rain pounding against my window, and when I blearily opened my eyes, I was forced to close them again immediately. Even that slight movement caused intense pain. I was going to pay for my late night. My head throbbed, pain was shooting around my eyes, and my throat was dry and hoarse.

I opened my eyes again, slowly this time. The alarm clock was nowhere to be seen. I edged farther toward the side and looked down. There it was, lying sideways on the floor, the hazy green numbers blinking steadily.

I had no idea what time it was. And I needed aspirin. Fast. That meant having to make my way to the bathroom.

Okay, no big deal. It was only a few steps away.

But it was a big deal. My whole body ached as I sat up, and the pounding inside my head got worse. I looked at the crumpled sheet still lying at the end of the bed, and the events of yesterday came back in rapid succession.

First there was Eugene being hit by a car. Then my mother and Jilly trying to make me feel better but not succeeding. And then a man's voice outside my bedroom window, demanding to be let in. Eugene's voice. And then there was Eugene himself. And he walked through a wall. And so did his dog.

And that was when I decided I was completely insane.

I paused and quickly looked around, waiting for any sign of Eugene's presence. There was none to be found. I gave a deep sigh and continued to the bathroom, the pounding in my head lessening slightly.

There was no aspirin to be found in the bathroom, so I decided I must have left it in the kitchen.

My steps dragged as I headed for the kitchen, making me stumble slightly on the carpet. I looked at the clock on the mantle and gave a small gasp. It was past eight and I needed to be at a client's house at nine. That meant no breakfast and a very fast shower.

When I finally crossed the threshold into the kitchen, the sight that met my eyes made me stumble.

Lying in front of the table, her hind legs curled half under her, was Jezebel. And she looked to be in a playful mood. Her mouth was partly open, her tongue lolling about, licking her pink gums in a rather sloppy way. No wonder Nutter Butter had stopped as suddenly as I had, afraid to cross the threshold.

Just past Jezebel was Eugene. He was standing with his back to the door, trying ineffectually to open the top drawer of my cupboard. His hand, which appeared solid, kept slipping through the handle, preventing him from grabbing hold of the brass handle.

"I almost have it, my girl. I was very close this last time. Just a minute more and we can see whether or not it's safe to eat off her silverware." I had at first assumed he was addressing his speech to me, but after these last words I realized that the dog was his intended audience. I gave a loud gasp that was both outraged and frightened, and Eugene spun around.

He had not disappeared as I had promised myself he would. Instead, he was standing in my kitchen attempting to either make use of my silverware or abscond with it. If it was the latter, he should have known that no one kept the good silver in a kitchen drawer. It would get scuffed and dirty. I thought I should tell him so, but that meant actually admitting he was here.

And I was not going to admit that. Not yet. Not until I had seen a psychiatrist, and it was pretty obvious that should now become one of my top priorities.

"Good morning, Hope. Sleep well? I certainly didn't. Even if I could sleep, which I am not at all certain it is possible for ghosts to do, who could possibly sleep through all your muttering?" He sounded oddly cheerful for a dead man.

Maybe I should say something. Ask him what he is doing rummaging through my kitchen. Or even better still, ask him to leave me alone.

While I was debating the merits and drawbacks of addressing a dead man, Eugene again took the initiative and spoke. "I see you're still having trouble adjusting to my presence, so I have decided to be benevolent and give you all the time you need."

"You're leaving?" Drat. I spoke to him.

"No. What a stupid thing to say. Where would I go? No one else can see me. Didn't we have this discussion last night? I meant that I am willing to be patient and put up with your," he looked around him and gave a forlorn sigh, "homey apartment and pathetic person until you figure out how to get me wherever I need to go. I am willing to wait on your convenience, Hope, which is not an easy thing to do." My convenience? What was convenient about having a ghost living under foot? Nothing. Nada. Nil.

An insane thought suddenly popped into my head. (I mean more insane than the fact that I was talking to a dead man): I probably needed to hire an exorcist. I didn't want to have to sacrifice chickens on my own, but I would if I got desperate enough. How did you find a person like that? What would people think if I started asking around for one? There would go my professional standing. I would be forced to move to some foreign country selling t-shirts on a beach to arrogant tourists.

Still, I wondered if exorcists were listed in the yellow pages?

Oh, no. I am going insane. No one thinks like this. I need to get out of here, my mind screamed.

I turned back around, the aspirin having been forgotten, and ran to the bathroom. I locked the door, turned the water on, and stepped into the shower.

Maybe I am overreacting, I thought. Maybe once I accept Eugene's presence he will disappear. Or maybe I just need to work through my guilt issues. I bet that's it. He will go away as soon as I have done that, and my life can go back to normal. I bet they even have drugs that can make him go away.

With these satisfying thoughts, I was able to finish my

shower in peace.

When I was dressed in a beige suit, my hair brushed back, and my lipstick on, looking as normal and professional as possible, I headed for the door. Eugene was sitting on the sofa looking oddly relaxed. He got up at my entrance.

"You don't really eat leftover pizza, do you?" he asked, not waiting for a reply. "That was about the only thing left in your refrigerator. I wasn't able to open the door, so I had to stick my head through it. This ghost stuff is getting easier though. Hopefully I will soon be able to move any solid object I want. Then I can rattle chains and everything."

I stared at him in horror. Did he intend to make ghostly noises at night, preventing me from ever sleeping again?

"I did finally manage to open your silverware drawer. I must say, Hope, I've seen better. Maybe you should have the dishwasher fixed. You have water spots." When I didn't respond he looked me over and noticed my suit. "Are we going some-where, Pip-Squeak?"

I couldn't resist speaking to him. I had to set some ground rules--for my own sanity. "No. *We* are not going any-where. *I* am going to work. And don't go through my things when I am gone. It is very, very rude. Especially when you weren't even invited. And stop calling me that."

"You're not going without me. It's obvious I can't leave you alone just yet. Knowing you, you'll probably go get some whack job to try and get rid of me by sucking me through a vac-uum or a deck of cards, or some equally dumb thing," Eugene snorted. And then he looked at my red face. "Oh my God. You really are."

I didn't reply, wondering what had possessed me to even speak to him at all. I fairly jumped over the sofa, and tried to get to the front door and shut it in his face before he could cross the room. My mistake. Ghosts can walk through furniture and walls. By the time I had locked the door he was standing be-side me, gloating.

And he gloated. The entire car ride. My attempt to speed away before he had floated through the passenger-side door failed miserably. And he gloated. The whole ride. When I met with a photographer I had known for several years he sat there and smirked. Even when I ignored Eugene, as I tried to do frequently, I could feel him gloating and smirking behind me. Even the dog looked like she was gloating. As a matter of fact, the two of them then gloated all the way to The Bon Vivant.

And that was when the fun began. For Eugene, anyway.

"You look like crap," Jilly greeted me.

"I know. I didn't sleep much last night. And what's worse, I think I'm losing my mind." I moaned, ignoring the fact that Eugene had decided to sit across the booth from me and was making gagging noises every time a waitress passed with a tray of food. "Do you see or hear anything strange, Jilly?"

"Just you complaining. What's the matter? Are you reliving the accident? I thought your mom and I cheered you up a little last night. I know watching someone die is hard, but really, Hope, you didn't even like Eugene. Not to speak ill of the dead, as your mother says, but he was a bit of an ass." She turned away briefly to speak to a passing waitress, hopefully ordering up some food for us.

Eugene rolled his eyes at Jilly. "Who is she to judge? She's about as bright as the mold in your shower."

"Shut up," I hissed. "Don't talk to me. And you've never even seen my shower. I don't have any mold."

Note to self: Do not speak to invisible beings in a public place. It only makes you look crazy.

Jilly looked back at me. "What? I didn't say you had mold. Don't tell me you've started talking to yourself. That is definitely a bad sign. It'll be the asylum for you next." She gave a little laugh and winked, and I swallowed hard. If she only knew.

Eugene could see my annoyance, and decided to liven up the meal even more. "How do you know that I haven't seen your shower? Maybe you just didn't notice me."

I sucked in a deep breath, indignant at the insinuation, almost forgetting how humiliating it would be if I yelled at someone only I could see.

Jilly sat down in the booth, her body passing through Eugene's. He gave a grimace of disgust and slid over until he was at the far edge of the seat. He raised an eyebrow and then pretended to be brushing dust off his coat and pants. I doubted he had even felt her at all. He simply wanted to continue annoying me.

I can't respond to Eugene's taunts, I told myself. He just wants to embarrass me. "I was just going over a list of chores I have to do. Cleaning the shower is at the top," I mumbled. Oh great, I thought. Now I am lying to my best friend. But I can't tell her the truth because then she would *really* think I was crazy.

"Chores? You need to relax instead. I've ordered you some lunch—your usual Caesar salad with shrimp. And I'll even join you. How is that for a treat? You can tell me all about Colby's upcoming nuptials and how gaudy it will be."

I smiled. This would be easy to talk about. And I didn't particularly care if Eugene sat there and made faces. If they were directed at Colby that could only make me feel better. "It's not going to be as bad as I had anticipated. But Colby insists on having swans and doves. And the swans are going to have pink ribbons tied around their necks. Apparently that is a must."

Both Jilly laughed and Eugene looked at me in horror. "Swans and doves. Isn't that a little tacky. I would have thought better of your friends, Pip," he mocked.

"I don't care how tacky it is, since she isn't my friend," I said crisply, looking at Jilly, but addressing Eugene. "As far as I'm concerned, she can have gondolas and a champagne fountain."

"Well there isn't any reason to get defensive about it. I know how you feel. And it isn't as if anyone who knows you will think her taste reflects badly on you," Jilly said. "What else is she planning? Duck for lunch and a Rolls Royce limo?"

"No duck. She doesn't want to offend anyone, after all." I rolled my eyes as I felt swans with pink ribbons might offend a lot of people. "Salmon and chicken. The staple wedding meals."

"Ugh. And they will probably both be overcooked. I hope you know good caterers, Hope," Eugene intoned. "But I doubt you do."

"The caterer is excellent. And the food is never overcooked." Without thinking, the words were ground out of my mouth.

Oops. I had been looking at Eugene, and Jilly was now giving me an odd look.

"You didn't sleep much last night, you said?" Jilly probed.

"I'm sorry, Jilly. I'm not myself today." I could barely hear myself speak over Eugene's obnoxious laughter. "I'll feel better after eating." *If* I can ignore Eugene long enough to get through one conversation without feeling like a fool.

The waitress came up with our salads, and I was frightened that she would trip over Jezebel, who had positioned herself at the next table, where a gentleman was enjoying a steak salad. The waitress made it through, literally, without mishap, and I wondered if Jezebel could even smell or taste food.

My salad was set before me, and I found myself ravenous. I was also relieved that for a few minutes I would not be required to maintain a conversation. The pain in my head was slowly subsiding, and I was certain that a good meal would make it disappear completely. Unfortunately, food was not going to make Eugene disappear.

I guess the habits of the living don't die with you, because Eugene was looking intently at our salads. If he had mastered the art of picking up objects he probably would have poked at the salad with a fork. As it was, he had to content himself with sticking his nose right above Jilly's dish. I stopped myself from calling out in protest, and Eugene soon lost interest in our meals.

He hadn't lost interest in the restaurant though, and slid right through Jilly in order to critique the menu. He stopped at every table, rudely examining their plates, and watching them eat with a sort of mercenary gusto. I still wasn't convinced that he was not just a figment of my imagination, but this behavior made me wonder if he really was Eugene's ghost after all. I didn't think that my mind would conjure up anybody so incredibly vulgar. At least I hoped I not. Of course, Eugene had never been vulgar, just obnoxious. Maybe dying caused one's maturity to drop a few levels.

With Eugene out of the way for a few minutes, I felt that it was a good time to speak seriously with Jilly. I put my fork down and leaned forward, indicating that I had something private to say. "Jilly, I don't know how to say this, but I think..."

How do you tell someone that you fear you are insane because a ghost is following you around? The answer is simple: you don't.

"I think I should see a psychiatrist. I can't seem to forget about Eugene. It's like he is following me around." There. That was pretty much the truth.

Jilly looked at me seriously, frowning. "It's only been a day, Hope. Of course you haven't forgotten it. Who could forget so quickly? Maybe you just need a vacation? I'm not saying that a psychiatrist is a bad idea, but you might not really need one."

"I think I do. I know it sounds crazy, but I think my guilt is making me see things. And I don't just mean reliving the accident. Sometimes I think I see Eugene when I know he can't be there." I didn't mention that I was at present seeing him trying to stick his finger in a piece of chocolate mousse that a middle-aged woman, wearing a hideous purple jumpsuit, was shoving into her mouth.

"That's normal, Hope. Sometimes, when I'm in a crowd, I think I see my mom. But then I remember that she's dead, and it isn't her. I think everyone does that once in awhile." It was obvious that Jilly didn't see her mother constantly, though. My case was not the usual one. But Jilly sounded concerned, and I thanked God that I had such a good friend, even if I couldn't tell her the whole truth.

"I do know of a psychiatrist if you are really set on it. My dad saw him for several years after my mom died. I can get his number from him and give you a call. Maybe the guy can see you this week."

I thanked her, praying that this man would be able to help. I felt a sprig of hope bloom in my breast. This could be the way to get Eugene out of my mind and my life for good. And with that thought I was able to finish my meal in peace and even drive home with equanimity, despite Eugene trying to penetrate my indifference by singing along to every song on the radio in an off-key voice, with Jezebel joining in on the high notes.

Chapter Six

I waited three days before my appointment with the psychiatrist, and those three days were not spent in peace. Eugene haunted me day and night, despite the fact that I refused to acknowledge his presence most of the time, pretending to be oblivious to him or simply maintaining a cold silence. I even tried to escape him on the second day by climbing through a deceptively narrow window in the ladies' room at a local restaurant. I was unsuccessful. I found him waiting for me in the alley, looking annoyed. And that was when he decided to show me what an accomplished actor he was, reciting all of Hamlet's lines in the most dramatic way possible. This lasted for four miserable hours before I finally dissolved into tears and he stopped.

But he still didn't leave.

One time I found him trying to pick up a bag of flour that I had left on the kitchen table. He was practicing at the same moment Jezebel decided the time was ripe to chase Nutter Butter (who was still sadly confused) through the kitchen. Watching Nutter Butter run in circles and even occasionally run straight for Jezebel would have been funny under other circumstances. But just as Eugene finally managed to pick up the bag and hold it for several seconds, Nutter Butter jumped on the kitchen table and then straight through Eugene.

Eugene was understandably startled, having not yet gotten used to being walked through, and dropped the flour. Only the bag was open. If I hadn't ended up covered in white powder I might have been relieved that Nutter Butter managed to avoid concussing himself. But the worst part was that Eugene looked as spotless as before. And he made sure to point out for quite some time that I was definitely not spotless. To my dismay, ghosts don't get dirty. Ever.

I guess I should have been grateful that Eugene gave up on trying to pick up Nutter Butter, which I caught him at late one night when I had gone to the kitchen for some water. After that I kept a closer eye on the cat and also kept a full glass of water by my bed. I had my suspicions that Eugene was spending his nights trying to teach Jezebel to move solid objects too. And I suspected that Nutter Butter would be Jezebel's choice target.

So by the time the third day came around, I was eagerly awaiting my first visit with a psychiatrist.

I hadn't told Eugene about the appointment. Actually, I hadn't really spoken to him at all. I prayed he would stay at my apartment rather than join me. I was even willing to speak to him to accomplish this. "I'm going out now." I had my purse clutched in my hand and my car keys out, so Eugene wasn't surprised. He didn't even seem surprised that I had addressed him.

"I can see that. Where are we going, Pip?"

He could call me whatever he wanted so long as he stayed here. "You don't have to come. It's nothing special. It would probably bore you." I hoped he would decide to be polite and leave me to my own personal affairs for once.

That hope was quickly shattered.

"That's okay. You haven't gone out much the last few days and I could use a change of scenery," he said. "This place is rather small and..." he wrinkled his nose and sniffed audibly, "it's starting to smell a little."

The cat was understandably nervous. I had cleaned it all up. Several times. He was just being difficult for the pleasure of it. "Why don't you take Jezebel for a walk in the park? She can chase the birds," I suggested with a smiled plastered on my face. He looked at me like I had sprouted an extra head. "It's not like I can lock you out." Unfortunately.

"What are you up to, Hope?"

"Nothing," I lied. Well, technically it wasn't a real lie. I wasn't planning anything; I just didn't want him to know I was going to see a psychiatrist.

"You're obviously lying. I bet you've hired an exorcist. Don't think I didn't see you googling exorcists." He stood up and headed for the door. "I'm coming with you. Let's go, Jezebel."

Since there was no way I could get rid of a determined ghost, I gracefully acquiesced. Okay, so in actuality I pouted the whole car ride and refused to speak to him again. I couldn't seem to muster any more grace than that.

I parked the car on a small street running perpendicular to South Broad Street, and put an exorbitant amount of money in the meter. I didn't want to get a parking ticket if the psychiatrist told me I was certifiable and I had to make plans for admitting myself.

As soon as Jezebel jumped from the car, a poodle being walked by its owner paused and turned in our direction, barking incessantly. Jezebel was about to leap into action, looking for a quick tussle, when Eugene yelled at her. Jezebel relented, but the poodle continued to bark at us--at me, since I was the only one visible.

The lady apologized and yanked her dog along the sidewalk in the opposite direction, but not before several unleashed dogs heard the commotion. A small terrier and a much larger German Shepherd appeared at the corner, and sensing Jezebel, began to bound toward us. They paid little attention to me, but barked furiously at the air behind me, only a few feet to the side of Jezebel. They then proceeded to follow me (and Eugene and Jezebel), continuing to bark and circle the empty space behind me. Eugene seemed surprised but amused, and Jezebel looked ridiculously happy.

I looked ridiculous. There was a train of barking dogs following several feet behind me, running around in crazed circles. I hurried my steps even more, while Eugene called to me to slow down. Unfortunately, the spectacle had gathered a few onlookers, and I could hear one woman laughing, and an elderly man making insinuations about my scent. It was mortifying, but a few days with Eugene and I was starting to get used to humiliation. I acted as if I had no idea there was any commotion at all, which might have just made things worse.

The walk to the building was blessedly short, although Jezebel stopped at every meter for a sniff. Only she didn't actually sniff anything. She just sort of stared at the meters, as if she were an amnesia victim seeing something familiar but not quite remembering what she was supposed to do. It almost made me want to cry, except that the dogs following us were also sniffing, as well as doing some unmentionable things.

Sadly, Eugene and Jezebel did not wait outside, but followed me into the building. It was an older building with a strangely austere inside. The walls were painted stark white and boasted no paintings or plaques or certificates. The furniture was modern and sleek, upholstered in shades of gray and black, with a few colorful pillows randomly placed. (And by colorful I mean pale gray-blue and watery green). There were several floor lamps that stood about five feet high, and which gave off a soft yellow light. The carpet, a large abstract piece, was also done in shades of gray, and looked as if it had recently been vacuumed. Or maybe visitors were too intimidated to walk on it.

The only bright spot in the entire room was the receptionist's area, which was situated across from the front door. There were several colorful, unlit candles on the counter, some photographs of young children wearing overalls, and a wall calendar sporting beach scenes.

I approached the receptionist, and noted that she looked completely out of her element. Her hair might have been pulled back into a bun, but she was wearing a green dress with a palm tree pattern, large, dangling earrings, and a necklace that looked like it was fashioned out of bottle caps.

She looked me over, checked her calendar, and said, "You must be here to see Dr. Frank. He'll be out in a minute. His previous session is just ending."

No sooner did she speak then an average-looking man walked dejectedly out of the door at the end of the hall. He nodded a goodbye to the receptionist, pretended I couldn't see him, and left through the front doors.

Eugene, curiosity getting the better of him, read the placard next to the door. "Dr. Andrew Frank, Psychiatrist," he chortled.

The receptionist handed me some forms to fill out while I waited, and I tried to give Eugene the cold shoulder. "A psychiatrist? You're seeing a psychiatrist?" Eugene belted out. "I am *so* glad I decided to join you. This is going to be highly entertaining. What do you intend to talk about? Me? That'll go down really well." Eugene continued to laugh while the receptionist motioned for me to be seated and started filing her cherry-red nails.

I wanted to turn around and hit Eugene, but I thought the receptionist would probably report my lunacy to Dr. Frank, and I didn't want to start off on the wrong foot. Better not to have him think I'm crazy before he even meets me.

Eugene didn't stop laughing until Dr. Frank, a man several inches shorter than I, had greeted me and ushered me into his office. This room was as stark as the one before, with the exception of some intentionally blurry seascapes on the walls. There were two armchairs, a sofa, and a desk.

Dr. Frank didn't motion for me to sit anywhere specific, and I wondered if this were some kind of initial personality test. I decided I had better take one of the armchairs and hope that was acceptable. Dr. Frank sat down in the other chair and folded his hands in his lap, staring intently at me. Eugene decided to sprawl out on one half of the sofa, and then invited Jezebel to join him on the other half, just to put me off balance.

And it worked. I cringed as soon as Jezebel hit the cushions. It didn't matter that ghost dogs didn't spread dirt; it was the principle behind it.

Dr. Frank, who had seen my cringe, attributed it to his presence. "Is this your first time seeing a psychiatrist, Hope?"

"Yes," I said, all the while casting furtive looks at Eugene. He had better not ruin this for me.

"And you're nervous? I can tell. Is it difficult for you, feeling that you need to see a psychiatrist? Let me guess, you've been raised to think psychiatrists are like the big bad wolf. That normal people don't need to see them? Be honest. How does that make you feel?" he asked.

I wasn't sure how to respond. The idea of seeing a psychiatrist didn't make me nervous, but the idea of being proven insane did. "I'm not sure how I feel," I said with a bright smile.

He nodded. "We will work on that."

I had no idea what he meant for us to work on, but I let that go.

"There's nothing to fear. I don't bite," he continued. He then laughed at his own joke, which was not even a joke, just some trite expression.

Eugene snorted and I gave him a threatening glance.

Dr. Frank, oblivious to this interchange (and why shouldn't he be?), lowered his voice to what he must have thought was a soothing tone, "I know this can be an intimidating experience, but it will be well worth it in the end. By the time you are done with our sessions, you will be a well-rounded, self-actualized person, capable of handling anything life throws at you."

That sounded pretty good to me, so I let him continue to tell me all about the benefits I would receive from his expert treatment. He finally finished, and asked, "Now tell me why you're here, Hope?"

"Well, it's rather complicated. A few days ago I watched an acquaintance die. He was hit by a car. And ever since then I have..." Eugene was testing the buoyancy of the cushions, and throwing me off. Suddenly I couldn't remember what I had planned to say. "I can't seem to get rid of him, it, the entire thing. I feel like he's haunting me."

"I see. In what ways do you feel like he is haunting you? Are you continually thinking about him? Do you think you see him in crowds? Do you start to cry at the smallest things?" he inquired.

"Well, not exactly. I mean I can't stop thinking about him because..." How much did I really want to tell the man on my first visit? Could he put me away without my consent? "I sometimes think I can feel his presence."

Eugene burst out laughing.

"I see. And how does that make you feel?" Dr. Frank asked.

"Like I'm going insane." How was that for honesty?

"I see. That's not insane at all." He gave a low chuckle. "Now, Hope, there are several things you have to understand about loss. There are stages one goes through, including shock and denial. Could it be that you are simply trying to keep your friend alive in your mind?"

I know it looked like I scowled at the empty sofa, but I couldn't help myself. "I don't think so. He wasn't really my friend. Just an acquaintance. I believe I already said that. I really can't think of any reason why I would want him to remain with me. I would like nothing more than to never think about him again."

Eugene wasn't offended. He actually looked rather amused. It was the psychiatrist that looked a little put off.

"I see. Perhaps you're feeling guilty? Do you ever wonder why he died and you are still alive? Maybe you think you should have been the one to die? Survivor's guilt can happen in all types of situations. Or are you questioning your own mortality? That's not uncommon at your age."

He made it sound like I was either incredibly young or incredibly old. "No. I don't think that's it. I might feel a tad guilty about the fact that he was standing in the street because he was coming to get something from me, but I certainly never thought I should have been in his place."

"I see." He tapped his finger against his chair and just watched me.

"I see," Eugene aped. "Can't he think of any other response? He makes my mute grandmother's conversation seem stimulating."

I laughed. And then I covered my mouth in horror, wondering if Dr. Frank was about to become a witness to my obvious insanity. "I'm sorry. I didn't mean to laugh."

"That's okay. Lots of people laugh when they are nervous or a subject is too serious. Haven't you ever heard of people laughing at funerals?"

I answered in the affirmative and he continued, "Does death frighten you? Was your friend's death a painful one?"

I looked at Eugene, and he shook his head in disbelief. "What an idiot. Really, Hope, I can't believe you are even here. I died instantly, with no pain, no white light, and no heavenly voice. Satisfied?"

I turned back to the doctor, who looked at me sympathetically. He probably thought I had turned away to hide tears of grief.

"I don't think it was a painful death." It says a lot when I need to have the ghost I came here specifically to eradicate help me with my answers.

"You didn't answer my other question. Does death frighten you?"

"No, I don't think so. I don't know." Should I tell him how I keep receiving deathly predictions and for years have had a dread of death? Perhaps not on the first visit. "I don't want to die, but who does?" I responded. "And I don't want to be haunted, either," I added as an afterthought.

Eugene agreed with me wholeheartedly, voicing his opinion with an occasional slap of furniture. I was determined not to be distracted again, so I shot him a quelling look.

"And how does that make you feel?"

"Can you believe this putz? And how does that make you feel?" Eugene mimicked.

"I don't understand. How does what make me feel?"

"Ah, you're still unwilling to allow your deeper emotions to surface. Can you try to be honest with me, Hope? I'm here to help you. I won't judge you, no matter what you say." His eyes looked sincere, although I could see his fingers twitching against the chair.

"Don't listen to him, Hope. If you tell him that you now have a ghost living with you he will send you to the fruit farm posthaste. Trust me on this one. He can't handle real problems. He's probably only comfortable with bored housewives that have sexual fantasies about their neighbors." Eugene then moved directly behind the doctor and stuck out his tongue while crossing his eyes. It was childish but effective.

"Stop that." Oops. Slipped again.

"I don't understand, Hope. What do you want me to stop? Would you like me to stop questioning you? That is not how you are going to feel better. Denial gets you nowhere. Admitting you have a problem is the first step."

Forget denial, this conversation was getting me nowhere. "Do you believe in ghosts, doctor?"

"Ghosts? I think the real question is, do *you* believe in ghosts, Hope? Is that what you're afraid of--that you might be haunted by your friend?" His voice had taken on a slippery quality, which made the question sound both sinister and ridiculous. His eyes didn't look as friendly now.

"I don't know if I believe in ghosts. I would like to. If there aren't ghosts, then I am probably crazy." What the hell, I might as well go all the way now. "If I'm crazy, then I'm just imagining my dead acquaintance standing behind you pretending to be Dr. Evil. Or maybe he's picking at his teeth. It's hard to tell."

"Ah. I see."

"I'm sorry, but what exactly do you see? You're not being very helpful," I snapped.

"We need to establish the problem before we can fix it. Your anger is not unexpected. You think you are seeing the ghost of your dead friend. This tells me a great deal." He still didn't elaborate and I was beginning to wonder if he had any real training. Perhaps 'Doctor' was his first name.

"Does he talk to you as well?" he continued in his very reasonable and level-headed voice. It was as if he feared the wrong tone of voice might set me off on some murderous rampage.

"Yes, he does."

"And how does that make you feel? Does what he say make you feel guilty? Does he talk about his death? About you being alive instead of him? How often do you see him? At moments of stress?"

"For God's sake, Hope. Let's get out of here. This man is completely insane." Eugene was becoming aggravated and Jezebel, picking up on his mood, started to growl at the doctor. "I can't imagine what made you come here in the first place. This guy couldn't keep the Pope from swearing," Eugene bellowed. "My mute grandmother could give you better help." And with an emphatic thrust, he knocked over the small clock sitting on the desk. It landed with a thud, and the dial rang out.

Dr. Frank jumped out of his chair and picked up the clock. "Time has certainly sped by," he said. "It seems our session is over." I had paid for an hour, and if I weren't so relieved I would have questioned his ability to keep time. "Your problem is a delicate one," he continued, "and not in my area of expertise. I have a colleague who specializes in your kind of...problem, for lack of a better word." He opened his desk drawer, scavenged around for a minute, and then pulled out a card.

"You picked up the clock, so you know it fell. Eugene knocked it over. It wasn't either of us. So I can't be crazy, right? He is real?"

He just stared at me and then pressed the card into my hand. "Of course you're not crazy. You are just grieving. But the breeze from the window knocked the clock over. Can't you see the curtains moving from it? Lots of people who suffer from shock see the person who has left them behind. It is not uncommon, despite what you think." He reluctantly took my arm and led me to the door. "Call my friend. He will help you." And with that, I was ushered back into the reception area.

I sighed. Eugene was giving me another of his smug 'I told you so' smiles, and Jezebel was prancing around, weaving in and out of Eugene's legs, happy to be free of Dr. Frank's presence.

"Do you believe that I really am a ghost now? Not some figment of your imagination?" Eugene asked as we made our way back to the car.

Refusing to talk to Eugene seemed pointless now. He was determined to stay, whether he was really there or not. "I still don't know. Part of my mind thinks I might be crazy. And that's not a pleasant thought. But part of me thinks you have to be real. A little breeze like that couldn't have knocked over the clock. And I didn't imagine it falling because that idiot doctor actually picked it up." I sighed again, something I seemed to be doing a great deal lately.

I unlocked the car, but didn't get inside. I stood at the door, facing Eugene over the hood of the car.

He stared back, looking more serious than I had seen him since the night he entered my bedroom. "I wish I could convince you that you're not crazy, Hope. I know I'm dead yet still wandering around on Earth. That makes me a ghost. You aren't insane because I know I'm really here. And besides, people who are convinced they are insane rarely are. It's the ones who are convinced they're sane that usually aren't."

"Let's say you are ghost. Why are you haunting me? Why can't anyone else see you?" Hopefully it wasn't because I had committed a grievous sin in a past life and was destined to go through eternity with Eugene at my side.

"That's what I'd like to know. I was a little, um, upset, at the way my life so abruptly ended. Well, you were there. You saw how disturbing it was. But I imagine most people are upset when they die. There probably isn't anything special about that. So why am I still here? Or is this what happens to everyone? I need to know."

I spotted several dogs heading in this direction, and I quickly got into the car, urging Eugene and Jezebel to do the same. I didn't want another scene. And there was no reason for me to stand outside my car looking like I was talking to the air. For all I knew the doctor was watching me, reporting my every movement to some insane asylum.

"Well, what now?" Eugene asked. I was starting to think he might be real after all, and he was getting cocky because of it.

"There's a few people we could try, but one in particular comes to mind." I smiled at him, and for once he was the one who looked nervous.

Chapter Seven

Everton, situated about twenty-five miles northwest of Philadelphia, is a small town of approximately two thousand people. It boasts more churches than stores and has not yet acquired a stoplight. The main street is lined with old-fashioned buildings of a primarily colonial nature, though a few federal and Victorians were thrown in for variety. The town is picturesque and peaceful; exactly the sort of place one raised a family.

"You grew up here? I should have known," Eugene snorted.

"Everton is a very nice place," I snapped back. "Where were you raised, a traveling circus?"

"No. I was raised in Philadelphia, if you must know. Suburbia doesn't do much for me." Eugene, already looking bored with the conversation, looked behind him to make sure Jezebel wasn't chewing on the car.

"This isn't suburbia—it's the country. There's a big difference. And stop looking at Jezebel. It makes me nervous. Ghosts can't do any harm, right? She isn't going to slaver over the seats, is she?"

"No. She can't slaver. But I'm trying to teach her to move things with her nose. She hasn't succeeded yet, but I know she will if she really focuses," he said proudly.

"I doubt she will be able to move the car with her nose." I couldn't believe I was even having this conversation. Who in their right mind was concerned about ghostly dogs tearing up the upholstery in their car—besides myself, that is?

"It's not the car I was thinking of." He turned back toward me, and leaned back in his seat. "You left your purse back there."

I checked the rear view mirror, and could see Jezebel debating over whether or not to continue her assault on the seat.

All she had managed to do so far was push her head through the seat and into Eugene. Seeing the two of them merge was incredibly creepy.

"Is it much farther?" Eugene asked.

"No. It's just another minute or two. Hey, stop that." I slapped at Eugene's hand, only to find my own sinking right through his. "Don't play with the radio!"

"I was only trying to see if I could move the dials. Your conversation hasn't been very stimulating. Even you must admit that."

He really knew how to irritate me.

"What do you expect? I'm trying to cope with the fact that I have a snotty ghost and his dog on my hands. You could try to be a little more understanding." What did he want from me?

"And what about me? It isn't exactly easy finding yourself dead and stuck with an uptight female that listens to Neil Diamond."

He was probably right. I wasn't being sympathetic enough. He was most likely having as bad a time as I was. Not worse--because he didn't think he was going insane--but still bad. "Lots of people listen to Neil Diamond. And I'm not uptight. At least not usually."

"Yeah, yeah. Whatever." He actually looked like he was moping. I hoped God wasn't sticking me with a manic-depressive.

"We're here. St. Jude's Catholic Church." Hopefully the answers could be found here.

"A church? A Catholic church? Do they even let Jewish people in there?"

"I don't see why not. Jesus was a Jew. Besides, your dead. How can they stop you?" I really hoped he wasn't going to make this any more difficult than it was going to be.

"What if your God decides to strike me down with lightning for my blasphemy?" He eyed the church doors nervously, and sidled away.

"I think it's the same God. Don't worry. He can't kill you

twice. At least I've never heard of anyone dying twice. Come on," I urged.

Eugene looked wary, and incredibly suspicious. "Aren't all priests child molesters or serial killers?"

"Don't be ridiculous. You can't generalize like that. And I've never heard of a serial killer priest. But if you don't want to come in, you can wait out here. Maybe you can practice moving objects. There's a nice gift some dog left on the lawn right over there. Have fun." I abruptly turned around and walked into the vestibule. I didn't care if Eugene came with me or not. As a matter of fact, this might even be easier without him.

But God likes to toy with me—obviously—so, naturally, Eugene decided to join me.

The inside of the church was empty except for an older woman in a floral print dress with a white smock. She was standing at the altar arranging flowers, and turned around as soon as she heard voices.

It was Mrs. Mahoney. Just my luck. Of all people to run into, she was the one I would have most wished to avoid. Mrs. Maloney was the worst gossip in the parish, which was why she was eagerly welcomed into every house in town.

"Why, Hope. What a pleasant surprise. Your mother didn't say you were going to pay the church a visit today. If I had known, I would have made some muffins and brought them over." If I am to be totally honest, Mrs. Mahoney did make excellent blueberry muffins, which might also contribute to her being welcome everywhere.

"It's a spur of the moment visit. I wanted to speak with Father Martinez."

Eugene, who had kept mercifully silent up to this point, decided to try his luck with God. "What do you think, Hope? What if I yelled really loudly? Would God hear me and be angry? Or do you think he has a sense of humor?"

I was fairly certain God had a sense of humor—a sick one. And Eugene and I were living (or not living) proof of that. But I couldn't say anything, so I pretended not to hear Eugene, instead grabbing Mrs. Mahoney by the arm and leading her away. She nearly walked through Eugene as she knelt to genuflect, and arched her eyebrow at me when I forgot to do so. It wasn't my fault, though. Eugene had decided not to yell, but was instead searching for the wine and bread kept behind the altar.

"I just want to see what kind of quality they use," he said to me as I led Mrs. Mahoney to the side door.

"Have you come to see Father Martinez about a personal problem, dear? Confession? I would like to help if I could," Mrs. Mahoney coyly said.

Like I would ever tell her my personal problems. The whole state would know about them within hours. I bet she had a line to all the local newspapers. "No, nothing like that, Mrs. Mahoney. I am checking the availability of the church for some clients."

"Anyone I know?" she enquired.

"No. They live in the city but want a country church," I lied.

"You did check to make sure they were Catholic, didn't you? I know some other denominations aren't so choosy about who they let marry in their churches." She sounded like she had already taken up the issue with the Pope.

"They're Catholic. Is Father Martinez around?" I wanted to get this over with, especially since Eugene was catching up with us rather quickly. Apparently he had been unable to locate the bread and wine.

"In his office. You know the way? I'll just finish up with the flowers. Say hello to your mother for me. Perhaps we'll see you on Sunday?" she asked.

"Perhaps." Maybe if I had gone to church more I wouldn't be stuck with Eugene.

I reached Father Martinez's office and knocked. The slight pounding echoed loudly through the hallway, and made me wonder if I was doing the right thing. Father Martinez might not be able to put me into a sanitarium, but he might decide that I was the one who needed to be exorcised rather than Eugene. I had seen "The Exorcist", and I knew what happened to people unfortunate enough to attract the dead. They used to burn people at the stake for this kind of stuff.

But I was being paranoid, and deep down I knew it. Father Martinez was a modern priest, not some witch hunter. The worst he could do was assign me a lifetime of Hail Marys.

He opened the door and stepped into the hallway, his tall figure blocking out most of the light. I had known Father Martinez for several years, and his presence did not intimidate me, but Eugene seemed strangely nervous. He had lapsed into silence and was standing more erect than usual.

Father Martinez was in his late fourties, with dark hair that was graying at the temples. He was good-looking and had such a paternal air about him, despite his relative youth, that he was a favorite among the younger parishioners.

"Hello, Hope. I didn't expect to see you. As a matter of fact, I haven't seen you in quite some time. Too long, if I may say so." He smiled in such a benevolent way that I felt a coil of shame inside me.

"I know. I'm sorry. I've been busy." Wow! That sounded lame even to my ears. "Er, hopefully I'll be able to make it to church soon."

He just gave me a knowing smile and ushered me into his office, where he offered me a chair in front of his desk. He moved slowly around his desk and sat in his own chair, leaning forward so that I didn't feel the need to speak loudly. "What can I do for you today?"

Eugene was standing just inside the doorway, Jezebel at his heels, equally awed, and I looked at him for confirmation. Did I really want to tell another person about this? Soon everyone would think I was some kind of loony. Eugene just shrugged his shoulders, leaving it up to me, and I decided to go ahead. I was willing to receive a lifetime of Hail Marys if it would let me sleep at night.

"It's rather personal, Father. And, well, strange. I wasn't even sure if I should come, but I didn't know whom else to talk to," I burst out.

"You can trust me, Hope. I won't tell anyone—not even your mother. You know that. And if I can help you I will." He gave me such a genuinely good-natured smile that I thought this might just be the right person to tell.

"A colleague of mine was killed a few days ago. He was hit by a car, and I saw the whole thing," I said.

"Yes. Your mother mentioned it to me the other day. I am so sorry. That must have been terrible to see."

I didn't look back at Eugene, but I could feel his eyes on me. "It was terrible. Thank you. But that isn't quite the problem." I paused. Was the direct route the best way? I didn't know. Maybe I should get a feel for his stance first. "Do you believe in ghosts, Father?"

He looked at me seriously for a few moments before answering. "My old mentor, Father Douglas, used to say that the world was full of many mysteries and a priest should be open to anything. God can work in many ways and through many forms." He eyed me speculatively. "Are you seeing a ghost, Hope? Is this why you asked if I believe in them?"

Okay, here it goes. "Yes. I know it sounds crazy, but it's true. When my colleague was hit, I just stared. And then he suddenly stood up. Only he was still lying on the ground. At least one of him was. And he's been spending just about every minute with me since then. Talking to me and everything." Yeah, that sounded crazy all right.

Apparently Father Martinez thought so too. "It does sound crazy, Hope, but I don't believe you would make something like this up. I believe that you think you are seeing your colleague, but whether or not he is really a ghost I don't know. Have you thought about seeing a counselor?"

"Yes. I just came from him. He didn't think he could help me. But the truth is, Father, that for a while I thought I was insane. I thought that my mind had created Eugene from shock or guilt. But I don't really think so anymore. I think he must be a ghost. He actually moved a clock, and I saw it fall and so did the psychiatrist." I looked at him, wanting him to believe me.

Again he took a long time to answer, carefully choosing his words. "I am not going to say that I disbelieve you since the church has documented alleged ghosts, but you are asking me to believe something that most people consider impossible. Are you sure that he is a ghost, not a figment of your mind? Are you sure you aren't wanting to see him, from a desire to have him still be alive?"

I glanced slightly to my left, where I could see part of Eugene, pretending not to be interested in the conversation and picking that nonexistent lint off his coat. "Yes. Like I said, I thought I was insane for quite a few days. But now I think he really is a ghost. And it does sound crazy. And maybe I am crazy, but don't you believe in miracles, Father?" I wasn't sure this was a miracle, so much as a form of torture, but I wanted reassurance.

"Yes. I believe in miracles." He gave me a small smile, the corners of his mouth turning upwards just enough to make his teeth show. "But the miracles I usually witness are the everyday miracles—the birth of a child, a wedding, someone helping a stranger. Ghosts aren't everyday miracles."

"So you don't believe me?" I asked, feeling rather let down.

"I didn't say that. I am willing to believe you. Look at all the grand miracles the Church has witnessed. Jesus was resurrected from the dead," he said quietly. His eyes wandered around the room, alighting on his bookshelf before returning to me. "But ask yourself why this is happening to you." He reached over and patted my hand. "I don't think you are insane or that you need to be put away. And I am not going to call the mental ward as soon as you step out that door. Or your mother."

He laughed a little, and then continued, "Everything you have said will stay just between us. But I do think you need to really question why you are seeing what you think is a ghost."

"Yes. You're probably right, Father. I hadn't really gotten that far." He didn't really believe me. I could see it in his eyes. But I wasn't going to press it any further.

"Come back whenever you need to talk. If there is anything I can do, you need only to ask." He sounded almost repentant. Perhaps he felt bad that he didn't believe me.

"Thank you. I will."

"Father Douglas always says that God's plan is more like a jigsaw puzzle than a road map. If you are seeing a ghost, and I rather hope you are, then you'll get your answers in time," he encouraged.

"Father, if Eugene is really a ghost, and he assures me he is, then why is he still here? Why hasn't he made it to heaven?"

Eugene finally spoke up, though it was almost inaudible, "It's not because I'm Jewish is it? There is an afterlife, isn't there?"

I broke in before he could answer, wanting Eugene reassured. "It's not because my colleague was Jewish, is it? I'm not certain on their beliefs about heaven, but that couldn't be it, could it?"

"No. I believe that we all go to the same place in the end. If all questions were so easy...But I can't answer why your colleague is still here. Father Douglas claimed to have seen a spirit. As a matter of fact, that was why he entered into the priesthood. Or so he told me."

I was not about to become a nun because Eugene decided to hang around Earth for a while, but I kept silent, hoping some token of wisdom would peek through Father Martinez's reminiscing.

Father Martinez continued to hark back to Father Douglas, his soft voice growing a little more certain in this familiar territory. "But he never mentioned why the spirit was there. Or who it was for that matter. I did ask, several times actually. But Father Douglas had his secrets as well. But I've been straying from the topic." He gave me that smile that charmed his parishioners. "As for your question, I'm not sure. Doesn't all the literature say that it is either because of unfinished business, a warning, or a soul too afraid of death? Who knows? Your ghost hasn't issued you any dire warnings, has he?"

I knew he meant that as a joke, and that he meant it kindly, as a token of belief, and if he had said that he had no doubt I was seeing ghosts and was willing to participate in emancipating Eugene, I would have laughed wholeheartedly. As it was, I was feeling rather discouraged. Eugene, loafing against the wall behind me, gave a deep sigh, echoing my thoughts. I knew it was time to go.

"Goodbye, Father, and thanks," I said. I stood up and held out my hand, and he gripped it firmly, holding it longer than was usual, his paternal side coming out in full force.

"I only wish I could have been more of a help. Why don't you start attending services again? It might make things clearer. We have such a nice parish, with lots of charming men near your age. You could make some new friends."

He had definitely been talking to my mother lately. And I also suspected he thought that new friends might lessen my interest in ghosts.

I nodded and turned away. I wasn't sure there was anything more to be said. For now, Eugene and I were on our own.

Chapter Eight

If life were as Hollywood portrayed it, Eugene's funeral would have attracted a large crowd of weeping mourners, dismal in unrelieved black and clenching handkerchiefs, barely noticing the torrential rain. The women would toss single roses upon the lowered casket, while the men placed their arms around the weeping women's shoulders and led them away. And one person, a heavily veiled female or a pale-faced, serious male, would remain by the casket, making a momentous vow or proclaiming undying love. And for one moment, noticeable only to those well versed in trite Hollywood scenes, a small ray of sunshine would break free of the clouds, and the mourner would have an epiphany. Then, just as suddenly as it appeared, the sunshine would dissolve into the grey sky and the mourner would slowly trod back to the car, a silent, shadowy figure in a barren cemetery on an even more barren cliff-side overlooking a stormy ocean.

But I don't live in a Hollywood movie. There was no torrential rain at Eugene's funeral, no dark, forbidding clouds, and not one umbrella in case of just such an occurrence. In fact, the weather was beautiful. The sky was a deep blue, and the sun shone warmly upon the somberly dressed shoulders of all present at the cemetery. There was no ocean to gaze upon, just rows of headstones amid lush lawn and blossoming trees. And not one mourner wore a veil or carried a flower (Eugene told me that flowers and music go against Jewish custom). I had no epiphany and made no vows, and as far as I could tell, no one else did either. In fact, the only melodrama involved Eugene's running commentary (this was actually quite dismal) on his relations and coworkers and the poor choices his relatives made in regards to the pallbearers. And I thought my mother was hard to please!

"And that's my cousin, Ethan. If there is a black sheep in every family, he's ours. Barely graduated from high school, if you can believe it. And now he runs a laundromat. Or maybe it is a porn store. Anyway, he's an idiot," Eugene sniggered, as the pallbearers made their first stop. "And that other loafer, that's my cousin Jeremy. Not such a bad fellow, but very high in the instep. His mother's fault, no doubt."

I wanted to laugh. Who was Eugene to complain about someone being too snotty? He had been the forerunner of snobbery at the newspaper. And that was saying a lot, since there were several fierce competitors for the position.

But he was oblivious to my thoughts, totally immersed in his funeral. "And that's my Uncle David. He's a lawyer in D.C. He probably arranged the funeral. He is very good at that sort of thing. And he likes to be in charge. I bet he was furious it took them so long to bury me."

I was standing among a group of colleagues, and didn't want to set myself up as a loony in front of them, so I didn't immediately reply, only nodded in response, made a choking cough, and then squeaked out a soft, "Really?"

"Mm-hmm. Oh good, we're on the fourth stop now. Not too much longer. Can you believe they chose that prick Daniel as a pallbearer? What a schmuck! He would sell his own mother if the offer were good enough--or maybe for any price. He was my neighbor growing up." He paused, looking around at the crowd that had assembled, and then stood on his tiptoes to get a better look. "I wonder where Tim and Bill are? They were my college roommates. I was certain they would be here." He looked disappointed and I was glad I was unable to comment.

"Does anyone know what they're reciting?" a woman near me asked. "I can barely hear anything back here."

"A psalm," answered a newspaper employee that had only recently started, and probably only knew Eugene in passing.

A few other people quietly mumbled and grumbled, flushed guiltily (probably from their noticeable lack of interest) and then looked earnestly at the procession.

This was my chance to enter into Eugene's conversation

without being thought insane. "Does anyone know the immediate family? Or anyone else here?" I asked.

Ari, perhaps the only one at the paper who knew anything of Eugene's history, stepped closer to me and whispered, "That's his sister, Judith. And those are her two sons, but I can't remember their names. I don't think Eugene was very close to them. And those three are some cousins, I think. And his uncle and aunt."

"What about his parents?" I queried, despite Eugene frowning down at me.

"Both dead. I don't think he really knew his dad, and his mom died a few years back." Ari stopped speaking as the pall-bearers reached the seventh stop, and then continued hurriedly, "I don't think he liked his family much. As a matter of fact, I bet Eugene would be pretty pissed at the crowd assembled if he could see them. Not a lot of people--at least not as many as I would have expected. And not too many friends, either."

If he only knew how right he was!

Eugene wasn't looking happy. His face was set in a scowl, his body rigid, and his eyes dark with anger.

His reaction made me earnestly pray that I don't have to witness my own funeral. It's bound to be disappointing. You always think you have more friends than you really do.

Note to self: Plan your funeral ahead of time. And make sure to include a list of everyone you would like notified. This is handy for garnering larger crowds (which will make you feel as if you were extremely well loved) and cost-effective in regards to the amount of flowers the ones left behind must purchase. This would be good stuff for a column, I thought. My dad had already written out all his degrees and awards and community work, just in case. Not that I thought my mother would leave anything out if she were forced to write his obituary.

The pallbearers had reached the gravesite, and the service continued--at least for everyone else.

While the Eyl Malei Rahamin (Eugene tells me this is a prayer for the peace of the departed soul) was being recited, I was listening to Eugene enumerate on the possible reasons for his friends' absences, list the many crimes his Uncle Joe had committed against the family, and make several snide remarks about the attire of his attractive cousin John. While the earth was shoveled into the grave using a reverse shovel, I was entertained with a list of the follies of the police in allowing lunatics on the street that were bound to eventually kill an innocent and cherished member of society. And when the immediate family recited the Kaddish, I was tortured with a description of Eugene's many accomplishments throughout his life and the means in which God, and society, could make this up to him. I desperately wanted to tell him that as a dead man he was not likely to be given an honorary doctorate from Georgetown (I didn't get to ask what the doctorate would be for) or several hours in the White House in which to tell off the president. And I really wanted to tell him that God was probably not going to give him a seat at His right hand in Eugene's rather warped (in my personal opinion) version of paradise (in which there was lots of gourmet food and jazz music).

I opted not to attend the reception held afterwards, Eugene having become a strain on my nerves during his last recital of the many faults of modern society in so easily forgetting the dead. I imagined that I would suddenly turn on him in a fit of annoyance in the middle of the reception, thereby making it know that I talked to invisible people. That probably wouldn't make me popular, and would severely decrease the number of people willing to attend my own funeral, whenever that unhappy occasion occurred. I decided it was safer to see Jilly at The Bon Vivant and grab a fortifying cup of tea (maybe laced with something stronger).

Eugene's expression of disappointment made me want to laugh. I was quite certain he only wanted to attend the reception in order to see what kind of food was being served and whether they had gotten out the best china for the occasion.

But he was soon resigned to accompanying me—at least he was after I threatened to leave him here where he would be forced to take a bus back to my place. Apparently he has a fear of public transportation and the inevitable germs that one would acquire. When I told him dead people didn't catch diseases he wasn't mollified, assuring me that even the dead were likely to be affected by public transportation. Not particularly loving the bus system myself, I didn't argue. I had won the argument, after all. I was willing to be generous and let him have his point.

Chapter Nine

"Get away from there!" I hissed.

Eugene looked at me and smirked, but didn't budge.

"I mean it. I'm not going to take you anywhere ever again if you don't stop this right now," I murmured though clenched teeth. "You're behaving like a three-year old."

As Eugene bent down again, his leg blocking the doorway (at least it would have if people hadn't keep walking through it), I wondered how I had ever thought this man was dignified. Instead of giving him dignity, death had taken it away. He had become so intent on trying to touch and move objects, disrupting several diners by shifting salt and pepper shakers, that I had pleaded with him not to do anything that would scare people away from the restaurant. His compromise was to try to trip people as they walked through the doorway. He argued that this way they could only blame themselves for being clumsy. I hadn't been convinced, worried he was likely to cause Jilly a lawsuit when someone claimed they slipped on a wet or damaged floor. But Eugene was bored and upset from the funeral, and there was no arguing with him. I was just grateful I had convinced him to leave Jezebel at home this morning, though I dreaded returning home and finding Nutter Butter in a frenzied panic because Jezebel decided to play with the poor cat.

"Sorry it took so long, Hope. We had some trouble with the oven this morning and the repair man just left." Jilly sat down with a plop, and stretched out her arms, giving a large yawn. "How was the funeral?"

"Oh, you know how funerals are—dull and depressing," I remarked.

"Yeah. And especially for someone you didn't really like. You didn't need to go, you know," Jilly said.

"You're wrong," I replied, craning my neck slightly to

see if Eugene could hear us. He couldn't. Having tired of his game, he was meandering toward the kitchen. I hoped he didn't intend to move anything in there.

"Just because you saw him die doesn't mean you have any special connection--or that you needed to upset yourself by going to the funeral. I bet that not everyone from the paper went," Jilly added.

"No, of course not everyone went, although I saw a few people there I hadn't expected. That new guy in accounting was there, which was kind of weird. But everyone who knew him fairly well went. I guess I knew him fairly well. As well as anyone else did. And ever since he died I have begun to think he probably doesn't—didn't--have many friends and could use some extra bodies at his funeral." That was only half a lie, and everyone knew that telling half a lie, like a white lie, wasn't really a sin. And I couldn't very well tell her that Eugene had been desperate to see how people had reacted to his death. And if I were honest with myself, my own sense of guilt, coupled with a desperate hope that someone else—perhaps someone close to him--would see Eugene, had likewise prompted me to go.

"Well, it doesn't matter now. How are things going otherwise? You look kind of beat," Jilly added in her frank way.

"I'm a little tired, I guess. I haven't been sleeping well lately. But it isn't anything a few good nights of sleep won't cure." Okay, that was another half-lie. But I still wasn't used to sleeping while a ghost watched television in my living room. And once I got used to that, and had a few nights of decent sleep, I would feel better. I hoped so, anyway.

"Martin hasn't been sleeping well either. Maybe it's something in the air. Do you know if it's a full moon? My mom used to claim that no one ever slept well during a full moon," Jilly added a little distractedly. "Did you hear something break?"

God, why are you doing this to me? I really hoped Eugene was not responsible. "No. I didn't hear anything. And if something important broke someone would come tell you, right?"

"Yeah. I shouldn't worry about it. We were talking

about you."

"I thought we were talking about full moons causing people to lose sleep. And it isn't a full moon right now, by the way. Maybe it's bad karma floating around the universe or electrical disturbances in the area? Or maybe Mad Cow disease has infected local cattle?" I suggested.

Jilly laughed. "You never know," she responded. "Maybe it's a new torture device that aliens are trying out on us? Or, better yet, a new method of controlling the population that Homeland Security has thought up? By using television waves, or something like that?"

Jilly had long since been a conspiracy theory nut, and was often heard making random suggestions about secret government plots to control the populace—most of which involved spy satellites and the dumbing-down of people through television and an intentionally under-funded education system all to secure upper-class domination. I secretly agreed with her— except for her theory about listening devices being hidden in energy efficient flashlight bulbs, which I was still trying to make sense of.

"I expect it's nothing more than a failing economy which is making sleep difficult," I asserted. "People are worried about their futures."

"Nothing doing. It is definitely not normal. My neighbor told me he hasn't had a good night's sleep in a month, and that his wife hadn't either. The cause is definitely something out there—some supernatural phenomenon," Jilly declared triumphantly.

"Doesn't your neighbor work as a night security guard? And I thought his wife was always moaning about how she worried he was going to be shot by robbers?"

"So? That doesn't mean anything. I'm telling you, Hope, it's supernatural. That psychic on TV is probably right. You know, the one that communicates with the dead. John or Jeff something or other. He said that the dead could sense that something is going wrong with the planet. Or maybe that other talk show host said that--the one that's on late in the afternoon, with the red hair and beard."

"That's Bill McClean, the local newscaster, and I doubt he said anything like that. All he does is talk about how much crime is committed in this country and how the common man is suffering from delusions of grandeur." His newscasts contained so much commentary that he was becoming a local joke and thus gaining in popularity. He was now the most watched newscaster in the area.

Jilly wasn't going to be deterred, however, which I thought I might be able to use to my advantage. She continued eagerly, "But someone said it, and I believe it. This world is teetering on the brink and I have no doubt that all that bad energy is causing tons of people sleepless nights. Myself included."

"Do you really believe all that supernatural stuff, Jilly? About ghosts and angels and a spirit world?" I asked.

"Oh, I don't know," she responded. "I guess I'm like you. Don't you always say you're open to believing in anything? Well, I'm a willing believer. How do we know that some angel isn't sitting next to us, laughing at how foolish the living are?"

More like some ghost causing chaos in the kitchen.

"And I definitely think the world is heading downhill. I bet all that negative energy is causing bad things to happen." Jilly looked thoughtful for a moment before adding, "And didn't we read all about Nostradamus and his predictions years back, when people were freaking out about Y2K. I'm not sure I believe it, but you never know."

"No, you never know. If you wanted to find out more about the spirit world—and its predictions for the future," I added hastily, "who would you talk to?"

"A psychic like that John—Jeff—James person, I guess. Or you could read up on Nostradamus, although I gather there are quite a few possible interpretations of his writings." She looked at me, her face oddly serious. "Why do you ask? You're not still hung up on dying young, are you? Lately I thought you were getting better about that. Is there something wrong with you? Why would you need a psychic?"

The question I was dreading. I didn't want to say that I was planning an event that called for a psychic as entertainment because Jilly would insist on knowing more (probably so she could crash the party). And I couldn't say I was writing a column about ghosts because that subject hardly fell into the etiquette category.

Then an answer came instantly to my mind—something that had been nagging at me for awhile. "Oh, I don't need a psychic. I'm just curious. Actually, I was speaking with Colby about the wedding the other day, and I asked her why her grandmother wasn't going to be seated at the head table. She told me that her grandmother was an embarrassment because she claims that her dead husband haunts her. And Colby was quite serious about not having her grandmother seated near anyone of any importance. I guess it made me wonder if there actually were people out there who spoke to ghosts, or believed that they saw them? It occurred to me that all these people might have been very attached to the ghost when he or she was alive, or felt guilt about the person's death, or something like that. It might make a good column on dealing with grief." I paused and tried to gauge Jilly's reaction. "And I admit that Eugene's death has made me start to wonder about what happens when someone dies. That's not too unusual, is it?" Jilly gave a frustrated sigh in response, so I continued more lightheartedly. "And I will admit that when Colby told me about her grandmother I actually choked on my tea. I'm not sure if it was surprise that her grandmother might be nuts, or that Colby would admit it to me."

Jilly looked humorously blissful. "Colby's grandmother? She really talks to her dead husband. Boy would I love to hear that insanity really does run in her family. It would make my year." She smiled and leaned back, savoring the thought. "And seeing you choke on your tea wouldn't have gone amiss, either. Were you instantly smitten with guilt and plagued with thoughts of your mother finding out?"

I must have looked guilty because Jilly laughed. "You're getting too predictable, my dear. Your mother can't be in two places at the same time, and while she might be embarrassed that you had made such a faux pas, she is unlikely to hold it against you for the rest of your life."

I put on my mulish look. "I know that. But when something is drilled into your head for nearly thirty years, it's hard to forget. And I did look like a proper fool," I argued, "so it was only natural that I feel embarrassed. You would too. But never mind my sad social skills, what about the hauntings? Where do you think I could find out more?"

"I suppose you could do some research in the library, though I have no idea what you would look under. Psychology maybe? Or you could talk to a psychic, like the one I was telling you about," she suggested. "That show isn't filmed here, but maybe they have a hotline or something."

"I doubt their hotline is to answer questions about ghosts."

"Well, I don't know what else to suggest, other than the internet. And don't look so serious. It is nice of you to want to help people deal with grief or even to know how to talk to nut jobs, but this just might be taking your job and good manners to the extreme." She paused and looked at me thoughtfully before asking, "This is really just about you seeing Eugene, isn't it? I know we talked already about your seeing him in crowds and how that was normal for a while. You're not still seeing him, are you? Cause you guys weren't that close."

She looked hard at me. "Are you still thinking about that stupid fortune teller you saw on your birthday? Because if you think you are cursed or something I will have to beat some sense into you."

I looked away, wondering how much I could really tell me closest friend. "It's more than that. And she wasn't the only one to say something to me about death. Maybe I am just curious since it seems to be a running theme in my life."

"Let it go, Hope. That stupid prediction in high school wasn't real, and this one isn't either. You are definitely going to see your thirtieth birthday, no matter what some mean old bat implied at grad night. You can't keep believing a stupid prediction made over a decade ago. You're almost thirty, as your mother likes to point out. Definitely too old to believe anything that an old woman with a crystal ball says. Then and now."

"How do you know? The fortune teller from high school

talked about death. And then the one on my birthday mentioned death. Maybe there's just something about me that screams out, 'dead woman walking.' Or maybe I'm cursed and am going to be haunted by random people, like that TV show with the woman who spoke to ghosts." I sounded peevish, but Jilly just laughed. She didn't see how scared the thought of perpetual haunting made me. The psychic at grad night predicted Jilly would get married, have three kids, and drive a minivan. Not what Jilly wanted to hear at the time, since she had been sure she was going to be a famous artist and world traveler, but still nothing compared to what I got. Death, plain and simple. I can remember the eerie lilt of the woman's voice as she drawled, "Death will find you before you are thirty." Needless to say, I spent that night in tears in the bathroom. Not my most favorite high school memory.

"Hmm. I don't think you scream 'death'. Obsessively polite, maybe," Jilly responded, trying to make me laugh. "You know what I'm saying, Miss OPD. You are too nice and you should have told both the fortune tellers off as soon as the predictions were made."

I frowned. And then immediately straightened out the frown, hearing an echo of my mother's voice telling me I would get wrinkles that way. "You know I can't help being polite. It's my mom's fault. And I've been working on it. And don't call me Miss OPD. What is it with people calling me names lately?"

"You have gotten better. You only said 'excuse me' twice to that couple who bumped into you earlier. But then again, you did also attend a funeral of someone you didn't even like today. And I bet you told everyone how wonderful the guy was and how he would be missed."

I blushed. But I couldn't tell her that with Eugene standing next to me I didn't have much choice.

"It's the OPD coming out in you again." Sadly, she was being serious.

For years Jilly had teased me that I had what she calls 'Obsessive Politeness Disorder' (OPD), which was why I almost always felt a compulsion to be polite and well-mannered. I didn't seem to have a problem thinking impolite thoughts, just in getting them to leave my mouth. According to Jilly, courtesy was my killer; I was too nice and it needed to stop. She repeatedly told me it made me a doormat. She was right. But there was nothing I could seem to do about it.

Despite my OPD, Jilly's behavior never bothered me, no matter how inappropriate or foolish. And that was a good thing, since Jilly was clumsy beyond belief. And lacked a filter. And swore like a sailor. Sometimes I thought she was the kind of person I wanted to be. If only I knew how to let go of those hang-ups.

"Still," Jilly continued lightly, "you should live the year up because thirty is not far ahead. Just in case." She was smirking now. "Because when thirty comes, your life as you know it will be over. And I don't mean because you'll be dead like some fortune teller says. It will be over because your mother will probably disinherit you if you're still single. Or maybe if you're lucky, your mother will die of shame and leave you in peace." She made the sign of the cross and silently asked my mother, not God, to forgive her.

"So let go of all this death talk. Forget Eugene. His death was tragic and it is horrible that you saw it, but you need to move forward. And forget all this nonsense about psychics. You aren't cursed or going to die or anything like that. It's all non-sense and it's time you stopped obsessing about it."

I guess telling her that I was actually being haunted wasn't going to go over well.

Luckily, I was saved from responding when a large crash echoed from the kitchen and caused several patrons to look toward that door. Eugene glided through the door swiftly, a look of surprise on his face, and headed in my direction.

"Sorry, Hope. I had better go see what happened. We'll talk later, okay," and then Jilly was rushing to the scene of disaster that undoubtedly awaited her.

Eugene came up, all apologies, but I wasn't about to tell him that for once I was grateful for his pranks.

"It wasn't my fault. I wasn't even near that tray. I did manage to push the broom a little, but how was I to know that idiot of a waiter wouldn't see it. My blind grandmother would have seen it," he exclaimed.

I was beginning to like Eugene's blind grandmother, even though I was certain he had claimed she was mute. "Fine. I believe you. But next time don't move anything. *Anything,*" I repeated, in case he had failed to hear me the first time. "Now let's go before people notice that I'm talking to the air."

Besides, we didn't have time to dawdle since I had a psychic to locate.

Chapter Ten

"Where do you suppose she has gone?" I asked Eugene.

He just shrugged his shoulders and walked to a neighboring booth that claimed to sell every brand of cigar available.

Next to the psychic's tent was a burly man in a Grateful Dead t-shirt, selling inexpensive jewelry, hookahs, and oddly shaped candles. Or rather, upon closer inspection, genital-shaped candles. I pretended not to notice while Eugene did a more thorough inspection of the goods, shaking his head in disdain. He really should meet my mother, I thought. Heck, he could even compete with Aunt Maude for sheer haughtiness.

Since all the other vendors were all helping customers, and this vendor had a friendly face and no customers, I approached him with my nicest smile. "Excuse me, but do you happen to know where the psychic—" I tried to read the sign above the tent but was having difficulty deciphering the ornate letters—"Madame Hurcovy—Musevy—"

"Muscovy. Bit hard to read, isn't it? But the old broad likes it that way. Adds an aura of mystery, if you know what I mean," he divulged. "It makes her seem foreign, too, which is far from the truth. Born right here, she was. But she'll never admit to it," he said, while laughter gurgled up from that rather large belly. "Afraid it would make her seem like a common psychic, rather than a genuine gypsy."

"Well, she might have something there. I guess people would rather be told their fortune from a Madame Muscovy rather than a Madame Smith," I chimed in.

"That's the way of her sort of business. All flash and little truth. " He suddenly looked a little embarrassed, as if realizing that he might be deterring her customers, "Not that she isn't a genuine psychic. She knows her stuff. Over the years she has told me a lot of things that she couldn't have known would happen. It would make your hair stand on end to hear them."

"I'm sure she's as genuine as they get," I assured him. Of course that wasn't saying much from my point of view, since I had witnessed several psychics whose predictions had been about as likely as my hitting a target in China from here with a tomato and a slingshot.

Yet this particular psychic had seemed to recognize the presence of death surrounding me. Or was it something about me being a friend of death? That sort of suggested devil worship or serial killing in my book, but if looked at another way it could possibly mean that I was a friend with someone who was dead. Friend might be an overstatement, but I was willing to overlook that. And why I would associate death with the devil and murder was beyond me. Maybe Jilly was right and the government was indeed tampering with my brain waves.

"She is the true thing, all right. Were you looking for her?" the jovial man inquired, a keen look in his eyes. He probably thought I was some lovesick young female desperate to find out how my man felt and if marriage was in the future.

"Yes. Do you know where I can find her?"

"She's taking her lunch. Most likely you'll find her across the street at the Ye Olde English Pub. She likes their fish and chips." He winked at me and then turned back to his booth, which had attracted a teenager with several body-piercings and underwear sticking out from low-riding pants. I wasn't sure if the vendor thought the boy was a potential customer or a potential shoplifter from the way he was suddenly hovering.

Eugene, who had ambled over during my exchange with the vendor, was shuddering at the boy's appearance, and softly murmuring something about the end of the world and modesty.

I urged Eugene to follow me across the street to the pub with the faded wooden sign hanging above the door. A chalk board had been set up on the pavement declaring that nowhere else on this continent could better fish and chips be found, the special was Shepherd's Pie, and tea was served between three-thirty and four-thirty and included two scones for the price of one.

The inside of the pub was dark and dingy, with dark

wood paneling, large picnic-like tables with benches, and deep booths with brown cushions on the left wall. The right side of the room was covered in a smoky haze, and several waitresses were popping in and out of the smoke carrying pints of beer on a sticky tray. The pub appeared to be a haven where the work-ingman could buy a beer and chat with his buddies before heading back to complete a day of drudgery and toil.

Madame Muscovy was seated in one of the booths, sipping a half pint of beer and consuming a massive quantity of fried fish set atop some leaves of wilted lettuce.

Eugene looked like he was about to be sick. "People actually *eat* here?" he asked rather incredulously.

I had no desire to be noticed by a garrulous group of men in the far corner who were currently engaged in winking at every woman they saw (and there weren't many), pinching the good-natured (and presumably well tipped) waitress, and mak-ing rather crude jokes about female anatomy. I glanced at Eugene and indicated that we should go see Madame Muscovy, who still had one large chunk of fish left on her plate.

Eugene followed rather reluctantly, stopping every few steps to dodge a puddle of spilled beer. Ridiculous behavior since he couldn't get dirty. I was beginning to think he was a great deal more fastidious than I was, and probably as prim as my mother.

Madame Muscovy looked up when she saw me ap-proach, a questioning look in her eyes. "Do I know you?" she asked in her rough voice.

"Sort of. You read my fortune almost two weeks ago. It was rather terse."

"Ah-hah. I remember you. You're the one who claims to know how to tell a fortune better than I do," she said smugly, though most of the sentiment was lost as she bit off another piece of fish. "What can I do for you? Want another reading?" She gestured with her hand that I was to take the seat across from her.

Ugh! She was talking with food in her mouth, and I could see pieces of fish in her spittle.

Eugene shared my revulsion, adding, "You *intentionally* had this woman tell your fortune? I'm surprised at you, Hope. I would have thought you'd at least visit a psychic that chewed with her mouth closed." He looked back at the psychic who was now slurping at her beer, and bent closer.

Yikes! I thought. He is probably trying to look inside her mouth.

But I was wrong. He was examining the coating on the fish. "I've never actually tried to make fish and chips, though I did review some once. It was too soft and greasy for my taste. This one actually looks pretty crisp. Ask her if it tastes any good. And if she knows what kind of seasoning they use."

No way! I was not going to sit here and discuss her lunch, which was nearly gone anyway. I had better things to talk about. "Madame Muscovy, I don't really want another reading, at least not now, but I would like to ask you some questions, if I may?"

"Sure. I can't guarantee that I'll know the answers though, unless they come to me like the fortunes do," she spat out. Or maybe it was a laugh.

I smiled slightly and settled myself into the booth. "I want to know about ghosts. Why they are here? How they get to heaven? Why they haunt certain people? That sort of thing."

"Someone up and died on you and is now haunting you," she stated, not even blinking.

I was surprised into a slight gasp. Maybe she wasn't such a charlatan.

"I knew it when I first read your fortune," she continued. "It's there, all around you--Death. Plain and simple. D-E-A-T-H. Death." She sat back and scrutinized my face. "Now I don't mean to scare you into thinking you're going to die soon or that wherever you go people around you are going to croak. It's nothing like that."

Rather than completely reassuring me, her words caused me to have visions of myself as the new Jessica Fletcher, a perpetually unwanted houseguest because someone was bound to up and get murdered when I showed up.

Madame Muscovy continued, interrupting these visions

of doom. "Some people have the ability to see ghosts. Others are just chosen. They can usually only see one ghost. Is that what you're seeing? One ghost?"

Eugene was looking as entranced as I was. "Er, yes. Well, one ghost and one ghost dog."

"A dog, eh? That's something new to me. I'll have to look that one up. Died at the same time did they?"

She was definitely smarter than I gave her credit for. "Yes. Do you know why they chose to haunt me?" At this, Eugene poked me, and he must have been intent on hurting me, because I felt it. "Ow. Stop that."

Madame Muscovy looked at me, slightly alarmed. "With you now, is he?" I could see her take several deep breaths. She was beginning to look nervous. She grabbed for her beer and took a big gulp.

Maybe she never really believed me and had been humoring me. Did she think I was crazy?

"I didn't choose to haunt you, you ninny. Ask her why we're stuck with each other?" Eugene demanded.

"I've never actually met a ghost, myself, you know. And nobody has ever brought one to see me," Madame Muscovy continued. She pulled at her neckline and cracked her neck. "I've learned everything from others, you see. I have a gift, I really do. I can sense things about people. But I have never been able to see a ghost." She looked at the empty seat next to me, staring straight at Eugene, who took the opportunity to make faces at her. "He's really there? You're not having me on, are you?"

"No. He is definitely here. Eugene, move something. I know I said not to, but this is an exception."

He gave me a smug look, puffed up his chest and pushed the salt shaker hard. And it moved—but only about a centimeter. Eugene looked a little crushed.

But Madame Muscovy had seen it, and appeared almost ecstatic. She was surprisingly easy to convince.

"He's not a dangerous ghost, is he? He's a nice one?"

"Yes--most of the time." Eugene glared at me, but I refused to look at him. "But he says he didn't choose me. I'm the only one who can see him though. And I didn't choose that either. We were wondering why this has happened and if it can be undone? How do we get Eugene to the," I paused, searching for the right words, "spirit world, ghostly plane?"

"I really don't know why you were chosen. Did you see him die? That happens sometimes. Ah, I can see I've hit the nail on the head. That must be it. I'll have to really look into that. And the dog, too. Imagine that, a dog." Her voice took on a speculative tone and I had visions of her holding fake pet séances for unsuspecting grannies.

I didn't want her to become fixated on Jezebel's presence in my life, so I sharpened my tone. "Madame Muscovy, I need some answers. How does my friend get to where he needs to go? Forget about the dog. Although I assume she'll go with him. (Please God!). Can you tell me what we have to do?"

"I imagine there's something left for him to accomplish. I can't be certain. Does he have a loved one he needs to apologize to? A debt left unfinished? What about a love child that he wasn't aware of?"

"I don't think he has any of those things. I'm not sure about the love child, but if he was unaware of one we wouldn't exactly know about it, would we?" The thought of Eugene with a love child made me want to laugh hysterically.

Eugene didn't think it was so funny, and he gave me a very nasty look.

"How did he die?" Madame Muscovy demanded.

"He was hit by a car." Too bad I couldn't hit him with another car right now, I thought.

"And did they catch the person? Maybe he won't get to where he belongs until that person is caught and his death is avenged. That's how it was in that Patrick Swayze movie." She looked like she thought Patrick Swayze was a god, and that the movie was the bible.

Eugene suddenly looked wary. "Hope, listen to her. She's getting all of this from movies. This is a waste of our time. We need to find a professional," he urged.

Where did he propose to find a professional psychic or expert on the paranormal?

"Can you tell us anything definite, Madame Muscovy?" I asked.

"Definite? No. But there is nothing definite about the afterlife anyway. I'll see what I can find out from some friends of mine that know some people with experience in this stuff. Here's my card. Call me if you need any help. Maybe I will have some answers for you by then." She pulled out a worn leather wallet and yanked a business card from one of the inserts. When I took it from her I first noticed the greasy thumbprint in the corner, second the large scrawl, and finally the Wicca symbols along the bottom.

This was getting creepy. Maybe I *am* becoming a head case. I'm talking to ghosts, contemplating exorcism, and am now having a strange conversation with a psychic who is into Wicca. When I start consulting the tarot cards I'll know I need to be committed.

Eugene gave his normal grunt of disgust, which was really beginning to get on my nerves, and I thanked Madame Muscovy politely. She waved goodbye, ordered another round of chips, and told me say goodbye to my ghost for her.

Eugene, grunting again, followed me as I exited the pub and headed back to the car, his head bowed in frustration.

Still no answers, I thought. Trying to find the man who killed Eugene was a job better left for the police, and I didn't for a moment contemplate calling all of Eugene's old girlfriends (assuming he had any) asking about a love child. And who used that expression nowadays, anyway? Not even my mother would use that euphemism. Love child? Please! I just wish people would call things what they really are.

Chapter Eleven

In the week following our visit to Madame Muscovy, Eugene became savagely determined to discover the extent of his ghostly abilities as well as the reason for his continued existence on Earth.

Moving objects had become an obsession with him, and occupied a great deal of his time. I didn't want to deny him what seemed like his only happiness, but I was getting tired of hearing loud thumps in the middle of the night followed by a hurried apology and assurance that nothing was broken. And since he hadn't progressed quite so far as to be able to return all the objects to where they had started, I often found myself tripping over vases and books, and on one occasion, a frying pan.

His attempts at teaching Jezebel to move objects were also progressing at an alarming rate. Usually Nutter Butter became slightly nervous when Jezebel would approach (though his fear of the seemingly invisible menace had subsided a great deal since the ghosts had first joined us) and then Jezebel would get bored toying with him and move on to alarming birds outside the window.

I am ashamed to admit that I began to ignore these incidents, having become tired of ineffectually yelling at Jezebel and then having to listen to Eugene defend his dog and insult my cat (who was not unattractive no matter what Eugene claimed). But one day Jezebel finally grasped the art of touching solid objects, and stuck her nose right in Nutter Butter's face. When Nutter Butter began screeching and hissing, and practically jumped across the room, I took notice.

The end result was that I yelled myself hoarse, and Eugene and Jezebel left in a huff, returning a day later, apologetic and miserable. The worst part was that instead of getting a decent night's sleep, I spent the entire night feeling guilty for having lost my temper and worrying that Eugene and Jezebel were out either causing trouble or getting into trouble. I tried to keep in mind that Eugene could not die a second time (a fate I had wished on him innumerable times) and therefore was in no real danger.

And so a renewed effort went into finding out as much about ghosts as possible. First, Eugene and I went to the library and did a great deal of research. Okay, I did the research while Eugene attempted to (I'm sorry to say successfully) knock books off of shelves.

It was not surprising that all the research said the same thing: haunting usually occurred because of a violent death, a desperate or unrequited love, or the spirit was just plain bad. The notion of a task left unfinished was relatively new, though based more in fiction than in eyewitness accounts. If Eugene and I were required to solve his murder (I actually think it's manslaughter in the first degree, or some such thing) we were very behind, and if he had a task left to complete we had yet to figure it out. He didn't need to assure me that there was no unrequited love, and I didn't think he was bad, per se, just annoying and toplofty. Surely that wasn't enough of a crime to require banishment to earth for all eternity? If it was, a lot of people, myself included, had to start mending their ways.

I had previously told Eugene about Colby's grandmother, and it was decided between us that if she wasn't completely dotty she might be a good source of information. So I agreed to take Eugene to visit her as long as he was on his best behavior, i.e. refraining from knocking things over or tripping people.

So, a few days later, when I went to Colby's to give her and her mother the caterer's sample fare, I was able to pay a call on Magdalena, Colby's grandmother.

She, it seems, had been avoiding her relatives by hiding behind a shrubbery, so it took some time to locate the rather odd woman. And when I did locater her, I immediately wondered if I wasn't Alice falling down the rabbit hole.

"I've been wondering when you would come." She blinked at me held out her hand.

I clasped the lacy glove and felt the small bones underneath. She had a strong grasp for someone so seemingly delicate. "I'm sorry. We met briefly before, but I'm not sure anyone actually introduced us."

"You're the wedding planner. And Colby's old friend. Or not a friend, if I read you right." She tittered. Yes, actually tittered.

"Hope Springs. And you are Mrs. Dupres."

"What a name you have. Not your parents' finest moment, I'm guessing." She sighed, and shook her head at the foolishness of parents everywhere.

"Er, right. Not that I don't like Hope, but I do wonder at times what my mom had been thinking." I sighed too. Foolish indeed.

"Then we will forget last names and I will call you Hope and you will call me Magdalena. I know. Not my parents' finest moment either."

At first I thought she must be joking. Only saints and gypsies were named Magdalena, and even then only in the movies. Of course, my mother had the bad taste to name me Hope after a kind and lonely distant relative, which was, according to her, the expected thing to do. One would have thought that after marrying a man whose surname was Springs she would have changed her mind, not wanting to cause her daughter years of teasing, but my mother was anything if not steadfast in her certainty of what was right. I wondered what Magdalena's parents had been thinking.

Magdalena smiled at me and I thought that she might be eccentric, but certainly not be as crazy as Colby suggested.

Eugene, who had sidled up after having taken a leisurely yet still vociferously critical, stroll around the estate, simply raised an eyebrow at the woman.

"Tea? I'm in the old carriage house. It's this way." And without any ceremony she latched onto my arm and dragged me toward her humble abode, Eugene and Jezebel tottering behind us.

She directed me through the door and onto a heavily cushioned seat, where a steaming pot of tea was already waiting on an adjacent table.

"My dear girl," she chirped, "I am so glad I caught you. Had enough of the grand ladies with their swans and doves?" Her eyes twinkled with merriment. "I was so excited when I saw you." She raised her hands and clapped them lightly together in excitement. "There is so very much for us to discuss."

I wasn't sure how to respond, so I just nodded. Eugene sat next to me and started fiddling with fringe on the cushions.

"I'm sorry, I forgot to ask if you wanted cream," she asked, suddenly very proper.

"No, thank you. Just sugar. I'm also glad to meet you, Mrs. Duprés—"

"Magdalena, my dear," she gently remonstrated.

"Right, Magdalena. Sorry."

Eugene, already bored by the pleasantries, got up and wandered to a bookshelf and started scanning the titles. "Get on with it, Pip. We don't have all day."

God, he was annoying. It was not as if I could just flat out say, 'So, are you haunted or what?'

"So, Magdalena..." I paused. I really didn't know how to start. "You're Colby's grandmother." Okay, that was kind of pathetic.

"Yes. So different from her and her mother, I know. I hope you think it's for the better. Colby's not always pleasant to be around, is she? Her mother either. But what can one do? Relatives."

I just nodded. There wasn't much to say to that. I wasn't about to contradict her.

"So, you're not close with your family?"

She smiled kindly. "You don't have to be polite. Just ask."

"I'm sorry. Ask what?"

"What it is you wanted to speak to me about."

"Well, I..." I took a sip of tea to give me some time to think of how to phrase it.

"I'll tell you what," she began, "I'll start." She paused for effect. "My husband started haunting me three days after I killed him."

The dainty sip I had spent years perfecting turned into a choking cough, and I could feel the tea spill ungracefully down the sides of my mouth and fall onto the linen napkin, the soggy brown puddle marring the perfectly bleached white that my unusual hostess had taken obvious care to achieve.

Perhaps Jilly was right, and the entire Raines' family was insane, starting with this one. But then, who was I to criticize.

Eugene turned around and just stared. "Wait, did she say she killed him?" Jezebel gave an excited bark, almost mimicking Eugene.

I tried to respond, but she smiled brightly and speech momentarily deserted me. The only sound that erupted was a gurgle. And then it turned into a slight choke. Magdalena looked at me with concern, and for some inexplicable reason I felt that my reaction had both pleased and disappointed her. I consoled myself that at least the tea hadn't come out of my nose.

She waited until I had regained a modicum of control before continuing, letting her words penetrate my unsuspecting mind. "I never did find out what took him so long. To start haunting me, I mean. Not to die." She glanced at the cup perched between my lips and said with mundane civility, "More tea, dear?" Her voice seemed to echo through the small room, bouncing off the sofa and the walls. I carefully put the teacup down.

" I'm sorry? I must have misheard you." Please God, let me have misheard her. Perhaps the Raines family housed their sweet, but mad grandmother in the carriage house because they feared she might kill them too.

"Oh, no, I don't think you did." She reached underneath her voluminous shawl and handed me another napkin as mine was currently being used in lieu of a sponge. She waved away my thanks and continued airily, "Technically I didn't kill him. He fell two stories off a ladder and died instantly. He was cleaning the gutters and I bent down to pet the cat and bumped into his ladder. It was an accident of course." She gave me a sideways glance, and then seemed to change her mind about something. "Not that he ever held it against me. On the contrary, he was most kind about the entire incident, and never brought it up except once when...well, you don't need to hear about that. It was so long ago now."

My eyes must have popped out of my head because she gave a tinkling little laugh and patted my hand as if I were either slow of understanding or in need of condolence. "Don't think I'm crazy, dear. These things do happen you know. This is what you wanted to know about, isn't it?"

I looked surprised. Don't tell me she was yet another psychic. I was beginning to think there was one on every street corner.

"I heard you ask the gardener where I was. And before that I heard you ask the housekeeper about my husband. You should really be more discreet, you know." She was sitting across from me, placidly toying with the fringe of a pillow, while I was awkwardly groping for a semblance of a response.

Eugene was thrilled. "She's a hoot. She's like Miss Marple, but crazy."

"M-M-Ms. Duprés—Magdalena—are you telling me that your husband's ghost is haunting you?"

Eugene looked around, ostensibly searching for another ghost. It took all my will power not to turn around as well. Jezebel, who had been sniffing around the room, suddenly plunked down in front of Magdalena, his back mere centimeters from her dress.

"No, dear. Past tense. Haunted. I haven't seen him in years. Not since...well, not for a long time." She sighed and her whole body seemed to flutter with the movement.

I gazed in bovine awe at my hostess. She really was something else. If one judged solely on appearance, her words would not be so surprising. Her small frame was hidden behind a royal purple shawl whose frayed ends dragged along the carpet, concealing any attire she wore underneath. The heavy wrinkles around her eyes were eclipsed by bright red lipstick and dark blue eye shadow, and her hair was a startling shade of white. If I had to venture an opinion I would guess her age to be in the late seventies, though her shrunken, bird-like appearance could have attributed to her looking older than she was. She gave off the impression of being a gypsy, the kind found in old movies, which were gaudily decorated in lots of bangle jewelry and were constantly trying to read palms. If I had formed a picture of a psychic, it would not have been of Madame Muscovy, it would have been of Ms. Duprés in all her finery. She was quite magnificent in a theatrical way, and quite out of place in her genteel cottage crammed with beige furniture, a large, odd-looking silver birdcage, an unusual marquetry desk, and some pastel artwork.

I wasn't really sure if I believed her. And since I was being haunted, that somehow felt unfair of me.

It suddenly occurred to me that her family might have pensioned her off, leaving her displaced in this shabby-genteel cottage. She should be pitied really. Maybe she is just melodramatic, or lonely, and craves attention. But what if she is telling the truth?

"I can see you are unconvinced, but I expected that. People rarely want to believe anything that doesn't fit neatly into their ordered lives. Haven't you noticed that? Isn't that what you do—teach people to control their environment?" She was extraordinarily perceptive, and I began to feel a knot forming in my stomach. Where were my good manners? I looked over at Eugene, who also didn't seem to know whether or not to believe her.

She didn't wait for a response from me, just continued speaking smoothly, "When my husband died I was a disbeliever as well. But after living with his ghost for years, I now accept any and all manner of things. The neighbor boy told me just the other day that he had seen strange lights moving through the woods, and I wouldn't be surprised if those were ghosts too. He thought they were aliens, but I'm not sure about aliens. I haven't seen any of them yet. Not that I'm not willing to give aliens the benefit of the doubt."

She sounded as if she expected aliens to pop into the room for after-dinner drinks.

I have always found that anyone who starts off sentences saying, 'I don't mean to be rude,' usually does mean to be rude, and is simply using the expression as a means of making their behavior slightly more socially acceptable. But suddenly I could hear myself saying those very words, quite loudly. Perhaps too loudly. "Ms. Duprés, sorry, Magdalena, I don't mean to be rude, but are you serious? You're saying that your husband's ghost haunted you for years?" That sounded horribly callow, especially since I knew all about being haunted, and I could see she was offended, but it had come out before I could stop myself.

I clapped my hand over my mouth. I had stepped over into the realm of what my mother deemed the "manner-less masses." Maybe I wasn't as OPD as Jilly thought.

Magdalena sighed deeply. The idea of a ghost haunting this woman was suddenly very vividly back in my mind. And for a moment I thought, 'Another aspect of death, and I'm right in the middle of it.'

I again felt an impulse to turn around—but this time to see if my mother, definitely still alive and kicking, had somehow sent a ghostly specter to spy on me and scold me for being so rude to this quite-possibly truthful woman. A foolish thought, my rational mind knew, since my mother would never send anything as off-color as a ghost after me. She would send my Aunt Maude instead. And that was a sobering thought. My Aunt Maude was scarier than a dozen ghosts.

Magdalena continued as if communicating with ghosts was the most natural thing in the world. "Yes, I thought I made that clear. Roger—my late husband—stayed on this earth as a ghost. He haunted me. I wasn't terribly surprised that he returned to me." She paused and looked at some old photos on a nearby shelf. "It never seemed odd that he was a ghost. He was *exactly* the sort of person who would come back as a ghost. It just seemed...natural. Not the way he first appeared, of course, standing at the foot of my bed and howling like a banshee. He said later that he wanted to initially appear that way because he had always read that ghosts did that sort of thing. He always did like a good joke, but I have to say that I didn't find that one particularly funny.

"I must have jumped several feet out of the bed. And I screamed. Of course, women were allowed to have nerves back then. I don't suppose that if I saw a ghost for the first time today I would be allowed to have a fit of hysterics. Women have to be so much braver now. It is such a shame."

She gave me a look of pity, obviously mourning the loss of Victorian femininity that must be causing me untold suffering. If she only knew that I had a 'fit of hysterics' myself when Eugene showed up at my apartment.

"I remember that my aunt used to wave around a handkerchief when she was upset. At one time I thought I might pick up that habit, as an affectation to make me stand out, but I kept misplacing the dratted things." She gave a dramatic sigh.

I laughed. She was really quite charming, despite her current lapse in normalcy. Or maybe that was what was so charming about her.

"But that is neither here nor there," she continued. "I was frightened at first, but I knew it was Roger come back to me. He looked just the same as when he was alive, with not even a dent in his head or a kink in his neck. I suppose I thought I was dreaming at first, but he assured me he really was a ghost."

That didn't seem much of an assurance to me, but I politely kept my thoughts to myself. No matter how many reassurances Eugene gave me, there was still a part of me that wondered if I wasn't crazy.

"I just knew he was really there. I never considered the possibility that he couldn't be there. I mentioned it to my sons once, and they were rather horrified and seemed to think that I was imagining him. They thought it was a form of comfort or a way of easing my guilt. But they were wrong—that's why laymen should never act as if they are psychiatrists. Roger really was there.

"Oh, I won't deny that I had always wanted to see a ghost, so that made it easier for me to accept it. Maybe a part of me also craved some excitement to take me out of my humdrum life. Ghosts certainly provide that, don't they?"

"I suppose they do." I furtively looked at Eugene. I wouldn't have described his presence as exciting. Annoying maybe. Disruptive. Occasionally humorous, though I would never admit that to him. But I suppose some people might look at it as exciting. "Did he stop haunting you just recently?" I asked.

"Oh no, he stopped haunting me ages ago. I don't know why he stopped appearing to me. I have an idea, but it is just that and not worth mentioning. According to movies, ghosts are only given a certain amount of time, or have to accomplish something left undone."

Her mind seemed to suddenly wander. She smiled dreamily and I wondered if she was imagining herself as a heroine in an old black and white movie, and her husband the hero that dies, only to return to the woman he loves. Part of me again wondered if this wasn't a fantasy of hers, to help her cope living in a world without her husband.

"You've done a lot of research? Or just what you've seen in movies?"

She smiled but didn't answer so I took another sip of tea, not wanting my hostess to suspect I doubted her veracity.

"Is she for real, Hope? I don't know. This might be a waste of time. First she says she killed him, and then he haunts her for years and then suddenly just stops. It doesn't make sense. Maybe she is making this all up? Maybe she is just a lonely old woman?" Eugene was worried, as I was, that Magdalena was living in some fantasy. I think he feared he would never find his answers. "What if this is all a hoax? Like a practical joke?"

A joke? Suddenly thinking there might be a television camera hidden somewhere in the room, I began to surreptitiously look around. A camera could easily be hidden behind the grandfather clock, or even behind one of those oil paintings, or the mirror above the mantel. And I bet a camera man could hide behind the curtains. They did drape down to the floor after all. I could picture the entire scene unfolding...an overeager talk show host popping out of nowhere and laughing at me. He would say, "Hope Springs, smile because you're on 'Candid Camera'." And then he and Magdalena would laugh while I sat there looking mortified. Of course I would have to laugh as well and act like I thought it was all in good fun, but I would probably never willingly have tea with any elderly lady again--or with anyone for that matter. And Eugene would never let me live it down—even though he was a real ghost. If I wasn't crazy, that was.

"You still don't believe me." She sounded as if she had made a grand prediction, and I left behind my fantasy television appearance. In truth, Eugene's blind grandmother would have been able to see my doubt. I wanted to believe her, but hearing how it sounded when she said she had been haunted made me question my own sanity. I needed to know if she was telling the truth.

Be nice, I told myself. Remember that virtue is its own reward. "Well, tell me more. Maybe you can convince me."

Ms. Duprés beamed at me in return. "I know it's hard to believe, but I am serious. I can't explain why some people see ghosts and others don't. It might even be the ghosts who choose. I've done some research since Roger died, but there don't seem to be any real answers. Roger says he didn't choose to stay. He didn't mind though. We had so much more fun when he was a ghost. The pranks we played on people." She smiled, a wicked gleam in those bright eyes. For a moment it seemed she had forgotten my existence, lost in some daydream all her own.

Eugene sat down at the window seat, and pretended disinterest in the conversation. He was still scared she was lying.

With a toss of her arm Magdalena recollected herself, and adjusted her position on the settee, her body suddenly stiff. "But I am getting off the subject. Where was I?"

"You were trying to convince me that your late husband was a ghost."

"Oh, yes. I didn't think you would be so hard to convince. I thought you might... Well, you seemed very receptive to psychic emanations when I first saw you. I knew as soon as my daughter-in-law pointed you out to me several weeks ago that you were special, that's why I invited you for tea. We are really very much alike, you know."

What do I say to that? I decided to go for something neutral. "Indeed? What makes you say that, Ms. Dupres?" Suddenly I wondered if Eugene would somehow cause me to end up like Magdalena, theatrically overdressed and desperately alone.

" I sense it. And please call me Magdalena. I do so hate to be formal with someone whom I know I am going to become great friends." She smiled at me again, and I set my teacup down on the table, worried that the remainder of the tea would soon be decorating the carpet if her next revelation were as startling as the first.

She clasped my hand across the table. "You are receptive to the other world. I sensed it in you immediately. We are of a sort. Great minds and all that."

I wasn't sure the phrase was apt in either of our cases.

She continued, "Yes, indeed. Your aura speaks very clearly to mine. You are a Chosen One."

Eugene snorted. "A chosen one? You? She must be kidding? I certainly didn't choose you."

He was right. I certainly wasn't anyone special. I'd eat my shirt if I had been chosen for anything other than a bleak future in an asylum.

Magdalena frowned at me and the wrinkles around her eyes bunched up into large folds. "You have to take it on faith."

I suddenly wondered if she had been talking to my mother? Did she know I had stopped attending church? "Even if I believe that your husband haunted you, I don't understand why you think I'm attuned to the spiritual world. That sort of thing doesn't happen to people like me." And if it did, they, unlike me, were probably smart enough not to acknowledge it or even talk about it. I glanced at Eugene. He didn't appear interested in the conversation at the moment. Maybe he really did think she was lying. "What makes you think I'm not just a normal person who has never had any, um—otherworldly experiences."

"I told you. I can sense it. Your future isn't going to be as boring as the life you're currently living."

That shut me up. I must seem a pathetic creature indeed if a woman who had known me for all of an hour noticed how boring my life was.

"I have a gift," she continued. "I'm not psychic--at least I don't think I am. I can simply sense things about people. I can't see the future in flashes of light when I touch people, or read palms or tarot cards. And I'm not related to the seventh son of a seventh son, or anything like *that*. As a matter of fact, I was born in a small Minnesota town, and I wouldn't say that my home state is famous for its psychics or its haunted houses. My family was of the most prosaic kind. My parents were shopkeepers. Quite ordinary. I thought I was like everyone else too—I mean I didn't think I would ever see ghosts. Well, just one ghost anyway. I saw a ghost but that doesn't make me crazy." She looked at me as if challenging me to doubt that she was once normal, not a mad old woman who claimed to see ghosts and sense what was going to happen to people.

Her dark eyes were pinning me to my seat, and I squirmed a little. There was just something about her eyes—her sincerity.

She knew. About ghosts. About me. And suddenly I knew I believed her.

And then she nodded, as if she had confirmed something she knew all along. "You can't escape death. You will be haunted."

And there it was. Death. Again. And again and again. I didn't believe I was chosen like Magdalena said. Not the way she meant it. But I did believe that Death had somehow fixated on me. Three women had now seen it, predicted it. And it scared me. Was there something wrong with me?

I needed normalcy. Now.

I sat there and thought up a pitiful apology and a long-winded explanation of why I had to abandon the poor mad woman and go to my other job at the newspaper. Why I had to get out of this cottage and back to a normal life. Why I had to leave immediately. But in the end, I didn't say anything.

I looked over at Eugene. I knew he was real. And he needed help. And God knew I couldn't take much more of him. And this woman might have the answers we needed. And if she *was* crazy, she wasn't any crazier than I was.

"Are you ready, my dear?" Magdalena was watching me,

half-smiling.

"Ready?"

"To talk. To tell me your secrets, of course." She laughed— a laugh that was little more than a smile with some puffs of air escaping.

"My secrets? Well..." I still couldn't say what needed to be said. "I actually wanted to ask you more about your husband first, if you have no objections?"

"My dear, why would I? So few people take an interest in my affairs. And no one ever wants to hear an old woman reminiscing about the past. Especially one that involves the dead. Most people think I'm absolutely insane without my even telling them about my husband. Can you imagine what they would do? Lock me up, no doubt."

I wondered if I would be locked up in the room next to her.

Eugene, who had been lounging on the window seat, wiping away that nonexistent lint he was so fond of, quickly looked up, showing a new interest in the conversation. He sensed something in the atmosphere between Magdalena and I had changed. Jezebel, who had been docilely seated at his feet, bounced up at his movement, looking around for whatever new sport her master had found.

"I am so glad you believe me. You weren't sure a minute ago, I could tell. But you do now. I knew you were special from the start. Oh, this is so exciting." She positively trembled with enthusiasm.

"I would certainly like to hear more about your ghost husband. For instance, why he stopped haunting you?"

She frowned at me. "Don't you want to talk about your ghost?"

I wasn't sure how to respond to that. Did I admit I had a ghost and take a chance that she would be able to keep her mouth shut ? She wouldn't think I was crazy, but it was still a bit of a risk. She had told quite a number of people about her husband's ghost after all. But then again, if people already thought she was crazy they weren't likely to believe her. It was a risk worth taking.

Eugene seemed to feel the same way, because he urged me to forget my fear of being labeled insane and get down to business.

"If you promise to answer my questions later, I'll tell you about my ghost." That sounded reasonable. Maybe I should embark on a career as a hostage negotiator or a lawyer and forget etiquette and events.

"Oh, of course. Do tell me. Is it a man or a woman?"

"A man—a colleague of mine. His name is Eugene Schreier."

"Eugene. Eugene," she purred. "Yes, a nice name. I quite like it. I'm not so sure about the last name, though. He might want to consider something like Bowers or Desmond. That sounds so nice. Eugene Desmond. Like an old-time film star."

Eugene pretended to be indignant, but was quickly snorting with laughter. I had to choke back a few giggles myself. "It does sound nice, but I think he is quite happy with his name."

"That's too bad, but if he changes his mind I have several other possibilities. I'm very good with names, you know. So many people are using the wrong ones. And it could make such a difference in their lives. There have been studies." She seemed to realize she was beginning to ramble. "But back to what we were talking about. Why is darling Eugene haunting you, do you suppose? He wasn't a..." she coughed delicately, "lover of yours, was he?"

Thank God I wasn't drinking my tea at that moment. It would definitely have come out my nose, and likely my ears as well. I don't know if my shocked denial was louder than Eugene's outraged cry of "give me credit for having some taste." That was a low comment, even from Eugene. "Er, no offense, Pip," he added, after I shot him a nasty look.

"I didn't mean to offend you," Magdalena broke in. "I was just curious. I gather he was just a friend then. But that is nice too. Women these days are too fast and loose I think. Besides, I see you with someone named Tom or Phillip, I think. Yes, definitely Phillip. It is such a nice name for a man. Strong yet gentle."

If Eugene didn't stop laughing and pointing at me, mimicking 'Phillip' over and over, I was going to take a lamp to his head.

"Actually, Eugene and I weren't even friends—just acquaintances. I'm not even sure I like him now. He's very pompous and likes to make fun of everyone around him." I glared at him, sending him into more hoots of laughter.

"My dear, is he here now?" she asked, glancing in the direction I had looked. "How exciting. I wish I had known I would be entertaining *two* people today. And one of them a man. I would have changed my dress had I known."

She amazed me. I was surprised I was still able to speak. "You look lovely as you are. But if we could get back to being haunted...I-- I mean we-- aren't sure why Eugene is still here, or why I am the only one who can see him."

"Oh. I don't know if I can help you in that area. I really did love my husband, and I saw him die. I just assumed that was why he haunted me. And maybe he wanted to pun—." She broke off and looked back to where Eugene was sitting.

With a flick of her shawl and a wave of her arm she had now moved on to another subject. "Has he learned how to move objects yet? Roger and I had such fun with that sort of thing. There was this one incident with a pie..."

I wasn't sure if Eugene was offended that Magdalena would desecrate a pie, or if he was simply agog that someone was taking us seriously, even if it was a batty old woman who was obsessed with her dead husband. I just hoped he didn't start getting any ideas about flying desserts.

"Tell her about the flour, Hope. She'll get a laugh out of that one. And the book that hit the librarian who was bending down. And don't forget to mention the knife I moved yesterday. And put back without slicing off one of your toes." He chuckled. "Boy, did I scare you." It was like he was gloating.

There was no way I would give him the satisfaction of bragging about his dubious accomplishments. "Eugene has been learning to move objects. He moved a bag of flour, with disastrous results. And lately he has moved larger objects, too."

"Can he move something for me now? How about that candlestick over there? The silver one next to the tissue box." She gestured at a tall, slender candlestick several feet from where Eugene was standing.

For a moment I was afraid that Eugene would refuse, thereby making me look like an idiot, but he was too proud of his new abilities to pass up such an opportunity.

And so, like magic, Magdalena saw the candlestick move up from the desk, teeter in the air, and then land back down with a slight thump a few inches from where it started.

"Oh, that was wonderful," she exclaimed, clapping her hands and nearly spilling her tea.

"So you saw it move?" I asked.

"Of course. Did you think you were going crazy and imagining your Eugene? Well, rest assured, my dear, I just saw the candlestick move. And quite expertly too. Eugene must have practiced quite hard," she said, sending a patronizing smile in his direction.

He positively preened.

"I won't deny that I have been wondering about my sanity," I admitted.

"Young people today are so cynical. It's really quite sad. A hundred years ago no one would think anything of seeing a ghost. My great-aunt saw one on a regular basis. A maid, I think it was."

"Ask her what else her husband could do," Eugene demanded. "I want to know if I am missing out on anything. There might be a myriad of abilities I could do."

"Magdalena, Eugene would like to know if Roger could do anything besides move things." I hoped Roger had been a particularly talent-less ghost. If not, I could be in for a hellish time.

"Not really. He did learn how to float. It took him a while to learn, but he was quite diligent about practicing. He used to practice in the garden. When he practiced in the house he would disappear through the ceiling and I wouldn't be able to see how high he could go. And I had to yell a great deal, which caused such a commotion." She paused, searching her brain for other stunts her beloved Roger had pulled. "He drove my car once, though it took a great deal of effort. I was never so scared in my life. I was certain we would crash and I would join Roger. If that had happened I was determined that I would haunt my sister, Rachel, who was such a catty woman."

Oh God! My fate was undoubtedly sealed. I had no doubt that Eugene would demand my car keys, or simply take them when I slept. My car would be spotted careening around the neighborhood and I would be arrested for reckless driving. It wouldn't matter that I wasn't in the car, or that the driver was invisible. I would be prison-bound in no time.

"My dear Eugene—you don't mind if I address him directly, do you Hope?—you haven't seen any other ghosts, have you?" She seemed particularly interested in this, clasping her hands tightly while waiting for a response.

"I don't think so. How would I know they were ghosts? Would they look different? How many ghosts are still on Earth?"

"Eugene says that he doesn't think he's seen a ghost, but he isn't sure he would recognize one if he did," I told her.

"Oh. I hadn't thought of that. I wanted to make sure that Roger really had moved on, and wasn't just loafing around. It's a fear I have. I don't recall Roger ever mentioning another ghost, but I don't suppose he really looked. Perhaps they look misty or have a light about them. Maybe you will just know," she mused.

"Do you know why or how Roger moved on? It would really help us."

"I'm not exactly sure. One day he just said it was finally time for him to move on, and then he was gone. And I never saw him again. It was just after I...but that couldn't be it," she trailed off.

Eugene moved forward and perched on the edge of the sofa. "Press her a little harder, Hope. It could be important."

"Magdalena, if you think you might know why Roger moved on, I wish you would tell us," I pleaded. I was wiling to beg on my knees if I thought it would get me the information I wanted.

"I don't think it would help your situation, dear. But if—
"

A knock on the door stopped Magdalena mid-sentence, and Eugene looked in annoyance at the guilty party.

"Oh, who could that be? I wasn't expecting anyone," Magdalena cried. She rose from the sofa, gave Eugene a wide arc, not wanting to walk through him, she told us, and opened the door.

A tall, well-built man with dark hair and dark eyes was lounging against the doorframe, a smile plastered onto his face. He immediately exclaimed over Magdalena's appearance and bent to kiss her hand. Eugene and I watched in fascination as she blushed and giggled and invited the man in.

"You sly rogue, making up to an old lady. You ought to be ashamed of yourself," she scolded, though it was obvious she enjoyed his attentions.

"What old lady? All I see is a charming, mature woman," he responded.

Eugene groaned.

"Fie on you. But do come in. I can introduce you to my guest. Yes, there are people who visit me besides you." Magdalena took his hand and led him forward.

My first good look at him showed me that he was in his early thirties, and while he wasn't handsome in a traditional sense, he was nevertheless quite good-looking, with perfect white teeth. He was dressed in a very expensive gray suit, with a shiny gold watch on his wrist and a large gold signet ring on his right hand. He looked like a charming flirt, who likely had all the ladies fluttering at his feet.

"And who is this lovely lady, Magdalena? Your daughter?" I knew that he intended it as a compliment to Magdalena, but it was really quite insulting to me. But then he winked at me, and I forgave him. He obviously hadn't intended any slur on my youthful looks.

Eugene gave another snort and mumbled something about a poser.

"Vincent, this is Hope Springs. She's an event planner. She's handling Colby and Evan's wedding and Angela's political dinner next week too. She's quite a help to both families. And isn't she sweet to spend her time with an old lady like myself?" She glanced slyly at me, and I feared she had matchmaking in mind. I should probably pull her aside and tell her he was too flash and suave for my taste. "Hope, this is Vincent Torrelli. He's a business acquaintance of Evan's. And I suppose he must be a friend, too, since he is around so often. Or did you say you were a very distant cousin?"

"How do you do?" As far as I knew all Evan's business ventures had been complete failures. This man did not look like he had ever failed at anything. As a matter of fact he looked like a dangerous predator.

"A pleasure. I hadn't expected to find two lovely ladies here. This must be my lucky day," he purred.

It was such a trite compliment I wanted to laugh in embarrassment for him, but he looked quite sincere so I managed to restrain myself. Eugene looked dubious, but I had heard him say similar things to our boss' wife, and he knew it. As a matter of fact, Vincent Torrelli reminded me of Eugene, though Vincent was obviously a much younger and better-looking version. They both screamed back-street-boy-turned-success-and-flaunting-it-with-expensive-suits-and-jewelry.

"You are such a flatterer, Mr. Torrelli," Magdalena cooed. "Hope is very pretty but I am just an old woman with more wrinkles than hair. I can handle the truth. 'No words suffice the secret soul to show, For truth denies all eloquence to woe.' Byron said that. Don't you just love the Romantics?" She winked at me and moved toward the tea tray. "But since you were so kind as to flatter me, sir, I will offer you a cup of tea. You can tell Hope and I all about your latest business." She remembered to make a wide circle around Eugene, who hadn't moved, causing Mr. Torrelli to look at her askance. But she just smiled at him and pressed him to accept a cup of tea.

"There's not much to tell. The man I work for is currently in the security business. We primarily produce high-tech computer software that the government purchases. And that's that—the highlight of my days."

"Is that how you met Evan?" I enquired. I wondered what Colby's fiancee was into now. Colby wasn't about to marry anyone without future prospects.

"No. My boss, Carl Gieppo, is quite an entrepreneur and has other business ventures as well. I met Evan in college and we have done some business over the years." Most likely shady business on your end, I thought.

"I certainly couldn't imagine Evan entering into anything that required more than a cursory knowledge of email. He's not really computer savvy, is he?" He gave Magdalena and I an apologetic smile, perhaps feeling that he might be doing Evan an injustice.

"No, I suppose not," I agreed.

Eugene wandered back to the window and began picking at his lint. "Don't believe a word of it, Hope. Everyone knows Gieppo is in the mob. This guy's a complete thug. He probably presses men, not weights."

I sent him a quelling look, though I wasn't about to argue. Besides, I had never actually met a member of organized crime (that I was aware of) and wasn't about to form a premature opinion on the matter. I couldn't imagine Evan becoming involved in anything criminal though. I bet he was honest on all his tax forms and never even jaywalked. His judgment obviously wasn't perfect since he was engaged to Colby, but organized crime? No way.

"Speaking of Evan...has either of you lovely ladies seen him? We have some business to discuss and he seems to have disappeared on me. I thought he might be visiting that fiancée of his, but no one is at the house. Which is why I decided to come see my favorite lady," he said, winking at Magdalena.

She blushed again, and in a flurry asked us if we wanted any more tea. The movement sent her oversized shawl into the cream, and we declined.

"So Hope—may I call you Hope?—you are an event planner?" he asked me.

"Yes. I also write an etiquette column for the Standard Press, and teach etiquette to socialites and their children, though that business declines more each year," I replied.

"I imagine it does. Nobody has the time to be polite anymore. Isn't that right, Magdalena? Didn't you tell me the other day that your mailman wasn't even willing to spend a few minutes to chat with you?" He gave her a sympathetic look that made Eugene groan.

If Eugene didn't care for our conversation, he could just go outside. And take Jezebel with him before she tried to see if she could chew the carpet.

"I did indeed. And to think, I have known him since he was a boy. And now he doesn't have the time of day for me. And all because this world is in such a hurry. I can't imagine what his mother would say if she could see him now. Nobody respects their elders anymore. Except you, my dears. And such a delight you two are," Magdalena pronounced.

A hesitant knock at the door checked Mr. Torrelli before he could respond, and Magdalena gathered up her shawl, which was now trailing in the sugar bowl, and went to the door. She looked at me questioningly before crossing the couch, and I realized she was still afraid of walking through Eugene.

I nodded at her, and she was reassured. If Vincent Torrelli thought we were a pair of nutcases, well, he probably wasn't far off, and I wasn't going to worry about it.

A man of average height and coloring stood hesitantly in the doorway. There was nothing remarkable about his appearance except for a pair of light blue eyes that were often cast downward. He muttered an apology for disturbing Magdalena, and she brushed it away, ushering him inside.

"Look, my dears, it's Evan. We were just talking about you, Evan. I believe you know everyone."

Evan Whittington's eyes were immediately drawn to Mr. Torrelli's. They grew slightly larger, and he walked forward, nearly stepping on Magdalena's shawl.

"I hadn't expected to see you here, Vincent. I shouldn't be surprised that you would be found with the ladies, though." He turned politely toward Magdalena. "I was looking for Colby and thought you might know where she is, Mrs. Duprés," Evan said.

Vincent stood up to shake Evan's hand. "I came to see you, but when I couldn't find you in the house I thought I would come next door and visit your future grandma-in-law." He paused, then added softly, "I thought I saw you on my way over here. Didn't you see me cross the garden? I was certain you must have. But maybe it was someone else skulking around the bushes. Do you have a new gardener?" Vincent asked, his voice dripping with sarcasm.

"You'd have to ask my step-mother about that. Angela takes care of that sort of thing. I've been out all day and only just got back. Colby said she would be home this afternoon, but I can't find her." He looked away from Vincent's penetrating gaze, and his eyes lit on me. "Hi, Hope. You're here, too. This is a pleasant surprise. It's awfully nice to see you. It's been quite a while--since the engagement party, right? No, wait, you were at that church picnic, weren't you? Well, it's been a long time, anyway." He seemed genuinely pleased to see me, which wasn't surprising since Evan had always been very shy and I was one of the few people who cared enough to make an effort to get to know him.

Evan Whittington was Marcus' Whittington's son from his first marriage, and, in his father's eyes, a complete failure. He was shy and earnest, failed miserably at athletics, and could never keep his checkbook balanced. He was smart enough, though not in business. But I respected him. He was idealistic in the extreme, and that was a likeable quality in my book.

His engagement to Colby was a bit odd, as Evan did not seem her type. I always imagined she would marry some high-flyer with more cash than moral substance. But I suppose one never knew when it came to love. Evan worshipped Colby, and if he knew all of her faults, he either didn't care or he ignored them. I'd like to think that having grown up with us, he was quite aware of the fact that she was extremely high-maintenance, but still loved her anyway. He would have to love her the way she kept pushing him forward at social events, trying to introduce him to all the important people.

"It's nice to see you, too. How are you? Are you getting excited about the wedding?" I asked. I had never met a man yet that did.

"Oh, sure. Luckily I don't have to do anything for it. Just show up, which isn't too hard," he answered, grinning slightly.

"You are such a sweet boy. I can't imagine how someone like Colby managed to get you," Magdalena chimed in.

How does one respond to a comment like that? I secretly agreed, although I was a little shocked Magdalena would say something so unkind about her own granddaughter. I decided that the best response was to remain silent. Evan looked startled and started stuttering something about not understanding, and Vincent Torrelli turned his face to the side to keep from laughing.

But the worst was Eugene. He guffawed loudly and said that he couldn't wait to meet this paragon of virtue called Colby. He then asked me if she looked like a horse and carried a riding whip.

The party broke up shortly after that, Magdalena getting tired and Vincent subtly maneuvering Evan into walking back to the Whittington's house with him.

When the gentlemen had departed, Magdalena held me back. "You will come again soon, won't you? We can finish our discussion. I would so much like to talk more with your Eugene," she said.

"Of course. There is still a great deal I would like to ask you about Roger. I won't have time in the next few days because of the fundraising dinner Angela Whittington is throwing, but after that I should have some more time."

"Will you be at the dinner? I hate fundraisers, or whatever this one is, but I promised my son Dean I would go. And be on my best behavior," she tittered. "Maybe you can keep me company."

"That would be nice, but I'm not sure how long I will be there. I'll be there at the beginning to make sure it all goes smoothly, but I don't really need to remain," I said. "And I wasn't really invited in that way."

"Of course. You will be working. I don't know what I was thinking." She looked so sad at the idea that I couldn't keep her company that I was quite flattered.

"I suppose I could come up with some reasons for staying. Watching over the caterers and making sure they clean up properly. That sort of thing. I usually don't do that, but I could make an exception for you."

"Oh, thank you so much. It will be so nice to see a friendly face there. Angela is nice enough, but she forgets about everyone when a good-looking man appears. I don't know why her husband puts up with it. And as for my family...they don't much care to talk to an old lady."

By the time Eugene and I left I was feeling like a saint. Eugene, on the other hand, was grumbling about thugs and socialites and how to choose a proper caterer.

Chapter Twelve

"No, for an odd number of males, the lady needs to be placed on the host's right, not his left. Ladies placed on the left were usually designated as..." What is a nice way to put this? "Let's just say that they weren't usually considered ladies. Or if there is an even number of ladies and gentlemen, the lady of highest rank, excluding the hostess, goes on the host's left. If you really want to be traditional, we'll have to switch those cards around, which means moving all the names on this side."

"Is that why gentlemen are supposed to walk on the lady's left side? Like on streets and stuff? So you would know they were ladies?" Angela, the latest Mrs. Whittington, and Evan's stepmother, asked, curiosity causing her to stop and look up from the table arrangements.

"Not quite. In that case they are supposed to make sure the lady walks on the inside of the street. But that was so that the lady wouldn't be hit by traffic or any dirty water being tossed out of windows," I replied. She would have loved The Sylvia Pearson School For Young Ladies (Who Suffer From Delusions of Grandeur).

She raised an eyebrow. "By dirty water you mean...?"

"Exactly. An unpleasant thought, isn't it?"

"Yes. Thank God for modern plumbing." She looked back down at the table, and then at me. "I think I do want to go traditional. Oh, I know that no one does it like this anymore, but I don't care. I don't want anyone to say I didn't know how to correctly set a table." By 'anyone' I assumed she mean Susan Raines, her nearest neighbor and future in-law once Colby and Evan were married. "Which cards did you say needed to be switched?"

"Every card on this side of the table. We'll have to make sure the other side is correct, too," I replied, wondering how I had become a glorified table-setter.

"If only Evan hadn't insisted I invite that Vincent fellow. He has completely ruined my seating arrangement, and I know you worked hard on it, Hope," Angela said. She lowered her voice so that the caterers and serving staff could not hear. "I adore Evan, and I'd do anything for him. He is the best step-son imaginable," she divulged, though I knew quite well that Evan was an annoyance in her home, disturbing the peace by upsetting his father and bringing unwanted guests. As a matter of fact, Angela had expanded at length on this topic only the day before.

"He always takes my side against his father—not that we argue a great deal. I know just how to please Marcus." She looked around furtively before turning back to me and giving me a conspiratorial look. "I admit that sometimes I wonder if Marcus' first wife didn't die from shame. Marcus can be hard to please if you don't know how. But then he rarely takes his temper out on me. Poor Evan, though. He's too much like his mother, I gather. And he is such a disappointment to Marcus. I feel quite badly for him. If only Evan were a successful businessman or academic or something." She sighed and flipped a place card between her manicured nails before placing it back where she had found it. "And Marcus doesn't bother to hide his disgust of the boy. He'd probably like a son more like that Vincent—smooth, successful, and deadly. I had heard that Vincent was the son of a second cousin of Marcus', but he denies it. He would probably love Vincent to be his relative. He likes sharp business men."

I waited for her to move farther down the table before repositioning the place card she had held. She merely picked up another and stared at it, her eyes glazing over.

"Vincent is good-looking though, so it might not be such a bad thing after all. Maybe he can keep Mrs. Mayfair occupied, or better yet, Susan. If I have to have him here he can at least make himself useful," she purred.

God help anyone who stood in Angela Plumber Whittington's way!

She had for several moments really been talking to herself, and I went back to neatly rearranging the name cards. No one used name cards at small, formal dinners nowadays, but Angela wanted everything perfect, which meant arranging the conversations ahead of time. By positioning like-minded people next to each other, she was guaranteeing at least a modicum of success, and possibly larger financial contributions to Dean Raines' political campaign.

And that thought caused me to rethink the seating arrangements yet again. "With these numbers we will have to put Dean Raines at the head of the table in your place, and your husband at the foot. We can seat you to Dean's left in this instance because this way the lady on his right will be served dinner first. And it is always wrong for the hostess to be served first," I said, reciting rules my mother taught me long ago. "It doesn't make you less of a lady."

She laughed. "I should hope not. I'll trust your judgment in this." What she really meant was that she was quite willing to sit next to Dean, whether on his right or left.

I stared down at the elaborately decorated table, and my mind began to get fuzzy. I hated arranging tables. At least Angela didn't require that the service staff measure the distance between plates with a ruler. Still, the number of different utensils and carefully arranged napkins at each place setting had taxed even my anal retentive abilities.

This dinner party was to be an intimate affair of eighteen (now nineteen) guests (the wealthiest), followed later by a larger cocktail party for approximately sixty additional guests, and Angela had made it fairly easy on me. As long as it looked good and she didn't need to put in a great deal of effort she was happy—the best kind of client.

After several more switches Angela was satisfied with the arrangement, and headed upstairs to finish dressing. Since she had been wearing a flimsy negligee with high-heeled slippers in front of the caterers, I wondered what she planned to wear to the party. No doubt something strapless, backless, or braless. I could hear the click of her heels on the marble in the foyer, and I chuckled to myself. Her shoes would probably be changed from one-inch to four-inch heels.

Eugene sauntered in at that moment, having refused to stay at my apartment with what he referred to as "that blasted cat", and I could see that he was glad he had insisted on accompanying me. "This is actually a very good catering company, Hope. How did you find out about them? Their scallop puffs look excellent. And so do the truffles. I haven't seen the main dishes, of course, but they just might be decent." He suddenly looked pathetic and weepy, and he sighed before adding, "I just wish I could taste them. I don't feel hungry, but I would still like to taste them."

I actually felt sorry for him.

That feeling lasted for about five seconds. It ended when he casually remarked, "I wonder if I could...I can certainly pick them up. Maybe I can actually eat food. I'll have to try it."

"Don't you dare," I hissed. "Wait until we get home. I'll make you anything you like, just don't cause trouble here."

"Anything? Coq au Vin, for instance? No, Beef Bourguignon. Or how about Beef Wellington?" he beseeched.

"Couldn't you think of something a little simpler?" Who makes Beef Bourguignon at home, anyway? Or Beef Wellington? Those were restaurant-only dishes for me. I'd never made either in my life. And as for Coq au Vin, well, that was not something I was prepared to make late at night for a ghost that probably couldn't even eat it. What was the matter with a nice peanut butter and jelly?

"You said anything," he retorted rather petulantly.

"Fine. Just behave!"

The door to the butler's pantry swung open and a woman poked her head out. "Is everything okay, Ms. Springs? I thought I heard you talking to someone."

"Everything's fine, Jeanine. Sometimes I talk to myself to help me remember things." I smiled innocently at her, and she nodded and returned to the kitchen.

"People are going to start thinking you're crazy soon. You should really stop talking to yourself like that. Maybe you should make lists instead," Eugene suggested smugly.

"You can go to hell, Eugene. Or won't the devil take you? That would explain why you are still here." I snapped back.

"Who knows? Maybe I'm already in hell—stuck with you." he said, a mocking look in his eyes. He laughed when I didn't respond, and sauntered back into the kitchen, his form disappearing into the wall.

Damn! I forgot to ask him where Jezebel was. I hope she isn't running around the house scaring any cats! I didn't need a distraught animal running into the party and tripping guests. I have no doubt that the blame would fall on the serving staff or me.

I wandered back into the kitchen, pretending to oversee the caterers and servers, but really shadowing Eugene. Through the hallway leading to the foyer I could hear the men of the house coming downstairs, obviously in disagreement over something. The words "money" and "fool" seemed to be pronounced with devastating effect by Marcus Whittington. I wondered what Evan had done to incur his father's wrath this time. Or, perhaps more accurately, how much money he needed.

With a final, emphatic, and rather disparaging, "fiancée" and "father-in-law", Marcus' side of the conversation ended. Evan lamented softly for several more seconds before the voices faded away into nothing.

They really needed to have thicker doors built into this place.

Several of the newer servers followed me into the dining room, curious about the eating arrangements and uncertain as to what was expected of them. After a short explanation they moved back to the kitchen to begin gathering their cocktail trays, leaving the echoes of their soft laughter behind them.

The dinner guests began to arrive before Angela had returned downstairs. I could hear Marcus and Evan greeting them, some laughter, and then footsteps and soft voices as they entered the living room on the other side of the foyer. A few of the voices I recognized: Dean Raines, who was the guest of honor as the party was a fundraiser for his political campaign, and his wife, Susan Raines; Dean's brother John, who ran the Raines' steel company; Colby, Dean and Susan's daughter, who sounded like she was gushing over some new piece of statuary; Magdalena, who was barely audible over Colby. The Raines family was closely followed by Allan and Rosemary Tate, neighbors on the other side of the Whittington's (and members of my mother's illustrious bridge group) and the possibly-mobster —but still charming— Vincent Torrelli.

Angela was still nowhere to be seen. If Marcus had married Angela in order to have a hostess, she was failing miserably in her job. The guests were being greeted by the host alone--a fatal faux pas, and one that Susan was bound to point out to Angela. I wondered what could possible be keeping Angela from her guests. Probably she was still primping, making sure she outshone both Susan and Colby Raines in looks and dress.

A few of the men remained in the entry hall, postponing the moment when they would join the other guests, eager to conclude their conversation. "He seems a likely for governor, if he gets the financial support. The other candidate is a putz, and his party has suffered a lot this year because of that DUI scandal," the first voice said.

"True, but I'm not sure he is going to get the support. Marcus was saying that he wasn't sure if or how much he would contribute. It seems that Raines may be falling out of his favor," said the other voice.

"Is that so? I thought the families were pretty close. Isn't Marcus' son going to marry the Raines girl? I would think he'd support a future in-law, especially one that would make policies that could only help his business."

"Well, maybe Marcus is just being cautious. Still, we can't have the other guy winning. The state would really suffer then. And Raines isn't a bad sort. Nothing fishy about him— good-looking with a stable family life. Exactly what the voter's like," the second voice responded.

The voices faded and moved toward the living room, and I returned to the last minute details that were required.

Angela joined the party several minutes later, her voice trilling loudly over the dresses of the assembled ladies. Comments like "How divine" and "What a beautiful ensemble" drifted toward the dining room and kitchen and several of the servers snickered before taking their refilled trays back to the living room. Angela tried to fit in with the upper echelon, but never quite seemed to fit. She was simply trying too hard.

I was sitting in the kitchen, enjoying a good chat with the owner of the catering company, while furtively watching Eugene ogle more of the food, when Angela flung open the door in a rather melodramatic fashion.

She had placed her hair in a sleek bun on top of her head, and was wearing a tight black dress that ended at mid-calf. I was right about her heels. How people could walk with their heels inches above the floor was beyond me. If I had been wearing them I would undoubtedly have fallen flat on my face—despite the excellent training from The Sylvia Pearson School For Young Ladies (Who Seek to Mimic Beauty Pageant Winners).

"Hope, thank goodness you're still here! How clever of you to know I would need more of your help. I found several large bouquets incorrectly placed in the foyer, when they should be in the living room and dining room. Please come and help. I can't imagine where in the dining room they will fit," she pleaded.

"All right. I'm sure we can find room on the sideboard since it isn't really being used. We just need to rearrange a few things. Do you need help with the flowers in the living room, or can you handle those?" I asked, not sure whether I wanted to enter that domain, dressed as I was in a causal dress with little make-up. Vanity is a trait that can't be helped, and even I am susceptible to it—especially if one's high school nemesis was present and undoubtedly wearing an expensive cocktail dress.

"No. I asked Susan to fix those. I thought she would be flattered that I asked," Angela replied. She looked so pleased with herself for her thoughtfulness that I was certain she believed a halo had suddenly appeared atop her head, making it obvious to all present that she was heading for sainthood. I hoped she wasn't doing it just so she could make Susan look bad. And having known Susan Raines most of my life, I could just about guarantee that being asked to help move a floral arrangement wouldn't be considered flattery but more of an insult.

I looked through the door of the dining room and could see directly into the marble-tiled foyer and the living room beyond. Angela, after fetching the two massive bouquets, unburdened herself by handing them directly to me, and stood peering through the door, careful not to be seen by the guests.

"Only a few more need to arrive and then we can start dinner. Did I tell you I invited Mr. and Mrs. Arbuthnot? You know them, don't you?" she asked, though she obviously didn't expect me to answer, as her next words cut off any possible response. "They are so nice, though I don't think they are very fond of Dean and Susan. Or maybe it is just Susan they don't like. She can make one feel very inferior at times. She doesn't make me feel that way, of course. I just let her comments roll off my back. But I have seen her do it to other people. I can't imagine what Evan sees in her daughter. Colby isn't exactly the nicest girl in town, either. So like her mother."

I wondered if she was trying to trap me into saying something unflattering about one of her guests. I preferred to think, rather than say, unflattering things. It caused so much less contention that way.

"But I forgot. You've known Colby forever," she said apologetically. She sounded so sincere; I began to think that I had misjudged her again.

"Not forever. We did go to high school together. And our parents are members of the same club," I responded, my voice as neutral as I could make it.

The flowers, which were harder to place than I had foreseen, absorbed most of my attention, and Angela went back to peering out the door. "Oh, no. Do you see where she has put the flowers? Exactly where I didn't want them. Excuse me, Hope, but I have to intervene." She quickly walked out the door, initially wobbling slightly in her heels, and I could hear her voice clearly say, "Susan, not there! I don't want the guests to strain their eyes and necks. Why not put them in the corner?" Her voice trailed off, and before I had finished satisfactorily placing the flowers, the doorbell had rung once again, and an older couple, presumably the Arbuthnots, joined the group in the living room.

When I finally finished with the flowers, deciding that anyone foolish enough to walk so close to the sideboard deserved a mouthful of leaves, I noticed that I had garnered several nicks on my hands. I headed to the powder room, situated across the kitchen hall from the dining room. The powder room door was closed, and I was about to knock on the door, when I heard voices from the other side.

It is incredibly rude to eavesdrop, and I could have easily washed my hands in the kitchen, but the topic of conversation kept me rooted to the spot. Curiosity isn't a sin. And while it may be in bad taste, who was here to see my lapse?

"Would you stop, Susan? There is nothing going on between Angela and I," Dean said through what sounded like clenched teeth. "I don't know why you are acting like this. And stop crying!"

"Then why was Marcus hinting at the fact that he wasn't going to support you? And don't tell me that wasn't what he was doing, because it was pretty obvious to everyone. The only reason I can think of is that he suspects, or knows, you are having an affair with his wife," Susan said, her voice muffled by tears but still audible.

"I don't know why he has been making those hints. We haven't talked about it yet. But I'm not having an affair with Angela. Get that idea out of your head! You're just making a fool of yourself."

"I am not. She hates me and is always trying to make me look bad. Did you hear how she behaved about the flowers? As if I hadn't asked everyone where they thought the best place was," Susan harangued. "And I was doing her a favor, after all."

I quietly backed up, making sure my footsteps didn't give my presence away. How would it look if I were caught eavesdropping like a common gossip?

I was about to open the main door to the kitchen when a voice stopped me.

"What are you doing here, Hope? Did Angela invite *you* to dinner?"

Ah! My old nemesis had at last approached me. This was bound to happen. If I were dressed in Armani with a gorgeous man on my arm I would not run into a single person I knew. Wearing casual cotton and dateless (which should have been okay since I wasn't actually a guest) guaranteed that I would meet everyone on the planet that I most wished to avoid.

Colby Raines, arching a perfectly manicured eyebrow, gave me a look that spoke volumes. It was her favored sneer. Mostly it said 'You are pond scum and I can't imagine why I am being forced to associate with you.'

I returned her look for one of my own. Mine said, 'Associating with you makes me feel as yucky as pond scum.' Or so I hoped.

To give her credit, she was dressed elegantly in a long black evening dress, which accented her tall figure and pale hair; nevertheless, her lips were turned down at the corners in the same way her mother's did. It was a trait I had come to despise throughout high school, and which still set my nerves on end.

"She hired me to arrange the party, that's all," I said rather defensively. I hoped she hadn't caught me eavesdropping on her parents.

"I didn't think these kind of parties were your thing," she said rather vaguely.

What did that mean? What did she think my kind of thing was? Granted, this sort of party did bore me, but did she think I only mixed with the lowest of the low."

"It's not. I usually prefer more intimate gatherings." There was no way you could make fun of that.

"I understand completely. Mixing with larger groups takes an entirely different set of social skills, and can be very exhausting for those without experience in it," she smirked.

Okay, so she could make fun of that. Time to just smile and leave.

Before I could make my escape, a booming voice hailed us from the entrance to the hall. "Colby, wait a second. Hope! What luck! Glad to see you! It's been too long, my dear. What are you doing here? Not joining this group of old fogies are you?" I was crushed in a bear hug before I had time to hold out my hand to be shaken. The bear was Allan Tate, the neighbor of the Whittingtons and Raines, and a casual friend of my parents. Still, the hug felt awkward. To me, Allan Tate was nothing more than an acquaintance, albeit a genial one.

Allan was a solidly built man in his early sixties, with an Alec Guiness face—the kind that always looks familiar yet nevertheless blends into the scenery. He was devoted to two things: his wife and arguing about politics. He always played devil's advocate and no one was really sure how he voted, and he certainly wasn't giving away any hints.

"Hi, Allan. It's nice to see you too," I said, trying to keep my voice lowered so that Dean and Susan wouldn't be forced to reveal themselves.

"Hope isn't here for the party," Colby said. "She planned it."

"Is that so? But of course you did. It's absolutely lovely. You're working on Colby and Evan's wedding too, right?" He winked slyly at me. "And a wonderful affair it will be I have no doubt." He grinned at Colby and she smiled slightly in response.

"I hope so, Allan. You and Rosemary are coming, aren't you? I know how fond you both are of Evan, besides being neighbors of ours," Colby chimed in, knowing quite well that they had accepted the invitations long since.

"Wouldn't miss it for the world! You'll be there too, of course, Hope." He winked at me again. "Who are you going with? Some nice young man I haven't met?"

That was not a very subtle way of asking if I was still single, and it was definitely not appreciated. Why did one's elders always feel that it was quite proper to question one on marital prospects? I would never dream of questioning a single sixty-year-old female about her sex life.

"I haven't decided yet," I said. It occurred to me that I probably had to find a date soon, even if the wedding was a few weeks away, or my mother might find one for me.

"Too many men to choose from, eh?" he asked.

He has now made up for his abominable lapse, I thought, bestowing my most brilliant smile on him. I was now all forgiveness. "Hardly. All the good men are taken, otherwise I'd have asked you," I said.

Allan just laughed while Colby looked bored. "Have either of you seen my parents?" she asked in a rather curt manner. I would almost have said that she looked nervous.

Allan responded that he had come looking for them, as almost all of the dinner guests had arrived. I merely gave a blank shrug. If she hadn't heard their voices arguing, then I was not giving them away. Or my own lapse in manners for that matter.

"Come say hello to Rosemary, Hope. She would love to see you. It has been such a long time," Allan cajoled.

I looked down at my hands, with their scratches, and wondered if I would ever reach a sink. "All right, but only for a minute," I agreed.

"Good. Come on, Colby. Let's go get another cocktail before Angela decides to start begrudging us and saving everything for the big donors," Allan joked.

Colby was as susceptible to Allan's charm as I, and she smiled at him while sending me a blank stare. She might as well have pinned me with a sign that read 'I don't exist. Ignore me'.

The three of us made our way back down the hall and into the foyer, where John Raines was carrying on a low-voiced discussion with Marcus Whittington.

"You can't be serious, Marcus. What possible reason could you have?" asked John.

"I won't talk about it now. We can discuss it after the party. But I won't change my mind. I'm not going to—" he stopped as we approached, and John swung around toward us.

"Hello, Hope. I didn't know you were here," John said, while Marcus gave me a nod indicating that he recognized my presence but had nothing to say.

I wasn't too familiar with John Raines, knowing very little about him except that he headed the family's steel company, was very ambitious, and liked to pat young women on the head as a sort of welcoming gesture. The company had expanded under his leadership, and rumor said that it was possibly headed for international recognition.

"Hello, Mr. Raines. It's nice to see you again." I shied

away from his hand, aware that I didn't look good enough to allow my hair to be mussed.

"Uncle John, have you seen my parents?" Colby asked, her voice starting to take on a panicked note when she still didn't see them mingling with the assembled guests.

"I think I saw your father head toward the kitchen a few minutes ago. Didn't you see him?" John replied.

Before Colby could respond, Dean and Susan entered the foyer from the kitchen hall. Dean looked slightly nervous and kept glancing at Susan, ostensibly because she appeared to be emotionally unstable. The tears had been wiped dry, but her eyes were red and slightly puffy, and her nose looked like it had been blown several times. Next to Angela she would look a wreck. Knowing Angela was likely to use Susan's appearance to advantage made me feel sorry for Susan.

Marcus, once more the friendly host, led Colby and Susan back into the living room, inquiring as to the progress of the wedding plans, while John gave Dean a slight negative shake of his head. Dean said nothing, but promptly ushered Allan and I into the living room, leaving John remaining in the foyer.

The living room was a long, rectangular room fronting the north side of the property. It stretched from the foyer to the patio on the west, and had several different seating arrangements so that conversations could be kept intimate. I noted that the flower arrangements, which had so concerned Angela, had been placed unobtrusively in the background, blending in with the floral sofas and curtains. Other than a faint scent lingering in the area, they were almost unnoticeable. Susan's placement had been much more dramatic.

Marcus quickly deposited Susan and Colby with an older man sporting a rather distinguished moustache and a colorful tie, before obtaining a drink from one of the servers. Dean joined a youngish couple and an older man who were discussing the gubernatorial campaign, and John had yet to return to the room. He probably headed outside for a cigarette, I thought, and didn't want anyone to discover that he actually smoked.

Left to ourselves, Allan and I made our way to the far

side of the room, where Evan was speaking with a tall, thin, blond woman in an understated green dress. She had friendly blue eyes and almost no wrinkles, and knowing she was in her mid-fifties, I thought she looked quite good.

"Look who's here, Rosemary," Allan drawled. "I told Hope she couldn't escape before seeing you."

Rosemary gave me an affectionate, if slight, hug, and asked me how my life was progressing and if I had found a decent man yet. That topic is apparently inexhaustible in most people's minds.

Evan, sensing my frustration, stepped in by saying, "Oh, Hope's too good for most of the men around here."

I could have kissed him for that except Colby would probably slap me silly if I did.

"True," Rosemary added, smiling at me. "I didn't find Allan until I was about thirty or so. And things are different now anyway." She said it like it was a hopeful consolation prize. At least I was saved from having to answer.

"So what has Evan been telling you that has kept you so enraptured?" Allan asked Rosemary.

"Just about some new business ideas he has. Why don't you tell them about the idea for a small shopping center on Route 9 past Little Fullerton?" Rosemary prodded at Evan, and he blushed and stammered a little.

"Yes. I'd be very interested in hearing about it. My boss is always looking for new investments," Vincent said, having wandered over to stand behind Allan. There was a twinkle in his eyes and a sarcastic tone in his voice that made me wonder what he really wanted from this strange conglomeration.

He looked very handsome in his tuxedo, and with his cocktail in his hand almost resembled a movie star from the forties. More of a Clark Gable than a Cary Grant, but without Clark Gable's ears. Still, I preferred Cary Grant.

Rosemary didn't seem to appreciate Vincent's debonair style, and stiffened in response to his presence. "I'm sorry, but I don't think I've met you," she said in a formal tone. Her tone was so icy I was surprised the royal 'we' hadn't been used. I was surprised. Rosemary was usually quite approachable.

"How remiss of me. Vincent Torrelli, at your service, ma'am." For a second I thought he might bow, but I was disappointed when all he did was shake Rosemary's hand. Apparently he was already known to Allan, and simply gave him a bland smile.

I was more fortunate.

"I thought I saw your pretty face over here, Hope. I didn't expect to see you. Maybe this party won't be so bad after all," he pronounced. Rosemary sneered a little, which I decided not to take personally, since it was obviously directed at Vincent.

Vincent was not a stupid fellow, and could sense that he was not the most popular person in this group. After exchanging a few mild pleasantries with us, mainly about the over-exaggerated (and rather humorous) faults of the rest of the assembled guests, he asked Evan to join him outside for a cigarette.

"I don't smoke," Evan replied in a brittle voice.

"But I do, and I want some company. And I'm going to need a cigarette in order to get through the remainder of the party," Vincent said, his voice brooking no disagreement.

Angela came over at this moment, looking flushed and pleased with herself. "Here you are, Mr. Torrelli. I need you to come entertain some women whose husbands are being very remiss."

"Call me Vincent. And I would be delighted, but first Evan and I are going out for a cigarette," he purred.

"But Evan doesn't smoke," Angela said.

I wanted to laugh at her comment and the frustrated expression on her face, but everyone else was looking entirely too serious. There is definitely something going on here and I am the only one out of the loop. It occurred to me that I was a fly in a room full of spiders.

"You'll be late for dinner," Angela argued.

"Don't worry. It will be very fast. I'm trying to quit so I don't smoke the whole thing. We have a minute or two, right? No problem. I just need a quick puff." Poor Angela had met her match here. Vincent wasn't about to be cajoled by her pretty face and figure.

Vincent, foreseeing future arguments, touched Evan lightly on the arm and jerked his head in the direction of the patio doors. Evan followed reluctantly, and Angela went off, deciding that Rosemary and Allan, however wealthy and nice, weren't in need of her attention.

Rosemary, a strained look on her face, watched Evan and Vincent disappear through the doors. "I can't like Evan associating with a man like that. And those ridiculous rumors that he and Evan are cousins. He will bring nothing but trouble," she murmured, half to herself. "I hope it's not too late." And with that ominous comment she walked away, heading toward Marcus and the Arbuthnots, who were engaged in talking vociferously while waving their cocktails about in a haphazard manner.

And the party has just begun, I thought.

I looked at Allan, who was watching Rosemary as intently as she had watched Evan and Vincent, and sighed. This could be a long night and I wasn't even a guest.

"I should probably get back to the kitchen. Angela wants me to keep an eye on things just in case anything goes wrong," I said. With the servers and the food, my mind amended. The guests could work out their own problems.

Allan looked back at me, finally realizing I was still present. "Of course. It's nice to see you again, Hope. Tell your dad that I'll call him soon for a game of golf. He beat me last time, and I can't let that challenge go unmet. I've been practicing," he joked. Allan was an enthusiastic, if not superior, golfer, and almost always lost with good humor.

I returned to the kitchen, glad of the respite and eager to check up on Eugene. When I had last seen him he was standing behind a caterer complaining about how the food was being displayed on the trays. And I still hadn't seen Jezebel. That thought made me shudder.

When dinner was finally served I found little to do, and I gestured Eugene to follow me into the kitchen hall. "Where's Jezebel? The Whittington's have two cats, and I don't want any trouble."

Eugene just shrugged, obviously not as concerned with flying cats and shattering vases as I was.

"Let's go find her. And then I think you should put her outside. The yard is big enough for her to run around to her heart's delight." Dogs liked to run about pointlessly, didn't they?

"Why? She can walk right back in through the walls. The door isn't going to keep her out," Eugene argued.

I knew this was true, but I had noticed that Jezebel rarely walked through walls, and usually waited for a door to be opened for her. She hadn't quite grasped the benefits of being dead, and I was hoping it remained that way for quite some time.

Before we entered the foyer I slipped off my shoes and indicated that Eugene should follow me up the stairs. The door to the dining room was open and I didn't want to be discovered prowling around someone else's house like a common thief.

From the dining room I could hear a discussion on politics, the primary debaters being Dean and Allan. I could imagine Angela leaning in toward Dean to catch every word he uttered, revealing far too much of her breasts. That would be the Plumber coming out in her, I thought, and then remonstrated with myself for having a thought worthy of people like Susan and Colby Raines (and, to an extent, my mother). It also was easy to imagine Susan sitting across the table watching this byplay while drinking heavily. I was thankful that I was not blessed with the necessary fortune that would have made me an invitee to this drama. At least I was thankful that I wasn't an invitee. If I had the fortune I could have refused the invitation without fear of social reprisal. And used it to go on a vacation far, far away.

Would I be required to bring Eugene on vacation with me? The thought made me pause and I stumbled slightly before returning to my present predicament—the missing dog.

Before I had completely passed out of earshot I heard Colby's voice exclaim that her father was quite right and Evan second her with a description of Dean's views as being "exactly what this state needs." Evan agreed with almost everything Colby said, so this wasn't surprising.

Marcus, though on the far side of the room, could easily be heard with a strong declaration of "that remains to be seen" and an even louder comment that "politicians can't make it on ideas" and "money buys the office."

"What a putz!" Eugene declared. "Where did you find these people, Hope? Her, Pip-Squeak, I'm talking to you." Eugene practically bellowed.

"I can't talk to you here. Someone might hear me," I whispered. I didn't want to announce my presence.

Eugene just rolled his eyes at me and kept going. In the dining room I could hear the discussion getting louder, with Marcus telling John Raines what he felt the political climate was and how it would impact the steel industry. And every time John tried to respond, Marcus just kept talking over him. This started several other background conversations that didn't sound altogether pleasant.

I decided I had better pick up the pace before the dinner got vicious and was abruptly ended because someone threw wine at another guest (or the host or hostess). Besides, the other guests for the cocktail party would arrive soon, and I couldn't imagine anything more humiliating than being caught searching the closets and under the beds by sixty strangers. Being caught skinny-dipping by strangers might be more embarrassing, but I wasn't prone to that sort of thing. Of course, I had thought that I would never secretly search the house of an employer. My life was taking some weird twists and who knew where it could lead? Prison or a mental institution were the most likely candidates, but if I lost income from event planning, my mother's house would still be a possibility. I needed to get this done fast.

I knew Jezebel was not in the living or dining room, and I was loath to open the door to Marcus' office or to the billiards room, both of which were connected to the back foyer. The library could only be reached through the office, so searching that was out for now, too. That meant the bedrooms were my best option.

The stairway runner was a plush oriental carpet, and my feet sank into its soft texture. The carpet continued to the top of the steps, where it met up with a pale beige carpet that lined the entire hallway and the bedrooms. I debated setting my shoes down at the top of the stairs, but decided against it. Eugene, ahead of me, was commenting on the furnishings. I couldn't tell if he liked them or not, as most of the comments contained the word 'interesting'. That was usually a word I used for an object that was horrible but could not be insulted in front of the owner. Occasionally I applied the word to objects that were truly unique, but I didn't think anything in this house was unique. Most of the furniture looked like antique reproductions except for the vases and clocks, which appeared authentic and rather ostentatious. And what kind of people kept a suit of armor? This wasn't a castle, for God's sake!

Eugene obviously agreed with me, because he was clicking his tongue and shaking his head from side to side. "When you buy one of these I'm finding someone else to bunk with, Pip," he declared.

For a moment I seriously thought about scouring antique shops until I found the most ostentatious suit of armor I could find. But with further consideration I realized that Eugene probably wouldn't stick to his word and then I would be stuck with both Eugene and an outdated pile of scrap metal that probably wouldn't even fit in my living room.

We turned into the first bedroom on the left, which must have belonged to Angela and Marcus, though little of Marcus' presence could be found. The room was like a softer version of the living room, decorated in a soft floral pattern, with matching bedspread, curtains and love seat. The bed was overly large and strewn with more decorative pillows than found in a harem. A vanity held a large jewelry box and a portrait of Marcus, as well as another photograph of a regular-looking family, which must be the Plumbers.

Angela's robe and negligee were thrown across the end of the bed, and several dresses were lying in a heap at the door of the closet. Marcus' business suit lay across the back of a chair, with a handkerchief, some business cards, and some small scraps of paper pushing out of the pockets. A neck tie and scarf were lying across the fireplace mantel, tossed there as if someone had picked them up and placed them on the nearest piece of furniture.

The room was in a state of partial disarray--Angela's doing without a doubt--but there was no sign that Jezebel was in here. I refrained from checking the closet or the bathroom, knowing Jezebel was not likely to be content with a closed-in space.

The next bedroom was a guest room decorated with a double bed and blue coverlet, a blue settee and mahogany coffee table, and oversized draperies. It was a much nicer room than Angela's, and I wondered why anyone would choose to sleep in Angela's ridiculous boudoir over this. Eugene liked it enough that he stopped to inspect the coffee table.

The room across the hall from Angela and Marcus was Evan's room when he stayed here. It was notable for its three portraits of Colby (one had the two of them but Colby's face blocked half of Evan's). This room was done in navy blue with gold accents. I doubted Evan would have chosen pillows with gold tassels, so it was safe to assume that this was what Angela thought a man's bedroom should look like.

Several sheets of paper were tossed on the bed, and when I crossed the room to check the other side of the bed, I noted that several were letters with Vincent's name typed across the bottom. There was also a small pile of hand-written receipts and a date book.

I didn't look in any more detail, feeling guilty for simply being present, but Eugene had no such scruples. He moved some of the papers around with his hand, while simultaneously priding himself on being so dexterous. "Your friend Evan is having some serious financial problems. I thought his dad was super wealthy. You'd think he would bail him out."

"You shouldn't be reading that. Leave it alone. It's none of our business," I reprimanded, thinking that Eugene was right and Marcus could easily bail Evan out of any difficulty. Maybe he was the kind of father who believed independence was learned through strife and hardship. I doubted it, though. Most likely he was just a jerk.

Again, there was no sign of Jezebel. That dratted dog was going to be the death of me—if Eugene didn't get there first.

"Jezebel isn't here, so we should go," I said, wishing I could yank Eugene by the collar or even bop him on the head with my shoes. That would certainly be satisfying.

He stole one more glance at the papers before following me out of the room and into the next bedroom.

I saw that the door was partially open and guessed that this was where we would find Jezebel. And I was right.

Jezebel was lying across the bed, a worn, loose photograph wedged under her paw. I really never understood how Eugene and Jezebel could sleep on a bed or sofa, yet somehow other pieces of furniture and small objects passed right through them. I wondered if it was a psychological issue.

When Jezebel saw Eugene and I she jumped up and started wagging her tail. The photograph went flying and landed at my feet. I had no idea where Jezebel had found it, but guessed she had taken it as a prize.

While Eugene congratulated Jezebel on her progress with moving things, I grabbed the photograph, which was of a rather blurry blond woman, and wondered how Jezebel had managed to get this from Evan's room to here. She was progressing indeed. I felt a small sense of pride but quickly squashed it. There was no sense in encouraging the dog to start running around moving objects. My apartment would be a disaster if Jezebel became too adept.

Eugene managed to instantly round up Jezebel and send her flying out the door and down the stairs. I hastily shoved the photograph back in Evan's room next to the others and fled down the stairs toward the kitchen. When I reached the kitchen hallway I put my shoes back on, and looked around for Eugene and Jezebel.

Jezebel was seated under the kitchen table, cleaning her paw, and Eugene was leaning against the counter, waiting for me.

"I was thinking that I might enjoy attending this party, after all," he said, a gleam in his eyes. It was more than a mischievous gleam; it was the kind of gleam that the wicked witch had when she said, "I'll get you, my pretty, and your little dog, too." Thankfully Eugene didn't add the cackling laughter. That would have certainly caused me heart palpitations. And while I had a fat cat rather than a little dog, I sensed trouble. Eugene was definitely not going to get any Coq au Vin from me later.

Chapter Thirteen

Instead of spending the party relaxing on the patio with a Long Island Ice Tea in my hand and a purloined tray of hors d'oeuvres at my feet, I spent the greater part of the evening on tenterhooks, lamenting the fact that my mother had succeeded in preventing me from ever biting my fingernails. Every clatter of a dish caused my head to snap up in fear that Eugene had tripped a server, and every hoot of laughter made me wonder if Eugene had tried lifting up women's skirts just for a laugh. Deep down I knew he would never be that horrid (although his sick sense of humor had gotten the better of him lately) and would be horrified if he knew I even entertained the thought. I hoped God gave me the satisfaction of having people walk right through Eugene and that it was, for him, an uncomfortable sensation.

I could easily have slipped into the party, grabbed those hors d'oeuvres I was thinking about, and cornered Eugene (if you can corner a ghost). I doubted that anyone would notice if I joined the guests, and if they did notice, that they would care. But something prevented me from taking that step. My mother would say it was a well-bred desire not to put myself forward; Jilly would say my vanity had taken over and I was ashamed of my casual attire; Eugene would say it was my fear of making a fool of myself if I inadvertently started yelling at invisible people. They would all be right.

'I am turning into a paranoid, pessimistic party-pooper,' I told myself. What happened to your kindness and sensitivity toward others? One part of me wanted to say 'Screw that!' but the better part of me decided to give Eugene the benefit of the doubt. Being dead was probably no fun. And to do him justice, I probably wasn't making his life (actually his death) any easier. Didn't unhappy people resort to desperate measures just to get attention?

Eugene returned, surprisingly sedate, when the food and wine had started to run low, no longer feeling the party was worth his time. It was, as he said, "A bunch of schlemiels talking politics and ignoring the more important things in life." I had no doubt that those important things included food, wine, theater, mystery novels, and classic films. Considering how highbrow Eugene was, it amazed me that he didn't care for discussions about politics.

I ushered Eugene outside so that we could talk in privacy, and asked him what, if anything, he had done at the party.

"Nothing, Hope. You worry too much. What could I possibly do? I just walked around and avoided getting walked through. And it was pretty difficult, too. One overly large woman nearly sat on me," he moaned.

Jezebel had spotted us and ran up to Eugene, her tail wagging gleefully. He bent down to pat her on the head and I feared he would be distracted from my inquisition.

"So you didn't try to trip people or eat any food? The last thing I want is for people to start seeing food flying around the room." I imagined a scene from an old comedy, with people screaming and fainting and food flying everywhere.

Eugene laughed. "It would be pretty funny though. Can you imagine the looks on the faces of all those pompous windbags?"

I laughed too. And for a moment I wondered how I had ever considered Eugene one of those pompous windbags. He was pompous, though when his sense of humor emerged he could be rather unaffected. And he certainly wasn't a windbag. When I wanted answers, rather than explicate on the subject, he usually just ignored me instead. Eugene gave out his pearls of wisdom on his own terms.

"Some of them were drinking so much wine they would probably just think they were slightly intoxicated. Though, if we were lucky, they might all panic, run out, and call in a Ghostbuster," he said, snorting a little when he laughed.

"That wouldn't be funny, Eugene. Have you forgotten you are a ghost? What if the Ghostbusters succeeded in sucking you into their little machine or setting a giant marshmallow man on you? You wouldn't be laughing then," I noted.

He thought about that for a minute. "I suppose you're right," he said. "I doubt they sent those ghosts to heaven. They kept them in a machine in a basement. That would be even worse than your apartment."

"Thanks for the compliment." What an ungrateful toad! And here I had been having such nice thoughts about him.

"You're welcome. I'll tell you what I did see, though. That old friend of yours who is not a friend—the one whose face is plastered all over that room upstairs—was having a pretty hard time of it charming our not-so-charming host. He cut her twice. Isn't she supposed to become his daughter-in-law? What a boob!" he declared.

"Really?" That *was* interesting. "Well, maybe he's had a taste of her bad side or he doesn't like women. That wouldn't surprise me. He screams misogynist," I proclaimed. "He doesn't pay much attention to his wife, either. Not that she cares." Angela probably cared more about Marcus' money than his body or soul—and I almost couldn't blame her.

"Well that would explain why she was all over Raines. She was actually gushing. I'm not sure who I feel sorrier for, her husband or Raines," he snickered. "Now that I think of it, she might have been what their argument was about."

"What argument?" I asked, curiosity getting the better of me.

"Well, maybe it wasn't an argument, but Dean Raines stormed out of Marcus Whittington's office and practically ran down Mrs. Whittington, who, unlike myself, had been eavesdropping."

Eugene's moral fiber was so outstanding I was thinking of filling out an application with his name on it for the city's community service award. For a person with integrity like his, I was sure they would consider posthumous awards. Right after they granted Colby sainthood and I won the Miss America pageant.

Several of the servers came out of the kitchen bearing

large garbage bags, and I quickly leaned back against the wall near the service entrance, pretending to be absorbed in checking my nails for cracks in the polish.

I must look like an idiot, I thought. Who checks their nails outside in the dark, with only a porch light for illumination?

As soon as the servers deposited their loads and went back inside, Eugene turned to me and said, "Since I've been such a good little ghost, I think I deserve Beef Wellington and a chocolate soufflé."

"Are you out of your mind? You're not even sure you can eat. So what happens if you can't eat? I'm stuck eating it all, that's what. And Coq au Vin is one thing, but forget Beef Wellington, and definitely forget the soufflé," I replied.

"What's the matter, Hope? Can't you make a chocolate soufflé?" he sneered.

I can't make a perfect soufflé, but neither can eighty percent of the population. It's not like I eat soufflés on a regular basis anyway. Again, that's the sort of thing one dines out for, which is why I refused to baited into an undignified response.

"I'll tell you what, if you're a good little girl I'll teach you how to make one," he generously offered. Well, if one ignored the snotty tone it was pretty generous for Eugene.

"Ha-ha," I said, secretly wondering what ingredients one needed for a chocolate soufflé. Chocolate actually sounded pretty good to me at the moment. "I think I can leave soon. I just have to oversee the clean up and say goodbye to Angela. Will Jezebel behave if we bring her inside with us, or should we leave her out here?"

"She always behaves," Eugene responded tartly.

I was courteous enough to turn around before rolling my eyes, and we headed back into the house while Jezebel ran circles around Eugene's legs.

The caterer informed me that almost all of the guests had departed, and that the clean up was nearly complete. All that was now required of me was to do a final check and make sure everything had been put back in its place (not usually my job, but I wasn't about to complain since I was being paid extra for all those little details).

The kitchen, the ovens and stovetop being the only part used by the caterer, was fairly clean. The silverware (Angela had insisted on using her own) was being washed by hand, and placed back in its tray, while the dishes (again Angela had wanted to use her own china) were stacked neatly in piles by the sink; the caterer's dirty napkins (Angela was smart in this instance) were stuffed into a bag to be laundered and all the trays were stacked on the island, ready to be taken to the van.

Eugene followed me into the dining room, where I did a quick inventory. The dining room table, which had been cleaned after the dinner and reset with trays of hors d'oeuvres for the party, now held only the bouquets of flowers, which had been moved from the sideboard. A few crumbs littered the carpet, and I was thankful that I was not required to vacuum. I would never have heard the end of it from Eugene.

Just as I was about to return to the kitchen via the butler's pantry, Magdalena came floating into the room in a cloud of purple and gold. Her dress was long and wispy and looked like something out of the Byzantine Empire, and she had a gold shawl draped around her shoulders. She wore a thick gold necklace and several gold bangles, though she did not have on any earrings. Her hair was done in her usual bun, but look tidier than normal. She was obviously trying to convey an aura of sophisticated elegance. And if she looked like a child playing dress-up, it went unnoticed when one saw her animated facial features.

"I've been waiting for you to emerge all evening, Hope. Why didn't you join us? Not because of your dress, I hope? Half the people who came were wearing sports jackets. Can you imagine? In my day no one would dream of attending an evening party in such attire. But then we dressed for dinner, too," she rambled. A faint emanation of brandy lingered around her and I hid a smile.

"That's nice of you to say, but I would have felt terribly awkward since I wasn't technically invited," I answered.

"Nonsense," she spat. "You probably knew half the people there. Not invited? Angela wouldn't care. The more the merrier in her view, which is one of her more endearing traits." She leaned closer to me, as if whispering a secret. "She probably wouldn't have noticed. She was far too busy hitting on all the men, especially my son."

I pretended surprise. "Really?"

"Yes. It was quite outrageous. She could have had the decency to wait until her husband was out of the room."

Eugene gave a snort of laughter while I merely nodded.

"I doubt she'll get anywhere with him, though," Magdalena continued. "Susan watches him like a hawk. And he's too wrapped up in this election to think of anything else." She leaned in closer and it became apparent that she might have had a little too much wine as well. "Come and see for yourself. They're all in the living room like a pack of wolves trying to devour each other."

I glanced to the side, to see what Eugene thought about this idea, and Magdalena caught my look. "Is *he* here with you, Hope? Eustace, or was it Ernest?" Definitely a little too much to drink.

"Eugene, actually, and yes he is here. Just over there." I pointed toward the doorway of the butler's pantry and Magdalena looked in that direction. Her eyes bulged with excitement and she waved cheerily at Eugene.

"Hello, Eugene. I'm so glad to be in your presence again. How nice of you to keep Hope company." She turned back to me and whispered *sotto voce*, "Do you take him everywhere with you?"

Eugene took offense at this and stood up a little straighter. "I'm not a dog," he growled. "I go where I choose and with whom I choose. You can tell her that, Hope."

"No, I don't take him everywhere. Sometimes he gets bored and likes to come along. He is a very independent ghost," I explained. If Eugene took a pet and left in a huff I would have a hard time finding him. There was no way I could think up enough excuses to remain here all night prowling around the house talking to myself.

"That's for the best. It would be very uncomfortable if he accompanied you everywhere. Can you imagine going on your honeymoon and having to take him along? Quite intolerable. Instead, he is like a friend that you can take to lunch and the movies. And you won't even have to pay for him to get in. Isn't that so much nicer?" she asked.

"You aren't likely to go on a honeymoon at the rate your going, Hope. And you haven't taken me to the movies. Now that she mentions it, I do feel slightly cheated. Mrs. Duprés took her ghost to interesting places and let him play tricks on people. I've been jipped, it seems," Eugene groaned melodramatically. "We need a real outing, Pip. One that I choose. It's not likely to cut into your social life, after all."

Great! All I needed was a ghost that not only thought exactly like my mother but had a theatrical streak as well.

"That's true, Magdalena. I never thought about getting two people into a movie theater for the price of one. Once Eugene learns to behave himself in public I will be sure to take him," I said with a touch of asperity. "I think there's a new sci-fi movie coming out next month. It's supposed to have wonderful special effects."

Eugene looked horrified. I felt pretty good.

"That's very nice of you, my dear. Poor Eugene must be very bored and lonely--even with his dog. And how is his dog? Is she here, too?" she asked.

Before I could respond, the click of heels on marble announced that Angela was approaching the dining room. Just as her hand was placed on the molding of the door and a shoulder became visible, another click of heels, softer than Angela's, approached. Susan, her voice sounding hard and broken, said, "Are you sure you can't do anything? This is serious."

"I don't know. Give me some time to think about it," Angela responded, clearly annoyed by Susan's demand.

The remainder of Angela's body appeared as a silhouette in the doorway, and she gave Magdalena and I a bright smile. "There you are. I've been sent to find you, Mrs. Duprés. Your sons are worried that you have tired yourself out." This was obviously a polite way of saying that they were worried she had imbibed too much and was liable to fall down at any minute and embarrass them.

"Thank you, dear, but I'm fine. Hope and I were about to join the others in the living room," Magdalena cooed. She grabbed my arm and dragged me across the room with her.

We followed Angela into the living room where several small groups were assembled at the rear of the room. The lighter cocktails the caterers provided had been replaced with stronger and larger drinks that every man but Vincent held in his hand, and the discussions were getting proportionately louder.

Marcus Whittington was arguing with Allan Tate about corruption in the White House and Dean and John Raines were discussing the problems with the public education system with Mr. Arbuthnot, who kept interrupting them by saying, "That's why I sent my kids to private schools," but seemed unable to offer any solutions. Mrs. Arbuthnot stood slightly outside this circle, nodding her head sagely at whatever words came out of her husband's mouth. Susan was standing sluggishly next to Colby, who had her arm wrapped around her mother, while Evan talked softly with them between large gulps of brandy.

Rosemary Tate, who had been chatting amicably (surprisingly so) with Vincent Torrelli, abandoned him and came toward Angela, Magdalena, and I. "Mr. Torrelli can be quite charming despite his, uh, business. You should ask him to tell you about his visit to Russia and the mistake customs made. It really is quite an amusing story."

Since Rosemary had not addressed anyone in particular, no one responded to the comment. Angela, seeing an opportunity to capture Dean's attention, said overly loudly, "The Arbuthnots said they were leaving in a few minutes, and I daresay they wouldn't mind taking you home, Mrs. Duprés. It's just a short walk, after all."

Magdalena grabbed at my hand and made a deprecating sound, but Angela ignored her. "I don't need to leave just yet. I thought someone mentioned a card game."

Angela looked horrified at the thought of having to sit down to a game of cards this late at night, and Rosemary just smiled condescendingly.

Mr. Arbuthnot, who had just finished explaining again

that lack of funding and large class sizes was why he had enrolled his children in private schools, turned around at the mention of his name. "Did you call me, Angela?"

Angela had successfully interrupted Dean and John's conversation without being impolite, achieving her desire, and was beaming with triumph. I wondered how she was going to get Dean Raines alone, now that she was about to dispose of the Arbuthnots and Magdalena in one swoop. "Mrs. Duprés was wondering if you and your wife would walk her home. It's just next door. She's rather tired, and I know her sons would appreciate it."

Again Magdalena made a sound of displeasure, but it was drowned out by Mr. Arbuthnot exclaiming that if the others were still meaning to stay he would escort Mrs. Duprés with the greatest pleasure. As an afterthought he mentioned that his wife always enjoyed Mrs. Duprés' company.

Had they ever even met before tonight? Poor Mrs. Arbuthnot was another (albeit willing) victim of male domination. And my mother wondered why I was still single!

Eugene gave me a significant look. Like me, he had hoped that tonight we would discover why Magdalena's husband no longer haunted her. Instead we were treated to a tipsy woman who was bombarded out of the house before any information could be had.

It wasn't long before Magdalena and the Arbuthnots were ushered out the front door by their hostess and the remaining company resumed their conversations.

"Can I have a word with you, Angela? I'm sure Hope won't mind leaving us for a moment. She can go and chat with Mr. Torrelli," Rosemary said. Angela looked surprised and a little disappointed, her flirtation with Dean being postponed a few minutes longer.

I was perfectly willing to leave them to themselves. A hurried departure was what I really wanted, but since Vincent had overheard Rosemary's remark, which was undoubtedly her intention, I was left with no choice but to head in Vincent's direction.

Vincent was in a good mood and eager to please. He smiled charmingly, setting up Eugene's hackles, and asked me how I had spent my evening.

"Doing very little," I replied. "I was supposed to oversee everything, but there wasn't really anything to do. I should have brought a book."

"Why didn't you join us? We could have used another pretty young female," he said, a gleam in his eyes.

"That's very nice of you to say. Did you enjoy the party? I imagine that after a few drinks the crowd lightens up a little," I said, a little smile escaping my lips. It wouldn't do to make fun of the guests in front of a stranger, especially when I was still in the house.

Eugene snorted yet again. A few more snorts and he'd make the Guinness Book of World Records. Maybe God is simply waiting for pig heaven to have an opening before taking Eugene.

"Are you kidding? The tension here is so thick a machete couldn't hack through it." Vincent glanced in the direction of the Raines brothers, careful not to be overheard.

"What's wrong? I've heard some bits and pieces of conversation, but nothing really informative. Has a skeleton dropped out of the closet?" I asked.

"The old man has decided not to fund any more of the Raines campaign, and he's not supporting him publicly either," Vincent said, a grim smile on his face. "And that means that Raines is going to have a difficult time winning the election if he doesn't rack up more funds. The problem is, once word gets out that Whittington has dropped him—especially since he is soon to be family--people are going to start wondering why, and the money is not going to flow the way it has been."

"Hasn't Marcus given a reason for withdrawing his support?" Remembering the conversation I overheard between Dean and Susan in the bathroom and Eugene's description of Dean's abrupt departure from Marcus' office, I wondered what skeleton *had* popped out of the closet.

"No, and no one else is talking. There is no reason that I can come up with. At first I thought it had to do with Whittington's lovely wife, but that doesn't seem to be the case. She obviously hasn't had much luck with Raines, seeing as she was looking like a disappointed flirt all night." He winked at me and added, "What does she expect with his wife looking daggers at both of them all night? And I imagine that Mrs. Raines is none too pleased that the governor's mansion may no longer be in reach."

It occurred to me that Susan Raines was not only socially ambitious, but devoted enough to her husband that she was willing to sacrifice her own happiness for his political career. I wondered if she actually wanted to be the wife of the governor. Socially it would be a coup, but it would also mean a frequently absent husband who would be a target for more women than just Angela. She would likely be consumed by her own jealousy. The image of a modern Joan of Arc flashed through my mind, but I brushed it aside. The only real connection I could make between Susan and Joan of Arc was that the latter was French and the former often did her nails in a French manicure.

Rosemary finished her conversation with Angela, and approached Marcus and Allan. A few words were said between them, and then Rosemary left the living room. A few moments later I heard the front door open and close, and I supposed Rosemary had decided to leave before her husband.

The lucky woman! I wish I could make my escape that quickly.

Marcus chose that moment to leave the room, and Evan, who had been deserted by Susan and Colby a few minutes earlier, followed him. The only other remaining people seemed to be Allan, Angela, Dean and John.

Not wanting to pursue a conversation about the guests in the Whittington's home, I decided to broach a new subject. "I'm surprised you're still here. Your business with Evan must be quite complicated."

He laughed and I knew how foolish that question sounded. Not only did it sound like I was fishing for information, but no intelligent person was likely to associate Evan with complicated business. His role was usually that of investor or front man.

"Evan's business with my boss was more in the line of a personal investment. Evan had some interesting ideas for some real estate development and needed funding and my boss took a liking to him. But liking him doesn't exclude him from repaying the loan. I'm here to work out the payment arrangements," Vincent said, smiling ruefully.

No surprise there. Eugene had been right. Vincent was a thug, albeit a nice one. I wondered if he actually beat people up or just used his presence as intimidation. "And you're not really his cousin?"

"No. I can't even imagine who started that rumor. We're just old friends, and on occasion business associates."

Eugene, who had no interest in hearing about the business ventures of Evan Whittington and Vincent Torrelli, walked over to the open liquor cabinet and bent down to examine the labels. After a few seconds I could hear him exclaim, "You must be joking. There's more vodka here than in a Russian bar. It's probably for the little wife. The old guy looks more like a whisky drinker."

Ignoring Eugene, I continued my conversation with Vincent. "I'm surprised Evan needed a loan. His father is very wealthy and could easily give him the money."

"Yes, but he has little faith in Evan. He's probably right, too, but Evan is a nice guy and my boss took pity on him," Vincent explained. "And if it had worked out it would have made them both quite a bit of money. But..."

"But pity only extends so far?" I prompted.

"Exactly. Evan asked his old man for a loan to pay back his own loan, but the old guy said no." Vincent looked disgusted by Marcus' lack of paternal sympathy. Or maybe it was because it made it that much harder to collect his boss' funds.

I'm becoming too cynical, I realized. Vincent just likes Evan, that's all.

"They've got a Remy-Martin in here. Pretty old, too," Eugene called out, momentarily disturbing my thoughts.

"Evan's plan still can't work out?" I asked.

Vincent shook his head and looked toward the door.

Evan hadn't returned. "I highly doubt it. The deadline hasn't passed though, so it still could, which is partly why I'm here. I've been showing Evan some new ideas that could revamp the project, but he would need some more funds to continue and Mr. Gieppo won't contribute any more. It could still turn out a very profitable venture if there were more investors. But it's too risky for the average investor."

"Hah, Hennessey, too," came from the direction of the liquor cabinet.

"But I imagine the money will turn up soon. Maybe Evan's pretty stepmother or his fiancées father will pitch in. If not, Evan and I will make a payment schedule for the old loan. Evan is trying to convince me that he has another brilliant, moneymaking idea, but it's a definite no-go for my boss. And I'd hate to see Evan in any more financial difficulties than he is already."

I nodded, wondering what Evan and Colby were going to do for finances when they were married. Maybe they expected their parents to support them. That would certainly be the life!

"Drumgray. I was right about the old man. This an excellent bottle of Scotch." Eugene's voice was getting more muffled the lower he bent.

"How much longer do you intend to stay?" I asked.

"Another week or two. This business with Evan is only a small part of why I am here. My boss has a lot of interests around the country, especially in this area. After Philadelphia I head to Chicago and then to Seattle and San Francisco."

I looked at Vincent questioningly. Seattle? Chicago made sense. Didn't the mafia (and I couldn't imagine his boss was anything but mafia) have business in places like Las Vegas and Miami?

He read my look correctly. "Yeah, Seattle. Mr. Gieppo has a lot of money invested in computers and electronics."

"Do you know if they have a wine cellar, Hope? I'd like to check it out before we go." Eugene yelled out in anticipation.

Angela approached us, eager to know if Vincent wanted

to join in a game of billiards before he left. When he declined she looked hesitantly at me.

"Don't look at me. I have no idea how to play," I joked.

"That's what Allan said. And the truth is, I don't either," she responded. "Dean and John will have to play by themselves. Maybe Marcus will join them, but the way the evening has gone I doubt it."

I smiled sympathetically. "I'm just going to finish checking the kitchen. I'll let you know when I leave so that you can lock up the kitchen door." Escape was finally in my sight.

Angela didn't demur, claiming that she was ready to retire, and Vincent very flatteringly looked disappointed. Eugene, now bored with examining the contents of the liquor cabinet, was eager to return with me to the kitchen and discover if there was a wine cellar.

As soon as I stepped out of the living room and into the foyer, Eugene stopped me. "Listen."

" I'm not going to eavesdrop on a private conversation." Not tonight, anyway. More accurately, I am not going to eavesdrop on another conversation. The less I know about these people the happier I am.

Eugene shushed me. "I can't hear over you talking."

The voices were coming from Marcus' office, so I knew the identity of at least one of the speakers.

A soft, feminine voice was pleading with him. I was still walking toward the kitchen and away from the office, so all I could hear was 'son'.

"You don't have any right to interfere in this business," Marcus hurled at the woman.

I couldn't hear her response, but Marcus' was quite clear. "I can do what I want with my money."

Eugene was hesitating between sticking his head through the wall and returning with me to the kitchen. The kitchen and possibility of a wine cellar won out.

We reached the door to the kitchen and heard a rather audible, "You disgust me, you always have," in Marcus' strident tones.

When I entered the kitchen, Eugene still a few paces

behind me, a scene of disturbing proportions met my eyes. The dishes were still piled on the counter, not yet returned to their places in the china cabinet, the silverware was being recounted by a nervous looking server, and the three remaining servers and the caterer were arguing amongst themselves. But that wasn't what was so disturbing. In the middle of the floor was a crumpled tablecloth strewn with several broken wine glasses and a plate of left over hors d'oeuvres. To be precise, it was really just the plate, as the hors d'oeuvres were scattered across the tiled floor. And to top off the scene, Jezebel was sitting underneath the table looking like the devil was after her.

I was not going to be leaving anytime soon.

I gave Eugene an I-told-you-so look and gestured that he was to take Jezebel back outside. If Jezebel were now capable of grabbing tablecloths with her teeth, a bleak future would stretch before me—a future of chaos and crumbs.

Stepping between the caterer and the servers, who were arguing, I was able to pacify the caterer and soothe the nerves of the servers.

"Someone had to have done it, Hope," Nathan Burke, the caterer said.

"I'm sure it was an accident and the individual responsible didn't even realize what happened," I responded. Drat that dog!

"But the wine glasses are ruined and they weren't cheap" he complained, giving the servers a baleful glare.

"It looks like only a few actually broke. And you can't tell me that you don't loose a few glasses at every party. We all know that they disappear as frequently as socks in the dryer," I noted.

"True," he said, "but it shouldn't have happened. And I'm not cleaning it up."

The servers, grateful for not having lost their jobs, eagerly volunteered to clean up the mess, and I agreed to put the dishes and silverware back in the dining room.

"Thanks, Hope. At least you aren't an idiot. The servers also lost some silverware. You haven't seen any lying around, have you? Some forks, a knife, and a three spoons are missing," the weary caterer moaned. His food might be excellent but he was in need of a lecture on remaining calm and poised under stress. But then again, I seemed to be in need of a refresher course myself. "They aren't ours and I don't want to get in trouble if they are lost."

"I'll see if I can find them. They probably ended up on the floor near the table legs," I replied. "People are always too embarrassed to retrieve silverware they have dropped."

The next ten minutes were a flurry of activity. I found myself continually moving between the kitchen, the butler's pantry, and the dining room. Each time I entered the kitchen Eugene would look sheepishly away, which made me less and less enthusiastic about reprimanding him and Jezebel when we got to the car.

The mess on the floor was soon cleaned up, a mop and bucket being found and pressed on the nervous-looking server.

As I picked up the last stack of dishes that needed to be put away in the dining room, Colby entered the kitchen through the mudroom, looking rather pale. She ignored the caterer and the servers and approached me. "Have you seen, Evan?" she asked in a rather clipped voice. "He was supposed to meet me here at the side entrance to walk me home."

"No. Sorry. Maybe he's still talking to his dad or playing billiards with your father and uncle." Something about that statement wasn't right, but I was too tired to think about it.

"Thanks anyway. I'll go around back and see if he's on the patio or in the billiards room."

"Why don't you just go through here," I suggested. "It's faster."

Colby looked guilty. "I know, but I don't want to run into Angela, or my mother for that matter. There was a bit of a tiff."

I didn't know if she meant that she had had a fight with her mother, if she and her mother had a fight with Angela, or if she herself had a fight with Angela, but I didn't ask her to explain any further. These families needed serious group therapy. And I knew just who to recommend.

Colby left through the kitchen door without another word, and I was able to continue uninterrupted to the dining room. I had placed several large piles of dishes on the table, and was in the process of returning them to the china cabinet when Eugene glided through the wall to my left.

"Okay, I admit it. I was wrong. Jezebel can misbehave on occasion. I'll start taking her for more walks and training her not to touch things," Eugene said apologetically.

It occurred to me that he might possibly think I would throw him out of my apartment. I would never be so cruel! Besides, if he refused to leave I could hardly call the police to have them evict a ghost. And exorcisms really were out of the question. If they worked, which was a big if, where would Eugene end up? I didn't want to be responsible for sending him to an alternate universe or hell or something like that.

"It's all right. It was just a few glasses. It's not like anyone knew who did it," I reassured him.

He remained by me, thoughtfully watching me stack the dishes. "Do you usually do this sort of thing?" he asked.

"Nope. This is a one-time deal, I hope. Why? Are you thinking of taking up a new career when you reach your final destination?" I joked.

"Hardly. When I get there I intend to spend eternity relaxing."

"Sounds good. Maybe they have ghost food up there and you can eat your way through eternity."

"A lovely idea. I could have all the Steak au Poivre I want. And a chocolate soufflé," he said, the customary gleam returning to his eyes.

"So what kind of ingredients do I need to make a chocolate soufflé? If you can't actually eat it, which I'm sorry to say seems likely, I'm going to be stuck eating it. And in that case I would like it to be good," I reasoned.

"There are surprisingly few ingredients. Don't worry, Hope, I'll have you cooking like a pro in no time," Eugene said. He rubbed his hands together in anticipation and I smiled. He could be surprisingly easy to please. Sometimes, anyway.

"Okay, I'm done here," I said as I slid the last dish into the cabinet. "If the clean up is finished the caterer and I just need to get our checks and we can go. Maybe Angela can give them both to me, and we can speed up the process." As an afterthought I added, "You haven't seen any of that silverware laying around have you?"

Eugene refused to get down on his hands and knees, telling me that was my job, but he willingly searched from a standing position. When none could be found I stood up, brushed a few crumbs off my dress (luckily they were all dry crumbs) and we headed for the living room.

We entered the foyer just as Rosemary was heading down the stairs.

"Hi," I said. "I thought you went home."

Rosemary jumped at the sound of my voice. "What? Oh yes. I went to get a book Angela lent me. She was thinking she might want to read it tonight, though I doubt she'll want to. She's probably exhausted from having walked around in those shoes all night," Rosemary said, trying to smile, but failing.

When she reached the bottom of the stairs she looked sadly dispirited and was drooping slightly.

"I think we're all a little tired," I said. I just hoped I didn't look as tired as I felt, as Rosemary obviously did.

"True. I could fall asleep right now."

We headed into the living room, but could see no one until the light reflecting off of an empty glass caught our eyes. Allan was sitting in the far corner in a lounge chair, leafing through a magazine. He glanced up when he saw us and smiled. "Ah, the ladies have returned. I was beginning to think I had been deserted permanently."

"Where is everyone?" I asked. "I wanted to say goodbye to Angela and get the check for the caterer."

"Which means you are as eager to depart as we are. As fond as I am of Evan and Angela and all the others, I hate this kind of party. There is always too much boring conversation, too much alcohol, and too much hostility," Allan complained. "But to answer your question, I'm not sure. Torrelli went out for a cigarette a few minutes ago, hence why I have positioned myself away from any smoke that may come in through the door. I believe John and Dean are playing billiards and that Marcus is in his office. As for the rest of them," he shrugged, "who knows."

Rosemary decided to chime in, adding that Angela was up in her room changing her shoes and dress. "We'll probably see her in a few minutes wearing a shockingly revealing night-gown with an open robe. I'm surprised Magdalena hasn't tried to adopt her, since they both share a passion for acting like film stars from the golden era."

"You're right," I agreed with a laugh. "Magdalena is like an Ava Gardner and Angela is more like Lana Turner."

"Nah, Magdalena is more like a Bette Davis and Angela is more like a Lauren Bacall," Eugene declared.

"Lauren Bacall?" I squawked. Where did Eugene get that idea?

"Lauren Bacall?" Rosemary repeated.

Oops! You can't keep slipping up like this! I chastised myself. "I was thinking that maybe Angela was like Lauren Bacall," I lied.

"How? I always thought Lauren Bacall seemed like a nice girl-next-door with a sultry side. But I guess Angela also has a nice girl kind of feel, though I think Angela's sex appeal is a lit-tle more blatant. Almost thrown in your face," Allan argued.

"Well, I hate to leave you, Hope, but I'm pretty tired and would like to go. Angela was changing when I went up and should be down in a moment," Rosemary said, gesturing to Allan with her hand.

As he stood up and stepped forward to take Rosemary's hand, Allan tripped and fell, bumping into Rosemary and the vase of flowers Angela had moved. Rosemary, already weary, slammed right into me, knocking us both down.

"Damn! I'm sorry. What a clumsy oaf I am, tripping over my own shoelace, I guess I should lay off on the bourbon next time," Allan said while he stood up. He brushed off his pants and held out a hand for each of us.

I could see that Rosemary's hand was shaking as it took Allan's, and I began to worry that she had either drunk more than I realized or was about to have a diabetic seizure. And I didn't think she was a diabetic. Was I the only sober person around here?

Allan steadied her when she got to her feet, and the two of them walked out into the hall to pick up their coats and leave. I heard the door close behind them and was about to make my way upstairs, giving strict instructions to Eugene not to follow me, when Vincent entered through the door to the patio, holding an ashtray that had a few cigarette stubs in it.

"Hi there! Still here, I see. I thought you would have been long gone by now," Vincent said as he set the ashtray down on the nearest table. His shirt and jacket sleeves were rolled up to his elbows, and he rolled them back down and checked his watch. "Time for me to head out. Have you seen Evan or his stepmother? I'd hate to leave without saying goodbye."

"No. I was looking for Angela myself. Rosemary said she was upstairs changing. I can't imagine it can take more than a few minutes," I ventured, though I suspected that Angela could take a great deal of time changing clothes.

"Maybe she'll be down in an hour or so then," Vincent mocked.

But we were wrong in our estimates because Angela walked in through the living room doors a few moments later, resplendent in a silky black negligee and matching robe. Allan had been quite correct in his guess. I only wish he had remained to see how right he was.

Angela paused at the doorway, prolonging her entrance, but when she saw that Vincent and I were the only ones present, she gave up the theatrics and came inside hurriedly. We probably should have applauded, but she seemed satisfied with our responses. Vincent looked quickly away so that Angela wouldn't see his cheeky grin, but I suspected she thought she had overpowered him and he was blushing. I just stared rudely at her, in complete awe. How could anyone not regard such a brazen person with anything but awe?

Eugene, though she couldn't have known it, gave an appreciative whistle although he made a derogatory comment about her modesty.

"Where is everyone else?" she asked, turning to look back into the foyer.

"Allan and Rosemary just left. And I think Colby went to look for Evan. I'm not sure about anyone else," I responded. "I was about to leave as well, but I wanted to get the check for the caterer."

"Of course. I completely forgot. I had Marcus write the checks out this morning. They're still in his office. Why don't you come with me, Hope, and we'll get them? I'm sure Marcus would like to thank you personally as well. Maybe we can round up the others and send them home too," she said, leading the way out of the room. "There weren't any problems were there?"

"Nothing more than was expected. It was a very lovely party. Much nicer than most," I assured her. "Did Dean get a great deal of donations?"

She hesitated before Marcus' door. "Not as much as he should have, but I think he got enough to keep the campaign going a little bit longer," she confided.

Eugene waited impatiently by the living room door with his arms folded across his chest and an eyebrow raised.

Angela knocked at the door to the office, and waited for a few seconds before opening the door.

She stepped into the room, her negligee brushing against the doorframe, a flirtatious smile on her face. But the smile suddenly vanished, and she let out a panicked, inelegant wail.

I moved in behind her and felt my stomach lurch. The sight that met my eyes was so horrible I had to clutch the doorknob for support.

Note to self: Never use your own silver and dishes at a catered party. You never know where they might end up.

Okay, that was a completely inappropriate thought. Sometimes I can't help myself. Murder is so shocking one can hardly think straight, let alone control one's thoughts.

Marcus was lying face down on his desk, a dinner knife stuck in the back of his neck, and an expression of shock frozen permanently on his face. A deep red stain spread down his neck onto the desk before forming a deceptive red halo around him.

Even the dark mahogany of the wood could not cloak the thick burgundy pool that marred its smooth surface. The bones in Marcus' fingers appeared incredibly white against his blue veins. This was heightened by the fact that his right hand was tightly clutching a gold ballpoint pen. An open checkbook was resting near his hand, but the only other objects on top of the desk were the telephone, sitting at the far left edge, an appointment book, and an ornate Edwardian desk clock.

Evan and Colby, alarmed at Angela's cry, hurried into the room through the library entrance, but halted at the threshold. Colby started crying fitfully and clutched at Evan, whose face seemed expressionless.

I lost track of time, completely engrossed in the scene before me, and didn't realize that a crowd had gathered behind me, until Vincent shoved me aside and was quickly followed by Dean and John.

Eugene came up to me, his hand held to his mouth, but I hardly noticed. I backed away from the scene, knowing the sight of Marcus' desecrated body would haunt me forever, just as I knew the image of Eugene being run down would always be with me.

Maybe I *was* like Jessica Fletcher, or even Miss Marple, with death following in my wake.

Chapter Fourteen

"I don't suppose you see another ghost wandering around this place?" Eugene half-heartedly joked.

He was lounging against a windowsill, and would have appeared to be at his ease if it weren't for the fact that he was cracking his knuckles repeatedly. This habit would normally have offended me, but since Eugene's bones made no noise when they cracked, I ignored it.

I glanced quickly at the closed doorway into the foyer, worried that the specter of Marcus would suddenly appear through its thick oak panels. Can people collect ghosts like they do hats or shot glasses? I certainly hoped not.

"No, thank goodness. One is definitely enough for me. Though it makes me wonder why he seems to have gotten off this earth and you remained," I retorted in a strained whisper.

"I know. I was thinking the same thing. Maybe he donated a lot of money to charity. That's hardly fair if it's the case. I didn't have a lot of money to give to charity," he mused.

The living room was beginning to feel chilly, and I gave the others a surreptitious look, wondering if they felt the cold as well.

A young trooper was standing near the door to the foyer, his gaze alternating between the assembled group and the door. He looked nervous, tense, and slightly bemused. We must be wearing the same expression, I thought.

Evan and Colby, looking strained, were comforting Angela and Susan, and it was hard to tell which of the women were more disturbed. Angela wore an unreadable expression, while Susan was wheezing and dabbing at her tear-laden eyes. Considering she hadn't even seen the body, only arriving on the scene after everyone had been ushered out of the library and the door closed, her behavior was rather excessive. Dean and John were talking together in an urgent, low whisper, looking annoyed, and Vincent was tapping an unlit cigarette against his palm, looking somber.

He caught my gaze and sauntered over, a grim expression on his usually smiling face. "The coroner arrived a few minutes ago and that young trooper has called in a homicide detective. He will undoubtedly want to question all of us in more detail," he sighed. "So it looks like we might be here for quite awhile."

I nodded, remembering all the questions I had to answer when Eugene died.

I should have left earlier and picked up the checks another day, I inwardly groaned. I could be asleep right now, dreaming of a date with Chris Hemsworth or an unending supply of brownies. But no, I'm stuck in the middle of a murder investigation with a bunch of people that care as little about me as I do about them.

Note to self: Never put money before personal comfort and well-being—unless you need the money to attain that comfort and well-being.

"Are you all right, Hope? You look a little weird," Vincent said, obviously concerned.

"What does he expect?" Eugene mumbled.

This time I thought Eugene was right. What a dumb question! Of course I looked weird. Murder tends to do that to people. Maybe if I were a hardened criminal or a resident of some South American country whose largest export was fingers and toes I wouldn't be disturbed.

Nevertheless, the number one rule of etiquette in regard to times of misery and anxiety is to fake cheerfulness. When someone asks you how you are doing, and you've just fallen down the stairs and broken both your leg and the priceless Ming vase that was on the side table, you say, "Very well, thank you." All those people who believe that their friends and acquaintances want to know when they are miserable are completely mistaken. No one wants to hear how awful someone else feels. Not only does this lower the mood of the discussion but it necessitates the inquirer to delve even further into matters which are best left alone. Misery might love company, but the well mannered know to keep this misery bound and gagged until a mother, best friend, or psychiatrist is available for unloading.

"I'm fine, Vincent. Just a little shocked," I said. More like incredibly shocked, but I didn't think he was up to comforting me, and I was equally sure I wouldn't have accepted comfort from a stranger.

"That's understandable. Hopefully they'll figure which one of us did it, and we can get back to our lives." The cigarette was slowly being crushed at the tip and now resembled a miniature volcano.

"What do you mean? You don't think it was a burglar or something?" I was horrified at the thought that I could be sitting in the same room as a murderer.

Vincent gave me a long look. "It's unlikely. I suppose someone could have wandered in through the back door and made his way into the office without anyone seeing him enter or leave, but I doubt it."

Eugene abandoned his ridiculous posture and glared at Vincent. "I hope he doesn't mean to imply that you are a suspect, Hope."

Was Eugene actually defending me? But, of course, he knew I couldn't have done it.

"Are we all suspects?" I asked.

"Don't worry, Hope. I'm sure no one will suspect you. You don't have any motive," he said, and then added as an afterthought, "unlike the rest of us." He gave me a cheeky grin, and I was disturbed at how calmly he had accepted the situation. If he ranted and raved I would have felt more at ease. What exactly did he do for his boss?

Vincent finally tossed the unused cigarette into the nearest ashtray and took a seat next me. As he swung into the delicate French chair his left arm swung right through Eugene, who harrumphed and turned to look into the blackness outside.

"I can't believe anyone would have reason enough to kill someone—even Marcus Whittington." But he *had* been murdered, and in a very personal way. He must have known the person because the way the chair was positioned behind the desk made certain no one could enter the room without being seen. The murderer had obviously been standing behind Marcus, who appeared to be about to write a check. He would hardly write a check for a stranger.

"Money can make the nicest person do the most heinous things," Vincent argued. "Don't you watch the ten o'clock news?"

I'm sorry to say that I often watch the ten o'clock news. And every day it seems less news and more horror.

I lowered my voice and leaned closer toward Vincent. "You said I was the only one without a motive. What's your motive?"

"Easy. I need to get back the money Evan owes. And if I haven't mentioned it before, I need to get it back soon. I was the one who introduced Evan to my boss, and he has a long memory. It isn't impossible to imagine that I would kill the old man so that Evan could inherit," he admitted with a cheeky grin and a wink. "My boss doesn't like failure."

I smiled back, but I suspected he was quite serious.

I could think of other people's motives for murdering Marcus, almost all of them involving money. It wasn't a secret Evan was desperate for money, though I doubted he would kill for it.

It was easier to believe that Colby would kill Marcus so that Evan could inherit, especially since Marcus had recently decided that Colby wasn't someone he wanted in the family. But to do Colby justice, she was more likely to hire a hit man than do the work herself. Okay, that's not really doing her justice. But I couldn't really see her killing a person for any reason other than jealousy or betrayal. I could see it now...Colby dressed to perfection in a pink business suit (I didn't want to picture her in a negligee), facing down her surprised lover. "How dare you betray me!" she would scream, pulling a gun out of her matching pink purse. And then she would shoot him several times just to make sure he was really dead. And like a wronged heroine she would drop the gun on the floor, put her hand to her mouth and cry brokenheartedly.

But this was reality, not a vindictive fantasy, and Colby was not having an affair with Marcus and had probably never done anything as messy as stick a knife in someone's neck.

Angela didn't look as if Marcus kept her on a tight spending leash, and he seemed to disregard her affairs as long as she was discreet, so she didn't have much of a motive either. It was possible that she killed her husband in order to be with a possessive lover, or, like Evan, was in dire need of a large sum of money. Marcus might even have been threatening to divorce her without a penny. Who knows? Maybe she was a psychopathic killer hiding under a façade of pretty naivety. She certainly wasn't lacking intelligence. She could be one of those merry widow killers ready to move on to another victim.

Dean seemed to have the best motive in my opinion. He wanted to win the election, and Marcus, for reasons unknown, had refused to support him. Marcus' disapproval would mean less donations and a lot of questions. With Marcus dead, it wouldn't be too hard for Dean to convince Evan or Angela to give him the financial backing he needed. Of course, just being involved in a murder inquiry would hurt his chance of being elected.

John Raines could have killed Marcus so that Evan would continue the funding, then his brother would win the election and eventually use his political station to boost the family business even more.

Susan could also have killed Marcus in order to aid her husband.

Overall, I was sitting in a room with a large group of greedy, devious potential killers. This was enough to make my hair curl and my stomach do back flips and swan dives.

"Buckle up, Hope, here come the big guns," Vincent announced.

And he was right. Sort of. The living room door opened and instead of seeing a staunch, older gentleman with a badge sticking out of the front pocket of a cheap suit, a youngish man with light brown hair and a personable face entered.

I breathed a sigh of relief. There would be no harsh grilling in front of a bright light for me. Thank you, God! Salvation was here at last (or so I hoped).

"You know him," asked Vincent, seeing my relieved expression.

I nodded, my attention still on the policeman. "His name is Peter Jameson. He grew up down the street from me. We used to play together when we were little," I clarified. "He's a nice guy. He's a favorite of my mom." Which was why I usually avoided him like the plague. The mean part of me thought that if my mom was so fond of him, there had to be something deeply wrong with his character that I hadn't yet discovered. Still, he was an old friend, if no longer a close one.

"Lucky you. Maybe you'll get special treatment, like being let out of here before the rest of us with nothing more than a warning to be more discriminate in your choice of dinner companions," Vincent said in a falsely jovial tone.

I wanted to point out to him that I hadn't attended dinner, but refrained. Any hunger I had experienced earlier in the evening had disappeared.

Peter looked over toward Vincent and I, gave me a surprised look, turned to the young trooper and spoke a few inaudible words. The trooper nodded solemnly before stepping back to allow Peter and Angela to leave the room.

"Looks like she's first to be questioned," Vincent said.

"What kind of things are we going to be asked?"

"Where we were and what we were doing. I can't imagine they'll need to know much more than that." Vincent picked another cigarette out of his pocket and started twirling it.

"Well that shouldn't be too bad," I declared resolutely.

Eugene snorted for what must have been the hundredth time that evening. "Should I listen in, Hope? It might be interesting to find out which one of this lot is a murderer first hand," Eugene commented. "I'll be back shortly. I just want to see what everyone says." Without another word he strode across the room and through the wall.

John Raines, looking haggard, approached Vincent and I, a frown creasing his thick brows. "Detective Sergeant Jameson— I think that's his name-- is going to question all of us quickly before letting us go home. And then a Lieutenant Strand, the sergeant's superior, is probably going to do some follow up questions tomorrow or the next day," he forewarned.

"What about the caterer and servers?" I asked.

"I thought you'd be worried about them. Another trooper is asking them some quick questions and then letting them go since they all have alibis. It's the rest of us who are of interest," John answered, sounding a lot like Vincent.

The police had requested that no one leave the house until all the questions had been completed, so I spent the following hour chatting inconsequentially with Vincent and later with Angela, who, having returned from her interrogation, was eager to discuss something unrelated to murder. She favored the topics of fashion trends and suspense novels, subjects to which Vincent and I had little to add.

Susan, whose tears had turned into panicked squealing and loud denials when she was told she would also be questioned, thankfully lapsed into silence once Dean had left the room for his interview. Evan, John, and Colby talked around Susan, perhaps feeling that speaking directly to her might set off another wave of hysteria. Their discussion was held in hushed voices, the only audible words being 'wedding', 'funeral' and 'cold'.

I was the last suspect to be questioned, so when my turn finally arrived I was impatient for the interview rather than anxious. The drinks had flowed freely after a half hour of waiting had passed, and I could not handle being asked yet again by Angela if I didn't think it was amusing that she was questioned by the police wearing only a nightgown. At which point she would burst into tears, then cheer herself up again before repeating the whole drama again. Added to that was Susan's hateful glare and ridiculous mutterings about the entire thing being Angela's fault, and Evan's effervescent repetition of trite phrases like 'at least we still have each other' and 'what doesn't kill you only makes you stronger'. It is my belief that Evan was either halfway to La-la Land or not actually aware of the connotation of his words. John must have shared my opinion because he assured the group that what doesn't kill you only prolongs the inevitable. I thought it a pity Eugene had decided to temporarily abandon me to this crowd because he would have appreciated John's caustic humor.

By the time Vincent returned and the diffident trooper called my name, I practically bounced out of my chair and rushed to his side like a schoolgirl eager to win her teacher's approval.

I was ushered into the dining room, where Detective Sergeant Peter Jameson sat with a notepad, pen, and cell phone placed in front of him. He smiled at me shyly (he had always been incredibly shy, even after we were forced to take baths together at the age of three or four), and motioned for me to take the chair opposite his.

Eugene stood behind him, looking pleased with himself. He briefly acknowledged my presence before continuing his study of the notepad. Several times he raised an eyebrow or shook his head and muttered softly to himself.

"Sorry to keep you waiting, but this shouldn't take too long," Peter said apologetically.

"That's okay. Sleep is for weaklings, right?" I joked. I freely admit to being a weakling. My mother is convinced you can't trust people who squander sleep, and she just might be right. Vampires are a perfect example.

"Weaklings like you and me?" Peter quipped.

"Exactly." I looked him over and realized he had probably been abed when he got the homicide call. Or maybe he just stopped combing his hair in the last few months. "Were you already asleep?"

"Yep. I was in bed like all normal people when my phone rang telling me that a homicide had been committed in our sleepy little town—hence the poorly put-together outfit." Fashion played a part in etiquette only when it was outrageously inappropriate. I wasn't about to impugn somebody's chosen style, but Peter did look like he had hurled himself out of bed and pulled on whatever was closest. His slacks were slightly wrinkled, which wasn't so bad, but his shirt looked as if it belonged with a jogging suit. A dark leather jacket had been thrown across the far end of the dining room table, with Peter's identification placed nearby.

"You were promoted," I said, remembering the rank John had mentioned.

"Last year. Do you mean to say that my mother didn't put out an announcement in the newspaper? I was certain the whole state of Pennsylvania knew," he exclaimed, feigning a look of surprise.

I laughed. Peter's mother never missed an opportunity to praise him in public, which embarrassed Peter so much that as a child he had been teased ruthlessly about it by all the local kids. "I must be out of the loop," I said apologetically.

"Don't worry, I'm not offended that you don't assiduously follow my career. That's what my mother is for," he said.

"Sounds like my mother," Eugene interjected. "She used to brag about me to the entire community. Boy, was it embarrassing," he quickly added.

Did Eugene expect me to believe that he didn't live for praise? He probably encouraged his mother's boasting.

"We should get back to business. Like I said earlier, this shouldn't take too long."

"What do you need me to tell you?" I asked, thinking how strange this whole scenario really was. Who would have ever thought I would be interrogated in a murder case? And by Peter Jameson of all people? Didn't he once have to dress as a donkey in the church play?

"Please give me your full name, with spelling," Peter said seriously.

"Is that a joke, Peter? You know my name."

"I haven't seen you in so long I've forgotten it," he lied.

"Ha, ha. I saw you at the Christmas service—"

"Which was months ago, Hope," he interrupted. I didn't say anything, and Peter blushed. I'd been avoiding him since Christmas when my mother appeared to have forced him to ask me on a date, and I had refused. "I don't know your middle name, and I do need that," he finished lamely.

"Genevieve." I secretly suspected I had been named 'Hope' as a punishment for all the long hours of labor my mother had to go through, and not after a distant relative. Genevieve was the name of my grandmother, as well as the patron saint of Paris, where my mother swears I was conceived. She never told me which I was named after, but I have my suspicions.

"That's a nice name," Peter said, trying to make amends for his social gaff.

"Thank you," I replied politely. One should never refute a compliment because they get scarcer the older one gets. And when they vanish altogether all that will be left is their memory. How much nicer it is to tell yourself that people admired you than to recall that you never believed the kind things people said about you. And while it wasn't a compliment about my looks or intellect, it was still a compliment and these days it seemed like I had to take them when I could get them.

"When was the last time you saw the victim?" he asked.

I thought about it. "After the party. We were all in the living room and then Marcus left, maybe to go to his office, I don't know. And that was the last time I saw him."

"When you say we, do you mean everyone who is currently in the house?" Peter asked, though I suspected he knew the answer already.

"Yes. But Allan and Rosemary Tate were also present. I remember because Marcus and Allan were discussing political corruption. And Magdalena—Mrs. Duprés—and the Arbuthnots were present, too. But the Arbuthnots walked Mrs. Duprés home right before Marcus left the room," I said, hoping I had gotten it correct.

"Why don't you tell me everything you did after that point?" he asked.

Eugene gave him a look of disapproval. "Don't worry, Hope. He can't suspect you. This is just part of the job," he reassured me.

"I stayed in the living room a little bit longer, talking with Vincent Torrelli. Angela came over and asked if Vincent or I would like to play billiards. We both said no and I left."

"And what happened after you left the living room?" Peter inquired gravely. His dorky side was coming out, the one that belonged to the chess club in middle school, and I suddenly wanted to laugh.

"Tell him about that argument, Hope," Eugene urged.

Eugene was right. Every little tiff suddenly took on a sinister aspect. "When I was in the foyer, I heard Marcus in his office arguing with a woman, but I couldn't tell you who the woman was except that it wasn't Angela. The voice was speaking too softly."

"Did you hear what the argument was about?"

"Not really. I heard the woman mention Evan, at least I assume she was talking about Evan since she said 'son', and Marcus yelled something about his money and the person not having any right to interfere. That's about all I heard," I admitted.

Peter looked at me for a moment, and then continued the questions. "And then what did you do?"

"I went to the kitchen. Some glasses and food had been knocked onto the floor and I helped clean them up and then went back and forth to the dining room to put some dishes away."

"Did anyone see you when you were in the dining room?" Peter inquired.

I wasn't about to tell him that a ghost had accompanied me. He'd probably have me locked up for the murder on the basis that I was insane. "No—not the last time I was in there. The caterer and servers saw me go in and out, and Colby Raines also saw me just before I went into the dining room the last time." I hoped that was a good enough alibi, but from the disappointed look on Peter's face, I suspected it was not.

"How long were you in the dining room that last time?"

"About five minutes. I had to place the dishes in the china cabinet."

Peter wrote down some more notes on the pad. "And then what?"

"When I was done, I went to the living room to find Angela in order to get the check for the caterer. Allan Tate was there reading a magazine, but no one else." I paused, suddenly remembering that it wasn't just Allan and I. "Oh, wait, Rosemary

Tate was coming down the stairs just as I left the dining room, and she went with me into the living room."

"Did she say where she had been?" Peter asked, his gaze sharpening.

"I think she said she had returned a book to Angela, who was upstairs changing."

"Into that nightgown she was wearing?" Peter asked, suddenly smiling. "She seemed to think it rather amusing to be questioned while wearing it."

I laughed. "I know. She told me so several times. She doesn't have any modesty issues."

Peter smiled and nodded, and Eugene added an emphatic "That's for sure!"

"Was the door to the office closed when you returned to the living room?" Peter said, though I suspected everyone else had told him it had been.

"Yes."

"Was this door open when you were in here?" Peter asked, indicating the door that led to the foyer.

"Yes," I said. "As far as I'm aware it hasn't been closed all night."

He nodded. "Did you hear any noise coming from the foyer when you were in here?"

"No, nothing at all. But I was stacking dishes, which can be somewhat noisy."

"Noisy enough to block out any other sounds?" he asked, that serious look returning to his face.

"I couldn't really say. My mind was occupied," I confessed.

Eugene looked pityingly at me. "It's too bad you can't tell him you have an alibi. Or even that you didn't hear anything because you were talking to yourself—I mean, talking to me," he prattled.

"Where were you standing? Could you see out the door into the foyer?" Peter asked, gesturing to the china cabinet.

"No. I spent most of the time bending down in front of the cabinet. And the view from this side of the room is limited. Even if I had been looking out that door, I would only have been able to see the area near the front door," I admitted.

"And you didn't see anyone go in or out that door?" he asked.

"No, but I suppose someone could have used the back door," I hypothesized.

Peter added a few more notes to the pad and then looked up at me and smiled. "Okay. Would you give me your opinion on Mr. Whittington's mood?"

"I guess you could say it was bad. He was pretty argumentative all night."

"With anyone in particular?" Peter asked.

"With Dean Raines. He and Marcus argued in the office earlier in the evening and Dean left and slammed the door behind him. And I think Marcus also argued with John Raines. I can't be sure because I didn't hear any argument between them, but something John said to Dean suggested that they might have had one." I didn't want to implicate anyone, but I wasn't about to let a possible murderer wander around my hometown.

"Were the other guests behaving uncharacteristically? Mrs. Whittington, perhaps?"

I shook my head. "Not really. Angela almost always behaves like this. She was flirting pretty outrageously with Dean Raines, and was annoyed that he wasn't responding. But that wasn't too unusual either."

"And what about Evan Whittington?"

"No. He owes Mr. Torrelli a lot of money, and he's been stressed out about that lately, but I didn't notice anything else." I almost wished I had kept my mouth closed because Peter looked interested, and I didn't want to put Evan under any more suspicion than was customary for the heir.

"What about the others? Did any of the Raines behave oddly?"

"Dean was upset about Marcus deciding to no longer support his campaign," I said. Peter nodded, and I realized that none of this was new information to him. "Susan was upset all night--almost hysterical half the time. I think she's worried that her husband is cheating on her."

"Do you think Dean Raines is having an affair with Mrs. Whittington?" Peter asked, before looking at his watch. I could tell that he was holding back a yawn. Maybe he saved me for last because he knew that if he started to fall asleep I wasn't likely to report him.

"No. If he were, Angela wouldn't be trying so hard to get him. I don't know her too well, but I gather that she drops men almost as soon as she gets them." Or so the dour women in the Everton Ladies Auxiliary claim.

"And what about," he looked down at his notes, "John Raines?"

"He was also a little upset about Marcus not supporting the campaign, but his behavior wasn't really odd or disturbing."

I hoped he wasn't going to ask me about personal habits, too. I was tired and if he started to yawn again, I would consider dropping down headfirst onto the table fair play.

"Okay. Almost done. What about Colby Raines and Vincent Torrelli?" He was obviously anxious to end this interview. He might be tired, I realized, but the coroner's loud voice exclaiming over the "nitwit" assistant was probably the more compelling reason for his haste.

"Colby was her normal self. She did say she argued with her mother, or maybe it was Angela, I'm not really sure. But that was it. And I don't know Vincent Torrelli well enough to give you an opinion," I acknowledged.

"All right, Hope. Thanks. If we need any more information I'll let you know," Peter said as he stood up.

He rushed out of the room without another glance, and I could hear him questioning the coroner.

"Let's go home," Eugene said, trying to take my arm to lead me out the door but failing. Instead of grabbing my upper arm, his hand went through me and he stumbled slightly. "Oh well. I've almost got the hang of making contact with people. I made some progress this evening. I'll tell you about it in the car. And about everything I heard that detective of yours and that motley crew in the living room discuss."

I nodded bleakly.

"You look pretty tired. Would you like me to drive?"

Eugene asked with an innocent and sympathetic expression.

We had crossed through the butler's pantry and into the empty kitchen, so I knew I wouldn't be overheard. "Are you crazy? You can't even grab my arm, let alone steer a car and use the pedals. We'd be dead in minutes." He looked at me with an incredulous expression and I realized what I had just said. "Okay, I would be dead in minutes. And then where would you be? Left alone on earth with no one to talk to."

"That's if you made it to heaven. How do you know you wouldn't get stuck here like I did?" he asked petulantly.

"I just wouldn't," I asserted. "Now where is that darn dog?"

Chapter Fifteen

"You tripped Colby!" I squealed.

"Don't act so outraged. I did it for you, after all. I know you can't abide her," he exulted.

"You didn't do it for me. You did it because you were bored and like making trouble," I countered.

"That's not fair, Hope. You're probably just upset because you weren't there to see it," he reproached me.

"It's not nice to trip people, Eugene—no matter how much you dislike them." Oh God! I really was turning into my mother. Where had my sense of humor gone?

"I simply stuck out my foot and wondered if it would work. I hadn't really thought she would make contact with it," he exclaimed. "This is the first time I've been able to do that. It's a milestone, Hope, not something to moan about."

"Huh. A milestone indeed! Sit back down, Jezebel," I commanded.

He smirked at me. "So it wouldn't interest you to know that she went down like a hippo on ice."

"I'm not listening to this, Eugene, so don't bother." Taking pleasure in another's grief was absolutely, unconditionally, without question wrong! And I didn't need to have OPD to know that.

But everyone has their own personal devil that tempts them into sin, and it seemed that my devil just happened to be a fifty-ish ghost with a snotty personality and an alarming sense of humor. And I am admittedly weak. And if not a huge sinner, I'm certainly not without sin. I would have loved to see her fall. "Did she really fall like a hippo on ice?" I asked, wondering why the voice asking that question sounded so much like my own.

"She most certainly did. And broke a nail. You should have heard her holler. You'd think that particular fingernail belonged in the Met," he cackled.

I managed to restrain any laughter, though I couldn't hold back a smile at the thought of Colby flat on her stomach wailing about a broken nail. "We shouldn't be too hard on her, I suppose. Her future father-in-law did get murdered tonight."

"So? I doubt she was all that fond of him. Come to think of it, I doubt anyone was that fond of him. He seems to have been a bit of a turd."

"Eugene! That's horrible. You shouldn't speak ill of the dead," I admonished. Yes, the OPD rears its head again in just a matter of moments.

"That's your mother coming out in you," he retaliated. "He's dead. What does he care?"

Was he reading my thoughts now? If ghosts could read thoughts he was leaving posthaste.

"How would you feel if I started saying mean things about you?" I asked.

"You're always saying mean things about me," Eugene retorted.

That's true. "Well, how would it feel if you heard other people saying mean things about you?"

"Okay, okay. But unless people in heaven, or hell, can really listen in on our conversations, I don't think he knows. But I will refrain from saying mean things about dead people in your presence if it upsets you so much." He reached back and patted Jezebel, smirking a little.

I seriously doubted he would stick to that. "Let's just drop the subject," I beseeched.

"I thought you were curious about those schmos' alibis. Do you want to know what I heard or not?" Eugene demanded.

"Oh, all right. If I'm going to be stuck in the middle of a murder investigation, I should probably know as much as possible." Saying that was somewhat plausible and also sounded much better than admitting I was actually extremely curious.

"Well the first person that detective interviewed was Mrs. Whittington, and what a show it was. If she shed any tears all evening, I'm the Tooth Fairy," Eugene muttered.

He was too cheap to be the Tooth Fairy. "Maybe she was just in shock," I argued.

"Huh, and maybe Hanukah comes five times a year. No, Pip, she wasn't all that upset. Granted, she didn't look cheerful, but she was still well enough to flirt a little and kept drawing attention to her attire. That poor cop did all he could not to laugh."

"Okay, okay. I could have guessed that. What did she say about her alibi?" I demanded.

"Gees, and you're always saying patience is a virtue. If you want me to try and remember this verbatim you are going to have to stop interrupting me," Eugene snapped.

For the next few minutes Eugene related everything he had seen and heard during the interviews in meticulous detail, as follows (with only a few side comments):

"It started out with the detective asking how old Mr. Whittington was," Eugene began.

"Just get to it, Eugene," I entreated.

"Okay, okay. Here goes, Miss Speedy-pants."

"What? That's 'smarty-pants', you idiot."

"Really, Pip-Squeak, you think you're smart?" Eugene shook his head in a sympathetic way. "Well, you just keep believing that. Now, can we get back to the interviews?" he admonished. "You're holding me up."

"Get going then." He was impossible! He couldn't drive me any crazier if he tried! Of course, he was actually trying.

"The detective had just asked Angela Whittington how old her husband was."

'Fifty-six last November,' Mrs. Whittington responded.

'And what was his occupation?'

Angela looked surprised at the question. 'Oh, he was into lots of things. I mean he had several businesses. I don't really know that much about them, but if you want more details I can give you the name of his lawyer,' she admitted.

Peter nodded. 'Can you tell me about the party you held tonight?'

Angela was quite eager to do so. 'A few months ago Marcus decided to host a party in support of Dean Raines' gubernatorial campaign. We invited about seventy or eighty wealthy or influential people from the Philadelphia area, mostly older friends of my husband. I have a guest list somewhere if you want it,' she added. 'But I don't suppose it really matters because he was still alive when they left.'

'Why don't you tell me about what happened after the party?' Peter urged.

'Not much, really. Marcus was arguing with everyone, which wasn't so unusual. He had also decided earlier in the day, or maybe it was a few days ago, not to give any more money to Dean's campaign. He grumbled a lot about political scandals and stuff, but never really gave a reason. He left the living room around the same time as a few other people: Rosemary, Evan, Susan, and Colby. I remember because after that Hope and I were the only women left in the room. And then Hope left, and Dean and John decided to play billiards, and I went upstairs.'

'How long was it before you returned downstairs?' he asked, taking copious notes.

She puckered up her lips and brow. 'About fifteen minutes, maybe a little more or less, certainly more than ten, but not more than twenty minutes.'

'What were you doing upstairs for so long?'

'Changing my clothes. See," she said, pointing to her nightgown. 'I never imagined I would be questioned by the police. It's so embarrassing.' She tittered slightly, though was restrained enough not to bat her eyelashes

"But she obviously wasn't embarrassed," Eugene added. "She didn't bother closing her robe, and intentionally let her shoulder straps slip off. You would have died laughing, Hope." Eugene chortled.

"The interview, Eugene?" The fact that he found so much humor in a murder was both disturbing and ironic.

"Right, sorry. Where was I? Oh yes, she was changing."

'You spent the entire fifteen minutes changing? You didn't stop and do anything else? No one visited you?' Peter asked, obviously surprised that it could take someone fifteen minutes to undress and put on a nightgown.

'No. I went up to my room, undressed, put this on, brushed my hair, powdered my nose—that sort of thing,' Angela said. 'If I had known what was going to happen I would have stayed downstairs. I just can't believe it. I was changing while poor Marcus was being killed.' She scrunched up her face in an expression of mingled sorrow and frustration, but managed to hold back any tears.

'Will you tell me what happened when you went downstairs?'

She sniffed even though her nose was not running. 'I went straight to the living room, but only Vincent and Hope were there. And then Hope asked for the check for the caterer and I told her Marcus had it in his office. So we went to his door and knocked. He didn't answer so I opened the door, and that's when we saw..." her voice trailed off and Peter nodded.

'Can you tell me what check he had last written?'

'Check? I don't know. I suppose the one to Hope. I had him write it earlier today, right after the one for the caterer. There shouldn't have been any other checks he needed to write today.' She looked concerned, as if Marcus had handed someone a check for all his money and she was going to be left in the cold.

'Why?'

Peter didn't answer right away. 'No reason. We just need to gather as much detail as possible. Can you remember the number of the last check?'

'Yes. It was 5784. At the 85 of every hundred they have a reminder to reorder. I remember seeing the reminder. And I'm actually very good at remembering numbers. Especially telephone numbers.'

The detective just nodded. 'Okay. That's enough for now. My superior will be in touch with you tomorrow, so please make yourself available. And we will need to collect the clothes you wore this evening. The corporal will accompany you to fetch them.'

"And when she left her robe was hanging off of her shoulders. But I think the effect was lost on the detective because he was looking at his notes and not at her. She was a little peeved," Eugene snorted.

There he goes, snorting again!

"She probably can't help it. And no matter how she behaved,

I think she must have been somewhat fond of her husband. We shouldn't judge," I pontificated. Secretly, I thought she would be remarried to another wealthy man within a year. But then again, I have been wrong about people before.

"Excuse me, Miss Perfect," Eugene retorted. "Why don't I just finish telling you about the interviews? "

Oh! Now he is so eager to finish. "I'm sorry. I didn't mean to moralize," I apologized.

"I know--it's a combination of guilt and your mother coming out."

I hated that he could accurately read my character.

"Let's get back to those interviews," I suggested, wanting to turn the subject away from my own faults.

"Okay. Let me think. The next person to come in was Evan. If you ask me, his interview was the most suspicious."

"Why?" I asked, curious as to why Eugene thought a mild-mannered fellow like Evan was capable of murder.

"Because his story was so unlikely. He claimed to have gone straight from the living room to the library and fallen asleep reading a book. Please! And I don't think that detective of yours thought much of the story either. He certainly didn't sound convinced," Eugene asserted.

'Where did you go when you left the living room?" Peter asked.

'Colby, my fiancée, and her mother left to qo to the ladies room, and since Susan, that's her mother, looked pretty upset, I figured they wouldn't be back for a while. Colby and I had agreed to meet later for a walk, so I thought I could spend the time in between reading,' Evan answered.

'You didn't want to remain with the others,' Peter asked.

'No. I knew I would be forced to play cards or billiards or some other game I'm terrible at. And Vincent was there, and I sort of wanted to avoid him,' Evan admitted.

'Why did you want to avoid Mr...,' Peter looked at his notes, 'Torrelli?'

'I owe him some money, and he needs me to repay it soon. I suppose that makes it sound like I had a good reason to kill my fa-

ther, but I didn't do it," Evan argued, clenching his fists.

'Why didn't your father lend you the money? I gather he had enough,' Peter said quietly, his eyes shifting from the notepad back to Evan and then back to the pad again.

'I asked, and he said no. He thought I was a bit of a failure, I guess. And just so you don't find out from someone else and think I'm hiding it, I'll tell you that he threatened to disinherit me earlier today," Evan divulged.

Peter looked up. 'And did you believe him?'

'I don't know. He's threatened me before like this, but never done anything about it.'

Peter considered Evan and his newfound belligerence. 'Alright. We will drop this subject for a time. Finish telling me about what happened after you left the living room. You went to the library by means of the office??' suggested Peter.

'Yes-- it's the only way you can enter from inside the house. The other door to the library is from the patio.'

Peter nodded in understanding. 'Was your father in his office at the time?'

'No. I think he might have been on the patio smoking a cigar because the back door of the foyer was slightly ajar.'

'Did you smell any cigar smoke? 'Peter asked.

'No,' Evan admitted.

'Then why do you suspect he was smoking a cigar?'

Evan flushed. 'He just did that sometimes.'

Peter just nodded. 'Did you hear your father enter the office anytime after that?'

'Yes,' Evan said. 'Almost directly after I entered the library I heard the office door close. But I didn't hear anything else. I picked up a book and sort of dozed off. I didn't wake up until Colby came in through the patio door. And then a few minutes later I heard Angela cry out. And that's all," he added.

'You didn't hear anyone else enter the office, close the door, or speak?'

'No,' Evan affirmed.

"And you know he must be lying, Hope. We both heard an argument in there from the foyer. He was even closer. He had to have heard the voices," Eugene declared.

"But if he was asleep he might not have heard," I argued.

"Asleep? Not a chance. He's hiding something. And that detective friend of yours thought so, too. It was pretty obvious that little Evan Whittington knows more than he is saying," Eugene assured me. "I didn't tell you the detective's last question. It made the whelp's story look like a bit of fluff."

'What book were you reading?'

'I'm sorry?' Evan looked blank again.

'You said that you were reading. What was the title of the book?' Peter spoke slowly, as if he were speaking to a child.

'Oh. Well, I just grabbed a book off the shelf. I really didn't open it. I can't remember the title. I can get it for you if you like.'

'No. Don't bother,' Peter responded, clearly not believing him.

"What did I tell you? He's as suspicious as a nun in a sex shop," Eugene preened. "My blind and deaf grandmother would have spotted the lie."

Blind *and* deaf. His grandmother was really something else.

"What about the others? Did you think their alibis just as suspicious?" I inquired.

"I don't know. It could be that they are all lying just to protect each other."

"Tell me what Colby said. I know she went in right after Evan." That little devil in me, while not really hoping Colby was guilty of murder, wouldn't have minded her being an accessory or something.

"She's a slippery character. She'd do anything to protect her family and her fiancé," Eugene responded. "And she's a pretty poor story-teller, too."

'Can you tell me where you went when you left the dining room, Ms. Raines,' Peter said, twirling his pen around his fingers.

Colby looked annoyed at his lack of deference. 'My mother was upset so I took her upstairs to one of the empty guest rooms. I stayed with her for a few minutes, and then I went downstairs to find my fiancé. Is that all you need to know?' she sneered.

'How long were you upstairs? You said a few minutes.

Could you be more specific, please?' he said, still not giving her his full attention.

'I suppose it was around ten minutes. Probably a little less than that,' she responded.

Peter looked directly at her. 'And you were with your mother the entire time—until you went downstairs to look for your fiancé?'

'Yes. And then I was with him. So you see, I have an alibi for the entire time. Questioning me is pointless.' She gave Peter a defiant look before turning her head slightly to look toward the door.

'Where did you meet your fiancé?' he questioned.

'In the library,' she said on a big sigh. 'We were supposed to meet by the kitchen entrance and go for a walk, but he fell asleep in the library.'

Peter nodded. 'You first went to the kitchen entrance?' At her nod, he continued. 'Did you meet anyone on your way there, or on your way to the library?'

'I met Hope Springs in the kitchen, along with a bunch of caterers I didn't know. But I didn't meet anyone else,' she told him.

'Since you claim not to have seen the body earlier, I assume you entered the library through the patio door. Did you smell any cigar smoke?' Peter was once again twirling with his pen and staring off into space.

'No,' she said in her clipped voice.

"I think he was getting rather tired at this point, and that Colby character was being so snide I'm surprised he didn't arrest her for impeding the investigation."

I smiled slightly. That sounded exactly like how Colby would behave under interrogation.

Eugene looked thoughtful. "If you know the detective sergeant, why doesn't she? Didn't you say you went to school together?" he asked.

"Colby didn't play with us as children. I met her off and on at club dinners and stuff, but I didn't really get to know her until high school, which was a private all-girls school," I explained. "That's the only reason Colby acknowledges me. While our parents are members of the same club, my parents don't make nearly as much money as Colby's dad."

"Figures. She looks like a spoiled witch. And that's why I tripped her. Hey, I had to do something to relieve the tedium of the interview. Tripping her was as satisfying as a chocolate eclair..." He looked dreamy for a few moments, probably remembering how delectable éclairs were.

"You like chocolate éclairs?" Maybe we had something in common after all.

"Doesn't everybody?" He gave me a pitiful look. "Don't keep distracting me. I don't want to forget anything. Let's see..."

'How long were you in the library before you heard Mrs. Whittington call out?' Peter asked, again looking directly at Colby.

'Two or three minutes,' she stated abruptly. 'I doubt it was any longer than that.'

'And in that time, you did not hear any noise at all in the office?'

'No. Besides, I was talking to Evan and not paying attention to anything else.'

'Thank you, Ms. Raines. If we need any more information I will be in touch. Please leave your personal information with the trooper stationed in the foyer.'

She got up to leave, annoyed at being so summarily dismissed, and walked a few steps toward the door before turning around. 'No one in my family could have done this,' she said. 'And I know Evan didn't, and probably not Angela either. I suggest that you look at the strangers that were wandering around--the caterer and servers, and Hope. Any one of the them could have done it as well.'

Peter looked annoyed at the suggestion. 'I assure you that I know how to conduct a homicide investigation. Anyone without an alibi during the probable time of the murder is being investigated.' He looked back down at his note pad and started writing.

"I was so irritated by her that I had to do something," Eugene declared.

"She actually accused me of killing a man I barely knew?" Outrage didn't describe how I suddenly felt. The fact that I hoped she was an accessory was irrelevant. Murder was a heinous crime, one that is simply not socially acceptable. Wishing your high school nemesis ill is only natural. If I wanted, perhaps I could justify her behavior by saying she was scared for herself, her family, and her fiancé, and was simply trying to protect them. But I wasn't feeling particularly generous.

"Ridiculous and petty, right? Your detective friend was annoyed when she mentioned your name, too. I just had to trip her," Eugene exclaimed, grinning broadly. "Really, Pip, you should thank me. I did it for you. And it was a beautiful sight. She started walking again, and I rushed over and just stuck out my foot. I really hadn't expected it to work, just hoped it would. And boy did it.

"She gave a great big gasp, then plummeted downward, her hands flailing in the air. The detective had looked up by this time and was trying to get up to help her, but it was too late. With a loud 'thunk' she landed on the floor. If it were a cartoon, there would have been a 'splat' appearing on the screen." Eugene looked positively giddy.

"The detective reached her and was about to help her up, but before he could, the trooper rushed in and nearly tripped over her arms. And when he tried to stop himself, he landed with a thud on his behind. That was a double bonus.

"And that viper Colby was wailing about her nail, waving her finger around and swearing. I'm surprised you couldn't hear it." He paused, savoring the memory. "I thought she might cry from embarrassment at first, but she just got really angry. She slapped away the detective's hand, gave the trooper a nasty look, and practically ran out of the room, clutching her finger." Eugene chuckled to himself, and leaned back in his seat, pleased with his exploits. Jezebel nuzzled against him and he started stroking her nose.

If Colby truly hurt herself I was sorry, but it still would have been amusing to see. Everyone needs a little public humiliation once in a while. It keeps people self-effacing and sympathetic toward others. I should know. I seem to have had a lot of humiliation lately.

"What about Dean, John, and Vincent?" I asked, hoping the change of subject would prevent Eugene from encouraging

Jezebel to hop into the front seat. The last time she did that her body went right through me (which was probably better than knocking me around) and I was so startled I nearly ran into a ditch.

"Their interviews were all pretty boring. Dean and John both swore that they went straight from the library to the billiards room and didn't come out until Angela screamed. Of course, one of them could have done it and the other one is just protecting him. I wouldn't put it past either of them. They both have a lot riding on this election," he mused.

"Mr. Torrelli claims that he was in the living room and then went outside for a cigarette, and stayed out there for several minutes before returning," he continued.

"And Susan Raines said she was in an upstairs bathroom powdering her nose the entire time. Gees, how long does it take the woman to go the bathroom?" Eugene questioned.

"She was probably being sick the whole time. Didn't you notice how much she was drinking? And she was crying a lot, too. I heard her get in a fight with her husband earlier in the evening," I explained. Group therapy might not be enough to help that family. Electric shock treatment might be in order.

"What a pack of rotters," Eugene exclaimed. "I'm glad I'm not stuck with any of them."

And that was the nicest thing Eugene had ever said to me.

Chapter Sixteen

"Weasel," I hollered, "leave that alone."

Eugene snickered. "It's your own fault, you know. Why would you have ever agreed to look after that dog?"

"I'm not looking after him. I'm just feeding and walking him. And he's really a sweet dog," I challenged. "If Jezebel would stop barking at him and rushing him, he would be fine," I continued to argue.

Jezebel, upon hearing her name, skidded to a halt and waited for Eugene to catch up with her. Once he had reached her, she took off again, running circles around Weasel.

My hand was beginning to ache from the pull of the leash and I wondered how such a small dog could manage to pull with such force. He must be part mule.

Weasel chose that moment to try and tear apart the base of the stop sign at the corner. "Stop, Weasel. Leave it," I ordered. All Weasel did was look at me stupidly before trying again. "The pole is made of metal, you dumb dog. You can't chew it."

"And you complain about Jezebel," Eugene scoffed. "She's an angel compared to this mutt."

"Weasel is not a mutt, and he is just letting out some pent up energy," I explained, not really believing it myself. "Sally wasn't there to walk him this morning. He'll be better after a few more blocks." Yeah right, I secretly thought. If he has any manners at all, I'll eat my shoes.

Eugene just grinned at me and kept walking.

I was wary of this particular section of the neighborhood because there were a lot of dogs around, and according to Sally, Weasel was terrified of other dogs. His reaction to Jezebel's ghostly presence had even topped Nutter Butter's. First, Weasel barked hysterically and hid behind my legs, he then followed with wetting the floor. That was when my daily store of patience ran out. I had not expected to spend my day cleaning urine off of someone else's kitchen floor. And to make matters worse, Jezebel decided that continually running through Weasel would be amusing, which caused Weasel to prance around in small circles, trying to see what had disturbed him. When Jezebel decided to stop torturing him, Weasel's muscles must have been severely strained, because he wet the floor again.

"Come on, Weasel," I beckoned. "Let's hurry up." I wanted to pass this corner as quickly as possible.

"You need to relax more, Hope. You're stressing yourself out over nothing. He's just a dumb dog."

That dumb dog had now decided to try and dig up the stones lining someone's lawn. "Stop that, Weasel," I bellowed and yanked on his leash. He decided to give up this round without a fight, and pranced quickly ahead. He still wasn't used to Jezebel, and avoided the area around her, but the feel of her presence must have lessened somewhat outdoors, because he had at least stopped peeing when she was near.

"It's not just the dog, is it? If it's the murder that's bothering you, you should let it go for now. There is nothing you can do about it," Eugene said somewhat compassionately.

"I know, but I wish it had been solved already. And I wish even more that the guilty person was some random burglar that just happened to wander into the house."

"It must be horrible knowing you are friends with a murderer," Eugene said in a mock-sympathetic voice. "But we all can't be excellent judges of character."

"How kind of you to look past my numerous imperfections," I said sarcastically.

"You are very welcome," he simpered, stepping forward.

"Wait, you're about to step in..." My voice trailed off. At least there was one benefit of being a ghost. The pile of dog poop that Eugene had walked right into made no impact on his shoes. Instead, he was standing in it—literally—and not even noticing. I knew he couldn't get dirty, but this really was unfair.

Every person on this planet has probably stepped in dog poop at least once in his or her life, with the smell and embarrassment likely remaining for several days. But not Eugene. Even in death he retains some dignity. Life just wasn't fair.

Eugene was just looking at me, expecting me to finish my sentence, oblivious to where he was standing. I was tempted to say something more. I knew that if I did he would probably squeal like a girl or jump back quickly. It might be worth it. He couldn't get hurt after all.

Just as I was about to tell him that he was standing in a pile of crap, a loud yelp jerked me around. Before I had time to react, two large St. Bernards plunged out of nowhere (it was actually an open garage) and headed straight for Weasel and I. Eugene jumped out of the way, not wanting to be run through by an unknown animal, but I had no such luck. The St. Bernards halted directly in front of Weasel and barked frantically before trying to roll him over with their noses. Poor Weasel was beside himself with terror—which explained why my shoes were suddenly wet and smelly and Eugene was practically rolling on the ground laughing.

This must be God punishing me for wanting to get a good laugh out of Eugene's discomfort. And for all those other sins that I can't remember because they are just becoming too numerous. Oh well! At least I was wearing thick socks.

Luckily the St. Bernards were good-natured animals and did not object too strongly to my yanking Weasel into my arms and yelling for them to go home.

Unfortunately Jezebel, eager to join in the fray, pounced onto the largest dog, but instead of knocking him down, ended up flat on the ground with a sadly confused expression. This caused Eugene to laugh even harder (which wasn't unexpected despite the fact that it was his dog making an ass of herself) and caused the St. Bernard to swing around and start yelping.

The commotion must have disturbed the slumber of several other neighborhood canines, because soon an entire chorus of barking could be heard the length of several blocks. The only positive aspect of all this drama was that the owner of the St. Bernards came out and rounded them up, allowing me to at least put Weasel back on the sidewalk.

"Do you think he's able to walk?" Eugene asked me, looking curiously at Weasel, who was sitting on his hind legs with a traumatized look in his eyes.

"I hope so. We're definitely turning back now. I think Weasel has had enough exercise for one day," I noted.

"And you need to clean your shoes," Eugene sniggered. "I hope the smell will come out."

"I'll take them to my mother. She swears she can get stains and smells out of anything," This was the perfect opportunity to test her claim. Of course, it also meant I would be given a disappointed look for allowing a dog to pee on me (as if I asked for it), but that couldn't be helped.

"Does she have a Beef Wellington recipe?" Eugene asked nonchalantly.

"I don't know," I said. "She might. But about this Beef Wellington thing...I'll keep my word and make it for you, but I don't know why you want it. And I thought you wanted Coq as Vin?"

"Maybe I want both. And I want some Bouillabaisse, too."

"Now you are being completely ridiculous. And I thought Jewish people weren't supposed to have shellfish?"

"Yes, but I've had to make one or two exceptions because of my line of work," he admitted.

Hah! I knew it—his religion was sidelined by his monstrous appetite. "But that's cheating!" I declared triumphantly. At last I had something to hold over him. Going against the dictates of one's faith was pretty serious.

"It's not cheating. That isn't a very strict rule, anyway. I have no doubt that lots of Jews eat shellfish. What about all those vegetarians that eat eggs? Are you going to call them hypocrites? And what about those people who eat beef but refuse to eat veal because they don't like the thought of killing a little calf? Are they all hypocrites?" he exploded.

"Calm down. I'm not calling you a hypocrite. You admit that you don't always adhere to the rules. Hypocrites are people who don't practice what they preach. If you want to eat shellfish—er, try to eat shellfish-- that is fine with me. I was just thinking that it might not be a good way to impress God— breaking the rules and all," I expounded.

"You eat shellfish. Do you think God is going to deny you entrance to heaven because of that?" Eugene asked guilelessly. "Besides, how do you know God didn't leave me here so that I could experience the joy of shellfish?"

"I'm not sure God rates shellfish that high," I chuckled. "I guess we'll be having bouillabaisse at some point, just to see what God does—but without squid." I had issues with chewy, squishy seafood, and I wasn't ashamed to admit it. "But let's start off small, okay? Coq as Vin first. Though I wouldn't really call that small."

"I'm more in the mood for bouillabaisse."

Oh, please! "You aren't even hungry. You don't eat anymore. How can you be 'in the mood' for something?"

Eugene gave me a belligerent grin, and started walking away. I knew that at some point I would somehow end up purchasing all manner of shellfish, including squid, if just to keep peace reigning in my apartment. God only knew what tricks he was liable to teach Jezebel if he felt the need for new forms of entertainment.

We crossed the intersection, Weasel keeping so close to my legs he nearly tripped me when I stepped off the curb. "Maybe Jilly will teach me how to make bouillabaisse," I said, half expecting Eugene to object. But he was hardly listening. Something on the other side of the street had captured his attention. Now I was of less importance than a garbage truck and a dented old Ford. The vehicles weren't even foreign! Talk about a slap in the face!

"Eugene?" I prompted. "I said—"

"Do you see that car, Hope? Doesn't it look a lot like the one that ran me down?" Eugene sputtered, clearly upset.

I looked in the direction he was pointing, and I saw a dark blue sedan stopped at the light. "I don't know, Eugene. It all happened so quickly. Most of it was a blur," I apologized. Actually, I was grateful that a lot of it was a blur. I didn't want to remember most of the details.

"It wasn't a blur for me. I will never, ever forget. It's as clear to me now as if it had just happened," he said absently. "Come on."

Eugene rushed across the street, oblivious of the traffic careening through the light. I was amazed that he hadn't been hit by any cars. It wouldn't have made a difference if he had been hit, but I doubted that seeing a car pass through his body would have lightened either of our moods.

I hurried to catch up with him, but Weasel was not being very cooperative and slowed me down. By the time the oncoming traffic had cleared and I had joined Eugene on the other side of the intersection, the car had turned right and disappeared down a larger thoroughfare.

"I know it was that car, Hope. I just know it. There was even a dent in the hood," he moaned. "What if I'm still here because I need to discover who killed me? That might be the reason. I've been thinking that I still needed to learn something or was being punished, but finding out who killed me could be a possibility. Isn't that how it is in all the movies?" he said, turning to me with a look of appeal.

"It's one possibility, I suppose. I had thought we agreed that the police were more likely to find out who hit you than we were. Shouldn't we let them handle it?" I asked, already knowing his answer.

"But they haven't learned anything!" he thundered.

"We don't know that. Maybe they have information we just haven't heard about. It's not like we've gone and asked," I countered. "I'll call the police and see if they've learned anything. Would they have told your relatives anything?"

"I don't know," he admitted. "I wasn't very close to any of them. They might not have asked the police to keep them informed."

That was one of the saddest things I had ever heard.

"Later on you can tell me everything you remember, and I'll pretend that I suddenly remembered it. I daresay witnesses sometimes remember things weeks later. Did you get the license plate?" I asked.

"A few of the numbers. The first part was BG93, but I couldn't see the rest."

"Okay, we'll just have to work with that. But, Eugene, what if this isn't the reason your still here? You could be here for any number of reasons. I don't want you to be disappointed if we find out who hit you and you don't go anywhere."

"Don't worry, Hope. I won't have a nervous breakdown if we find that bastard and I still don't get off of Earth," he responded.

I just hoped he was right. It was difficult enough living with a nit-picky, temperamental ghost; if he started talking to himself and dancing around wearing garlands and tutus I'd probably have to call in the Ghostbusters for my own sanity.

Our journey to the best laundromat in Pennsylvania— my mother's—was accomplished in silence. That wasn't so bad, since Eugene seemed depressed and I was dreading showing up smelling like urine.

My parents' house was a two-story brick federal with white trim and a well-manicured lawn. The front door was black with a brass knocker in the shape of a lion and a knob that only worked if you pushed and pulled with a great deal of force. Like the other houses in the area, the driveway was composed of dirt and gravel, and meandered along the side of the house before ending at a converted barn/carriage house. A stone wall separated the house from its neighbors, though the wall was so low it served more as a long, uncomfortable bench than a barrier. What my mother loved most about the house was that it was undeniably proper, and exactly like almost every other respectable house in Everton. For some reason, she was scared to veer from the norm.

A petite Asian woman with a glowing face greeted me across the stone wall as Eugene, Jezebel and I pulled into the drive. "Hello, Hope. I haven't seen you in awhile. What have you been up to lately? Too busy fending away men to come and visit?" she asked exuberantly.

"Hi, Ling," I greeted her. "How are you?"

"Oh, I'm doing the same as always--great! My business has been flourishing lately, and my ex-husband has stopped calling. Life can't get much better than that," she joked.

Ling Suen was currently a Feng Shui consultant, having sold her last business—a clothing boutique--around the same time she and her husband got divorced. She had marvelous business acumen, always benefiting from the latest trends. She was in her early forties, dressed in all the latest trends, and always had something positive to say. The neighborhood adored her, and often referred to her as "The Angel of Albemarle Street". Exactly the opposite of my mother (I don't mean the angel part, but all the rest). She had been my role model when I was younger, and I still envied her ability to do exactly as she pleased, regardless of what others thought. Too much like my mother, I hadn't yet broken through my fears.

" You look wonderful and your place looks great as always," I said, thinking that the façade of my parents' house might benefit from a few of Ling's spiral-shaped hedges.

Ling owned the liveliest house on the street. While the architecture of the house was in the typical Queen Anne style, that was where convention stopped. The house was painted a bright yellow with a purple porch, green trim around the windows, and blue trim around the doors. Strangely enough the color combination worked, and the house was more of a town focal point than an eyesore—at least according to everyone who wasn't a member of the Everton Women's Auxiliary League. And who wasn't my mother.

The front yard held the typical lawn, but was bordered on all sides by large clumps of tall, brightly colored flowers. A massive elm tree was located in front of the left side of the house, and a path of colored tiles in a floral pattern led up to the front door. The house was an artistic masterpiece.

"How's my little Nutter Butter doing?" Ling asked. Whenever I went out of town, Ling, who was a cat lover, watched Nutter Butter for me. She spoiled him to such an extent that I could swear every time I returned from a trip he had gained another pound.

"He's up for sale, if you want him," Eugene called out.

I sent him a warning glance, and he laughed and shrugged. "It's not like she can hear me," he observed.

Maybe not, but I suddenly had a vision of Eugene managing to pick Nutter Butter up and ditch him under an overpass. Of course, Eugene would never really do that, but he might think it funny to lock Nutter Butter in a closet and pretend the cat had gone missing.

"He's fine. I think he misses you. I haven't been able to get him to stand on his hind legs and dance the way you always can."

"That fat slug does tricks?" Eugene bellowed. "I don't believe it." Jezebel didn't believe it either, and started barking, stopping only when Eugene let her off the invisible leash.

"I'll come visit soon," Ling promised. "I just found a new on-line store that sells specially made cat treats," she said, her enthusiasm growing.

"If that's the case he'll probably go into a depression when you leave," I predicted.

"Oh, no. Don't try to convince me that cat isn't devoted to you, Hope."

"All right, I won't." Nutter Butter might have gotten used to Jezebel's presence, but he still wasn't happy, and he blamed me. Instead of sleeping at my feet, Nutter Butter had recently taken to sleeping under the bed and then demanding loudly that I wake up extremely early and accompany him into the kitchen. "But he does like visitors."

She nodded, and then leaned farther over the stone wall until she was practically lying across it. "I heard that Marcus Whittington was murdered, and that you were there," she said.

Oh God! That meant my mother probably knew. I knew I should have called her and told her immediately. Now I was going to be in trouble for not informing her before strangers did.

"Yes. It was horrible," I mumbled.

"The Tates told me about it. It seems the police went and questioned them as well. Poor Rosemary was quite upset," Ling explained. "Allan is so devoted to her, and he was furious at the way the police upset her. He was livid when he told me about it."

"That's too bad. Peter Jameson is handling the investigation, and I can't believe he would be insensitive."

"I know. He's such a dear boy. I think Allan is a little over-protective because before Rosemary met him she was involved in a bad relationship. Allan is one of those men who thinks women need to be coddled," she said in an exasperated voice. "I like Rosemary a lot, but sometimes I wonder if Allan's role as her protector isn't making her hypersensitive."

"I didn't know you were so-well acquainted with the Tates." No real surprise there. Everyone in this town knew everyone else. Avoiding people in Everton is about as easy as avoiding somebody else's body parts in a game of Twister.

"I've known Allan for a number of years. We used to buy from the same clothing companies, although we bought for different types of customers. I only met Rosemary about four years ago when they moved back to Everton and Allan went into semi-retirement."

"I thought they had lived in Everton for a lot longer than that," I said.

"Allan did. He moved away when he was in his early twenties. He didn't meet Rosemary until he was in his late thirties or early forties. I'm not really sure. They both moved back to Philadelphia after that, and then, like I said, back here. I guess people always feel an affinity for their home town," Ling commented.

"I think you must be right," I said, looking at the house that had seen me through all my childhood and teenage years. It was as much a part of me as anything else in this world. "I should probably get inside. My mom must be wondering why I am being so rude as to keep you here talking when your arms must be hurting you by now."

"Don't be silly. And I doubt your mom is thinking anything of the sort. She is probably thinking what a nice daughter she has to keep a bored, middle-aged woman company," Ling replied.

Ah, the delusions of the tender-hearted! If only I were so naïve.

"You're not middle-aged yet," I laughed.

"Flatterer," Ling retorted.

"She's right, Hope. She's probably getting close to forty-five. Technically, that is middle-age," Eugene noted before shrilly whistling for Jezebel. "A mid-life crisis would explain her house," he added softly, in a deprecatory voice.

What did he know about style? He might know a lot about food and wine, but I doubted he had more than a passing knowledge of decorative arts. His apartment had probably been filled with black leather sofas and chrome appliances.

I said a quick goodbye to Ling, and walked into the house through the front door. "Mom, are you home?"

"In the kitchen, Hope," came her perfectly enunciated voice.

Eugene gestured to the antiques spaced perfectly throughout the living room, "Family heirlooms, right?"

"Of course. My mother wouldn't have it any other way." And if they weren't heirlooms, she wasn't about to admit it.

"I can appreciate someone wanting to preserve their history," Eugene acknowledged.

"You're going to love my mother, Eugene. The two of you have a great deal in common," I pointed out. The first thing was that they both loved to lord their superiority over me (though in my mother's case it wasn't intentional); the second was that they both were finicky about food to the point of being obsessive.

When we entered the kitchen through the swinging door, my mother was seated at the breakfast table, a complete tea service for two spread out in front of her. "I saw you pull up and start talking to Ling, so I knew I'd have the time to make a quick pot of tea."

Eugene looked first at the steaming teapot, and then at the fresh cream and the sugar cubes. When his gaze rested on the scones and clotted cream, the dainty dish filled with jam, and the napkins folded perfectly atop the plates, he smiled with enthusiasm. "Finally, someone who knows how to serve a proper tea. Did she make those scones herself, Hope, or are they store-bought?"

"This looks great, Mom. Did you make the scones yourself?" The things I am willing to do for Eugene continually astound me.

Her mascara-free eyes narrowed and she looked at me as if I had lost my mind. "What a ridiculous question, Hope. You know I always make my own scones. It's my mother's recipe, if you recall," she said peevishly.

"I'm just amazed that you managed to find the time to make them. I know how much work you have to do during the week. I know I couldn't manage to run a school, take care of Dad, and keep the house in order," I said, aware that she loved people knowing how much she did. She would never boast about it herself, but it was quite acceptable for others to point it out and compliment her on her management skills.

"I'm sure you could do just as much if you put your mind to it," she asserted. "It's just a matter of listing what needs to be done in order of priority. Then you allocate certain amounts of time in which to complete the tasks, you work diligently, and voila, it is all done."

Eugene nodded his agreement and then bent down over the scones and sniffed.

What is he doing? He can't even smell!

"I'm quite proficient at making the lists, I just can't seem to accomplish everything. There are always too many distractions." Like a high-strung ghost and his vexing dog.

"You just have to ignore them, dear. If you refuse to let them interrupt you they will either go away or wait until you do have time," she said sagely and then proceeded to pour me a cup of tea.

She must be kidding! The last time I checked one couldn't avoid things like grocery shopping or murder.

"I see she used currants—that's the proper English way. Does she make crumpets, too?" Eugene asked, finally removing his nostrils from the scone that my mother had just deposited on her plate.

"Sugar? One cube or two?" my mother asked, and before the two cubes of sugar had even plopped into my cup, she added, "I spoke with Sarah Jameson yesterday."

Here it comes! If my mother doesn't start a diatribe on the importance of sharing information with one's family and the true value of a mother, I will eat my shoes. Well, maybe not the shoes since they were still covered in urine. My pants would suffice.

"She said that Peter told her Marcus Whittington had been murdered and you were there when it happened." She glanced up at me, deeply concerned. "You should have called me immediately."

Not a true diatribe, but it was enough of a reproach that my pants were safe from any gnawing in the near future.

"I didn't want to upset you," I lied. The truth was, I didn't have the heart to listen to a speech on the continual horrors enacted against innocent victims in their own homes.

"Upset me? Marcus Whittington was an acquaintance of mine, and often played golf with your father. I was bound to be upset when I heard about his death. But to hear about it from Sarah, and have to admit that my own daughter hadn't seen fit to tell me was rather embarrassing. You should have realized that." She sipped her tea and fixed me with a tragic look. "With that horrible death of your colleague, and now this, I imagine you are rather over-wrought. It would have been nice to think that if you were upset you would automatically come to me—and don't tell me a murder didn't bother you."

Over-wrought was right! How many violent deaths could a person witness in the space of a few weeks before wondering if she was cursed? I could give Miss Marple a run for her money.

"I'm sorry. You know you're the first person I call when I'm upset." And after speaking with her I usually need to call Jilly to ensure that any further damage my mother may have caused is undone.

"It's all right. I suppose you were simply in a state of shock. Who wouldn't be? The atrocities committed against innocent people these days are growing at an alarming rate. And to think he was killed in his own home. You can't feel safe any-where..." she prattled. I started to tune her out after she declared that the news was only watched by criminals these days in order to learn new ideas for committing crimes.

Eugene, fascinated by my mother's embellished account of burgeoning crime in Everton, was staring open-mouthed at her. If he believed that an entire family of six (containing four teenagers) had been robbed of all their alcohol in the middle of the night by bandits that came through a loose attic window, I had a large bridge in Brooklyn to sell him.

"Was he shot, dear?"

"Excuse me?" I said, startled out of my reverie about Mission Impossible-like ways of getting into a house through the attic.

"Was Marcus shot? Sarah didn't say," my mother ex-plained.

"No. He was stabbed in the neck with a knife." I wonder if there is a euphemism for that?

Eugene gave an involuntary shudder and tried sitting down on one of the empty chairs. Unfortunately, the chair was still pushed in to the table, and a large portion of his body ended up merged with the wood. In disgust he stood back up and walked to the counter, where he was able to lean back in com-fort. It amazed me again that some things were solid to him, like chairs and counters, but others were insubstantial.

I suppose it has a lot to do with the mind. If you believe something is solid, it is. Isn't that the Zen way? Or am I thinking of the Jedi way?

"How awful. Poor Angela. She must be beside herself with..." My mother paused, searching for an appropriate word, and finally came up with, "anxiety. Just imagine how terrifying it must be to wonder if the murderer is going to return to the house and stab you in your sleep. And I'm sure she was very fond of him," my mother added, feeling that it would be horribly rude to deny Angela of any tender emotions.

"The police don't think a stranger killed him. In fact, they think it was one of the guests that remained after the party," I clarified.

"Maybe they were all in on it," Eugene theorized. "Birds of a color and all that."

"One of the guests?" she gasped. "I can't believe that. Why would one of his friends kill him?"

"Money, I guess. And it might not have been a friend, but a relative." If she still thought I was a bad daughter after hearing that Marcus' only son may have killed him, I had best give up now.

"What? That's ridiculous. Evan couldn't hurt a fly. And as for Angela, well, I think she is too smart to murder someone. She would know that it wasn't worth the risk of getting caught," my mother argued.

"Maybe," I shrugged. "But if it isn't one of them, it has to be a member of the Raines family, or even the Tates. Oh, or me."

"You? Don't be an idiot! I doubt the police suspect you. You wouldn't have any reason to kill Marcus Whittington. You barely knew the man," my mother declared, her maternal instincts raised.

"I know you didn't do it, Hope, having been there, but you might have had a motive," Eugene theorized. "Maybe he was stiffing you on your fee, or you were having an affair with him. Or maybe you're secretly a lesbian and are having an affair with Angela," Eugene popped out. When I gave him the nastiest look I could muster, causing my mother to gaze at me with concern, he apologized. "I don't actually think any of that, Pip. And I wouldn't have suspected you of killing him even if I hadn't been with you. The only thing that might be true in all of that is that the old man might have tried to stiff you on your fee. He looked like a tight-wad," Eugene somewhat apologized.

Where did Eugene come up with these things? He was only a few years younger than Marcus, so calling him an 'old man' was a bit much. He wasn't British! And as for Marcus being a tight-wad, did Eugene look at the furnishings in the house or the clothes Angela was wearing? Not even he could have been so engrossed in the canapés that he failed to notice.

"Peter would never suspect you, dear. Don't you remember how fond of you he has always been?" Hints don't get much broader than that.

I nodded. She was practically gushing when she said his name. I had to get out of here fast. Mrs. Lancaster down the street just received her first grandchild, and my mother had been looking rather put out since seeing her holding the infant.

"I don't know why you don't date nice men like Peter," she chided.

I take it back. Hints can get far broader. Some of my mother's could span an ocean.

"I do date nice men, Mom." Did she think I only dated men who belched at the dinner table and had criminal records? Maybe that one guy belched at her dinner party, but he had overdone it on the sodas. But certainly none of them had criminal records. That I knew of.

"Then why are you single again?" she asked.

"The sixty-thousand dollar question," Eugene chimed in. "Though I suspect it's because of—"

Whatever reason he suspected was drowned out by my mother. "Jilly is married to a nice man."

"You don't expect me to marry a man just because he's nice, do you?" I didn't mention the fact that my mother had disapproved of Martin right up until the vows were spoken.

"Of course not, but you could look a little harder."

"She's right, Hope. You're practically a hermit. All you need is the cave," goaded Eugene.

"And Peter is so nice. Just look at what good care he has taken of his mother since his father died. He even bought a house a mile away just so he could be around if she needed anything," my mother insisted.

If that was a hint that I should move a mile away from her in order to kill spiders for her when Dad was out golfing, she truly was delusional.

"He looks after his mother?" Eugene questioned. "Now that I think about it, he did look like a nice fellow. You could certainly do a lot worse, Hope."

Oh God! Now Eugene was meddling in my love life! If he started writing my phone number in bathroom stalls he was going to have to go.

"I won't talk about it anymore today if it upsets you so much, Hope, but I think you should seriously consider going out with Peter. He has a steady job, a nice house, and he knows all your friends." She sipped at her tea, her eyes never leaving my face. "He's also become quite good-looking and athletic, not at all geeky like he used to be, and I know looks and physique are what all young women look for these days."

"True. I've noticed that women are becoming increasingly fickle. It's advertising. You probably can't help the way you are, Hope," Eugene decided.

I was not solely interested in a person's looks. I just didn't want to date Peter.

"Forget it, Mother. I've already turned him down once. I like him too much to date him. I would probably end up causing him to have a complex or something. Can we please change the subject?" I moaned.

"Of course. I promise I won't mention the fact that you are too picky."

"You just did."

"Did what?" She gave a frustrated sigh. "It's obvious you're in a churlish mood. Let's talk about something else. Why don't you tell me how your work is going? Skipping the murder, if you don't mind," she said. "And give me those shoes of yours. They smell like a barn."

I settled back in my chair. I was quite willing to talk about work. She'd get a good laugh out of my latest column—she always had a hard time believing that people don't know what jewelry it is and isn't permissible to wear before sunset. This was one of my mother's pet peeves—and one that was so out-of-date it made me laugh every time I thought of it. As far as I knew, she was the only person left on the planet who felt that wearing diamonds (other than engagement rings) before sunset was as great a crime as adultery.

Chapter Seventeen

"Are you sure about this?" I asked, nervously eyeing the soup bowl I had set before Eugene. "Maybe I should put newspapers on the floor before you start. I don't want the whole place to smell like fish for the next few weeks."

"If I spill, I'll clean up," Eugene promised me.

"Oh, please! You have trouble picking up a spoon. How do you expect to be able to mop a floor?" I demanded.

Eugene looked momentarily nonplussed. "Okay, go get some newspapers."

"We really should have started with the Coq au Vin. It might be easier to clean up."

Eugene didn't bother to respond.

I rummaged through my recycling bin until I had found a large stack of week-old papers. "You weren't planning on finishing this crossword, were you?" I asked Eugene. The crossword I held in my hand had three words filled in, written in an illegible scrawl, and the rest of the spaces were glaringly empty. When Eugene had tried to work on the puzzle he had such a hard time moving the pencil that he had given up in frustration, slamming the paper into the recycling bin whilst professing that he had always hated crosswords.

"No. But save the movie section. I might want to go see a movie this week," he announced. It would be the first time he had decided to (willingly) venture out on his own. The farthest he usually went by himself was to the end of the block, and that was only when walking Jezebel. This could mean freedom for me. Several hours of it anyway.

I spread several sections of newspaper across the kitchen floor, and sat back down at the table, my spoon and fork at the ready.

Eugene was staring at his spoon, his face wearing an expression of deep concentration. He looked so much like Yoda I wouldn't have been surprised to see the spoon rise of its own accord and dip itself into the soup. I was tempted to say something along the lines of, "Do, or do not; there is no try," but managed to restrain the impulse. I didn't need Eugene storming out of the house and leaving me to eat an entire pot of bouillabaisse by myself.

"Are you ready?" I asked, slightly nervous myself. I had no idea how Eugene would react if his experiment failed. I only owned one mop.

He nodded and reached for the spoon, his hand hesitating only a second before it closed around it. When he successfully lifted the spoon he gave a squeal of triumph.

"Now aren't you glad I'm using stainless steel silverware, instead of the real, heavier silver you demanded?" I inquired. Even my mother used the stainless steel for everyday usage.

"Shhh. You're distracting me," he grumbled.

I grinned knowingly. If he failed I would be blamed as the culprit; if he succeeded I would be accused of not having the proper amount of confidence. And whether he managed to taste the soup or not, it would be held as horribly inferior and dreadfully flavorless.

The spoon glided into the broth, picked up some liquid, a tiny piece of fish, and a finely chopped piece of celery. He slowly moved the spoon away from him before pulling it out of the soup bowl. The tremors from his hand caused a little soup to drop onto the tablecloth and splatter into several yellowish-brown worm-like shapes.

By the time the spoon reached Eugene's lips I was so tense my hand was clutching the edge of the table. Eugene gave several gulps and then tipped the liquid into his mouth.

The expression on Eugene's face when the liquid went pouring right through him before landing in an undignified heap on the floor was priceless—a combination of surprised disappointment and hygienic revulsion. When the liquid first touched his lips Eugene looked ecstatic, but upon realizing that it wasn't actually going to be digested his eyes widened and he looked down in horror, watching the broth and those small pieces of fish and celery tumble to the ground before being absorbed by the newspaper. He quickly ran his hands over his suit, making sure it hadn't been soiled, while keeping his eyes focused on the dark grey spot swelling and obscuring an advertisement for a department store.

I braced myself for an explosion of anger, a clenching of the fists and an admonishment to God, but none came. When Eugene finally took his eyes off of the floor, he looked at me and said, "I guess we should have started with crackers."

I didn't want to laugh at his misfortune, but I did. I couldn't help myself. Here was Eugene standing before me with a sheepish expression on his face, a dirty spoon still grasped in his fingers, and a large pot of bouillabaisse still needing to be consumed. I guessed I wouldn't be able to feed it to the dog, either. Maybe Nutter Butter would eat some and save me the trouble.

"It isn't that funny, Hope," Eugene said peevishly.

"I know. I'm sorry. You must be very disappointed," I sympathized.

He looked at me defiantly, a militant smile on his face. "Not really. It probably wasn't very good soup, anyway. I'm not criticizing your culinary skills, but you really aren't Julia Childs. You're not even up to Emeril's standards, and that is saying a lot."

Exactly how *did* he define criticism?

"It appears as if you added too much saffron. It shouldn't be this yellow," he claimed. "And the broth is awfully thick. That doesn't look natural."

I was willing to overlook his comments since I knew he was undoubtedly very disappointed. Food had consumed his life, and now he was denied even a smell of it. Death is a lot tougher than I had previously thought! I sent up a quick prayer to God that when Eugene reached heaven he would be able to taste food again.

Eugene looked at his soup dish and then at me. "Since I can't eat it, I expect you to tell me how it tastes."

I just stared at him. Did he truly want me to describe how it tasted? That was going to be hard.

"Go on," he urged. "Take a sip."

I obeyed reluctantly. It wasn't too bad considering I had never made bouillabaisse before. I might not be a professional like Eugene or Jilly, but I wasn't completely incompetent. My mother had insisted that any female wanting a husband had to learn at least the rudiments of cooking. "It tastes pretty good," I said, giving myself an imaginary pat on the back.

"I don't want to hear your untrained opinion on its quality, I want you to tell me what you taste," he said in the voice of an exasperated adult who has had to repeat instructions one time too many to a daft child.

"Well, it sort of tastes like fish broth and saffron," I enlightened him.

"Of course it does, you idiot. What about the other flavors—the fish, for instance, the vegetables? Do they blend well?"

"I think so. It tastes good, at any rate." What more did he want me to say? I knew I should have researched culinary terminology as soon as Eugene looked like he was becoming a permanent fixture.

"Do you have any Pouilly-Fumé or Champagne Brut? Either one would be an appropriate accompaniment."

"No. And don't ask me to go out and get any when you can't even drink," I told him.

"I wasn't thinking about me," Eugene said in a saintly voice. "I was thinking that the right wine might improve the meal *for you*," he emphasized petulantly.

I wasn't about to fall into that trap. If I started bringing home special wines Eugene would probably expect me to start describing bouquets and nutty flavors, and whatever other qualities wine connoisseurs sought--and I didn't have time to take an Internet course in viniculture.

Before I could argue with Eugene about my simple culinary needs, the doorbell rang. I quickly tossed the soiled newspaper in the garbage bin, told Eugene to stay in the kitchen and keep Jezebel with him, and rushed to the door.

To my surprise, Peter was standing on the threshold

looking embarrassed.

"I hate to bother you, Hope, but I have to do follow-up interviews with all the suspects," he apologized.

I nodded. So I was still a suspect? The police were not nearly as effective as I had hoped. Maybe there were more innocents on death row than I had realized.

"Come on in." I beckoned him inside, stepping aside so that he could pass by me. "But I'm not sure there is anything more I can tell you."

A floating head suddenly emerged in front of the kitchen door, and I realized that Eugene had stuck his head through in order to find out who had arrived, but left his body inside the kitchen. It was undoubtedly his way of annoying me and eavesdropping without allowing me to chastise him for leaving the kitchen. I would have to start being very specific in my instructions.

Peter seated himself on the sofa, so I took the chair opposite him. "Have you been cooking? I hope I'm not interrupting anything."

I assured him that he was not, and he took out a much smaller notebook than the one I had seen him with last time. "What is it you wanted to ask me?"

"First I need to ask you for the dress you were wearing that night. We have warrants to get the clothes and shoes from everyone who remained after the party."

"Sure. It's in the laundry hamper. Do you want me to get it now?" I asked.

"No, I can get it when I leave. I have a bag for it right here." He indicated a medium-sized paper bag that bore the state police insignia.

"If someone did get blood on their clothes, wouldn't they have already had the clothing cleaned?" I asked. This was beginning to sound like a bad murder mystery.

"Probably, but my lieutenant wants me to collect your dress anyway. He thinks I should have demanded everyone's clothes that night," he groaned. "Truthfully, I collected just about everyone else's on the night of the murder." His voice trailed off and I waited a moment before breaking in on the silence.

"What else do you want to know?" I wasn't particularly eager to return to the bouillabaisse, but Eugene's discombobulated head was making me uncomfortable. A few more minutes and I would grab a large object and try to pummel his head back into the kitchen, like those bop-the-gopher games at fairs.

"Do you remember if the back door of the foyer was open or unlocked?"

I thought about it for a moment, while Eugene's head began to sway. He must be losing his balance, I thought with a little bit of guilty satisfaction. "I don't know if the door was unlocked, but it wasn't open when I was in the foyer. Why?"

"We found a bloody napkin hidden in a corner by the back door. It had been shoved behind a potted plant," he disclosed. "I'm trying to determine if the murderer walked around the patio and came in through the back door, or was within the vicinity of the foyer."

Eugene gave a loud gasp and toppled through the door. His hands flailed out in front of him and he careened through a table and lamp. In his own words, he had gone down "like a hippo on ice."

I had to turn my head aside so that Peter wouldn't see my smirk and think I was laughing at the notion of murder.

"And you still don't know who killed Marcus? There weren't fingerprints on the knife or DNA on the napkin, or anything like that?" I questioned him while simultaneously watching from the corner of my eye as Eugene straightened his body and brushed off his suit. I was just waiting for him to start picking off that imaginary lint again.

"You've been watching too much CSI," Peter joked. "Seriously though, they dusted the knife and room for fingerprints and nothing surprising came back. There were no fingerprints on the knife, so we suspect the napkin was used to wipe it off. And there were numerous fingerprints throughout the room and doorknob. We even found your prints on the doorknob," he said mildly. "As for DNA, the napkin was sent to the state lab, but the results won't be in for a couple of weeks. Even then there are no guarantees. A lot of people probably handled that napkin."

I nodded in agreement. I might even be one of them. I really hope they don't arrest people on circumstantial evidence alone.

Eugene decided that listening in on my conversation with Peter was more important than his dignity, and he swaggered over to a chair and sat down. He proceeded to give me a defiant look that I chose to ignore.

"Can you tell me if all the napkins and silverware had been accounted for after the dinner was finished?" Peter asked, though he didn't sound particularly hopeful.

"No. I didn't collect the dishes or napkins, the servers did. The napkins are tossed into a laundry bag right away, and the dishes and silverware are washed and set aside. No one counts them until the end of the evening because silverware has a tendency to disappear. You find it all over the house at the end of a party." For instance, in people's necks.

Peter and Eugene must have realized my verbal blunder because Eugene let out a sound that was half snort and half laugh while Peter grimaced. "I meant that you find them under sofas and tables--things like that," I said lamely.

Eugene rudely kept on laughing, but Peter simply nodded and moved on. "Was any silverware other than that knife missing at the end of the evening?"

"Yes, some spoons and some forks, too. As a matter of fact, almost an entire place setting went missing and we still—." I broke off what I was saying, suddenly realizing my mistake. Peter looked at me expectantly, his pen in his hand, and I gave him an apologetic smile. "I was going to say that an entire set was missing and that we still hadn't found it, but the knife was found, wasn't it? I didn't associate the two because when an entire setting goes missing you assume you just miscounted the number you started with."

"So you are saying that besides the knife, some forks and spoons disappeared as well? This raises a lot of new questions, Hope. I wish you had told me sooner," Peter chided.

"You fool," bellowed Eugene. "You're supposed to tell

the detective all the little details." I wanted to tell Eugene that he knew about the missing silverware as well, and he hadn't made the connection either.

How exactly does one look ditzy? I tried to look as appealing as possible by widening my eyes and tilting my head slightly. "I'm sorry, I must not have been thinking straight. What sort of questions does it raise?"

"There are a few possibilities: the first is that the murderer stole the entire set hoping that the caterers wouldn't notice they were missing until it was too late to see which place they came from; the second possibility is that the murderer found the setting lying around the house somewhere and decided to use it as a weapon. Either way, I need to find the missing silverware."

Boy, am I glad I don't have his job! It didn't sound like investigating crime was a lot of fun—rather a bunch of tedious errands and exhaustive searches.

"Is there anything else you wanted to know?"

"That argument you overheard between Evan Whittington and his father—do you remember how Evan responded? Was he angry or upset?"

"I couldn't really hear his response," I admitted.

"If you were a tad less polite you might not be a suspect in a murder investigation!" Eugene threw in.

"And you didn't recognize the female voice that was arguing with Mr. Whittington about his son either?" inquired Peter.

"No," I bristled. "I'm not holding anything back, I just didn't think it was any of my business so I didn't pay attention."

"I'm not accusing you of holding back, Hope," he said soothingly.

"I'm sorry. It's just that it sounds a bit skeptical even to my ears."

Peter looked thoughtful. "Do you remember anything else? Any noises you didn't remember before? Someone walking around with a knife in his hand?" he joked.

"I wish I did. I hate to think that someone I know is a murderer, but the thought of a murderer running around loose in even worse," I exclaimed.

"Do you remember seeing any checks on the desk or the floor when you and Mrs. Whittington found the body?"

"No. Sorry."

"Any check pieces?" he asked.

"No. Is it important?"

"Look, don't say anything to anyone. I probably shouldn't be telling you, but there was a small piece of a torn check under the deceased's shoe, and one check seems to be missing from the book."

I nodded, but didn't say anything.

"And I don't suppose you saw the victim smoking a cigar with anyone?"

"No. Let me guess? You found one of those too. Wouldn't it have DNA on it or something?"

Peter smiled and shook his head. I wasn't sure of he was denying finding a cigar or whether they identified any DNA. "I don't suppose the idea of it triggered your memory?"

It hadn't, but I did suddenly remember that I hadn't offered Peter any refreshment I made up for my lapse in manners by offering him every refreshment I had in the apartment.

"Too bad you can't offer him Champagne Brut," Eugene grumbled.

If Peter accepted a glass of wine while on duty I would eat my other shoe.

Peter finally agreed to at least taking a glass of water, and I went into the kitchen to fetch one. Eugene stayed behind, perusing Peter's face and attire. As I was entering the kitchen I heard him say, "Hmm. He could use a little work."

The kitchen was exactly as Eugene and I had left it, with one exception—Jezebel had decided that anything in a bowl must be dog food, whether it was on the floor or the table. The good news was that she hadn't managed to knock anything over. The bad news was that she was standing on top of the table, pushing her nose in and out of the bowl of bouillabaisse—literally. Every time her nose would move right through the dish and soup, she would lift her head, shake it off, and then try again, moving closer to the bowl each time. My kitchen table wasn't large, and Jezebel was now practically sitting on the food. While she wasn't actually contaminating the food, the sight of her sitting in it was enough to dissuade me from consuming that particular bowl of soup. It might be best to foist the soup off on the neighbors, I thought.

I shooed Jezebel off of the table as quietly as I could, picked up the rest of the newspapers before I forgot they were there and tripped on them. I retrieved a glass of water for Peter, and when I reentered the living room he was still seated on the sofa, though he now held my date book in his hand. He was examining Colby's wedding invitation with interest. He looked up. "You have a paper calendar. You don't see that very often. Sorry, it fell off the table from right behind me. You must have a window open."

I looked at Eugene, who looked entirely too smug for my comfort. He shrugged, and sat back down, his lips fixed in a gloating smile.

"It's a back-up in case my phone dies or my lap top breaks. You can't be too careful." Okay, forget the OPD, now I'm sounding OCD.

Peter examined the wedding invitation that had been sitting on top. "I didn't think people actually put cherubs on wedding invitations," he commented. "It seems a little...tacky."

"I know. They thought it was very baroque. Colby and her mother have gone overboard. It's strange but I always thought Colby had good taste before I started planning her wedding. I guess her good taste only goes as far as clothing."

"You've known them a long time?" Peter asked, curious. He returned the book to the table and placed the invitation neatly on top.

"Yes," I admitted with a rueful glance at Peter. "Through my school and the country club."

' He nodded. "I think my mother mentioned meeting them on several occasions through your parents. She didn't have many positive things to say about them."

"No, I imagine she didn't." Peter's mother was the typical small-town housewife, and having never desired anything more, could not understand socialites with dreams of grandeur. "How is your mother?" I continued. "I forgot to ask you about her the other day."

Peter smiled. He was such a mama's boy. "She's fine. You should come see her—she would love it. She's retiring this year, you know. She finally decided that she wanted to do more traveling and gardening and learn a new language. She's actually taken up Italian."

I was surprised that Mrs. Jameson wanted to retire. She had been a legal secretary for a local attorney since graduating from college over thirty years ago, and used to joke that she would retire on the day she could no longer walk to work.

"He spends a lot of time with his mother now that his father is dead?" Eugene asked. "I think that's what your mom said."

I nodded in response to both Peter and Eugene

"I should probably get going. I already visited everyone else, but I need to get back to the station and do some work there." He checked his watch and stood up.

"I'll go get that dress. Did you want the shoes as well?"

"Yes, please."

I found the dress rather quickly, as it was near the top of the pile of dirty laundry, and retrieved the shoes from the closet. It seemed a shame to hand them over to the police, as the only thing they were liable to learn was that I was fond of vichyssoise (there was a spot near the waist line) and that I had no compunction walking across a lawn in heels.

When I returned to the living room both Peter and Eugene had disappeared. I could hear the sink being run in the kitchen and when I pushed open the door Peter was standing at the sink, his empty glass full of soap suds. "I thought I'd wash it for you since I had a minute." He rinsed it off and gestured to the table set with two bowls of soup. "You told me I wasn't interrupting. Are you having a guest over? I hope I didn't take up too much time."

"Not at all. He already left," I lied.

"Oh." He looked embarrassed and quickly started looking around for a dishtowel, but I stopped him.

"Don't worry about it. I'll do it later. I have to clean up this mess anyway."

Eugene, who had been kneeling on the floor and petting Jezebel, looked up at me. "You should invite him to a movie. That way the three of us can go. The ads for that new western film look pretty good."

I have never particularly liked western films. And the one he was talking about starred Clint Eastwood. Harrison Ford or Sean Connery might have made me consider Eugene's suggestion, but Clint Eastwood was not good-looking enough at his age to make me start encouraging Peter.

"Here's the dress and shoes," I said to Peter, paying no heed to Eugene's suggestion.

"The bag is in the living room." Peter led the way back into the living room, snatched up the bag and let me deposit the clothes inside.

"If I need any more information, I'll call and set up a time to meet," Peter assured me.

"At least ask him about my death before he goes. That way the afternoon won't have been a complete loss," Eugene remarked woefully.

Eugene was right. Peter was a good person to ask a favor. "Before you go, Peter, can I ask you something?"

He paused at the door. "Sure."

"A few weeks ago a friend of mine was killed in a hit-and-run. I was a witness and this morning I thought I saw the car that hit him. I'm pretty sure it was the same car—it had a dent in the hood and everything. But I can't remember the officer's name that was handling the case." I stopped, uncertain as to how to continue.

"And you want me to give him the information?" Peter asked, taking out his notebook.

"I can get him the information, if you can find out who the officer is." But I would prefer you to do it for me, I thought.

"You got the license plate?"

"Only part of it. Is that going to make a difference?" I asked, hoping that it wouldn't.

"I don't know. Why don't you give me the plate number, and the location and date of the accident and I'll see what I can find out. I'll run the plate number before giving it to the investigating officer, though," Peter said apologetically.

"In case I'm completely wrong about the car?" I suggested.

Peter smiled, "It's happened before. So what is the information?"

I gave him all the required information and he told me he would get back to me by the end of the weekend.

As I waved Peter off, Eugene stopped and admired himself in the hall mirror. "Do you think your appearance changes when you get to heaven?"

"I have no idea, Eugene." I eyed him speculatively. "We talked about not getting our hopes up, right?" Getting Eugene to heaven was definitely a shared hope, and I didn't want us both to end up crushed with disappointment.

"I know, I know." He gave me a disapproving look, and added, "I just want to be prepared for the occasion whenever it comes, whether it be tomorrow or in ten years."

Ten years! God forbid!

"You don't need to worry about that," I pointed out. "Your appearance never changes. I don't even think the wind blows your hair."

"No?" He moved his hair around with his fingers. "It's moving now."

"Maybe that's because you're the one touching it," I suggested. No matter how often Eugene played with his hair, it went immediately back to its former style once his fingers were removed.

"Do you own a hair drier?" he asked, his concentration now completely on his hair.

"Don't tell me you want to try and simulate wind?" Had he always been this vain?

"So? What does it hurt to find out for certain?" he argued.

Even if Eugene accepted the fact that his appearance

wouldn't change no matter what Earthly forces were thrown at him, I imagined that he would still pick at imaginary lint, avoid anything that would stain a living person, and fluff his hair when he was proud of himself.

"Okay, let's go get the hair dryer," I responded.

Eugene paused, his eyes wandering toward the kitchen door. "Hope, are you still going to make a chocolate soufflé?"

I looked at him incredulously. "You won't be able to eat it." Poor Eugene! He really was obsessed with food.

"It would be for you," he said gallantly. "You ought to learn how to cook more elaborate meals than baked chicken and lasagna. It would be helpful in getting a man. You know what they say, the way to a man's heart is through—."

I cut him off before he could finish the cliché. "Thank you, Mother, for that lovely piece of advice," I said sarcastically. "When you return from your voyage to the 1950s let me know."

Eugene pulled his fingers out of his hair and stood tall enough to look down on me. "I'm just trying to help, Pip-Squeak. You don't have to be so ungrateful!" He then went all melodramatic. "I'm just a poor ghost who is willing to teach you how to cook like a gourmand, and all you can do is make fun of me." He looked at me in mock reproach. "You are not a very good hostess."

"Did you want me to get the hair dryer or not?"

Eugene was willing to trade his silence for the hair dryer, and he spent most of the afternoon trying to alter his hairstyle by means of the dryer, the comb, the brush, the mousse I had purchased several years back, and, as a last resort, the curlers. I was particularly entranced with the sight of Eugene's head topped by fat pink and green rollers. He so closely resembled an old woman startled out of bed that I had to leave the bathroom in order not to choke on my laughter. And for some reason he was deeply offended when I asked him if he would like to try and see if make-up would stay on his skin.

But in the end none of the items were successful in maintaining a new style and Eugene finally gave up, insisting repeatedly that his original style was more attractive anyway.

I had managed to eat a fresh bowl of bouillabaisse for

supper, not wanting to waste it (having made sure Jezebel's ghostly fur didn't touch it), when the phone rang. Eugene, who had been trying to teach Jezebel to play fetch with one of the curlers he had broken in his earlier frustration, glanced up at me. "It's probably Jilly, or your mother," he said matter-of-factly as I moved past him to reach for the phone. "They are the only ones who ever call this late. And if you're going to talk about something personal or related to women's issues take the phone into the other room. I don't want to have to listen to another conversation about why men should be extra understanding when their wives are suffering from PMS."

I sent him my most withering look. Just because he trivialized the time when Jilly was forced to dine with her in-laws while she was suffering from severe cramps didn't mean it wasn't a crisis. What did he know about women, anyway? He died single, didn't he?

"Hello," I said into the receiver, slightly distracted by Eugene's imitation of Jilly having cramps.

"Hope, it's Peter."

"Hi, Peter. I hadn't expected to hear back from you so soon. Did you find anything out about my friend's accident?"

Eugene got up and stuck his ear next to mine. "Move the phone over a little, Hope. I can't hear with you hogging the whole receiver."

Peter, unaware of the interruption, continued to speak. "As a matter of fact, I did. I ran the plates and the description of the car you gave me, and it matched a car that belongs to a man who is wanted for assault and suspicion of armed robbery."

"I knew he had to be a criminal," Eugene bellowed in my ear.

"As it turns out," Peter continued, "his car was used in one of the robberies. Unfortunately, the man and car disappeared right after that robbery, and until now, the investigators haven't had any other leads. He had abandoned his house, which also held a surprising amount of drugs, and he is presumed to be using yet another alias."

"Another alias? He was using one before?" I inquired.

From the description of this guy, I wasn't sure I did want to find him.

"He was using the name Sam Nelson here in Philadelphia, but that doesn't appear to be his real name. They have his fingerprints on file but they don't match any in the state or in the federal prison system," Peter noted, his voice suddenly sounding tired.

I could hear several people in the background having a loud discussion and then the high cackle of a woman. He must still be at work, I thought. No wonder his mother is so worried about him all the time.

"And they can't check other states?" Eugene gasped, outraged that his death wasn't ranked high enough to warrant a full-scale investigation. Where were the G-men when you needed them?

"They only check Pennsylvania? Will they check other states?" I asked.

"Normally, no, but since he was most likely involved in a vehicular manslaughter the detective in charge said he would file the necessary paperwork. We are short on manpower and funds,' he explained.

"I appreciate your telling me all this." I daresay Eugene would have expressed his appreciation as well if he weren't foaming at the mouth and muttering about unnecessary government expenditures that prevented the common man from receiving what was his due.

"No problem. I asked Detective Collins to let me know if they come up with any more leads."

"Thanks, I owe you for this."

"I know. I'll hold you to it another time." He paused for a moment. "Hope, I was thinking, I mean, are you sure it's healthy to take such an interest in this? He wasn't a good friend of yours or anything."

"I know. But I watched him die and I would like to know that the man who did it is behind bars." And I wanted Eugene out of my stuff before he decided to use my razors to see if he could shave his head.

"As long as you're keeping it in perspective, I won't say

anything more about it." He suddenly switched into a more business-like voice. "You haven't remembered anything else that can help in the Whittington murder, have you?"

"No. Sorry." His superior must have walked by, I thought.

"Okay. I will talk with you later then. Goodbye." He hung up before I had completely finished saying my goodbye, and I was left cradling a dead receiver.

"Did that satisfy you, Eugene?" I hoped he didn't expect me to track down this Sam Nelson's friends and start grilling them like a detective out of film noir.

"For now. Make sure your friend keeps you up-to-date. I want to know if they find out his real identity," he urged.

"I will. I want this to end as badly as you do," I reminded him.

"So I was killed by a criminal on the lam," he mused. "I suppose that's better than being done in by some old lady who was having trouble seeing over her steering-wheel."

I wasn't sure that it was, especially since the end result would have been the same, but if Eugene wanted to imagine himself the sympathetic victim in a crime story, he was welcome to do so. I intended to put the matter behind me—at least until tomorrow.

Chapter Eighteen

"I don't want to go." I didn't stamp my feet and add, 'And you can't make me,' but I was sorely tempted.

"You have to pick up your fee, and the check for the caterer," Eugene argued. "You promised the caterer you would give it to him tomorrow, and you can't shirk your duties."

Eugene was especially annoying when he was right.

"Why can't I just call Angela and ask her to mail me the check?" What sane person would want to venture back into a house that might possibly be sheltering a murderer?

"That would be cowardly," Eugene noted.

Hah! He was already dead. What did he have to fear?

"And while I've noticed that you dislike scenes, I didn't expect you to be so spineless. It's not like the murderer wants your blood. You don't have any money, and even if you did, it wouldn't be left to any of them. There is nothing to worry about."

"I'm not worried about being knocked off; I'm worried about being sucked into their hairy drama. Are you willing to be forced to listen to all of them whining about how dreadful everything is, and how the police have no respect for their situation?" I moaned.

"You are not being polite, Pip," Eugene said in a sing-song voice. "And here I thought you were always well-mannered."

"I don't have to be well-mannered in private. That's the beauty of the system. Good etiquette does not prevent you from thinking and saying whatever you want in your own home." He was smirking like a spider about to trap a fly. "And for your information," I continued, "I have been nothing but polite to that entire family--to both families, actually. And now I am tired and need a break. Just think how much easier it is to be polite over the phone."

"And how much duller. By going over to the Whittington's house we can see if the police have made any progress. Maybe someone will let something slip."

Oh my God! I am living with an Ellery Queen wannabe. Next he'll start insisting we carry around magnifying glasses and plastic gloves.

"We could be like Nick and Nora or Sherlock Holmes and Dr. Watson," Eugene added dreamily. "If we were Nick and Nora, Jezebel could take on the role of Asta."

That was fine as far as I was concerned. If I recalled correctly, Asta never did much but look cute and go for walks with his master. But if Jezebel actually decided to follow Asta's exemplary behavior, I'd eat my socks.

"I could see us as Cagney and Lacey, too," he added, his gaze unfocused and his mouth slightly ajar. He had obviously entered La-La Land.

"Cagney and Lacey? You watched 'Cagney and Lacey'? I would have thought that show was a little too...feminine...for you."

"My mother used to watch it," Eugene said in a defensive voice. "And they *were* fairly macho women," he added.

"I thought only one of them was tough. Wasn't the other one distinctly feminine? Wasn't that the point—that they were opposites?"

"Does it matter?" Eugene snapped out at me. "My point is that you have to go to see Angela, and while we are there we should try to find out what happened to the old guy. It would be good practice for finding my killer. And you are a suspect in the old man's murder. It would be a shame for the police to nab the wrong person."

"We both know that is extremely unlikely. I'm the only one of the suspects without a motive. Your clutching at straws here."

Eugene looked at me expectantly.

What would happen if I don't go? I doubted Eugene would resort to putting a horse head in my bed. More likely he would simply gripe and moan for all eternity.

When looked at from that perspective, what did I really care if Eugene wanted to go poking his nose around someone else's house? It wasn't as if anyone would ever know.

"Fine, but Jezebel can't come this time. It's bad enough that I have to worry about you knocking things over and tripping people," I muttered.

"When have I ever knocked anything over? Intentionally, that is?" Eugene argued somewhat ineffectually.

I could think of several instances, but decided that the wisest course lay in silence. I didn't want another bag of flour decorating the kitchen floor.

With some minor primping (by Eugene) we were ready to depart for the grief-laden Whittington home.

Since I hadn't expected the Whittingtons to set out a black wreath and close the curtains in a Victorian manner, I wasn't disappointed. The house was neither somber nor unwelcoming. It was surrounded on all sides by blooming flowerbeds and a vast, deep green lawn, the east portion of which was in the process of being mowed by a large-bellied gardener with a tattoo of a skull on one arm and The Virgin Mary on the other. He waved when I pulled up, and indicated that I should enter the house through the west patio.

As Eugene and I approached the patio, it became evident that Angela and Evan were entertaining. Several chairs and chaise lounges had been set out on the patio, and five figures were sprawled atop them, drinks in hand. A stereo was on somewhere in the house, and the sounds of Bach came tumbling through the windows.

"It looks like that older Raines is there. Jim, Jack?" Eugene queried.

"John," I corrected. "And the Tates, too. Maybe they're all here for the same reason you are—to find out what the police suspect."

The first to notice our approach was Angela, who bounced out of her chair and then proceeded toward us with a languishing walk. 'The performance is about to begin,' my devil whispered in my ear. Or maybe it was Eugene. Lately the two voices had become analogous.

Angela was wearing a black day dress, which made her look incredibly feminine and weak, and while she wasn't carrying a black-trimmed handkerchief that she wept into hysterically, she had lessened the amount of blush she normally wore, and refrained from lip-stick altogether. Her hair was held in a bun by a black clip, and the only jewelry she wore was a gold chain around her neck and her wedding ring.

"Oh, Hope. How sweet of you to come by. All the neighbors are avoiding us except for the Raines and the Tates. But of course they are suspects as well and are receiving the same ghastly treatment. The police keep coming by and demanding documents and asking more questions. If I weren't such a strong person, I would have collapsed into hysterics long since."

I pretended a look of confusion (for Eugene's benefit) and added, "So the police haven't figured out who killed Marcus yet?"

"No. As far as I can tell, they don't have a clue—excuse the pun." She gestured to the small group seated on the patio and raised her voice so that she could be heard by everyone. "We were just talking about forming a club—something like the Society of Suspects. I thought Criminal's Club sounds much more dramatic, but John assures me that it simply makes us all sound guilty."

I assured her in the politest terms that although Criminal's Club did indeed have a nicer ring to it (some white lies don't really count as lies), Society of Suspects was more appropriate. Angela waved her hand in the air in a sign of capitulation, and, after seating me, leaned back in her chair, her legs extended in front of her.

"It is all so dreadful," she disclosed in her ultra-feminine voice. "It really is very good of you to come. That wasn't just an act when I said that. Everyone but the curious and the gossipmongers are shunning us. I know you just needed to pick up the checks, but you could have just had them mailed. It shows what a dear you really are."

Eugene, leaning on the rail across from me, gloated.

Rosemary appeared in better spirits than when I had last seen her, and she enthusiastically joined Angela in defaming her friends and neighbors. "She's right. Yesterday several people stopped by simply to ask what the police had been doing at our house," Rosemary contributed. "And my lunch date at the club cancelled today. She said she was sick with a cold, but I doubt it." She frowned at the group in general, her nose twitching slightly.

Allan laughed at Rosemary's grimace. "My dear, she probably did have a cold. Helen adores gossip and nothing short of pneumonia would have prevented her from getting all the dirt on Marcus' death."

"Humph," Rosemary snorted. "If the police come back to our house one more time I will probably lose all my friends."

"I suppose the police are just doing their job," I suggested. "They probably don't like forcing their presence on you any more than you like it."

"You are too good to them, Hope. Police thrive on the misfortunes of others. Why else would they have entered that particular profession?" Allan argued.

"The policeman that visited me was very polite and apologetic," I disputed. Okay, so I left out the fact that he was also an old friend. He probably would have been polite and apologetic even if he weren't.

"Don't tell me you've been bothered by the police, too?" John asked incredulously. "What reason could they possibly have for suspecting you would kill Marcus?"

I shrugged. "I don't know. I think they are just checking out everyone who had the opportunity to kill him."

"Exactly. They have questioned Rosemary and I twice now," Allan said. "They came to our house the night of the murder, demanding to speak with us. Poor Rosemary had already gone to bed."

"It's true," Rosemary affirmed. "They actually dragged me out of bed the first time. Literally. They insisted I talk to them then and there. Nothing Allan could say would convince them to leave it until the morning. And they learned nothing that could help them."

"No? What did you tell them?" Angela asked, her face a mask of naive curiosity.

"Just the truth, me dear," Allan said in an equally dulcet voice. "I told them that I was in the living room the entire time, speaking with that Torrelli fellow, dozing a little, and reading a magazine. In short, just like a typical evening spent at home, except that I usually fall asleep to the television rather than to a hireling for some mob boss."

Evan looked sharply at Allan, and the latter apologized. "Sorry, Evan. I know he is a friend of yours. I meant no disrespect to him, but rather to the job in which he has found himself. He seems like a nice enough fellow."

"You are being too flippant about the whole thing," Rosemary admonished. "The police grilled us for hours. Nothing would do but they knew our every movement and how long going from here to there took and if anyone saw me. As if finding out that our closest neighbor had been murdered wasn't bad enough."

"What did you mean about going from here to there?" John asked.

"Oh, because I left the house to get that book from Angela. They wanted to know how long it took me to fetch it, how long to get back here, how long to get to Angela's room, and which door I used--that sort of thing. I told them I came back through the front door, gave the book to Angela, and went back downstairs."

"It was really unnecessary," Allan piped up. "I told them the same thing--that she was only gone for a little while and that I heard her come through the front door, then she said a quick hello to me before going upstairs to give the book to Angela. Why they needed to double check her story in the middle of the night is beyond me."

My mind snapped into action. That couldn't be right. Surely I would have heard anyone coming in the front door and calling out a greeting. I looked questioningly at Eugene, who shook his head and confirmed my suspicion that Rosemary was not being totally honest.

"My dear, you should have come in and given me the book. I nearly tripped over it on my way downstairs," Angela laughingly reprimanded.

"Your door was closed and I didn't want to intrude. Besides," she added a little guiltily, "I knew that if I saw you, Allan and I would be forced to remain even longer, and I had completely exhausted my store of political information for the evening. Any more discussions on politics and everyone would have known that I have no idea what I'm talking about."

Everyone laughed dutifully except Evan, who had been quietly sitting and watching us all intently. "Couldn't anyone have done it?" he blurted out. "Some stranger could have come in through the back door. I think the police have it all wrong. It was probably some lowlife high on drugs who entered the house thinking he could rob it. He probably had Dad write him a check at gunpoint, and then realized it could be traced, stabbed Dad, and tore up the check. I don't know why they think any of us did it."

Evan's vehemence startled the entire group, and John, sitting next to him, patted him on the shoulder. "That is probably exactly what happened," John said. "I'm sure the police are beginning to realize it was a stranger. The police just have to look at every angle, that's all. It's nothing personal."

"It *is* personal," Rosemary threw in. "The police think that all of us are capable of murder. I'm sorry, John, but I do take offense at that."

"I doubt it could be a stranger," I argued, mainly addressing Evan. "Your father was killed with a dinner knife, and unless the stranger found one lying around in the back hall or Marcus took one into his office with him, there would be no way for a stranger to get his hands on one."

"You tell them, Hope," Eugene cheered from the sidelines.

"Then it must have been one of the catering staff," Evan argued mulishly.

"But they all have alibis," I continued. "The police aren't dumb. At least not any dumber than the rest of us."

"So you think one of us did it?" Rosemary asked, her voice suddenly brittle.

Uh-oh! I didn't want to alienate these people unnecessarily. This was going to be tricky. "No. Maybe it was someone who came to the dinner or the party, took the knife or hid it, and came back later." I didn't believe that, but it sounded somewhat plausible and seemed to mollify the rest of the group.

Note to self: Do not accuse a family friend of murder. That is a fast way to social ruination and will infuriate well-bred yet implacable parents. Also, do not accuse your clientele of murder. That is a fast way to lose business.

"You're right, Hope," Evan said. "It wasn't a stranger per se, but it wasn't one of us."

You just keep telling yourself that, I thought.

"What a putz!" Eugene added.

Angela, fluctuating between nervous high spirits and morose sentimentality, abruptly changed the subject. "This is too morbid to discuss any longer. Let's talk about something else—anything else. What is going on in the world? I haven't read the paper or watched the news in days."

"I thought you didn't want to talk about a morbid subject," Allan said laughingly. "The news is never anything but depressing. I did once watch a news story about a newborn baby being raised by wild dogs for almost a week before someone found it, but that was a while ago."

"There are some new studies on the negative effects of global warming," I added. "Apparently the soil is also being contaminated by chemicals and is contributing to the phenomenon. And now the sexual orientation of birds has been affected, but I can't quite remember what caused that exactly."

"I had heard that too," Rosemary said. "The amount of carbon in chemically treated soil is far greater than they previously thought. But I didn't hear about the birds."

Rosemary and I seemed to be the only ones interested in discussing environmental damage, and the conversation lagged for a moment.

"Why don't you tell us how Dean's campaign is going?"

Angela asked John, her voice radiating enthusiasm.

"Not very well right now," John admitted. "It got out that he was present at a party where his host was murdered and the papers had a field day with it. Luckily, the other guy might have cheated on his taxes and definitely lied on his resume, so it might turn out all right in the end. Newspapers have a short memory."

"But the public doesn't," Eugene commented. "Who would you rather have as governor, someone who cheated on his taxes or someone who was a suspect in a murder investigation?"

"As a matter of fact, that was partly why I came over today," John continued smoothly. "I was wondering if you, Evan, and even you, Angela, were intending to donate to Dean's campaign?"

Evan assured John that since his father's will had left him almost three-fourths of Marcus' vast fortune, he most certainly intended to donate to his future father-in-law. He even went so far as to say he was offended that John even needed to ask such a question.

"I didn't want to take anything for granted," John declared, though it was fairly obvious to the rest of us that he hadn't expected anything less.

Evan, in a good-humor now that he had been able to do something beneficent for his future family, admitted that Colby would probably have made his life a living hell if he didn't give money. That was something on which everyone present agreed.

"What about you, Angela?" John asked. "Do you intend to make a decent contribution?"

In my opinion, a decent political contribution was about fifty dollars. You had to have a great deal of trust in the candidate to give more than that, and politics and trust were not usually bed partners.

"I have to think about it. Marcus left me very well provided for, but I have expensive tastes and need to think about my future. I'll discuss it with Dean when I see him next," she purred.

"I wonder what she's up to," Eugene said. "A little tit for

tat?"

No one else seemed to be bothered by the comment, and I wondered if Angela made a habit of keeping people waiting. It could even be a form of control.

"Marcus' funeral is scheduled for four days from now, Hope," Angela said, turning her attention back to me, "and Evan and I have finished all the funeral preparations. Marcus was rather specific in his will about his funeral. But I was wondering if you knew of a caterer that could be found at the last minute. I had planned to have the funeral reception at a restaurant, but Evan thinks we should have it here."

"I have the names and numbers at home of some caterers that might be able to help you," I replied. The last caterer had no desire to ever set foot back in this house. I was lucky if he would ever work with me again, actually.

"Thank you, that would be wonderful. I don't have to serve anything elaborate, do I?" she asked hesitantly.

"Not unless you want to. I don't usually deal with funerals, but at all the funerals I've been to most people serve hors d'oeuvres or have a light buffet. Some people even ask the mourners to bring a dish with them, though that is rare."

"I couldn't do that. Can you imagine what people would think if I made them do a potluck for the funeral? I would be the laughingstock of Everton," she giggled. "Not even the Plumbers would do that."

Rosemary smiled at Angela's bantering form of self-deprecation. "All anyone would think was that you were too busy to find a caterer."

"That's kind of you, Mrs. Tate, but we both know that's not true. I'm sure Hope only mentioned it to give me a laugh. Isn't that right, Hope?" she asked me.

I just smiled blandly. Her view of life was actually as warped as Susan's. I had met several people in reduced circumstances who were forced to rely on the charity of their relatives and friends when unexpected expenses arose.

"I've already received a ton of flowers for the cemetery and for the reception, so that shouldn't be an issue. Do I have to write thank-you notes to everyone who sends flowers and a card?" Angela asked me, her eyes pleading for a negative response.

John, who had gotten the information he needed, was looking bored, and Evan stared blankly at the nearest flowerbed. Rosemary was sending Allan exasperated looks that either said 'Where was she raised—a barn?' or 'Young people today lack the most basic of manners!'

"You definitely need to write personal letters of thanks to people who send flowers as well as to people who wrote you personal letters of condolence. If you have time you can also write thank-you notes to everyone who simply sends a stock bereavement card." That reminded me that I still needed to send Angela and Evan a card. I must be slipping!

"Forgot to send a card?" Eugene asked, watching my shifting expressions.

I hated it when he did that! He deserved the frown I sent him.

Before I could mentally chastise myself for forgetting the card and for letting Eugene make me feel badly, a figure approached the house from the direction of the Raines place.

Vincent Torrelli was easily recognizable by his dark hair and height, and Angela jumped up with only slightly less enthusiasm than she had when she greeted me.

"Hello, Vincent," she cooed. "Have you decided to lighten our moods or have the police been bothering you as well? They drove Hope into our arms, as you can see."

That was a blatant lie since she knew I was only here to pick up the checks, but Angela reveled in the dramatic.

"They came by and asked a few more questions yesterday, but nothing terribly alarming. I am here to see Evan, actually—not that I don't always enjoy your company," he added politely.

Evan, rather than looking nervous or annoyed, welcomed Vincent with enthusiasm. "I'm glad to see you, Vincent. Things have been very dull around here. If it weren't for Rosemary and Allan, as well as Colby and John, we would be without any amusement. And Hope, too, but she only just arrived," Evan clarified.

Vincent, amused at his warm reception, sent me a con-spiratorial look. "I'm glad I can help entertain you. It must be awful to have lost a father, and a husband."

Since no one looked sad or upset the comment was ignored and Vincent was offered a drink, which he declined on the grounds that he was only here for business.

"In that case I will take myself off. I should pay a visit to Dean since I'm in the area," John said. "I'll hold you to your word about the campaign, Evan."

Evan just smiled. "Of course. Send my regards to Dean and Susan, will you? Oh, and will you tell Colby I'll be over later to take her to dinner?"

"Sure. A pleasure seeing you Angela, Rosemary, Hope." He nodded at Allan and Vincent and strode toward the front of the house and the path that led directly to the Raines' front lawn.

"I hope my arrival hasn't spoiled the party," Vincent said with a mischievous grin.

"No, of course not," Angela assured him. "John was really just here on business, too. And Allan and Rosemary aren't leaving yet, are you?" she said, turning to them.

"No. We don't intend to leave until you've run out of iced tea," Allan assured her.

"Good heavens! I hope you don't mean to stay that long!" Angela exclaimed with feigned alarm.

"If you are going to be here for awhile yet, Vincent and I will go in and discuss our business. It shouldn't take long," Evan said, rising from his chair.

Vincent, who had just settled himself, was forced to rise as well, and accompanied Evan into the house.

"If you have the checks, I should go. I have a lot of work that needs to get done for the paper," I commented. If the party was breaking up, I wanted to take advantage of the opportunity.

Eugene winked at me and yelled, "Don't leave without me," before sprinting into the house behind Evan and Vincent.

"I'll go get them. The police still have the office closed

off, so I put them in my room. It'll be just a moment," Angela said as she gracefully swung her legs to the ground and rose out of her chair. "That poor caterer must wonder what kind of house this is, what with the owner being murdered and his check being held because it was locked in a drawer at the crime scene. I doubt he'll ever cater another of my parties." And with those final words Angela walked through the living room doors and disappeared from sight. She was so right.

Allan burst into laughter once Angela was no longer in earshot. "She's quite a character. I wonder how long she will stay in Everton. She would probably do very well in New York or Los Angeles."

"She'll stay until she finds a new husband or decides to look for one elsewhere," Rosemary answered. "I don't think she's the kind of woman who can be alone for too long."

No one said anything more until Angela returned to the patio, two checks flapping wildly in her left hand. "I was worried I had misplaced them, but here they are. Please tell the caterer how sorry I am."

"Thank you. I will. I doubt he holds you responsible. He is a very reasonable person," I lied. It was more likely that the caterer was calling all of her friends and telling them never to take a job in Everton because the people here were all insane.

"You will be at the funeral, won't you?" Angela asked, handing me the checks.

"Yes. And my parents will be as well," I answered.

She nodded. "That's nice. Thank you. Most of Marcus' friends were a great deal older than I, so I don't have much to say to them. The more people I know I can say anything to, the better I will feel."

Eugene dashed out of the house, running through Angela and her chair before coming to a halt. "Okay, let's blow this joint," Eugene said in some weird slang which sounded like it came straight from the mouth of a nineteen thirties gangster. Or was that how teenagers spoke now.

I am definitely going to have to cut back on the amount of television he is allowed to watch, I thought.

I said my goodbyes and slowly made my way back to the

car, Eugene urging me to hurry. When I reached the car and opened my door (allowing Eugene to crawl across my seat first because he was touchy about having to walk through the car door), Eugene blurted out, "They are all suspicious characters in my opinion."

"What makes you say that?" What wouldn't make him say that?

"I just heard Evan Whittington agree to pay a hefty sum of money to his friend almost immediately. And he sounded quite relieved to have the matter dealt with. That sounds like a motive for murder to me. And he didn't seem all that upset about his father's death. Or didn't you notice that his whole de-meanor has changed?"

"I did notice," I acknowledged. "He seems more cheer-ful and confident. It's amazing the affect one's parents can have." How would I behave if my mother died? The same? I might dread her disapproval but she hardly kept me under her thumb or lambasted me for every little thing.

"And that Torrelli fellow was very relieved to get the money. I think he is a little scared of his boss. Or maybe he just fears losing his job and being stuck with a large amount of debt."

"What about Rosemary Tate?" I queried.

"There is definitely something there. She told the police that she entered through the front door and called out to her husband, but that's got to be a lie. We would have heard her. And besides, when the two of you entered the living room her husband looked surprised to see her. She had to have come in through the back door, and I can only think of one reason for her doing so," Eugene said ominously.

"To think that any of them did it is ludicrous," I com-mented.

Eugene just shrugged. "Isn't it always the person you least suspect who did it—hence the idea of the butler?"

"I would have thought it was the person you most sus-pected that ended up doing it." Wasn't that usually the person with the biggest motive and opportunity?

"No, never that. Unless some strange character with a

weird past suddenly emerges into the spotlight, the killer has to be one of them. My vote is for Rosemary," Eugene deliberated.

Chapter Nineteen

The dead have no respect for the wishes of the living. If they did, they would die at a time that best fit the schedules of their friends and family. Their deaths would be expected and planned for, allowing the grief-stricken to properly mourn rather than be buried in funereal details. But this is almost never the case.

It certainly wasn't the case for Marcus Whittington. After Eugene started haunting me, I came up with a saying: "Difficult in life, difficult in death." Marcus Whittington was a prime example of this but in a different way from Eugene. I had no idea how Marcus was behaving in heaven (or wherever he ended up) but his departure from Earth was incredibly inconsiderate.

The evening before Marcus' funeral the weatherman announced that we were going to have record highs for the season. Eugene, who could not feel hot or cold, laughed himself silly at the thought of a bunch of self-righteous socialites wearing black and standing out in the hot sun while a priest delivered a lengthy sermon. I prayed that God would spare me from that ordeal. In this instance, God took Eugene's side.

I still had hope of a moderate day on the morning of the funeral, but that hope quickly vanished when I opened my front door. The temperature had already reached eighty, and by noon it would be in the nineties.

I slipped on a dark gray dress that was almost sleeveless (I wasn't going to be so crass as to wear a sleeveless dress to a funeral) and a pair of black sandals that had enough straps to make them look almost like regular heels. If the priest looked at me askance it wouldn't be because of my attire but because I was trying to pommel an invisible man.

I met my parents at their house, my father postponing his day of golf to attend the funeral (all his buddies were as well, since Marcus usually made up the fourth and they had yet to find a replacement). Eugene liked my father instantly, claiming he was "a fine man with a good sense of style." He also liked the fact that he was a doctor, since, according to Eugene, it showed that my parents were at least intelligent, and that somewhere deep down I probably had "some brains, though not too many".

We drove to the cemetery together, my mother expostulating on the new trend of fashions some of her students were attempting to adopt. Since everyone at The Sylvia Pearson School (For Silly Socialites) wore uniforms, I was certain this was simply a generalization about the teenagers she saw in the city. Eugene, now my mother's devotee, agreed wholeheartedly with everything she said, adding emphatic nods throughout the recital. It was a pity my mother couldn't meet him; she would love his utter devotion to "the old ways".

When we reached the cemetery it was to find that so many people were expected a valet service had been hired and uniformed ushers were directing mourners to the gravesite. I almost suspected that I was a part of some Hollywood extravaganza.

The casket, which had been placed next to the grave, was a dark mahogany with brass handles and white satin lining. It was ringed with large purple and yellow bouquets that were so massive that many of them could not stand on their own, while others were tilting dangerously close to the grave.

Angela had explained that Marcus wanted to combine his funeral and memorial service, which accounted for the nearly three hundred people sitting stiffly in rusty folding chairs at the edge of the lawn.

How many graves are being trampled in order to hold this monstrosity? I mused. Fifty? One hundred? That could be a lot of annoyed skeletons.

Eugene was looking particularly moody, and I wondered if he was disgusted with the size and ostentation of the gathering, or by the fact that his own funeral had been so poorly attended.

"I knew a lot more people than showed up at my funeral," he grumbled. "And I had to be more popular than this guy. It just shows you what money can do."

Ah! So it was the latter. Poor Eugene! I hope God spares me from witnessing my own funeral. I would be devastated if the only people who showed up were Jilly and her husband Martin (who would probably only attend because Jilly would force him to).

"Can you find us some seats?" my mother asked my father, who was already looking over the crowd for some gaps in the rows of chairs.

"Over here," he beckoned, and my mother and I dutifully followed.

"He was so well liked," my mother said, as she tried to wedge between a hefty man wearing a pin-stripe suit with a white carnation and the back of another chair.

I thought this comment might shake Eugene's faith in my mother, but he was too busy trying to assist her through the crowd. Every time it looked like she would stumble, Eugene would reach his hands out to steady her, only to find that he sailed right through her. As silly as he looked, his intention was honorable, and if it weren't for my father performing the same feat (and succeeding) my mother would likely have stumbled and torn a stocking. I was left to fend for myself, being young and spry, and managed to find the empty chairs with only a few minor mishaps to other people—but I'm sure the man with the large oval glasses was wearing thick shoes and socks, and didn't suffer too much.

When we were all settled in our seats, Eugene moved out of the crowd and stood near a beech tree. He didn't particularly enjoy the feeling of people walking through him, and as he told me later, the idea of someone sitting on—through—him was too much to bear.

While we waited for the service to start, my mother questioned me in a low whisper about the murder. "The police haven't found the killer yet?" she opened.

"No. But they still think it was one of the people at the dinner party," I responded, my voice equally low.

"Did Peter say whom they suspected in particular?" she

asked, her gaze furtively searching the crowd for Angela and Evan.

"No. Even if he did know, he wouldn't tell me. That wouldn't be professional." She probably expected that Peter would simply tell anyone who asked him politely.

"Do you see them?"

I knew she meant Angela and Evan, since everyone who attends a funeral is anxious to see how the bereaved relatives appear. If they are miserable, sad, or tear-stained, they are objects of pity, which make everyone still alive and in possession of their loved ones grateful. The guests get the opportunity to make token comments they are certain will bring a smile to the face of the bereaved, creating a sense of satisfaction in both parties. If the bereaved look nonplussed, the crowd is given the gratification of privately berating the relatives while telling them how strong they are to put on a brave face. Either way the onlookers go home satisfied (as satisfied as one can be by a funeral).

My father pointed out Angela and Evan, who were seated near the casket, though Angela was nearly hidden by a large grouping of yellow roses and calla lilies. She looked attractive and incredibly serene in her short black skirt and coordinating jacket, with not a trace of sweat on her. Her hair was coiled on top of her head and a shiny onyx necklace circled her throat. Every so often she would smile and nod at an acquaintance before returning her attention to the still casket. However, on closer inspection one could see that despite the outward calm, her hands were clasped tightly in her lap, causing Evan to keep whispering in her ear and pat her hand.

Evan was also wearing a dark suit, though traces of sweat could be seen gathering at his brow. He looked the picture of a dutiful son quietly mourning a beloved father. His face was neither deeply shadowed nor giddy, but rather accepting of his father's unfortunate fate. Colby sat on Evan's other side, silent and brooding. Her eyes rarely left the casket, and her mouth drooped more noticeably than usual. When her eyes did stray, it was to furtively seek out her mother's drawn and tired face. At each glimpse of it she would flinch and turn hastily away before repeating the process.

When Father Martinez rose to begin his sermon, the assembled crowd became eerily silent. I could hear a few nervous giggles from some elderly ladies seated to the rear of me, and some murmurs of haughty protest from the men seated to my left.

Father Martinez delivered a passionate, if terse, eulogy, ending with a denunciation of all sinners and criminals and a reminder to follow the Ten Commandments. Half of the audience began to look uncomfortable, several men pulling at their ties and hastily checking their watches. I would eat my skirt if even half of the audience could recite all ten, though in all fairness, I could only recall eight or nine of them myself.

I wasn't the only one to notice the tension in the crowd. Eugene started up from his undeserved place in the shade (it's not as if he even sweats) and hollered, "Take a look at the lot of them, Hope. I bet one of them makes a sign of guilt." I practically jumped out of my chair in fear that someone else had heard him, but the remainder of the crowd continued sitting docilely, waiting for the priest to end the service.

"Stop fidgeting, Hope. You're making people stare," my mother chastised. "If you are having so much trouble remembering the Ten Commandments you should start going to church again."

How is it that I am so easy to read?

"I do remember them." At least I was pretty sure I could list them all if I were handed a piece of paper. Well, maybe not all. Is eight out of ten good enough? The Sylvia Pearson School (For Bank-account Babies) kept a poster-size copy in the entrance hall, right next to a poster entitled "The Supreme Laws of Etiquette". That particular wall-piece had been added by my mother's predecessor and had been given a place of honor, surpassing even God's laws.

I focused back on the service, but Eugene was behaving in such a manner that I could not help but look his way. My eyes dutifully followed his dramatic gesticulations, but detective work was obviously not my forte. All I saw was Dean looking slightly pinched, while Allan and Rosemary bent to whisper to Angela, and Susan silently cried. Why she would cry over a man who hadn't liked her was difficult to comprehend, but I put it down to my mother's favorite reason—nerves.

Father Martinez came to an abrupt conclusion, startling everyone who had lost focus during the bit about lambs being led to slaughter (or maybe it was wolves in sheep's clothing). The only person who seemed unperturbed by the heat and the somberness of the occasion was Magdalena, who stood up and clapped her hands while shouting, "Amen, Father." A few people laughed at this, and someone in the back asked rather audibly if she was insane and thought she was at a church revival. She ignored the aspersion on her character and smiled graciously at the offender, causing him to admire the edge of his tie in a noticeably unnoticeable manner.

"Thank goodness that is over," my mother exclaimed. "It isn't healthy to be out here in this heat. Hopefully the reception will be air-conditioned."

And on that note we departed for the Whittingtons' abode.

————

"It's not that Evan and I don't mourn the loss of his father, it's just that all the plans have been made and the invitations sent out," Colby whined.

"I'm sure that still having the wedding is perfectly acceptable, despite the circumstances. Has someone been saying otherwise?" I asked politely.

"No. Not really. It's just that we don't want to do anything that would be considered gauche."

Too late for that, I thought. "Everyone will understand. You can hardly cancel all the plans at this date." Part of me thought I should be more understanding about her predicament, since holding a wedding so soon after a funeral was a bit odd, but it was hardly a newsworthy matter.

"Well, if you agree with us..." Her voice trailed off and I could sense that she was prepared to depart my company and seek worthier pastures.

"Don't let me keep you. I know you have a duty to Evan," I urged.

Without a response she walked away, though not in the direction of Evan, but toward her mother, who was looking slightly ill, no doubt from the large glass of whisky she was gulping.

"She just gets friendlier and friendlier," Eugene commented. "Is it too soon to depart? I'm beginning to tire of these socialites. God knows they certainly can't throw a good wake."

I didn't agree with Eugene on this point. The reception was vastly more entertaining than That Fateful Evening had been. Obviously the alcohol was flowing freely, because most of the guests were smiling and laughing and overindulging in lobster patties. Not standard funeral fare, but tasty nevertheless.

If one discounted the overwhelming amount of black, the event was almost festive—which was undoubtedly what was bothering Eugene. He had a very close-minded view of funereal gatherings. If people weren't crying, he wasn't satisfied.

Since Eugene knew I couldn't respond to him verbally, he continued to bluster on about the insincerity present in the modern family unit, lambasting that invention of the devil—television—which he himself was above watching. At least on a regular basis, he amended.

Magdalena strode over to me, a large, but untouched drink in her hand. "How are you, my dear? You look very nice in black." She glanced at the people around us and then lowered her voice. "Did you bring your *friend*?"

The way she said 'friend' made me cringe. He sounded imaginary, or worse.

"Yes, he's here. Just to the left of me."

"Oh, how marvelous. When are you going to come see me again? We have so much to talk about. You and Eugene have given me a new purpose in life—to discover all I can about the afterlife. I do so wish to find out if I will be reunited with Roger one day." She winked at Eugene, only missing his direction by a few feet, and then continued. "I expect you both to help me.

Perhaps we can start a weekly club---like bridge, but for ghosts and their earthly friends."

I gave her a slight chuckle. "And how do you plan on advertising for this club? If you put an add in the paper for a club that is exclusively for people haunted by ghosts, you are likely to get the wrong sort of members."

"You're right. Nut jobs. We don't want any crazy people joining us. That would completely destroy our credibility." She looked thoughtful for several moments, and then her face lit up. "Eugene will have to find the ghosts. And if he can't, we can consult a psychic. I'm sure a real psychic will be able to locate the kind of people and spirits that would be appropriate."

Eugene looked at Magdalena in amazement. "She's lost it. Maybe she won't be as helpful as we hoped."

"We shouldn't rush into anything just yet," I said quickly. "We don't want just anyone knowing about this."

"I suppose so. We'll wait and see how far we get on our own first." She looked slightly disappointed that she wasn't going to immediately become the center of a psychic network, so I abruptly changed the topic.

"This is a lovely reception." Good one, Hope--completely inane. Are you brain dead?

"Yes. People seem to like Marcus better now that he is dead," Magdalena added.

What does one say to that?

"That's a lovely dress. Where did you get it?" Hey, I tried.

Eugene snickered. "I'm out of here if you two are going to start talking about women's fashions. What are you, Pip, the poster-child for polite inanities?"

The fact that I had recently had a similar thought depressed me. What had my mother done to me? What had I done to myself?

I remembered why I hate funerals—they make one introspective. If I didn't leave soon I would be questioning every decision I had made in the last twenty years and start bemoaning my wasted existence. People joined the Peace Corps so that when they attended funerals (and weddings) they would be able to claim that their life had not been wasted and that they had actually done something to better the world. Was it really too late to join the Peace Corps? Was I going to have to live out the rest of my life as a social nonentity with a sneering ghost trailing behind me? Was I indeed destined to become the next Miss Marple?

Magdalena, not as in tune to my inner thoughts as she claimed, rambled on about a small boutique a few towns over, and how the owner of the store was a close friend of a close friend of a cousin of some famous actor that I must have heard of but couldn't place. Eugene departed rather abruptly--ostensibly to admire the food, but more probably to see what gossip he could gather.

Magdalena was claimed shortly thereafter by John, who, determined to prevent his mother from making a social gaffe, escorted her to the library on the basis that she must be exhausted and in need of a short rest. She left with a wave of her hand and fluttering of her limbs, all the while exacerbating John by stopping every few feet to exchange social pleasantries with everyone she saw, most of whom I suspect she didn't know.

Left to myself, I wandered over to the living room doors, hoping for some fresh air and a glimpse of my parents. I had stayed long enough to become sick of the color black, and I hoped that my father had come down with the same illness. With a little luck, I could be on my way home in a matter of minutes.

The front balcony was crowded, the outdoors seemingly cooler than the interior, which was crowded with overdressed, sweating bodies. I managed to wedge my way between an obese man dressed head-to-toe in dark grey and a petite woman wearing a massive hat adorned with ostrich feathers that had been dyed black. The effect was rather stunning, though purely in the style of a British soap-opera-gone-bad. It was the kind of hat Princess Diana used to wear to royal gatherings—the kind of hat that was continually bumping into the overdone coiffeurs of the surrounding women, and thus creating a mass of snarling socialites. Luckily, I was not a socialite, and was still learning how to snarl.

With little grace and no ease, I avoided several direct collisions, stepped on only a few toes, and parked myself safely in the rear of the balcony, directly outside the open library doors. While I was debating whether the air-conditioned interior of the library would be cooler than the bright outdoors, my suddenly acute hearing picked up soft voices inside the library.

With only a momentary sense of shame (undoubtedly the lack of shame being a side-effect of living with Eugene) I inched my way closer to the voices, while remaining hidden by the draperies. Payoff was sweet. A quick glance past the curtains showed me that Angela and Dean were having a cozy little chat. At least it looked cozy on Angela's part, as she was practically falling off the edge of the desk, where she was draped, in her attempt to latch onto Dean's lapel. Dean was squirming away from her, but with little success. Angela had a rather strong grip, and I could see her hands turning white with the effort to hold on to Dean.

Angela, her voice lilting and bell-like, was laughing at Dean's vain attempts and teasingly shaking her head. "Meet me tonight at ten at The Oaks."

Dean cringed and his voice cracked. "You know I can't. I have a career to think of. And if Susan found out..."

"You can. I'll make it worth your while."

Dean almost looked tempted, but remained silent.

Angela looked at him thoughtfully, before a rather alarming smile lit her face. "I have such a loose tongue sometimes. The things that I might let slip..." Dean looked panicked, and there was a long pause before Angela continued, "You know you really don't have a choice."

Dean nodded. "I'll try. But I can't guarantee anything. I have to make certain that Susan won't be around. She's been rather suspicious lately."

"I'm sure you'll take care of it. You have such a knack for eliminating problems."

"I don't know what you mean by that, Angela."

"Don't you, Dean? I was certain you did." With a small pounce, Angela landed on the floor, disentangled herself from

Dean, and was quickly walking out the door, leaving a distraught Dean in her wake.

I slowly moved away from the door, hoping my eavesdropping hadn't been noticed by any of the other guests. Before I had fully turned around, a voice whispered in my ear, "Not exactly Shakespeare, was it? I always think the villain and villainess should have long, passionate speeches, just like the heroes."

I jumped at the words, immediately backing up and bumping into a solid wall of a man. I turned, a denial on my tongue, when I saw that it was Vincent who had caught me out. It was clear from his amused expression that he neither wanted nor expected an apology or an explanation. "I don't agree. Sometimes saying less is more sinister than saying too much."

He smiled and said lightly, "Are you a theatre aficionado, a studier of human psychology, or do you simply have experience with criminals?"

"None, I'm afraid. And you? Are you fond of dramatics, or do you simply have a long association with criminals?"

"Both."

"And psychology? Don't tell me it was your major in college?" If he had majored in psychology, I would eat the hat with the ostrich feathers.

"Let's just say that I find a knowledge of human nature useful in my line of work. Don't you?"

"I suppose so. I've never really thought about it that way, but there are some distinctive personality types that I have come to recognize over the years."

"For instance..."

"Eager social climber, doting parent, political machine, bored housewife." And a few more unmentionable ones, I thought.

"Grief-stricken widow?"

I blushed. I had no reason to be ashamed of Angela's obvious insincerity, but I somehow felt it looked bad for womankind.

Vincent didn't seem to notice my discomposure. "Jealous wife. Pampered daughter. Inadequate son. Pompous CEO. Have I missed any?" he joked.

I was not going to be drawn into this discussion.

"Fraudulent eccentric," he continued.

"Hey, that's not fair. Magdalena isn't a fraud. She really is eccentric." That didn't sound very complimentary, but it was true. It was definitely time to send some psychology his way. "You missed intimidating thug."

He just laughed. "Doesn't the nosy newspaper columnist mean an intimidating, yet charming, affable and acutely intelligent thug?"

"I believe that was what the inquisitive, yet polite, gracious, and attractive columnist meant." I responded just as jovially.

"Naturally, that was what I meant," he smirked back.

At least he thought I was attractive, which neutralized the 'nosy' bit. "But these are just stereotypes. No one is really black and white, but varying shades of gray."

"Of course," he agreed, a twinkle in his rather perceptive eyes. "Which is why Caesar's wife is not above suspicion."

I was about to argue the point, when Vincent stopped me rather effectively by simply speaking over me. "But we can debate it over dinner. Say yes. I believe you have already realized that I don't take no for an answer."

My parents materialized in front of me, and I was saved an immediate response. "I'll get back to you," I hedged.

My mother, seeing me talking with a good-looking man, was rapidly making her way to my side. "Hope, your father and I were about to leave, but if you wish to stay, we will understand."

Note to self: Never attend a social event of any kind with one's parents--especially if one has a husband-seeking mother.

"Actually, I'm ready." I gave Vincent a classic goodbye smile (the kind that is almost an apology, or at the very least an explanation without words) and moved off with my mother, who had thankfully spotted a dear, old acquaintance of about eight weeks, with whom it was absolutely necessary for her to converse.

Now all I had to do was gather my belongings, including the elusive Eugene, and make that mad dash for the car. With the funeral down, there was only one more major event to go—Colby's wedding.

Chapter Twenty

Time stops for no one. Not the living. Not the dead. Not the incredibly exasperated victim of otherworldly machinations who simply needs a long vacation in Tahiti. Sans ghost.

The week following the funeral was one of chaos. My editor decided to change some columns at the last minute, sending me into a flurry of activity. My piles of letters had to be resorted and reread, responses written, and then checked for the common mistakes an overworked person makes.

I don't want to lie and say that there weren't any mistakes in my work, but there were not nearly as many as Eugene claimed, which I was vociferously telling him when the phone at my apartment rang, halting my moratorium on grammatical changes in sentence structures in the last fifty years.

"Well, aren't you going to answer that?" the pudding-faced prat asked, all innocence. As if I didn't know that as soon as I turned my back on him I was going to find my desk in disorder and several key components of my work scattered on the floor. And if I uttered one complaint about the mess, I would have to suffer through Eugene's guilt trip about my not being a supportive friend while he was learning the intricacies of moving objects. Please! He couldn't convince Inspector Clouseau of his innocence.

"Don't touch anything," I warned.

"Who? Me? Really, Hope, you are so paranoid," he said, a large grin spreading across his face.

Uh-oh. What was he up to now? I hated to turn my back on him and cross the room, but I was left with little choice when the phone continued to ring insistently.

I managed to walk to the phone almost completely backwards, though I had to turn my back on Eugene to find the receiver. "Hello?"

"Ah-choo."

I flinched, holding the phone away from my face. Good thing germs can't travel through the phone lines. "Hello?" I repeated, having a good guess as to who this was. The high-pitched sneeze gave it away.

"Hope? Sorry about that." There was a slight pause, followed by a loud "Ah-choo," the surprise of which caused me to drop the phone onto the table. Eugene snickered, and I pretended not to hear him, turning my back on him completely.

" Is that you Veronica?"

"Yeah. Sorry. I have a horrid cold, and I could just kill my boyfriend for giving it to me. I should have known that I would get it. I mean, he was coughing and sneezing all over the place. And he keeps leaving his dirty Kleenex lying around. I mean, can you imagine? No wonder I'm sick, huh?" Even with a stuffy nose and clogged lungs she managed to get enough air to talk a mile a minute.

"That's too bad. I hope you start feeling better soon."

"Thanks. I knew you'd be sympathetic. My mom says it's my own fault for dating a man that can't spell his own name, although that isn't true. He can spell perfectly fine. Maybe he isn't the smartest guy, but that doesn't matter. I mean, I'm no Einstein either."

She sounded like she was about to start reciting all her boyfriend's accomplishments, so I mercilessly interrupted her. "I think you're very smart. Now what can I do for you?" Getting to the point was what was needed in situations like this.

"What? Oh, yeah. It's been pretty crazy around here, but I managed to do that research for you. You know? For that wedding announcement you have to write. I know you said the wedding isn't for a few more weeks, but I wanted to make sure I finished it all in plenty of time. I have all the info here, if you want to come get it. All the editors are in a meeting that should last the entire day, so it is pretty quiet too."

Bless her heart. Veronica might be ditzy sometimes, and talk too much all the time, but she was a nice person. And obviously an understanding one, because I most definitely did not want to see my editor today, or any other day this week, for that matter.

"Great. I'll come by in about an hour. I have some stuff to drop off anyway."

"Okay, see you then," she replied, pausing between each word. Before she had hung up, I heard a loud "Ah-choo" and then a murmured apology and a sniffle.

I turned around, prepared to pick up any papers Eugene had strewn across the floor, only to find the room perfectly tidy. My latest columns were sitting exactly where I had left them. The stacks of letters were still in neat piles and organized by subject. Nothing had been moved. Boy, did I feel like a jerk for even thinking Eugene would trash my desk just to annoy me. After all, I reminded myself, he is quite amiable most of the time; he just gets antsy when he is bored.

Eugene didn't say a word, just looked at me, the picture of ghostly innocence. "Is everything all right?"

"Yes. Veronica finished doing the historical research on the Whittington and the Raines families. I'm going to go down to the office and pick up the info, and I can drop off my columns at the same time." Since Eugene was obviously sorry for his earlier comments about my ineptitude at writing, and appeared to be behaving himself, I was ready to feel magnanimous. "Would you like to come?"

Eugene smiled brightly. "Okay. I wouldn't mind seeing the office again." He sighed deeply, undoubtedly about to launch into a self-pitying speech, when he paused and glanced at me, a sharp look in his eyes. "Have they found anyone to replace me? Well, replace probably isn't the right word since I am—was— one of a kind in the business. Have they found a substitute for me?"

"A substitute?" I paused to think about how to continue. Eugene would be hurt if he knew that within a week of his death he had been replaced, and by a well-known critic from San Francisco. I didn't want to cause him any pain, since he didn't really have anything to live for anymore. Well, 'live' might not be the right word. 'Exist' maybe? Let's just say that the reality of his former life was not nearly so grand as he had believed. "I daresay they have. I mean they probably had to hire someone in the meantime while searching for a critic—a gourmand—that would be able to live up to the standards you set." That sounded good. No one could fault me for being tactless in this instance.

"True. They do have a business to run. I imagine that it will take a while before they can find someone with the qualifications I had."

I wondered exactly what Eugene's qualifications were, but I refrained from commenting. He was beginning to look rather woebegone.

"Why don't we get going? I'll park near that new gourmet food shop you are always pointing out, and we can go inside and see what they have. But Jezebel has to stay here or in the car."

He agreed, and I grabbed the items I would need, and headed for the door, Eugene following close behind me. As I opened the drawer in the stand by the front door, where I always kept my car keys, Eugene and Jezebel went right by me, straight through the front door, disappearing from view.

It occurred to me that he was probably so excited about visiting the store, that he was impatient to be gone. That thought didn't last long. As a matter of fact, it lasted just until I realized that my car keys were no longer in the drawer. They were not anywhere in sight. They weren't under the stand, on the coffee table, on the kitchen table, under the sofa, or anywhere in the living room. My mother was continually drilling into my head the idea that ladies did not swear. She would have been sorely disappointed in me. And God probably wasn't going to be letting me into heaven anytime soon either. Of course I feared my mother more than God, so that thought was only slightly disturbing.

I silently cursed myself (again) for having turned my back on Eugene even for a moment, and I continued to curse myself for the five minutes more it took to discover my car keys, strangely enough, hidden underneath some lettuce in the refrigerator.

When I did arrive outside, car keys in hand, it was to

find Eugene sitting inside the car, tapping his watch, and demanding that I inform him if I was going to primp every time I left the house.

While his comment wasn't totally unjustified, since I had to change my skirt once I discovered that my living room floor was not nearly as clean as I had imagined, I nevertheless wanted to wipe that smug grin off his face with a dirty dishtowel. The picture of his perfect self soiled with dirty linens was so agreeable to me at that moment, that I simply smiled and ignored his teasing. It would take more than a childish ghost to make me lose my cool.

As it turned out, it would take a childish ghost, several broken jars of jam, a trail of loose dogs, and a skinned knee.

The broken jars of jam were from the gourmet food shop. They were a delicious blackberry, and prior to breaking had been stacked neatly in a pyramid along the sidewall of the store. Unfortunately, they met an untimely demise.

Maybe it was my fault. Maybe I wasn't firm enough with Eugene and Jezebel. Maybe I should have been watching closely to monitor that Jezebel did not escape the car. Or maybe it was the fact that I couldn't actually touch Jezebel to catch her when she did escape. Still, I'd like to think it was Eugene's fault, since the dog actually listened to him. But it would have been unfair to lay the blame solely on him. He couldn't have known that Jezebel would see a table stacked with samples of toast and jam and head straight for it. He couldn't have known that Jezebel was getting good at touching things and managed to lightly brush one jar of jam. He couldn't have known that that particular jar would be pivotal in keeping the pyramid steady. He couldn't have known that the pyramid would collapse, causing blackberry jam and shards of glass to go flying in every direction. He couldn't have known that I would be standing close to that pyramid in an effort to rein in Jezebel. He couldn't have known that several other people were also standing near that pyramid.

In the end, four customers ended up splattered with jam, myself included, though no one was actually cut by the glass. Since no one visibly touched the pyramid, there was no one to blame. But still, I felt guilty and embarrassed and hurried out of the store, Eugene dragging Jezebel by the collar directly behind me. He wasn't laughing or smiling, so I suspected that he was as embarrassed as I was. No doubt he thought I would never take him to another gourmet food shop again.

I wasn't surprised when a few stray dogs started barking at me as I walked by. I wasn't surprised when a few more dogs started following me, sniffing my legs, my skirt, and the air behind me. I wasn't surprised when a smallish dog took one look at my entourage and me and fled, knocking over several pedestrians in the process. I was surprised when one of those pedestrians turned on me and started lambasting me for my behavior. I wasn't certain what I had done wrong, but I kept my mouth shut, and let the older man have his say. I couldn't say who looked more a fool--me, being followed by the canine collective, or the man shouting at the top of his lungs that people who didn't put leashes on their dogs should be fined. Since none of the visible dogs were mine, and that fact was fairly obvious to everyone else, I simply walked away, shooting Eugene the nastiest look I could muster.

We managed to get to the newspaper building without further incident, and I decided to clean up a little before heading upstairs. I shouldn't have been surprised that Eugene and Jezebel followed me into the ladies' room, but I was.

"What are you doing in here?" I demanded sharply, frantically checking that all the stalls were empty.

"I've never been in the ladies' room before," Eugene said slowly, his eyes glancing around in curiosity. "It's much nicer than the men's room. Your mirror is bigger, and you have more stalls. I've never been a urinal sort of person."

Dying had obviously turned Eugene's brain to mush. Not only was he in the ladies' room, which the living Eugene would never have done, but he was making generalizations about what type of people use different waste disposal systems. Talk about an uncivilized comment. And what was a 'urinal sort of person' anyway?

"Would you get out of here, please? I don't want someone to come in here and see me talking to myself. It's bad enough that I am covered in jam, without having people think that not only am I sloppy, but crazy as well."

"I think your priorities are all wrong. Wouldn't it be worse to have people think you are crazy rather than sloppy?" Eugene quizzed me, trying to lighten the mood.

It wasn't working. "Just get out of here. You shouldn't be in here. It's wrong."

"Sorry. I just wanted to apologize. You make it awfully difficult, you know. If I had known Jezebel was going to cause trouble, I would have insisted she stay in the car. Although I am slightly pleased that she is making such progress," he added unabashedly.

"Apology accepted. Now will you go?" I asked, in a slightly better humor. It was rare to have Eugene apologize, and just knowing that he was capable of it was a relief.

"Sure. But Hope, don't bother to straighten up. It's really quite hopeless," he insisted, while he and Jezebel headed out the door.

That did it. I walked into a stall and slammed the door behind me. I should have known that the door wouldn't stick, but rather bounce back, hitting me hard in the legs, scraping me knee, and causing me to wince in pain. If I had hurt myself I knew it was my own stupid fault, but that didn't stop me from shocking God yet again.

Note to self: Always carry Band-Aids in one's purse. Along with toilet seat covers, extra Kleenex, and spot removers. An extra pair of stockings might come in handy as well. Of course, if one's mother is the headmistress of The Sylvia Pearson School (For Young Ladies Who Desire a Moneyed Marriage), these items, along with lipstick, foundation, and a hairbrush, should already be in said purse, and woe to the woman who is unprepared.

By the time I emerged from the bathroom, I had managed to wipe off most of the jam, although that left some bizarre wet spots on my skirt which I hoped would fade quickly, had put on some lip stick, washed my sticky legs (after having removed and discarded my stockings) and brushed my hair.

While completing these tasks, I had a few moments to ponder exactly what type of person preferred urinals to regular toilets. It was incomprehensible to me and I was secretly grateful that Eugene was not the sort of person that preferred urinals. In my feminine ignorance on the subject I could only imagine that urinals were incredibly smelly, messy, and unattractive. Not that toilets were attractive, but urinals were undoubtedly worse. Give me a toilet and a bidet anytime. While I was on the subject, I wondered how some of those European women could handle those strange toilets that were no more than a hole in the floor with swirling water. That was just too much for a clean person to take. Being able to pee standing up had never been a goal of mine.

While Eugene and I walked upstairs, he pointed out to me the minute changes that had occurred since his death: the sales department had added another member; the carpet on the first floor had been cleaned; Jerry had gotten a new computer; Winston was using a different coffee mug; and John the custodian had changed shifts. Eugene seemed greatly intrigued by these changes, and I realized how limited his life, or rather his death, had become. It was sad that I was the only person with whom he could speak (not that I wasn't a good conversationalist), and that he had no job to occupy his time. When Winston getting a new mug was the highlight of my day, I would probably kill myself out of desperation.

It occurred to me that maybe Eugene could take up art classes. He could practice at home (if he could really master holding a paintbrush) and maybe audit some at the local community college. I say 'audit' because that would be exactly what a ghost would have to do. It sounded like a good idea and I was determined to suggest it to him the next time we were alone. As a matter of fact, there were a lot of classes he could attend. They had film classes, cooking classes (although the thought of Eugene around cooking utensils made me cringe), language classes. They even had dog-training classes. Yes, I would definitely suggest it.

As I reached the top of the stairs, I was greeted by a loud

sneeze and a high-pitched apology from Veronica. She was dressed in pale magenta sweats, which closely matched her nose and eyes, and her hair was somewhat untidy. A box of Kleenex was clutched in one hand, and some papers in the other. "I'm glad you're here, Hope." She sneezed loudly, grabbed a Kleenex from inside her sleeve, and then seemed to choke on phlegm.

"Why aren't you home? You are obviously really sick. I hope it wasn't for me. This stuff wasn't that important. You being healthy is."

"I'm okay. Really, I am." Sniff, sniff. "It's just a cold." Sniff. "No big deal." This feeble declaration was punctuated by another loud sneeze that was powerful enough to send a spray of germs over the entire landing, despite her attempt to cover it. "Sorry."

"That's okay. Are you sure you don't want to go home? Everyone would understand."

"No. I don't want to waste a sick day if I don't have to." She moved in closer to me, and I resisted the urge to step back. It would be very poor manners to act as if she were a leper. Seeing that I remained still, she continued in a nasally whisper, "My boyfriend and I are going to the Caribbean later this year and I am worried that my vacation days won't be enough and I will have to use up some sick days as well."

"Good thinking," came out of my mouth, but I doubt it sounded sincere. I would hate to see her end up with pneumonia because she was worried she wouldn't have enough vacation days.

Eugene must have been thinking along the same lines, since he spat out "idiot" and stalked away.

Veronica and I walked back to my desk while she tried to chatter about the planned vacation, but only ended up squeaking out a few words between sneezes. When the sneezes had finally abated, her nose had been blown, her eyes wiped (with a different Kleenex, Thank God), and her papers put down, she began to gather up the research she had done for me.

"I did a background search on as many people in the family as I could, and especially on the parents and the bride and groom. I also tried to find out as much as I could about marriages and employment for all of them, in case the family wants a really drawn out announcement. I don't see why just mentioning names and locations isn't enough," she sputtered, before wiping her nose again.

I heartily agreed!

I could see the pile of Kleenex on the desk growing, and I slid the garbage can closer to her, hoping she would take the hint.

"They want everyone to know how wonderful both the families are, and how they have been important members of the community for several generations. Especially now, after the murder."

Veronica nodded and dropped another Kleenex on the desk.

I sighed. She wasn't getting the hint.

"I think part of the problem is that they read that obituary on Douglas Wilcox a few months back—you remember, the one that was spread over four pages--and they decided that their families are wealthier and older and deserve equal attention," I said, raising my eyes to the heavens.

Maybe I could take a blank piece of paper and push the Kleenex into the garbage can. I opened the drawer in front of me, searching for anything large to use as a sort of shovel.

Eugene had come up behind me while I was searching, and pointed out an index card. "If you hold the card vertically it should be tall enough that you don't have to touch any part of the Kleenex. It's thicker than computer paper so it should be even better."

Thank goodness Eugene understood cleanliness (personal cleanliness anyway). It would have been much harder to live with someone who required a constant explanation of one's actions.

"Even so, it seems," sniff, "a bit much. There were some holes in the research though. I could dig deeper if you want, but for one thing, I couldn't come up with the name of Marcus Whittington's first wife."

"Really? That shouldn't have been hard." Great! I just

know that Susan and Colby would insist on having the first name of Evan's mother in the article. If worse came to worst, I suppose I could just ask one of them. They had to know it. They had probably checked his pedigree right after the first date.

"Yeah. You'd think that. But I couldn't even find a copy of his marriage license or certificate. Maybe they weren't married in this state," Veronica said gloomily.

"There wasn't even an obituary for her? I think she died. Or maybe they were divorced. I just can't remember." I covertly slid a few of the Kleenex closer to the edge of the desk. Veronica seemed completely oblivious to what I was doing, and I debated simply doing one big, dramatic sweep. The only thing that held me back was that I would probably end up embarrassing the girl if she thought I was finding fault with her.

"Nothing at all. Maybe she died somewhere else, or was divorced somewhere else. I couldn't say. And the only obituary that was really relevant was for a…" she shuffled through the papers in front of her, "Roger. And I doubt that you are going to want to mention him in the article, at least not how he died. He was a big shot businessman apparently, but that intelligence didn't—"

She paused, holding her breath, and then let out a giant sneeze, blowing a few of the Kleenex back toward me.

Here we go again, I thought, pushing the Kleenex slowly back to the edge of the desk.

Veronica took a deep breath and rushed to complete what she had been saying. "Didn't convert into his personal life. He died by falling off a roof or a ladder or something. Apparently he was doing some patching on a roof."

That didn't seem right. Someone had told me differently. What had I been told? Something to do with gardening, perhaps? It took me a moment, but my conversation with Susan came back to me. "I thoght he was cleaning out the gutters."

"I don't think so. I'm pretty sure the story said he was doing some roof patching. Anyway, it wouldn't have been the right time of year to clean out gutters, would it?"

I couldn't answer that, having never cleaned out a gutter in my life, but I doubted it mattered. The truth was, it was a rather embarrassing accident, and Veronica was right in that the family was not going to want it mentioned in the article.

"Anything else of note? Skeletons in the closet? Anything like that?" I joked.

"Probably," said Eugene, who was watching me bat at the Kleenex with my index card every time Veronica looked away. "They're involved in murder aren't they? There are probably several other murders lurking in both families' history. Maybe a few Black Widows." He said the last with a bit of relish, and I suspected he had been watching more film noir while I was asleep.

He was right that one of them was a murderer, and that made me wonder if he was right about the skeletons. What other secrets did those families have? Were the skeletons in their closets real ones? It was a truly disturbing thought, and I decided that the announcement was only going to briefly touch on the family histories. I could probably find enough nice stuff to say about Colby and Evan--if I tried really, really hard.

"Not much. I pulled out any articles our paper has ever had on anyone in those families. There was a lot of business and political stuff, which I only glanced through. A few pictures from weddings and engagements, and a lot of short announcements, a fact which didn't seem to bother any of the other relatives," she said pettishly.

"I know. This is a real pain. But I appreciate everything you did. You went far beyond what I would have done," I said soothingly. She looked like she was about to fall over.

"Thanks. I just wanted to do a thorough job. And like I said when I volunteered, I had the time." She sneezed again, and then caught sight of me slowly moving the Kleenex. Her face turned beet red, although I suspect quite a bit of that was due to a fever, and she stammered an apology. "S-sorry. I'm such an idiot. I didn't even think about what I was doing." With a sweep of her hand she knocked all the Kleenex into the garbage can and gave me a sheepish look. Now I felt like the ass.

I was about to tell her that I was simply playing a form of basketball with her Kleenex, when a bellow from Eugene brought me up short. I looked to where he had moved, and saw that he was standing over a box on the floor. The box seemed to be full of a variety of odds and ends, including a frame, a large paperweight, some papers, and a couple of vases.

If Veronica noticed my abrupt turn she didn't say anything, although this could be because her face was currently buried in a Kleenex. A few more, and she would have finished the entire box.

"Veronica, what's in that box on the floor over there? The one with the picture frame?"

She looked up, her eyes watering while she tried to focus on what I had pointed to. "Oh that. That's Eugene's personal items. We had them boxed the other day and weren't sure what to do with them, so they have just been sitting there." She sneezed again, grabbed a Kleenex, and wiped her nose with it.

Eugene was reverently touching the objects, and Jezebel, who had skipped over to his side, was smearing her nose over the ones Eugene had missed. It was heartbreaking to see Eugene look so forlorn.

"Are they giving them to a relative of his, or something?"

"There is his cousin, at least I think he is Eugene's cousin. He works at the law firm with my uncle. He's going over everything in Eugene's apartment to sell or whatever it is they do with a dead person's things. I guess that box will be taken over there. I should probably call the guy to come and pick it up." She looked into the Kleenex box but it was empty, and she frowned, turning around to search other desks.

"I'll take the box and drop it off at Eugene's apartment or the cousin's office. I'd like to see what Eugene's place looked like anyway."

"Yeah, me too. I bet the walls are covered with nothing but pictures of Eugene. And I bet his bedroom has lots of mirrors," Veronica said, still searching for more Kleenex. "Not that I want to speak ill of the dead," she said quickly, looking embarrassed.

I doubted Eugene would have a bedroom full of mirrors, but it wouldn't surprise me if he had his own wall of fame, covered with awards and trophies and pictures of himself with famous people.

"I'll take the box with me today and you can call me with his cousin's phone number."

Eugene, who had sauntered back to me looking grumpy, had brightened at that and even deigned to smile on me.

"Okay. I appreciate that. It's been getting in the way of the filing cabinets, but no one had the heart to move it into the storage closet."

I really hoped that when I died no one moved my personal belongings into a storage closet. It did seem like a rather callous thing to do, even if the person was dead and couldn't object. Well, usually dead people couldn't object. Lately I was finding that dead people could object to a lot of things.

After helping Veronica locate another box of Kleenex, I picked up the box of Eugene's belongings and headed back to the car, Eugene and Jezebel trailing me contentedly. I somehow managed to get home without incident, and lugged the box inside with me, setting it gingerly on the coffee table.

Eugene was so excited that he couldn't manage to grab hold of anything, although I imagined most of the stuff in the box was heavy enough that he would probably have had to put in a lot of effort anyway.

"Hurry up, Hope. You're taking too long. How hard is it to lift things out of a box?" Eugene complained.

"Sorry, but I don't want to drop anything," I snapped back. If this is how he was going to repay me for my efforts, I was going to start acting childish and leave the room. He can get everything out on his own.

But the thought of the mess that he would probably make decided me against any childish course of action. I grimaced and began to sort through the box.

The first items were unopened mail and half-finished columns that I put aside, holding little interest for Eugene, and even less interest for me. Several awards were set in wooden frames, and Eugene smiled smugly at me, pointedly asking me where my awards were.

"I'm too young to have numerous awards. They don't give them out to the younger people because they don't want the older columnists to feel bad." I looked as smug as he had a moment before, and he just laughed and moved onto the next item.

It was a photograph of a plump woman in her mid sixties, wearing a dark purple pants outfit, with a small gold chain around her neck, and gold drop earrings. Her gray hair was pulled back into a bun, and she was genuinely smiling at the camera. I could see a few crooked teeth, but they all appeared to be hers, which made them seem endearing.

"Is this your mother?" I asked him.

"Yes. Beautiful, wasn't she?" he said reverently.

I looked at the photo. I would never have described the woman as beautiful. She did look cheery and pleasant and comfortable. She looked like the kind of grandmother little kids want--the one who would always have cookies and milk waiting, and a game of checkers going on the porch. In short, she seemed to be nothing like Eugene.

"She appears to have been a lovely sort of person," I said. That was quite close to beautiful, even if I was referring to her personality and not appearance. Hopefully Eugene would take it as the compliment I intended.

"Mmm. She was. She raised me by herself. She did everything for me."

I thought he was going to cry, but he held himself in check. I suddenly felt rather awkward. My own mother was great in her own unique way, a fact I had realized long since, even if we didn't always see eye to eye. Or ever see eye to eye. But Eugene held his mother up like she was a saint. It made me rather envious, but also rather uncomfortable. I hoped Eugene wasn't going to turn out all Norman Bates-ish.

"It sounds like she was a very devoted mother."

"Yes. It was tough growing up with only a mother, because I had to work to help support us since I was a kid. My family didn't pitch in at all. And I think my mother was too proud to ask for their help." He looked up at me, and said, "Did you know I intended to join the army?"

Whoa! That came out of nowhere. And it was the most ridiculous thing I could imagine. I could see Eugene in a circus before I could see him in the army. But I restrained myself from guffawing loudly, pointing at him, and flopping onto the floor in a fit of hysterics. "No."

"I did. I know it's hard to believe, because I am so...polished."

I couldn't help but smile at that. I'm pretty sure he had intended to say 'superior' but held himself back for my sake.

"But I wanted to join," he continued. "All the kids on my block joined. But not me. I stayed home because I had to support my mom, and army pay wasn't going to be enough."

I was surprised that he didn't sound bitter, since most people would be, but he sounded proud of himself. I guess he had a right to be. Not a lot of people would give up their dreams to stay home for their mother. I probably wouldn't.

"In the end it was for the best. I got a good job at the newspaper and worked my way up to a well-known columnist, became a respected community member, while all the kids on my block ended up as beer-bellied couch potatoes." He patted his slightly chubby belly as if to prove to me that his belly was superior to any other belly I could come across.

I wanted to laugh at the way he had puffed up like a peacock. "When did she die?"

"Three years ago. It was tough because she was really the only relative I had. At least the only one I could respect. The rest of my family is a bunch of schmoes. I think you saw that at my funeral."

"I didn't notice. They can't all be bad. What about your cousin? The lawyer?"

"The perfect cousin. The successful cousin. The slimy, cold-blooded cousin."

"If he's slimy and cold-blooded, he can't be perfect," I protested.

"You'd think that. But my family regards him as the cream of the crop. He is the best looking, the best educated, he has the prettiest wife, the nicest house. Do I need to go on?"

"No. Everyone has a perfect cousin. I do. Mine is a doctor in California. And she is on a medical news program once a week. And she is gorgeous." I hated that I sounded like I was bitter.

"Let me guess. She is also married and has kids," Eugene predicted.

"Only one kid," I protested weakly.

Eugene laughed. "And your mother holds her up to you as the epitome of everything you should be."

"Of course. Didn't yours with your cousin?"

"Nope. The rest of my family did, but not my mom. Everything I did was wonderful to her." He looked down at the photo again, moving his fingers over the glass. "If there is a heaven, I'll get there, if just to be with her again," he said with a sudden vehemence.

I hoped he was right, since I was counting on that fact as well.

"Let's put this stuff back in the box. Did you want me to look at your mail? And what about the unfinished columns? Should I throw them out?"

"No. Just shove it all back in there." He paused and looked at me uncertainly. "You don't suppose you could put up this picture of my mom, so I could look at it?" He sounded like a little child, and I realized that he didn't have a home anymore. Nothing here was his, and the sight of a few of his personal items was reminding him of all that he had lost.

Oh God. I am way out of my depth here! I should have been a psychologist. But if I had been, I probably would never have met Eugene and wouldn't be in this position. Of course that was what I wanted, and just reconfirmed that I should have indeed become a psychologist.

So what did I say to Eugene? I didn't want to insult him, but I just couldn't hang up his mother's picture. "The thing is, Eugene, how could I explain to people why I have your mother's picture out? People would really think that was strange, especially since I never met her."

"I suppose so." He sounded glum, and I actually thought that his hiding something from me, or knocking over a lamp would be a good thing.

"What if I put it in a drawer, face up, so all you had to do was open the drawer?"

He continued to look sour.

"I could hang it up on the side of the refrigerator in a magnet frame, I suppose."

He just stared at me, looking rather disgusted. That was just too bad. I wasn't going to hang up a picture of his mother where anyone could see. I was willing to hang it up where no one would look, but I wasn't sure he would go for that. But it was worth a try. "How about I hang it up in the back closet? There's a light in there, and I know you can turn on lights. That way you could go in there and not be disturbed."

"You want to put my mother's photo in a closet?" he said slowly.

Uh-oh. "Of course not. But when you think about it, it's not such a bad idea." Okay, think fast Hope, because you are about to talk yourself into a corner. "You should have your own private space, where you can put your awards and stuff. I could clean out the back closet and you could put whatever you want in there. It's a walk-in closet. I could even put a chair in there. It could be your own private sanctuary." Now I was just winging it.

But I seemed to have hit a chord with Eugene. "You would let me put whatever I want on the wall—my photos and awards. I would get a chair. And there is a light?"

"Yes. Definitely."

"What about a dog bed?"

"I'm sorry?"

"There's room for a dog bed for Jezebel in there, too. She should have her own space too."

I suspected that Jezebel slept on my sofa when I was out, and while I knew she couldn't get it dirty, the thought still bothered me. "Sure. Why not?"

"Just so we are clear, I am getting an entire walk-in closet, which you will empty. Your vacuum and broom and your junk will go somewhere else. I will get to put up whatever I want, and get a chair and a bed for Jezebel."

I knew where this was heading. "Yes. But I am not putting a TV in there. And you can't have any candles to make a shrine or anything."

Eugene smiled. "You've mentioned the candle issue once or twice before."

"Jezebel is sometimes hard of hearing," I said coolly.

"Fine. I agree to your terms. But under no circumstances am I sleeping in there."

I laughed at that. "There wouldn't be room for a bed in there anyway. And you're not Harry Potter. You can easily sleep on the sofa. That is, if you actually do sleep. But I will need to keep it locked, okay? I don't want my guests to wander in there. That would look really bad for me. So you would have to walk through the door. Jezebel too."

He smiled. "Agreed. And here I thought you didn't like us walking through walls."

And so Eugene and I amicably cleared out the back closet (Well, I cleared it out while he made fun of my efforts) and started hanging his photos and awards on the wall. "Can we go to my apartment and get some other things?" he asked.

"I don't know how much more will fit. And I don't know if everything has been packed away and sold or not. I'll call your cousin as soon as Veronica gets me his number. But don't expect me to hire a moving van or anything. I don't even want to imagine explaining to your cousin why I want some of your belongings."

"Don't worry, he's not quick on the uptake," Eugene assured me. But it didn't make me feel any better. What would people think if they happened to stumble into the back closet? I would definitely be institutionalized—a thought which seemed to echo through my mind quite frequently these days.

Chapter Twenty-One

Magdalena phoned just as the most comfortable chair in my living room was being deposited in the aforementioned back closet. She invited my 'dear ghost Eustace' and me for 'tea and gossip' the following day.

Eugene was determined to visit her for three reasons: The first was that he wanted to know more about his ghostly existence, and Magdalena was our best lead. The second involved the murder. Eugene had a morbid curiosity, and puzzling out the murder was giving him something to do with his time. The third reason was that there was a pet store on the way to Magdalena's, and Eugene wanted to get a fluffy pink bed for Jezebel. I know he wanted that particular dog bed because I had shuddered in horror when he had pointed it out on the Internet. The joke would be on him though, since he was the one who would have to look at it. I had no intention of setting foot in that back closet once his "study" was complete.

When we arrived at Magdalena's, it was to find her ensconced in a deep armchair, with the sunlight hitting her crystals and her silver birdcage through the window, casting rainbow colored specks along her petite frame. She had draped a thin blue shawl intermittently woven with silver thread across her shoulders, and another purple one across her lap. Beneath the shawls she wore a white housedress that had sparkles attached to the sleeves, neckline, and hem. Her hair was pulled back into a tight knot, exposing her thin neck, which was covered in a riot of silver chains. Her earrings were large, shiny, and dangled alarmingly when she moved. I suspected that she had just watched 'Saturday Night Fever' on the television, and was trying to single-handedly bring back the flashy sequins of the disco era.

She rose and hugged me in greeting and held out her hand so that Eugene could shake it. He probably would have tried to do so if he had been standing in that general area, but, as it was, he gave her a short bow, which I described to her in exaggerated detail. She whispered that since this was a proper tea, she had even rouged herself. While that was obvious from the two rather bright pink circles on her cheeks, smeared slightly upwards, I feigned surprise and shock, much to her delight, and sat across from her, carefully placing a napkin across my rather drab lap.

Eugene took a seat near the window, so that he could watch the gardens while we talked, occasionally exclaiming over the ridiculous amount of people wandering the grounds.

"Is Eustace---I mean Eugene, sitting on the sofa?" Magdalena asked, her eyes wandering the room as if a slight movement would betray his whereabouts.

"No. He is sitting over there, by the window."

Eugene looked over at us, and told me to tell Magdalena that he was honored to be in her presence yet again.

I did so, using his phrasing, and Magdalena preened with pleasure.

"It is an honor for me as well. To think of all those other people in the world taking tea right now, and most likely none of them are sitting with a ghost."

"There are few who would have been blessed with my presence when I was alive, so she is doubly honored," Eugene spouted.

Since that sounded arrogant in the extreme, much like something the living Eugene would have said, I refrained from translating. There was no need to alienate Magdalena before we could get any really useful information.

"I'm sure you have had lots of famous people to tea in your time."

"Oh yes. Tea is quite my thing. I had several famous actors from the forties and fifties, and their lovely wives, of course. I have also visited with several presidents, although I won't mention names; they didn't bring their wives, you know. I would hate to cause a scandal, even if one or two of them have gone to a better place." She smiled benignly, waiting for me to digest this latest information, before blandly continuing. "These days I get few visitors. Although that dreadful murder has certainly added some excitement to my life."

Eugene shifted to get a better look at Magdalena. I recognized that look in his eyes. It was the same look Jezebel got when the commercials for doggy bacon came on television.

"Has she learned anything new?" Eugene asked.

"Have you learned anything new?" I parroted.

"Well, I've had four nice young policemen visit me in the last week. And they were all quite handsome. It's enough to start my old heart beating faster."

"I meant about the case," Eugene mumbled.

Magdalena, oblivious to Eugene's discontent, continued gaily. "And the excitement, too. I've decided to start my own neighborhood watch program. I'm the only member right now, but I daresay it won't be hard to convince the rest of the street to start openly spying on their neighbors. It will give them a good excuse for their already shameless behavior," she tittered.

Look out, Miss Marple! Magdalena Duprés is on the case!

"That one detective—Johnson, or was it Jackson?—was particularly nice."

"Jameson," I automatically corrected.

"What? Oh, of course. I hope I didn't get it wrong while speaking to him. But I doubt he would care about something like that. He was quite understanding of my position here. At first I believed that he suspected me. But we got that straightened out."

"What does she mean, Hope? You should be interrogating her, Pip-Squeak, not sitting there like a mannequin in a dress shop." Eugene was giving me such a stern look that I was reminded of a particularly unpleasant gym teacher I had in grade school whose only coaching advice was, "Don't stand there like a lump. The ball isn't going to come to you!" The problem was, the more often I tried for the ball the more I got whacked in the face.

"What did you get straightened out?"

"The silverware, of course." She looked at me as if I had

just received a particularly nasty nosebleed from a flying soccer ball. "Such a nice detective. Not at all like one reads about. And quite good-looking for a police officer." She eyed me speculatively. "Do you know if he is single, my dear?"

"Isn't he a little young for you?" I asked facetiously. Heaven forbid I meet yet another matchmaker.

Magdalena frowned at me. "I won't bother answering that."

My old friend Guilt walked back in the door.

"I'm sorry. You were talking about the silverware and somehow we got off track. Can you explain about the silverware? I seem to be a little slow today."

"And everyday," Eugene murmured just loudly enough to be heard.

"You aren't slow. I am probably being vague. I do that on occasion you know. Roger used to say that in order to survive a conversation with me one had to be extremely good at holding several conversations at once. My mind skips around so."

"Which only makes you more interesting. Now what about the silverware? I know that a set was missing."

"Yes. That is what it was about. He wanted to know if I had taken the silverware. Somehow he learned about my habit."

"Good grief. She's not talking about drugs, is she?" Eugene bellowed, scooting closer to the window. "She doesn't look like a hard drug kind of person, but maybe she smokes medical marijuana. Or opium. I bet she is into opium. All those old movie stars did it, you know."

I ignored Eugene. Magdalena might tipple, but I doubted she did any drugs. Kleptomania I wouldn't put past her though.

"What habit?" I asked as nonchalantly as possible.

"My birdcages."

I was starting to feel out of my depth, wondering if I was now Alice caught in some web of verbal obstructions, when Eugene started to laugh.

"Don't you see, Hope? She means that literally. She makes birdcages out of silverware." He pointed to the birdcage near the window, which I had only given a brief glance when we entered.

It was somewhat attractive in an odd sort of way, and I stood up to view it more closely. The birdcage was about three feet tall and fashioned completely out of misshapen and mismatched silverware. It had a dome with a spoon as a sort of spire. There were three ledges, made solely out of bent spoons, and two doors made from forks. The actual cage was a rotation of spoons and forks. "You made this?" I asked in disbelief. It looked like it required some welding skill.

"Yes. It's my fourth. The other three I gave as gifts. This one is almost finished. Do you really like it?" she asked with an endearing child-like enthusiasm.

"It's very creative. I'm sure it would make a singular decoration to any home," I answered honestly.

"Then that decides it. When I am finished, it is yours."

Eugene laughed at my stunned expression. And laughed. And laughed. And then laughed some more. If he weren't a ghost, I would have suspected that he had wet his pants he was laughing so hard.

I smiled at Magdalena. "Thank you. I will treasure it. I know just where to put it, too—right next to my favorite chair." I sent Eugene a rather triumphant gloat, and he stopped laughing as quickly as he had started. It would make a lovely piece of ornamentation in the back closet. And the beauty of this idea was that Eugene was not yet able to move such large, heavy objects by himself. Where the cage went, it would stay, unless I decided to move it. And it really wasn't that unattractive. It was quite interesting. No doubt Eugene would grow to be very fond of it.

We still hadn't quite resolved the police questioning Magdalena, though, and I wanted to make sure that I wasn't going to be accepting gifts from a murderess.

"Because you make these cages the police thought you had taken the silverware?"

"Yes. And I did take the silverware. Not that knife of course. As you can see I only use forks and spoons. I wouldn't want some poor bird to be cut by a knife." Her face scrunched up tightly for a moment, as if she were picturing that exact thing, and then she relaxed and continued. "So the police, that dear, good-looking boy in particular," she shot me a glance, "were most interested. But they realized that I couldn't have killed Marcus, so they kept asking if someone had seen me take the silverware, and who was I seated next to, and so forth. Most of it quite boring and repetitive, I'm afraid."

Eugene and I asked simultaneously, "Who were you next to?"

"I can't really remember, dear. You set the place cards, do you remember?"

I thought about it, but couldn't seem to picture the table. I just remember it being rearranged at the last minute and Angela later commenting on the fact that a few guests had decided to change their seats for amorous reasons. I had never seen a group of less amorous looking people in my life. But then, what do I know? I'm still single after all.

"I can't recall."

"That's all right, dear. I remember there was a lot of talk of politics, and I believe I was sitting next to someone I knew, I just can't seem to remember whom. Or maybe it was one of my sons. Or both of them. And I remember talking to that senator and that oil man, and then Allan and Evan. But that could have been before or after. To be honest, it is a bit of a blur. I might have had a bit too much to drink that night."

Eugene laughed at the understatement, and then turned to look outside, deciding that the conversation was not as intriguing as he had hoped.

"And then they also wanted to know if I had seen anyone cross our grounds and go to the Whittington's house. Of course I saw no one and told them so, but they did keep asking. In the end I wasn't much help, and the best part of the interviews was simply meeting those nice men."

I was about to respond when I was interrupted by a startled exclamation from the window.

"Hello! Do you see that?" Eugene spluttered in amazement. His mouth was agog, and he inched his neck forward until the tip of his nose had actually passed through the glass.

I peered around him, to get a better view at what had

captured his attention. I had previously noticed the people wandering across the lawns, but had paid little attention to what they were actually doing. It seemed that in my absorption I had been missing a great deal.

A stream of gardeners, painters, and carpenters were simultaneously transforming the grounds into a virtual paradise. I had a suspicion the swans would be arriving any minute to complete the too idyllic picture.

Magdalena shuddered at a smocked man carrying a rather detailed statue of a youthful Cupid, begging Eugene and I to excuse her of any part in this onslaught of Vegas-like romance. "They are completely remodeling the gardens in preparation for the wedding. I told them they had several weeks to prepare, and we could do without the statuary until then, but no one listens to me. And I know you didn't have anything to do with it, Hope. Susan and Colby were quite definite on that score. Although they seemed to find that your objections were foolish. But then, those two don't have an ounce of sense between them. I did expect more out of Colby, but I fear I am destined to be a disappointed grandmother. It is just one more melancholy role that I am resigned to playing."

Since she said this last with such relish, I simply nodded, giving her my most believable smile of sympathy.

"But that is the lot of an old woman. Be thankful you haven't reached my age yet. Being old is quite difficult. And everyone treats you as if you were senile. Family especially."

"I'm sure that isn't their intention." How did one nicely say that the family in question was already patronizing in the extreme, and their behavior in no way reflected Magdalena's advanced years?

A few seconds of rational thought made me realize that one couldn't say that graciously, so I decided on the next best thing. "I can only hope that I am as..." I paused while sipping my tea. What was the right word to describe her? 'Competent' made it sound as if I thought her ancient, as did 'agile.' I didn't want to say 'blessed' either, for although having one's family near when one is older is a blessing, Magdalena obviously felt that her family was more of a curse. A moment more of thought and I had it, "...dynamic." As everyone knows, this is a distinctive and wonderfully vague word. I was quite proud of my ingenuity.

"Thank you, my dear. How lovely of you to say so. I do feel that I have retained a certain aura as I have aged. It is very astute of you to spot it," she purred.

Eugene gave a small chuckle and seated himself next to me on the sofa. "She is quite a character. I'm not surprised she was haunted by a ghost. You, on the other hand, Hope, are the least likely person to ever be haunted. Perhaps this is not about me at all, and is actually God's way of livening up your life."

"My life is lively enough, thank you," I retorted acidly.

Magdalena looked from me to the air next to me, her eyes lit up like fireworks. "Don't tell me the naughty boy is teasing you, Hope? But how droll. You must have such interesting conversations. Ah, how I wish Roger was still here."

This time I really did smile in genuine sympathy. Despite her ever-present family, Magdalena was quite lonely. "Eugene and I will just have to come by and entertain you more often."

"Would you? That would be so wonderful—like having my youth back."

"Then we would be most honored," Eugene said, giving Magdalena a gallant bow, which was completely lost on her, but pleased me immensely.

My pleasure was soon dimmed as a loud clap of thunder shook the small building, and fat drops of rain splattered against the window.

I had not seen this coming. But then, predicting the future was not my forte. Until Eugene had started haunting me, the only thing I was ever certain of was etiquette. I could recite the proper forms of address from the Pope to the lord mayor, explain the purpose of every knife and fork, even explain the difference between a tea dance and a dinner dance, but I could never get a grasp on that capricious beast called 'weather'.

That isn't to say that I don't know the appropriate attire for every form of weather--it's part of my job to know that--I simply never anticipate what freakish turn the weather will take next. In grade school my mother was certain that I would die of pneumonia, mostly because I would expect sun and, being a smart girl, would dress appropriately. Naturally the sky would then spit out freezing rain and hail. My mother still despairs of me, and I still get caught without an umbrella during the most heinous of storms.

Apparently Magdalena did not suffer the same affliction. Noticing my consternation (not Eugene's raucous laughter and smug smile), she opened a closet door to reveal every type of attire and apparatus ever made. Everything except an umbrella, that is.

There were neat piles of rain hats, sunglasses, parasols, sunblock, beach chairs, winter scarves, and galoshes. Hanging up were wool coats, raincoats, windbreakers, and shawls. Everything was grouped by type and then by color, the piles in order from largest to smallest. It was like heaven for someone suffering from obsessive-compulsive disorder. I loved it.

Still, there was something wrong with this picture.

I looked from Magdalena and then back to the closet. There was no way that this lively, shatter-brained woman would have a closet like this. Or was there?

Before I could voice my question, she answered me in as good-humored a way as imaginable. "I know. It isn't me, is it? I can see the look in your eyes. I am far too impatient for this kind of thing. Actually, Susan did it."

Susan? I couldn't see Susan sitting around organizing anyone's closet, not even her own.

"Well, she hired someone to do it anyway. She claims it was because my little abode here was too messy for her taste. I think it was just an excuse to annoy me while being able to look through my things. She didn't get all the family jewelry, you know. I still have a few valuable pieces hidden, which I am determined to hold onto until the day I depart this earth." She glanced over to where Eugene had formerly been seated, not knowing he was now standing directly behind her, and continued. "That is, if I depart this earth. We all know there are other possibilities. Maybe I will stay a little longer and haunt Susan.

Ha! Wouldn't that just kill her!"

I smiled lamely. Magdalena was probably right. Susan appeared to be on the verge of a nervous breakdown as it was. I could barely handle Eugene. If Magdalena haunted Susan (and I had no doubt that Magdalena would be even more obnoxious in death than Eugene), Susan would be in an institution in a matter of days. And most likely it would be the Betty Ford Clinic.

"I know I shock you dear, but sometimes these pleasant little thoughts are all that keep me going."

Heaven preserve us all from old women with too much free time and too much money. It is a lethal combination.

"I'm sure Susan meant it for the best." I didn't really believe that either, but it was still the right thing to say.

"How pleasant it is to meet someone who thinks nicely of everyone," Magdalena cooed.

"Yeah right!" Eugene snorted. "What she means is that these days you rarely meet someone who hides what they really think, not because they have ulterior motives, but simply as a matter of politeness. Or maybe just too scared to upset people."

Magdalena, oblivious to Eugene's subtle condemnation of my character, was busy rummaging through the closet. When she came across a bright yellow rain hat, she yanked it out with a triumphant "Aha!" and handed it to me. "I don't keep umbrellas in the house. It is bad luck to open an umbrella indoors. Did you know that? I am so scared that someone will do so and they will have bad luck, or maybe I will have the bad luck since it is my house, that I just can't bear the thought of keeping them indoors. So this will have to do."

I looked at the article she handed me. It was a replica of the hats the deep-sea fishermen wore—oversized yellow plastic.

"These were all the rage a few years back. Susan and Colby each have one as well. So does Angela. Or maybe Angela got hers first and then Susan and Colby followed. They are absolutely hideous, but most everything that is practical is." She looked closely at the hat, scrunching her forehead until it was nothing but wrinkles. "Still, I imagine all good Yankees have one somewhere in their closet."

I looked outside at the deepening gray sky and the

raindrops that showed no sign of abating. I looked at Magdalena with her expression of pleased benevolence and Eugene with his relentless smirk.

To hell with my pride!

My one consolation as I stepped out Magdalena's front door was that my mother was not around to see me.

Chapter Twenty-Two

By the time Eugene and I had exited Magdalena's front door three statues had been placed around the man-made pond, several hedges had been trimmed (thankfully not into heart shapes) and a wall of flowers separated the Raines' property from the Whittington's. I imagined the last was simply out of spite on Susan's part, since the wedding was to be held on the opposite end of the grounds. I doubted if any of the guests would see the newly planted flowers.

The rain had already caused a small stream of water to run across the paving stones and the wind was picking up. My car was parked in the front of the house, and I knew I would be soaked to the skin before I reached it if I ran directly across the grounds. Another option was to run for the side door and take shelter in the house until the rain abated, which I was loathe to do since I suspected that either Susan or Colby was at home overseeing the preparations, not trusting me to do it for them. My final option was to make a dash for the car by running along the edge of the house, where the building was acting as a buffer against some of the rain. I would still get wet, but the weather was still quite warm and I suspected my clothes would be dry before I reached home.

Hmm. Dealing with Susan and/or Colby, or getting a little wet?

Being the friendly, dignified, and self-respecting woman that I am, I chose the latter. After all, water was my friend. Didn't I enjoy water sports? And how dignified and self-respecting could I be dripping wet and imposing myself on others? No, avoiding the others was really the only option.

Having made my decision quickly and with only a little added dampness to my person, I held onto the hat and sprinted toward the main house, which I hoped would indeed block some of the rain while I made my way to my car.

Eugene, impervious to the rain, followed leisurely, laughing blithely at my discomfort.

He is definitely sleeping in that closet tonight!

While continuing my Olympics-qualifying sprint, I saw several other people running for the house, including two women with yellow hats similar to the one I was wearing—Susan and Colby, I imagined--a few workmen, one with a yellow hat and two with gray ones, and a man in a beige suit. All of them disappeared around the corner toward the side entrance, not noticing me, and I continued on undisturbed.

Just as I was about to reach the wall of the house, my foot caught on a clump of crab grass and I stumbled slightly. To my consternation, and almost immediate discomfort, only one of my heels continued with me. Apparently the other shoe felt the indignity of my situation and had decided to brave the elements rather than continue to accompany me.

Eugene clutched his side in what looked like pain, but I quickly realized was laughter.

That was too much!

I jerked to a stop and hopped the few feet back to my dratted shoe, pausing only long enough to yank it back on. Unfortunately, my foot was immediately covered with a rather thick, oozing slime that made slurping sounds with each step.

Obviously my shoe was out to get me.

With only a mild expletive at my particular shoe and the men who made women feel they had to wear such monstrosities in order to feel attractive, I moved on until I reached the house.

I had been correct in my assumption that the rain would not be as strong here. The massive structure blocked the worst of the onslaught, and the few balconies that graced this side of the house offered even more shelter, though the ground was not particularly dry and continued to suck at my heels.

I paused long enough to catch my breath, deciding that the US Olympic team wouldn't want someone who was in such bad shape, when I saw a man approaching from the opposite direction in which I had come.

When he got within ten yards of me I recognized the man as Vincent, looking rather dashing in a gray suit that was only slightly damp from the rain. He was obviously a faster runner than I was.

I smiled at him as he approached, and he stopped right in front of me, looking as if he had leisurely sauntered over rather than run through the rain.

"I wasn't sure it was you, Hope, but I'm glad I decided to find out. Don't tell me you're leaving?"

"I'm afraid so. I only stopped in to visit with Magdalena and check on the tents, but it looks like I will have to come back tomorrow for that. Not much can be done in this weather." God was definitely torturing me. Maybe if I pretended to relish the prospect of coming over here He would find reasons to keep me away.

"I noticed there was a lot of work going on. As a matter of fact, I'm afraid I trampled some of it on the way here. Don't hate me if the newly planted flowers don't take."

I laughed. "Don't worry. I had nothing to do with those. But Susan might hate you for it. I get the feeling it's her version of a fence."

Eugene reached us, gave Vincent what I feel is his classic disparaging look, and moved to stand beside me.

"Don't tell me you are going to allow yourself to get soaked just to talk to this guy?" Eugene asked contemptuously, although I'm not sure which one of us he held in contempt.

"You are probably right. Angela has been doing everything she can to annoy Susan, so I suppose Susan is retaliating in her own feeble way." He paused. "I think the best thing Susan can do to get back at Angela is to have a makeover and try to seduce her own husband. That would spike Angela's guns."

"You're probably right, but I doubt Susan would do something like that. She's too..."

"Passive?" Vincent finished.

"Actually, I was going to say 'proud'."

Vincent nodded, though I could tell his mind had moved on to another topic, and he was looking for a way to broach it. He must have decided on the direct approach, because he didn't do any of that beating around the bush.

"Has that policeman friend of yours told you if he is going to arrest someone for the murder?"

I probably shouldn't have been surprised at the question, since Vincent himself was a suspect, but I was surprised. Vincent struck me as the type of man who would laugh at a police investigation, even one that involved himself.

"No. I mean we are friends, but we don't talk very often. And Peter wouldn't talk about the investigation anyway. He's not that sort of person. He takes the rules pretty seriously."

"I suspected as much, but I was still wondering. It seems there has been a bit of a fuss over at the house, and Evan and Colby are rather panicked."

Gossiping isn't wrong when it involves a murder investigation. Even my mother would agree with me on that.

"What's the matter?" I asked, hoping I sounded less curious than I was. The rain no longer bothered me. I was immune to everything but Vincent's words. Even Eugene had leaned in closer and dropped his look of perpetual boredom.

"It turns out that the police came back for more of Evan's shoes. He apparently gave them the wrong pair the first time around. And the idiot didn't do a very good job of cleaning the right pair, because the police found blood on them."

Vincent paused, waiting for me to absorb this fact.

Evan? A killer? Was it really possible? "Have they arrested him?"

"No, because it could mean nothing. He might have gotten blood on his shoes when he walked through the library after Marcus was killed. And he could have given the police the wrong pair by accident."

Vincent didn't sound convinced, and Eugene scoffed at the notion.

"He's hiding something. Didn't I tell you that from the start, Hope?"

I ignored Eugene's comment (what else could I do?) and addressed Vincent. "But you don't think he did? Do you think he killed his father?"

"I don't know. Normally I wouldn't think so. It's Evan, for God's sake. But I know that he isn't telling the police something. I heard him talking on the phone the other day, though I don't know whom he was talking to. Probably Colby. All I know is that he said he didn't intend to say anything to the police about the matter. But that could be about any number of trivial things."

I raised my eyebrow at that. What was trivial in a murder investigation?

Vincent laughed. "I know what you're thinking, and Evan might be guilty of something. I still have a hard time believing it's murder, though."

I nodded. "So do I."

"Maybe the others have heard something more. Are you going inside at all?"

"I hadn't intended to. You caught me trying to make a break for my car without being seen."

"No such luck. I saw that hat of yours from the Whittington' s house. And Angela and Colby left before me, so they probably saw you too. But if you don't want to go inside, let me walk you to your car." He looked up at the rain that was still falling steadily on our heads. "Or run with you to your car. Whichever you prefer."

I thought about it. If I went inside I might be able to get some more information on the murder, but then again maybe not. The others might not want to talk about Evan possibly being a suspect. I could hear them now, exclaiming over the fact that the wedding might have to be postponed, or, God forbid, cancelled.

"The car," I answered with only a slight hesitation.

Vincent didn't look surprised.

I stuck my head out from the under the balcony, testing the amount of rain that was falling on my hat, and deciding that it was no more than before, stepped into the tumult.

Eugene gave me a look that clearly said he thought I was a party-pooper and probably a coward as well, but stepped out from under the balcony right behind me, while Vincent, probably sharing Eugene's thought, moved at my side.

Vincent looked up at the sky, clearly not bothered by the rain or the fact that his suit was being ruined. He turned back to me and linked his arm into mine. "Hope, I asked you before, but you didn't answer whether or---"

Before I realized what was happening, Vincent had grabbed me around the waist and swung me towards him. A moment later a large, gray object fell heavily toward the ground, and straight onto—through—Eugene. It seemed to rend him asunder as it fell through his head, chest and legs and then, with a sharp crash, shattered at our feet, sending chunks of plaster and moist dirt into the air.

For a moment I was in a state of shock, the picture of Eugene being split in two firmly lodged in my brain, blocking out reality. I cried out and tried to step out of Vincent's grasp so that I could make sure Eugene was unharmed, but Vincent's grip was too tight.

I took a deep breath and focused on Eugene's form, standing before me, still in one piece, and I relaxed slightly.

"Don't look so scared, Hope," Eugene chided. "I'm already dead. Remember? That thing fell right through me. I didn't even feel it." He looked down at his body and then held up his hands, turning them around in some sort of inspection. Overall, he looked damned pleased with himself!

Vincent was swearing behind me, and loosened his grip on my waist as he bent down to look at the pile of rubbish at our feet. "It's some sort of planter or urn," he said through clenched teeth.

"What?" Maybe I was still in shock, but nothing he said seemed to be sinking in. But then, I was beginning to feel like that a lot lately. Maybe I was a lot dumber than I realized. "An urn?"

I looked up at the balcony a good fifteen feet above us. It didn't seem to be missing any decoration. Nor did the roof for that matter.

"I suppose the rain could have knocked it over," Vincent was saying. "Still, if I hadn't seen it fall, it would have killed you, Hope. Or left you brain dead or paralyzed if you survived."

Why is it people feel it necessary to discuss all the possible ways one could have been injured or killed in an accident? I wouldn't have been surprised if Vincent has started going on about the number of bones that could have been broken, or exactly what it would be like to be left in a vegetative state. And if Eugene started talking about the parts of the brain that would have been squashed like a bug and the obvious damage that would have been done to face, I would have thought it par for the course.

As a matter of fact, if Angela hadn't rushed out of the house screaming, I might have begun to list all the unfortunate possibilities myself.

"Oh, my dear. I was on my way out and just saw what happened. Are you all right? Oh, how horrible. You'd think Susan would have the sense to make sure that everything that is supposed to be attached to the house stays that way." She reached up and grabbed at her own yellow hat, which was about to be blown off her head, and then proceeded to hug me as if I were her own dear little sister that had wandered into a construction zone.

Vincent stood up and gave Angela a puzzled look, but she seemed not to notice, continuing to blather on. "But what can you expect from Susan. I doubt she knows the least thing about home maintenance. Father Plumber made certain all his children knew about those things. It's just common sense, isn't it?"

Angela's scream had attracted Susan and Colby, John (he was the man I saw in the beige suit), a maid, a gardener, and a workman in some overalls. And none of them looked pleased to have been dragged outside in the rain.

"It's all right. Hope's fine. I'm going to bring her inside. She probably needs a drink. I know I need one," Angela rattled on, tugging my arm and dragging me behind her. "I know you don't mind, Susan."

The shock was wearing off, but I let her lead me, since I was now sopping wet and covered in mud and really would appreciate being indoors.

Vincent walked behind us, though I could sense that he

was continually turning around to look at the balcony and roof ledge. I really hoped he wasn't the type of person to get a morbid fixation on an incident, because I was most definitely that type of person and I didn't need anyone to encourage it. Eugene was beginning to follow in my footsteps, and if there were three of us it would be more than I could handle.

By the time we had reached the door, the only remaining people were Susan and Colby, both of whom looked slightly damp, from their hair to their shoes.

Colby was the first to greet us as we entered the house. "Did you trip and land in the mud, Hope?" She looked me over from my dripping yellow hat to my muddy heels. "You look horrible."

"Colby, where are your manners?" Susan said sharply. "It's obvious Hope has had some sort of accident." She also looked me over. "Would you like a drink?"

I noticed that I had not been invited to sit down, but I couldn't really blame Susan. I wouldn't want my wet person sitting on any of my own furniture either. I accepted the offer of a drink and took off my hat, clenching it in my fist.

Susan walked over to the bar and poured three drinks, though I couldn't tell what she was pouring, and then handed a glass to Vincent and I, keeping the third for herself.

I took a small sip, conscious of the fact that everyone in the room was staring at me. Where were their manners? Was I such a fright?

Susan had downed her drink in a few swallows and proceeded to pour herself another, much to Colby's dismay.

And because Colby was displeased, she turned on me. "What are you doing here, Hope? And why are you wearing that stupid hat?"

Both odd questions, but then, Colby *was* odd.

"I was visiting your grandmother while checking on the preparations. And your grandmother lent me the hat. I think it is rather stylish." I didn't think so, but I wasn't about to admit that I also thought it was stupid. My OPD, or maybe my pride, getting the better of me.

"Well, Colby must as well, since she owns the same one. And so do I. I think you have one, too, don't you, Susan?" Angela said haughtily.

Angela was really quite likable. When she wanted to be.

Susan didn't answer, being too busy pouring herself a third drink, which Vincent deftly grabbed out of her hand in thanks.

"Actually, Colby," Vincent said as soon as the drink was safely out of Susan's reach, "your house seems to be falling apart. A large pot or urn or something simply fell from the sky and nearly brained Hope."

John, who had come in silently, looked disturbed. He remained silent, his eyes focused on some point just beyond my shoulder.

"Thank God someone is mentioning it," Eugene practically cheered. "What a lot of shady characters. Close-mouthed ones, too." The Film Noir talk was coming out in Eugene again. I was definitely going to have to start limiting his television time. "My mute grandmother gave up more information than they do," he continued.

Susan practically collapsed into a chair (the one I should have been occupying if I wasn't still standing here dripping on the carpet) and Colby faked a laugh.

"Don't be silly, Vincent. Hope probably just knocked something over."

What a witch!

This is what I get for preferring a soaking to human company, I thought darkly.

"No, it's true," Angela said reproachfully. "I saw the whole thing." She looked momentarily stricken, and added, "Well, almost the whole thing. I saw something fall and crash right next to Hope. She could have been killed."

Susan clutched at the chair arm and winced.

"I am so sorry," John said to me, speaking for the first time. "I daresay it gave you quite a scare. I'm not surprised, though. Dean and I talked about having the roof redone this summer, as well as having the balconies reinforced. You know how it is with older homes."

In my career I have been into dozens of older homes—hell, New England seems to be nothing but older homes—and not one of those houses tried to fell me with a pot. And none of the owners did, either. And from the suspicious glances that both Eugene and Vincent were throwing around, I suspected that they were thinking along the same lines. Had someone tried to kill me?

I would have been affronted if I hadn't been so worried. Why would anyone want to kill me?

The answer was obvious. No one would want to kill me. It was all a big mistake. It was the fault of that damn hat. Someone undoubtedly wanted to kill Colby. Someone besides me, that is. They thought I was Colby because I was wearing a yellow hat. Didn't I see her enter the house wearing the same one?

But then, maybe someone wanted to kill Angela. She had the same yellow hat, too. And since she is always flirting with Vincent, maybe they mistook me for her. I could think of three people who would probably not object to her death, and they were all in this room.

Or maybe someone wanted to kill Susan. That seemed less likely, but one never knows. She might have pissed off the gardener with all those stupid flower demands.

Or just maybe someone had been aiming for Vincent.

"I don't suppose anyone else saw the incident?" Vincent asked coolly. "I only ask because if Hope is hurt she could sue, and witnesses would probably be helpful. That way we could know if the pot came from the roof or balcony, and how close to the edge the pot was."

"You're not going to sue, are you?" John asked laughingly. "I'd hate to have the home owner's insurance go up."

"I'm not going to sue. Although I admit that, like Vincent, I am curious about how the urn came to fall." If one of them didn't push that urn off the balcony I would eat this cursed hat!

No one said anything, but everyone looked guilty. Or maybe my increasingly suspicious mind simply thought everyone looked guilty.

Before I could ruminate more on the matter, the door opened and several more wet people walked in.

Amazingly enough, not one of them was wearing a yellow hat.

Evan was wearing slacks and a dress shirt, which clung to his chest in unattractive splotches; Allan was wearing slacks and a sport jacket, damp, but not as wet as Evan; and Rosemary was wearing a summer dress, which was wet on one side only. Apparently the umbrella dangling in her hand was somewhat ineffectual.

"But where did you all come from? You weren't here a minute ago," Angela asked, her face lit with curiosity. "Don't tell me you heard my scream?"

"We did. But we were already on our way over," Allan said, just a trace of impatience in his voice. "We met Evan on the lawn, and the three of us decided to head on over here and see why we weren't invited to the party."

"Not a party, Allan. Not with a murder charge hanging over poor Evan," Angela said, casting Evan a pitying glance. "And then poor Hope was nearly killed." She didn't shoot me any sympathetic glance, but sent a triumphant look toward Susan and Colby.

"What's this?" Rosemary said, looking a trifle panicked.

She really needed to be on tranquilizers or something.

"Nothing important," Colby said blandly. "A pot or something fell and nearly hit Hope. But as you can see, she is just fine so there is nothing to worry about. The only *real* problem is what those idiot policemen are thinking. As if Evan could kill anyone."

"That so, Hope?" Allan asked, looking me up and down.

I nodded slowly. For some reason, my mind seemed to focus more on the fact that John had ushered the three new guests onto the sofa. And they weren't exactly dry.

I wanted to slump into a chair, but Susan, looking tipsy and worried at the same time, was occupying the nearest one. It seemed the only available seat was next to Vincent on the divan. I say seat, but it was more like a small gap since he was rather large and the divan rather small. Still, it couldn't be much worse than standing like a clod pole in the middle of the room while everyone watched the mud slowly dripping off of me. I made my decision and moved swiftly toward the bar, grabbed a napkin, and then just as swiftly moved to the divan, laid the napkin on the seat and slid into the space before any one could stop me and insist I take off my clothes first.

Vincent looked rather gratified, which I suppose he should have been since we were now seated uncomfortably close. Eugene gave me yet another look of exasperation (I am going to start giving these looks names soon) and Allan winked at me. I'm pretty sure Allan's wink had everything to do with the napkin and nothing to do with my choice of seats, but I wasn't sure, and I didn't want to ask.

"I wouldn't worry about Evan," John was saying to Colby. "The police couldn't possibly arrest him on such flimsy evidence. Circumstantial evidence is what they call it, right?"

Susan got up and poured herself another drink. The glass was shaking rather badly, and I was worried that if someone didn't help her she would drop it.

Apparently I wasn't the only one with these thoughts, because John got up, took the glass from her hand, chugged it down himself, and helped her back to her seat.

It was obvious that everyone knew she had recently developed a serious drinking problem, which was somewhat understandable under the circumstances, but if her family didn't do something about it soon, she might end up really hurting herself and Dean could say goodbye to that political career.

"True," Allan responded to John, who had moved back to his seat. "But if the police really thought he did it, they would probably have arrested him by now." He looked directly at Evan, who wasn't paying much attention to the conversation, but was instead focused on Colby, who was looking alternately at Angela and I as if we had suddenly grown ten arms and a handful of noses.

"I wouldn't place too much stock on this whole shoe business," Allan continued. "We all probably have blood on our shoes."

I almost expected him to say 'hands', but he didn't, and the subject was quickly changed to The Wedding—a topic I hated even more than The Murder.

After a few minutes of listening to Angela facetiously exclaim over Colby's lovely taste, seconded by Evan, I was ready to leave.

Eugene, who had slipped out of the room shortly after I sat down, came back with a curious expression on his face. "Let's go, Hope. This place gives me the creeps. The front lawn looks like someone vomited up Valentine's Day, there is no interesting food in the kitchen, and that damn politician is smoking a cheap cigar in his office, making it difficult to do any proper investigating."

Since I had no doubt that Eugene felt rifling through people's drawers (as best as he is able) is 'proper investigating', I didn't hesitate to take my leave. I wanted Eugene out of here before he started scaring people or decided to reciprocate the hospitality we'd been shown by trying to drop a pot on Colby's head.

Despite my objections, Vincent offered to show me out, since he claimed he had to return to town as well.

When we reached the door, he stopped me. "Since I saved your life back there, you should really consider yourself indebted to me."

He was smiling, but I suddenly felt like I was in a scene from "The Godfather". Vincent looked the part, admitted to occasionally acting the part, and was a murder suspect. (I ignored the fact that some might consider me a murder suspect as well). If "The Godfather" was true-to-life, I was probably honor-bound to repay the debt to Vincent by spying on my neighbors and then leaving horse heads in their beds.

"I think dinner is a small price to pay. How about tomorrow? I'll pick you up at seven."

Dinner? That was how I could repay him? Either he was extremely desperate for female company, which I found hard to believe, or he already had someone to leave horse heads lying around and was going to pump me for information. Not that I was unattractive or boring. I just felt certain I wasn't his type.

This had to be some ploy to gather dirt on the Whittington and Raines families.

Uh-oh! I was beginning to sound like Humphrey Bogart. Soon I would be joining Eugene in his film noir fantasies.

"All right. But why don't you tell me where and I will meet you there."

"Worried that I will find out where you live? Or are you worried the evening will be a total bore and you won't be able to escape fast enough?" Vincent teased.

Since Vincent simply had to ask anyone in the living room for my address that wasn't much of a concern. And as for being bored, well, that seemed unlikely with Vincent. My biggest worry was Eugene. I knew he would insist on coming with me, and the idea of having him with me was rather frightening. God only knew what he could get up to. It would be so much better if I took my own car in case he managed to burn down the restaurant or make me talk to invisible people.

I glanced furtively at Eugene, trying to gauge his mood, but I wasn't furtive enough.

"I am definitely coming, Pip-Squeak, so get any ideas of ditching me out of your head. This is the perfect opportunity to question this thug about the murder. And I wouldn't miss seeing you on a date for the world," Eugene confirmed.

"I will probably be working late tomorrow. So it would just be easier if I took my own car," I said.

Eugene just laughed. "My deaf grandmother could come up with a better lie than that."

"Okay." Vincent gave me the name of the restaurant and the locale before seeing me off.

Eugene glanced at me, a sly look coming into his eyes. "I must say, Hope, I'm a little surprised you agreed to a date with this guy. If you really want some decent dates there are a few people I could recommend. As a matter of fact, it might add some entertainment."

"I'm not going to start dating strangers just to liven up your social life, Eugene." Did he think my life was his own personal soap opera, or was he trying to live vicariously through me? Either way it was disturbing.

"I'm hoping that dating will liven up *your* social life. Although I won't deny that it will liven up mine as well." He gave me a serious look. "Have you decided who you are going to the wedding with? It's less than a week away. I have some ideas if you don't. As a matter of fact, that Peter fellow seems quite nice, even if you didn't get my hint before. If not, I used to know a few decent men in the restaurant business."

He was a male version of my mother! God was definitely punishing me for a past misdeed!

Chapter Twenty-Three

"Don't say it. I'm fine."

"I don't know, Hope. You don't look so good. Your nose usually isn't *that* red," Eugene muttered.

"I'm f-f-fine," I spluttered right before the sneeze caught me in its vicious grip.

Maybe my nose was a little red, but Eugene didn't have to be so ungentlemanly as to point it out. And a little powder would cover it up perfectly. No one would even notice. The runny nose might be a problem though. But short of stuffing Kleenex up my nostrils and down my dress, there was little I could do about it.

"I bet you touched Veronica's Kleenex. It just proves that I am right, and you don't wash your hands enough. And now you have a cold."

"I wash my hands all the time. And I didn't touch any of her Kleenex. She must have sneezed on me," I argued.

It was too bad ghosts weren't susceptible to ailments. There were quite a few I would wish on Eugene at the moment-- if I were the sort of mean person that wished ill on other people, that is. Although, in Eugene's defense, he didn't actually wish ill on me, he simply laughed at me when it happened. He really did need to get out more! I would have to bring up the subject of auditing classes again.

"If you are done lambasting my character in your head, you might want to think about getting dressed. You don't want to look dowdy for your date," Eugene said with an air of comic gravity. "What are your options?"

Any hopes I had that Eugene was joking died an abrupt death as he walked through my closet door and started yelling to me from the other side. "The blue dress isn't bad. Nor is the lavender." There was a long pause and then a spurt of laughter.

"Good heavens, Hope. No one past the age of ten wears frilly pink dresses. Please tell me your mother bought this for you."

"It was a bride's maid dress, for your information," I snapped as I opened the closet door. "And who do you think you are to be going through my closet? You have your own now, remember?"

"Someone has to help you with your fashion," Eugene said, still peering through my outfits. "There are certainly a lot of pastels in here. Brunettes can wear darker colors, you know."

"If I didn't know better, I would think you were gay."

"Would it make you feel better if you thought I were? Would you sleep better at night?" Eugene asked me with that damn smirk of his. "You aren't really worried that I watch you sleep, or anything bizarre like that?" The idea seemed to afford him some secret delight. I had a sneaking suspicion I would wake up tomorrow to find him standing over my bed with a pair of my stockings in his hands.

"No." Although I did suspect him of rearranging my toiletries so that I couldn't find anything when I got up. I couldn't be so shatter-brained that I misplaced my hairbrush three days in a row.

"Straight men can have fashion sense. I watch "What Not to Wear". It's on The Learning Channel."

I daresay I should have been surprised, but I wasn't. Film Noir couldn't be on all the time, after all.

"I don't much care for this salmon-colored dress. I'm not sure that's a flattering color on anyone."

"That one my mother did buy me," I acknowledged. I had always hated the dress, but my mother searched my closet for it every time she visited. It might remind her of a favorite dress she owned during her school days, but it reminded me of Pepto Bismal.

"Well, let's start trying stuff on," Eugene announced.

"What?"

'How am I supposed to help you decide what to wear if you don't try any of it on?" Eugene asked impatiently. "Let's get to it. We don't want to be late."

There was no 'we' about it. I would be doing all the

work. I would be the one who was late.

"I know how they look. I don't need to try any of it on."

"But I don't know how any of the dresses look. And I'm the one who is going to have to tell you when you look bad. Now hurry up."

I wanted to argue some more, but decided against it. A second opinion always helped in deciding on clothes, and Eugene's taste was usually quite good. It would be best if I simply acquiesced nicely.

"Fine. But I expect you to stay in the bedroom."

Eugene nodded and walked back through the door, telling me to get a move on.

I have never enjoyed trying on clothes, and Eugene didn't make the process any easier. My figure was nice, my clothes tasteful, and my self-esteem average. And yet, after twenty minutes the only thing I was sure of was that Eugene was going to die a second time, right after I managed to get out of the seventh dress.

Eugene was at his finest when critiquing. His wit knew no bounds; his opinions gave no ground. He was a god among mortals dispersing his superior knowledge, and I was the lucky recipient.

According to Eugene, the lavender dress flowed too much and I looked like a fairy. The green dress was too short and made me look like a hedge. The silver dress was too shiny. Eugene insisted that I looked like a strobe light. The white dress was too casual and made me look like a meringue. The yellow dress was too long. I looked like a banana. The black dress was too sedate. I looked like I was attending a funeral.

"I don't want to be seen with you if you are going to look like a frumpy school teacher," Eugene argued.

I had never looked frumpy in my life. Not even my mother had ever called me frumpy.

"No one is going to see you! I'm the only one they are going to see," I reminded him.

"But *I* know that I am with you. How would you feel knowing that you were dining out with a drab spinster?"

How dare he? He was older than I was, and also single. And he was single when he died. Why is it men who haven't married by the time they are thirty are dashing bachelors and women are old maids?

"I am not a spinster. God, you sound like my mother!"

The floor of my closet was completely covered with discarded dresses by the time I was down to the last few remaining. And my patience, which I used to be practically famous for, was gone.

"The blue dress is nice, Hope. And at least you don't look like a piece of fruit in it," Eugene conceded when my eyes were beginning to water and my nose drip. "You don't look very alluring, but I suppose you don't have a lot of need for sexy dresses."

That settled it! I was going to wear the only red piece of clothing I owned—a rather skimpy dress that I had bought for hot dates. This might not be a hot date in my mind, but I wasn't going to give Eugene the satisfaction of seeing me looking less than gorgeous.

Unfortunately, it was not to be.

"I hate to break it to you, Hope," Eugene said dispassionately after I had donned the dress, "but the dress would be great if it didn't currently accent your rather red nose."

I glanced in the mirror and was disheartened by what I saw. The sneezing might have subsided, but the redness and runny nose had increased. I looked like a thin Santa Claus.

The blue dress it was.

By the time I had actually donned the dress, put on enough make-up to cover the reddest part of my nose, and gotten into the car, I was bordering on being late. I hated being late. It was the one thing my mother and I wholeheartedly agreed on. Every well-mannered person knew that tardiness was unacceptable (except for in cases of dire emergency and urgent bathroom stops). OPD didn't allow for tardiness.

For once in my life the streetlights were cooperative, and with just a tiny bit of speeding, I managed to arrive at the restaurant with two minutes to spare.

Vincent was waiting for me at the bar, a martini in hand.

Eugene eyed the drink dubiously, "Well at least he knows how to pick a good restaurant."

He was right. The restaurant was one of the nicest in Philadelphia. It was a blend of French and California Cuisine, with a hint of Asian. It was dimly lit, crowded, and incredibly chic.

"You look recovered from your near death experience," Vincent greeted me.

"Hardly that."

"No?" Vincent asked, though it was obvious exactly what he thought.

The host approached us, returning with a waiter and two menus.

The table to which we were escorted was covered with a white tablecloth and mustard-colored napkins. To my delight there were three forks, three spoons, two knives and only two chairs. Eugene would have to stand or sit at another table. I hoped for the latter.

I was disappointed. Apparently ghosts didn't feel exhaustion. Eugene assured me in a glib voice that standing was not tiring, and that he could stand all night if necessary. I ignored him.

As soon as I opened the menu, Eugene insisted that I point out what dishes I was considering. I dubiously did as he asked, looking a fool for moving my finger around the menu like it was in Braille.

"I wouldn't order that if I were you. It isn't one of their better dishes. I know. I did a review on this place last year."

I pretended not to hear him, focusing all my attention on the menu in my hands.

Eugene looked around at the forks loaded with meat and fish and smiled in appreciation. "You'd do better to order the Lamb with Mango and Papaya Salsa. And ask for a glass of Zinfandel with that. A better choice would be an Amarone della Valpoicella, but I doubt they have that. You don't see it on the menu, do you?" Eugene asked, maneuvering around me until he was partway through the table. I shifted slightly, still finding it difficult to have Eugene standing anywhere inside my body.

Vincent closed his menu, politely asked if I was ready and signaled for the waiter.

Eugene was still scrutinizing the menu when the waiter arrived, and I knew I looked like a fool with it sitting open in front of me. The waiter probably thought I was a moron and couldn't pronounce the items and was going to embarrass both him and myself by pointing at them.

No such luck. I snapped the menu shut, whizzing through Eugene's nose, and placed my order.

Okay, so I ordered the lamb. Eugene did know what he was talking about.

"Veal au Jus, eh? Well at least he ordered the California Merlot with it. That means he's not a total loss."

I gave a less than dignified sneeze in response.

I managed to lightly brush my nose with some Kleenex from my purse before the next sneeze hit.

"Allergies or a cold?" Vincent asked.

"I'm not sure." I wasn't about to admit that I was crude enough to go out with the beginnings of a whopping cold.

Vincent let the subject drop, and I put the Kleenex back in my purse, though it was no longer usable.

Since Eugene couldn't participate in the necessary small talk that started off every date, he decided to roam the restaurant, poking his fingers and nose at several different entrees scattered around the room.

"Have you been here before?" Vincent asked.

"No, though a friend of mine says it is quite good. And he should know since his expertise was food."

"A colleague from the paper?"

"Yes--I mean no. He was. He died."

"I'm sorry. Was it recent?" Vincent sounded all sympathy.

"Yes. As a matter of fact, it was just a few weeks before Marcus Whittington died." I had found the perfect opportunity to start questioning Vincent about the murder, and Eugene was on the other side of the room trying to dip his finger into something that resembled a mousse.

"At least Whittington wasn't a good friend, eh? That would have made it so much worse." Vincent said.

"True. I barely knew him. Still, knowing anyone who dies, and especially murdered, is upsetting."

"Of course," he agreed.

Eugene had moved on to a soufflé, and I was tempted to pull out one of my tissues and wave it unobtrusively in his direction. Common sense got the better of me. Waving around a tissue wasn't normal behavior, and I didn't want to give Vincent the idea I was less than sane. He was secretive enough as it was. I didn't think he would tell me anything if he thought I was bound for the sanitarium.

"Have you spoken to your police friend?" Vincent asked casually. " I was wondering if poor Evan were in for an immediate arrest, or if there was still a good chance the wedding would take place."

I was almost positive he was just being facetious.

"I told you that Peter doesn't talk to me about these things. For all I know, they could really suspect someone else altogether."

"Like who?" Vincent asked, his brow raised questioningly.

"I don't know. Anyone one of us."

"So he didn't give you any hint at what direction the investigation was taking?"

Had I not been clear the first time? "No. As a matter of fact, I haven't seen Peter since the beginning of the investigation. They could have made leaps and bounds by now. I was probably the last to hear about Evan's bloody shoes. The murderer will probably be tried and convicted before I hear about it."

"I doubt that. From what I have learned about Everton, information disseminates rather quickly."

He was right. My mother was probably leaving me a message right now telling me all about the person the locals most suspected of the murder and why.

"You know everyone better than I do, Hope. Who do

you think did it? And don't say Colby just because you can't stand her."

I thought I was supposed to be the one asking the questions. Eugene would be very disappointed in me right now. "I don't know. I think everyone is hiding something."

"Even me?" he asked with a look of mock horror.

"Most definitely you," I responded.

He laughed. "Seriously, though. Who do you suspect?"

"Evan would have the most to gain. And I suppose Angela as well. But then, so would Dean."

"That's not an answer," Vincent exclaimed. "What do you really think?"

"Well, the person behaving the most suspiciously is Susan. She seems to be doing a lot of drinking and looks scared. But maybe she just knows something. And Angela doesn't seem to be too upset about her husband's death. I heard her propositioning Dean in the most bullying way."

"Blackmail? Maybe she knows something, too. Is that all?"

"No. I know Rosemary lied to the police and to the rest of us about coming back into the house from the front door," I asserted.

"Really? Hmm." Vincent pondered what I had said for a moment before focusing his attention back on me. "I don't know, Hope. You seem to suspect all the women. If I didn't know you better, I would say you were just being catty."

Catty? What did he know about it?

I was beginning to really dislike him. Until he winked at me. Okay, so he wasn't so bad. And he was rather good looking.

"But perhaps you have something there," he continued. "Maybe the women are in it together. Or maybe one or more of them saw something. I suppose we'll find out one day."

"What about you? Who do you suspect?"

"John."

He was quite definite. There was no pause, no uncertainty, just the name.

"Why John?" I asked curiously.

"For one thing, he had easy access. All he had to do was

walk across the hall. And maybe Dean was in the room with him, maybe not. But Dean wouldn't rat on his brother. He wouldn't want the scandal." Vincent stroked his chin, picturing the scene in his mind. "And politically they needed Marcus' backing or his money. Both of which seemed to have disappeared rather suddenly. I have no doubt there are a few skeletons in the Raines' family closet."

I didn't look convinced, and Vincent smiled. "Besides, I know for a fact that the Raines empire is falling fast, and only some government contracts will save it."

"How do you know that? I haven't heard anything like that."

"I do a lot of research before making any move. And when Evan was short on funds, I considered getting it out of his fiancée's family." He paused for effect. "And if you still don't believe it, I heard John threatening Angela yesterday, telling her to keep her mouth shut about what she knew."

That sounded pretty damning, but I didn't want to jump to any conclusions. There were probably several reasons John would make a statement like that. Granted, I couldn't think of any, but that did not mean they didn't exist.

I looked around for Eugene, wanting to share this latest information with him, and saw him standing over a waiter who was setting fire to some dish.

Luckily, or perhaps unluckily, I sneezed at that moment. My eyes began to water and my nose to run rather haphazardly, sending me digging into my purse for the crumpled tissue. Realizing that there was no way I could gracefully blow my nose I excused myself and headed for the ladies' room.

As I passed Eugene, I sent a "psst" his way, causing several older couples to look at me askance.

The ladies' room was empty, so I felt comfortable sneezing quite loudly and yanking at the paper towels next to the sink. Eugene entered just as I was blowing my nose hard.

"Yuck, Hope. You didn't make me come in here to watch this, did you?"

In response, I blew my nose again, even harder.

Eugene looked around the bathroom curiously. "Do all ladies bathrooms look the same?"

"Sort of," I responded in a nasally voice before blowing my nose yet again.

"So, why did you bring me in here? There's a roast out there I would like to get a good look at. I don't recognize the spices offhand."

A woman entered the bathroom at that moment, undoubtedly wondering why I was doing nothing but staring at the entrance to the bathroom.

I blew my nose again, this time for good measure, and turned to the mirror as the woman entered a stall.

"Your nose looks really red now, Hope," Eugene declared with a little too much gusto.

The problem was, he was right. All my powder had been wiped off, and the harsh texture of the paper towels left red raw spots on my nose. I looked like Rudolph, just without the bells and harness.

Eugene walked around the room, looking into each stall (except for the one that was occupied), and making comments on the tiling, the cleanliness, and the bizarre methods of flushing that restaurants were now adopting.

I searched my purse for some powder and managed to finish touching up my nose just as the woman emerged from the stall.

She washed and dried her hands in silence, sending me a few curious looks. Had she never seen someone powder her nose before?

When she had finally left, I turned back to Eugene, who was sitting in a stall, and told him what Vincent had said about John and Angela.

Eugene did not look impressed. "Don't believe everything Mr. Suave says. He's probably trying to throw the trail away from himself and is using you because he knows you have connections. He probably thinks you are going to call up your police boyfriend and tell him everything."

I wondered if Eugene were correct. I had suspected that Vincent was using me to get information, but it hadn't occurred to me that he would use me to spread information. Apparently the attractions of my person were lessening by the minute.

"Are we done in here? That roast awaits."

I nodded, but before I could leave Ling walked into the bathroom, full of excitement. "Hope. I could hardly believe it was you when I saw you come in here. Your mother didn't tell me you had a date tonight."

"Wow. All this excitement over a date," Eugene snickered. "And a date with a thug, at that. Wait till your friend here tells your mother. I can hardly wait for the fireworks."

I shuddered at the thought.

"I didn't see you, Ling, otherwise I would have said hello."

"I know. You were so intent on your conversation with the good-looking gentleman. But this is better anyway because now we can talk in private."

Nothing was private when Eugene was present.

"There's not much to tell. He's one of the murder suspects."

That should put her off any idea of a romantic dinner out.

"Oh. How disappointing. And he is quite good-looking, too. But I shouldn't be surprised. Good looking men that are not married or criminals are so hard to find these days. Except for the gay ones, of course."

"I didn't say he was a criminal, just a suspect."

Ling nodded, but her hopes for me had been crushed, and she couldn't garner any more enthusiasm. "How are you doing otherwise? You look a little flushed. You're not coming down with something, are you?"

Why is it old friends can get away with asking questions that border on the insulting?

"A cold. Isn't it obvious?" I laughed at how ridiculous the situation was. "I was certain they could hear my sneezes in China." I turned and looked back in the mirror. I looked worse than I had realized. The evening would have to end soon or I would be forced to hide my head behind my napkin for the remainder of the night.

"It's not so bad. Really," Ling said kindly. "You just look a little feverish. But think of it this way— it's putting some color in your cheeks."

And then it hit me, clear as day. My life officially sucked. I was on a date with a man I wasn't really interested in, simply because I wanted to find out if he had killed someone, which I was only doing in order to keep my insufferable ghost tenant happy. And I was supposed to be grateful that I felt like a train wreck because it was actually improving my appearance. And to top it off, I had run out of Kleenex. I wanted to cry.

"What's the matter? You suddenly look much worse," Ling asked, grabbing my arm.

Oh, great! How much worse could my appearance get?

I wanted to tell her that my life was falling apart, all my preconceived notions of life and death had been shattered, I was living with a man that took pleasure in annoying me, and I was now involved in a gruesome murder that made me envy my mother's life. Instead, I decided to sum it up for her, "I'm out of Kleenex."

"I saw some next to the host. We can pinch it while his isn't looking." She understood, as only another woman could. This was the beauty of feminine communication. One female did not have to use concise description to get a point across to another. Vague references to toiletries, shopping expeditions or even naming kitchen utensils were all that was really needed.

Eugene, who had decided to poke his head in and out of the door to keep both an eye on both the roast and I, did not get it. "What's the big deal? It's just a little cold. No one is going to hold it against you."

Didn't Eugene get it? I didn't care what strangers thought of me; I cared what *I* thought of me. And right now it wasn't very much.

So Ling and I returned to the dining area by way of the host's podium (thankfully empty), where a small packet of Kleenex was deftly pocketed by Ling. Eugene, extremely interested in the reservations book, barely noticed, and certainly didn't comment.

Ling walked me back to my table, curious to meet a murder suspect, and stayed to chat for a few minutes, leaving her own date twiddling his thumbs several tables down from us.

It would probably have been the most pleasant part of the evening if Ling hadn't belatedly remembered that she had seen Peter and he had told her that he intended to visit me in the next few days. I looked rather embarrassed, having just told Vincent that I rarely saw Peter, and while he didn't comment, I could see his brain store away the information. Ling finally floated away with a resounding, "Give my love to Nutter Butter," which made several people at nearby tables stare. Undoubtedly, they assumed that I had an unhealthy relationship with Peanut Butter, or that I was besotted with the cookies.

Eugene, who had finally moved away from the host's podium, had returned to examining the dishes as the waiters brought them out.

By the time the coffee was served, I had sneezed twice more, finished my wine, as well as two glasses of water, and was wondering why I hadn't brought some Sudafed with me. Vincent kindly blessed my sneezes, and then even more kindly proceeded to ignore my hasty grabs for tissue, which placed him much in my favor.

I was trying my hardest to focus my attention on Vincent, who was giving me his opinion of Philadelphia and our hoagies, when Eugene roared in triumph and marched straight into the kitchen.

I strained my ears for sounds of crashing pans and shrieks of terror, but I heard nothing. I waited for the fire department to arrive, hoses in tow, but they never came. To my amazement, Eugene was behaving himself.

And just as I was smiling in delight at the progress he had made, the crash came, and Eugene hightailed it out of the kitchen.

He sat down in an empty chair at a neighboring table, which was occupied by three middle-aged businessmen, and looked at me defiantly. "It really wasn't my fault," he said, though he was at this point speaking to the side of my head. "I was so focused on the Sweet Breads that I didn't realize I was leaning against the counter. Besides, only an idiot would put a metal dish full of chopped vegetables at the edge of a counter where it could easily be knocked over."

I didn't respond, pretending to be absorbed in Vincent's conversation, when Eugene added, "You should actually be pleased that I am getting so adept at moving things. I keep telling you that, but you don't seem to see the significance of it at all."

I saw the significance of it all right. I saw it in my nightmares. Visions of ransacked houses, huge bills for broken items in stores, people tripping over Eugene's invisible feet and into puddles of mud. Did I mention I usually get splashed in those dreams?

"So I still think hot dogs are superior, though it is tough to decide whether I like the ones in New York or Chicago best," Vincent finished.

When did the conversation turn to hot dogs? I thought we were still talking about hoagies. "I'm afraid I don't know much about hot dogs. I'm more of a pizza person."

"An expert?"

"No. Just an aficionado." Okay, that's only half the truth. Pizza is more like therapy for me.

"You'll have to give me some recommendations for the rest of my visit. Or for my next visit, which I am sure will be soon." He smiled at the last part of his statement, and I got the distinct impression that I was sitting opposite a predator.

"Oh, please. If he starts to gush and suggest that you two are soul mates, or even that you are worth coming back here for, I am leaving."

Eugene had a real knack for being unintentionally insulting. But in one thing he was right: I wasn't about to be flattered by suggestive comments.

I smiled politely and said, "I believe you mentioned before that you move around a lot."

"My business requires a lot of travel," he replied noncommittally.

"To abandoned warehouses and deserted beaches," Eugene asserted. '

Vincent motioned to the waiter to bring the check, and I took the opportunity to dab at my nose with the purloined Kleenex. But I was not meant for subterfuge. The small tissue fell out of my hands and down the center of my dress, where it rested snugly between my breasts.

Just as I was about to reach my hand down my dress (a serious faux pas) Vincent turned back to me. My hand paused mid-air and I smiled, quickly brushing back my hair. The tissue was far down enough that he might not notice. But if he did notice, he might assume I stuffed my bra or was one of those coarse women that kept secret articles in their bra—things like wads of cash or stolen microchips.

He didn't notice, but Eugene did. In the typical Eugene style, he laughed until I could swear he was foaming at the mouth. He would never let me live this down.

"I would love to travel more," I said suavely (or as suavely as I could manage under the circumstances). I darted a quick look down my dress. "I'm not sure I would want to travel for work, though. Traveling for pleasure would be better." Like traveling to Tahiti right now. Alone. And when I say alone, I mean without my maddening sidekick.

"Well, I have seen some funny things while traveling, which makes the boring business side of it more bearable. Especially at airports. I think everyone has funny airport stories, and I probably have more than my share."

Eugene was still laughing, only now he was pretending to pull things out of his shirt. He looked like a drunk playing charades.

"I admit to being bodily searched more than my share," I said, which caused Eugene to actually fall over and roll on the floor. Three departing customers walked through him, and for once he seemed as oblivious to their presence as they were to his. "And I've had a few technical problems, though they mostly involved flying with one working engine, and the air conditioning going out. What has happened to you?"

Vincent sat back, obviously getting comfortable for

what was going to be a long oration. "The most humorous things usually involve airport security. Especially now that check points have so many ridiculous rules. I actually saw a man, a member of the military, who was allowed to have a loaded weapon on the plane go through security with all his papers and what not. Then they searched his luggage and confiscated his tweezers. Can you believe that? The man is allowed to carry a loaded gun onto an airplane, but had to leave his tweezers behind."

I could believe it. I recounted an incident that I had witnessed in which some security guards took a G.I. Joe doll from an old woman--who was presumably carrying it as a present for a child--and took away the little inch-long plastic gun. Apparently they couldn't tell the difference between an inch-long plastic gun and the real thing, because they checked the gun to see if it worked and then kept it. I guess G.I. Joe was going to have to defend himself using a cigarette lighter, because one of those was allowed on the same plane.

Vincent then informed me of a woman who had mistakenly gotten his luggage instead of hers, and held it hostage until the airline found hers and returned it to her.

Eugene, who had managed to pick himself up the floor by this point, looked outraged. "What kind of a person would hold someone else's luggage hostage? The nerve of some people. As a matter of fact, that sounds exactly like something my mother's old neighbor, Mrs. Frantz, would do. Ask him what her name was, Hope. There's probably a good chance it was her."

"Did you know that the most common item found in lost luggage is men's wedding bands?" Vincent asked, cutting off the last part of Eugene's speech.

If I said I wasn't surprised, I would sound like a bitter man-hater. If I asked why that was, I would sound like a naïve idiot.

I decided to go with polite interest.

"Really?

"Yup. Are you surprised?"

No. Some men *are* real pigs. "Maybe they were worried they would lose it if they took it off at a security checkpoint."

And pigs fly, too.

Vincent laughed. "I know you don't believe that, but I will respect that you don't want to criticize men in front of me."

I knew I liked this man.

Eugene just snorted.

As Vincent rose to leave, momentarily turned away from me, I grabbed the tissue out from my dress and dropped it on my plate, much to the surprise of the bus boy, who looked at my chest to see if any more would be forthcoming.

He was sadly disappointed.

Chapter Twenty-Four

Typically, the only person who really enjoys a bridal shower is the mother of the bride—at least according to Jillian. The single women feel resentful and envious, the bridesmaids disappointed they weren't chosen as the maid of honor, and the maid of honor wondering why all her work in planning the shower was wasted on a bunch of sulky bridesmaids. Family friends question why their daughters are not walking down the aisle, and if their daughters already have, they wonder what took this future bride so long. (It never occurs to them that the bride might not have been the problem). The soon-to-be mother-in-law is undoubtedly thinking that her son could do better, and the bride herself is so stressed out over the wedding that she is barely aware of what is happening around her. But the mother-of-the-bride is happy. Her daughter is finally being wed (to a man obviously not good enough, but that was bound to happen). Her daughter will have a great life, several adorable children, and a cute house just down the road. And if it weren't for the pesky in-laws, life would be absolutely perfect.

At least that is normally the case. Colby's bridal shower was no different in that it held a roomful of miserable women, though some for slightly different reasons; the big difference was that the bride's mother was without a doubt the most miserable person there.

When Jillian and I (undoubtedly last-minute invitees due to a decline in guests) walked into Susan's living room, a sorry sight met our eyes. And it wasn't just the decorations, which were indeed dreadful.

Susan and the maid of honor, a pushy woman named Meredith, had filled every nook of the room with white streamers, paper bells, and heart-shaped bouquets. A table was set near the door to hold the gifts, and another table at the far end of the room to hold some appetizers and punch. Both had white table-cloths with a heart border, and hearts interspersed across the entire fabric. The final touch was an ice sculpture on the far table that depicted two swans forming a heart with their necks and beaks. It was like walking into my own personal version of hell.

And I haven't even gotten to the guests.

Approximately twenty women of varying ages were clustered around the room, chatting amicably with one another while shooting nasty looks at some of the other clusters. And everyone, with the exception of Jillian and I, was wearing white or pink.

Eugene was right. I shouldn't have worn the green dress with the floral pattern; I was the only 7up in the middle of pink lemonade.

"I thought this was a bachelorette party? Isn't that what the e-vite said? This looks a little tame. I guess there aren't going to be any strippers." Jillian sighed in disgust. "I guess I shouldn't have bought her a sex toy as a gift."

I laughed (okay, more of a cough) at Jilly's look of utter embarrassment. "You didn't? What were you thinking? And I'm pretty sure the invite said bridal shower. Or bridal send-off. Or something bridal. I didn't really read it, to be honest."

"I was sure it was a bachelorette party. Who has a bridal shower just days before a wedding?"

I shrugged. "I think that Colby's mom thinks this is what a bachelorette party should be. Can you imagine how bad the actual bridal shower was? I'm just glad we weren't invited to that."

"Yeah. Wait, you think she had a bridal shower before this one? Really? Well, why wouldn't we be invited?"

"Maybe it was for close friends only."

"Oh. And that is definitely not us. You'd think she would want the extra gifts, though. I know I would." Jilly scanned the room. "Do you see who's here, Hope?" She pinched my arm when I didn't immediately respond.

"Uh-huh," I spit out before a racking sneeze erupted

from my small frame.

"Yep, you're right. Everyone in the world you are allergic to," Jillian agreed.

If one could have allergies to people, she was right in that these would probably be those people. Several of the women were acquaintances from high school that I had hoped never to see again, while a few of the older women were members of my parents' club, and disposed to criticize everything I did and then report back on it to my mother.

And then of course, there was Colby, who had heard my sneeze and seized the opportunity to come over and welcome us personally.

"I didn't think either of you would be able to make it," she pouted. The way she phrased her words didn't leave any doubt that she had hoped we wouldn't make it.

"We wouldn't miss this for anything," Jillian gushed.

Except for maybe a colonoscopy or a root canal.

"We are so happy for you," I added politely.

Colby just smiled smugly.

Here comes the comment about my still being single. I could tell she was just itching to get it out. A forklift wouldn't have been able to close her mouth.

"Thank you. You know, Hope, if you—"

"How lovely of you both to come," Susan interrupted a little too brightly. "And you brought gifts. How charming."

Either she had no idea what to say, or she thought we were barbarians storming the castle.

"Why don't you go sit with your friends, Mom? I'll introduce Hope and Jillian to the people they don't know." It wasn't a suggestion. Colby didn't make suggestions; she simply gave orders.

Susan, losing her false cheer and suddenly looking lost, nodded and moved to the far side of the room, where two middle-aged women were holding court with several younger women.

"Your nose is running, Hope," Colby said sharply before turning around and walking to the nearest group of women, leaving us to follow in her wake.

I quickly dabbed at my nose, which had improved over the last few days, while Jillian deposited our gifts on the appropriate table.

"This is Anna and Julia, friends of mine from college," Colby announced with a queenly gesture. "And I believe you know Dominique and Valerie. And of course, Rosemary," she continued, this time using her hands in the manner of Vanna White.

Jillian and I nodded, and Colby excused herself, walking over to Susan, who had been handed a glass of punch by a somber looking middle-aged woman.

"Colby is so worried about her," Valerie chirped. "Poor Susan hasn't been feeling well. It's probably menopause."

Ah, menopause! The younger woman's explanation for all erratic behavior in middle-aged women; the middle-aged woman's excuse for all behavior that shocks the older women; and the older woman's reason for losing all the hair on their head and growing it elsewhere.

Jillian looked at me with a question in her eyes but I just shrugged. I wasn't about to announce Susan's problems to the world. I could tell Jillian all about them in private later.

That sounded bad, but I needed to get Jilly's opinion on the murder. Eugene was talking about sending anonymous blackmail notes and seeing who acted in a guilty manner. I didn't doubt that the notes would have people banging on my door with carving knives, and I suspected that a new perspective would be helpful in curbing Eugene's enthusiasm. I needed to force Eugene's thoughts into another outlet--like ballroom dancing. He claimed to be quite good at it. Maybe Jillian knew of a class he could sit in on. Then he could practice all night long and leave off watching those darned crime films. Maybe he could convince Jezebel to be his partner.

I could hear the click of the front door as it opened and closed, and a slight breeze ruffled the dresses of the women around me. I turned to the doorway to see who had arrived, and held my breath in astonishment. Magdalena, wearing a red chip hat with a matching veil, and wearing a black, flowing dress, stood at the threshold. She held a thin, narrow box wrapped in silver paper, and tied with a red bow.

Jillian turned toward me. "She's wearing black. Can you believe it? Even I wasn't brave enough, or rude enough, to wear black." Jillian sounded awed rather than shocked.

I smiled. "I can believe it. The fact that Colby is her granddaughter only makes the drama more appealing to her." And boy was she creating a stir. Magdalena was probably elated over her entrance. I could imagine the triumphant way she would tell the story to the next person who took tea with her.

"I am here," Magdalena said loudly enough for the entire room to hear her.

Angela, looking amused, laughed heartily at Susan's horror. "Of course you are. And what an entrance! We've been waiting for you to liven up the party."

It occurred to me that Angela would certainly not have discouraged Magdalena from wearing black and red to Colby's bridal shower if Magdalena had chanced to mention the idea to her.

Susan hurried over to Magdalena, fluttering around her while she softly scolded her for her attire. "Colby is going to be so embarrassed. Why would you do this to her? You are the worst grandmother imaginable."

Magdalena looked frosty. "This has nothing to do with Colby. Can't I wear whatever I please, whenever I please," she said a little louder than was necessary. "I am a widow, after all. A hundred years ago widows wore black until the day they died or the day they remarried."

Colby strode over and urged her mother to stop making such a fuss. "Grandma just likes to stand out, which is just fine. Let her make a fool of herself."

At this point I thought all three had made fools of themselves. Boy, was I glad I hadn't been born into this family!

"What a show," Jillian said. "Now aren't you glad we came? I wouldn't have missed this soap opera for the world. And Martin said I wouldn't enjoy myself."

Angela, relishing any scene that placed Susan in a bad light, decided to benevolently take center stage. "Why don't we start eating? The food is just lovely. And while we're eating, we can pass around the recipe cards we all brought for Colby."

"Recipe cards?" Jillian and I said in unison.

Apparently the guests that received more formal invitations had been instructed to bring a favorite recipe. Since I didn't have a favorite recipe, I wasn't overly distressed at my lack of a card. Jillian, an actual chef, was not so placid.

"She doesn't cook. I doubt she could boil water," Jillian said waspishly.

"That's not the point. It's bridal shower tradition to bring the future bride recipes to start her off. Whether she uses them or not is besides the point."

"We still should have been told."

"Would you really have wanted to share one of your recipes with Colby?" I teased.

"You're right. I probably would have shocked you horribly by being so mean-spirited as to bring a fake recipe that I knew would send her guests running home in fear of their lives," Jillian half-joked. "And why didn't they bring recipes at the other shower? How many does she need?"

I shrugged. "Maybe this is it. They might have had to cancel the other shower."

"Right. Because of the murder. But still..." Jilly wasn't as sympathetic as I thought she could have been, but then Colby had been worse to her over the years than she had been to me.

I sighed. And it turned into a choking cough. Jilly hit my back several times, drawing the attention of several stern older women.

What were we even doing here? Surely we were destroying the sanctity of the institution of bridal showers by our very presence?

Jillian and I quickly grabbed some plates and joined the line that had formed around the food table, directly behind Magdalena, who was entertaining an older woman with thinning hair and a moustache.

"But I turned the film down. Love does the strangest things to people. To think, I could have been as big as Ava Gardner or Elizabeth Taylor," she was saying.

The other lady looked skeptical, but nodded politely before turning to the woman in front of her and asking for the spoon and fork to dish out some salad.

Magdalena, temporarily left without an audience, found Jillian and I and gave a gurgle of triumph. "At last. I knew you would be here, Hope. Angela assured me you would. Thank my lucky stars there is someone sane I can talk with." She looked Jillian over critically, decided she liked what she saw, and introduced herself with a flourish.

Jillian was stunned into silence, which was quite unusual, and I set about procuring utensils for us all.

When I reached the table, I grabbed a few mini quiches, some salad, and some cheese with crackers. At least the food wasn't shaped into hearts or swans.

Magdalena also filled her plate and pulled me away from Jillian and the crowd around the food and onto a solitary sofa.

"We only have a moment before your friend joins us, and I have so much to say to you in private. But first, how is dear Ewan? No, that's not right. It's not Ewan, it's Eugene, isn't it? I'll get it right eventually."

"He's fine. He's at home, probably watching television or trying to rearrange my desk."

Magdalena nodded in understanding. "I can't imagine how it would feel to be..." She lowered her voice and leaned into me, "...dead. It must be very frustrating and quite boring. Roger acted out at first, too. Looking back, he was so much more fun when he was dead."

Magdalena whipped her sleeves out the way as she used her knife and fork to plunge into the wiggling shrimp. A shrimp went flying, landing at the feet of a tall blond wearing a pink suit and matching heels. The blond turned around in horror, obviously fearing for the sanctity of her stockings, and Magdalena lifted an imperious eyebrow in response.

"That woman has the face of a mole," she said as the woman turned back to her conversation, carefully stepping away from the shrimp. Magdalena turned back to me, moving her napkin closer to her waist. "Do you object to my using my fingers for the shrimp, my dear?" she asked me with an apologetic smile.

I surveyed the plate Magdalena held with trepidation. There was a small mountain of shrimp with cocktail sauce, several pieces of lox, some loose greens that were dripping with dressing, a small portion of chicken salad slavered in red beets, and some caviar on crackers.

It would have been wise to sit on the opposite side of the hand she ate with.

Magdalena turned around to make certain that no one was taking notice of our whispered conversation. "I've been thinking about our club," she tittered.

"Club?" I asked in confusion.

"Yes. For people who have been haunted. We talked about it before. I was thinking that we should place an ad in one of those scientific journals. They must have one that deals with the supernatural."

Yeah, and it was probably monitored by the government so that they could keep tabs on all the loonies in the world.

I was saved from a response by Jillian's arrival with her own plate and a few extra napkins. "I saw that shrimp go flying, and I thought these might come in handy," she said laughingly. "And Hope, your nose is running again. You can use it as tissue.'

The cake, a chocolate creation with white frosting and pink roses, was served immediately after the food. It tasted like it came from a box, but I didn't object. Chocolate was chocolate in any form.

Jillian was more discriminating, and after one bite set it down on the side table next to her. "You'd think they could afford something a little better."

I supposed Jillian was right. Maybe Vincent was correct in his assumption that the Raines' were not so wealthy as was commonly suspected.

The last bite stuck in my mouth and I reached for my punch. I heard someone calling my name from the doorway, and I looked over to see who it was.

And then I spit out my drink.

Standing there, in the flesh, was Eugene. Okay, not in the flesh. But it was still Eugene. The same Eugene I had left at home with strict instructions to stay put and not touch anything. The same Eugene that had said a car ride with Jillian and I was more than he could bear anyway. The same Eugene that had claimed watching a 'B' movie would be more entertaining than a bridal shower.

And yet, here he was, looking around with a bemused expression.

And now I was burdened not only with a punch-splattered dress, but a disobedient ghost.

"Are you okay, Hope? Did the punch go down the wrong pipe?" Jillian asked, her hand in position in case she needed to thump me on the back again.

"Hmm? Yes. Sorry. Did I get you?"

Jillian looked down at her dress and shook her head. "Nope. I'm clean. But I am worried about you, Hope. You don't usually spit out your drinks. And you are looking a little pale. Is it your cold?"

"Probably. I should have stayed home."

"And miss all this excitement? And don't tell anyone, but Valerie has hinted that Angela Whittington, for some unknown reason, has hired a stripper. Can you imagine the look of horror when Colby finds out? Her poor dignity will go right down the drain. I am so excited!"

A stripper? Oh God! I had to get rid of Eugene fast!

"Did someone say something about a stripper?" Magdalena asked, appearing from somewhere behind me.

"Yes. I think Angela hired one," Jillian responded laughingly.

"Ooh. How fun! And to think I thought about staying home and pleading the headache." Magdalena looked like a child that had just been handed the keys to the candy shop.

There was only one place I could go and not be overheard.

"What is it with women having conversations in bathrooms?" Eugene asked jokingly after I had practically herded him in there.

"What are you doing here? I thought I made it clear that you couldn't come."

"You did. But then I got bored, and I started thinking. Here you are, practically at the scene of the crime, and you can't do any snooping because you are too busy playing nice with that horse-faced Colby. But I, on the other hand, can snoop because no one will see me. Some of the prime suspects live in this house. We should be searching their rooms."

"Eugene, I was serious. This isn't an appropriate time for you to be here."

"Why not?" he asked seriously. "If it's just because of lady-talk, I could care less. After listening to your phone conversations with Jillian nothing a female says could shock me."

"It's not just that. Besides, murder is a serious business. And you are an amateur."

"So? No one is going to kill me for learning something. You, on the other hand, are a different story. That is why I should be the one to be looking around."

There was no winning with him. "Fine." Something was bothering me. "Wait. Eugene, how did you get here?"

Eugene stood a little taller and sucked in his gut, and expression of disgust on his face. "I took the bus," he said dramatically.

I wanted to laugh, but he had started brushing off that invisible lint again, and I knew what that meant.

"How terrible for you. Did Jezebel come?" I asked, managing to hold back a sneeze.

"No. I know how you feel about letting her run loose around other people's homes." Eugene sounded snappish, as if my thought processes were ridiculous and I had no notion of appropriate behavior.

"Thanks. I'll make it up to her by taking her to the park later on in the week."

What was happening to me? I was feeling guilty about leaving an invisible dog at home so I had now promised to take her to the park. That wouldn't be a happy experience if her behavior on our last walk were any indication. The other animals simply weren't prepared for her ghostly presence.

"Are you in there, Hope?" Jillian asked through the doorway.

"Yes. Hold on."

"I will be very careful not to knock anything over," Eugene said. And then he walked through the door, probably through Jillian, and out of sight before I could respond.

I splashed some cold water on my dress and tried to rub out any remaining punch before opening the door to Jillian.

"Were you talking to yourself again, Hope?" Jillian asked as we walked back to the living room.

"Yes. I was just chastising myself for being so clumsy," I lied.

When we entered the living room there was a small pile of silver and white wrapping paper and tissue on the floor next to Colby, and a pile of colorful bows and ribbons were lying on a side table, ready to be formed into a bouquet. A small pile of kitchen utensils, books, and vases had accumulated at Colby's feet, and Susan was distractedly writing down names and gifts on a notepad. She looked like she could use a good drink, which wasn't surprising since Angela was sitting next to her and whispering into her ear with a triumphant smile on her face.

Rosemary handed Colby her present, and I was surprised to see that it was a silk nightgown that likely gave a clearer view than a window. I saw a few women wink at Colby, who smiled coyly.

Maybe I should have shopped at Victoria's Secret rather than Pottery Barn. Jillian looked at me and shrugged. Maybe these women were wilder than I had ever suspected.

A few shouts of laughter and some rather tasteless sexual comments were thrown at Colby as a slinky silver negligee with black lace was pulled from the box Magdalena had brought.

"What on earth is that? Is that even considered clothing? That wouldn't cover an infant, let alone a grown woman. But that's the point, isn't it?" Eugene exclaimed. He stepped into the pile of wrapping paper and got a closer look.

I shouldn't have been embarrassed since the clothes weren't mine, but I was.

"Her grandmother bought that for her?" Eugene was stupefied.

I put my head in my hands as pink underwear with red trim—did I mention it was Velcro?--was brought out of the next box.

Eugene's mouth dropped open and he backed away a few steps. "I really don't think I want to be in here," he said loftily before practically running out of the room. I was grateful, since Jilly's gift was next. And it didn't go down well. Colby was mortified and several of the younger women had to explain to the older ones what its purpose was.

When the last gift had been opened, and the bouquet of ribbons tied together, the guests began to wander about the room, chatting in small groups while Susan, looking even gloomier than before, stacked the presents in neat piles on the far sofa.

"Would a few games be too much to hope for? I suppose Colby doesn't do things like make wedding dresses out of toilet paper or games like on 'The Newlywed Show'. The sort of game that compares answers and shows how little couples really know each other?" Jilly was quickly getting bored.

"I would very much doubt it. I don't think the idea is for us to be entertained at Colby's expense."

Before Jilly could respond, a gorgeous man in a cheesy blue police uniform walked through the door, with Angela at his elbow. He was carrying a boom box and a bouquet for the future bride.

The stripper had arrived. And Jilly wasn't the only one who cheered.

I briefly wondered if Angela had insisted that the stripper dress as a police officer because she thought it was sexy, or she just wanted to stir up trouble. I dismissed the thought almost immediately as the stripper grabbed Colby and gave her a smacking kiss on the lips, much to the delight of her audience.

The party was suddenly getting more interesting.

The first item to come off was the man's walking stick, followed by his holster.

One of the older women started jumping up and clapping as his shirt came off. He threw it at her and she caught with both hands, swinging it above her head. The woman with the moustache jumped up as well, and shouted for the man to take his pants off.

And he did, but not before removing his belt and swinging it around like Tarzan. The belt was gently tossed to Magdalena, who shouted, "Is this all I get?"

The cop was nice enough to give her a smacking kiss too, before moving back into the circle of his admirers and continuing his strip tease.

The pants went soaring across the room and right through Eugene as he walked in the door. He stopped and stared in horror as the fake policeman, now wearing nothing but an extremely skimpy pair of Speedos and a cap, was gyrating to the music. Several women were crowded around him, stuffing wadded bills into his underwear.

Eugene was rooted to the spot, staring with a strange fascination at the scene unfolding before him. Most of the women had gotten into the fun, with the exception of Susan and Colby, who were looking slightly disgruntled that their classy shower had suddenly turned into a raunchy strip show. The shirt and pants were being tossed around from woman to woman, and the stripper was randomly kissing women and giving them a mild version of lap dances. He was beaming at the women, young and old, as they laughed and clapped in tune to the music. As a matter of fact, the stripper looked like he was enjoying the performance even more than the women. But then, who wouldn't be cheerful if twenties were being shoved down their pants?

"I can't believe you are actually watching this, Hope," Eugene yelled in my ear, trying his best to drown out the music. "Aren't you embarrassed to be here?"

Jilly and I had moved to the back of the crowd, not wanting to find ourselves being mauled by a stripper, no matter how good-looking. It was probably a safe move, since the women had started getting pushy in their attempts to attract the stripper's attentions.

I wondered if I should write a column on etiquette with

strippers. For instance, when you find yourself at a strip club, avoid the bored housewives. They can be vicious when you come between them and a handsome pair of cheeks. And on a side note, experience has shown me that the older a woman is, the freer she feels to express her admiration for a man through not-so-subtly placed bills. It would make an outrageously good column. Too bad my editor probably wouldn't go for it. And my mom would disown me out of embarrassment. In which case, it might be worth it. Ah, if only I dared.

"Cover your eyes, Hope. This isn't decent," Eugene moaned, trying to place his hands over my eyes, but only succeeding in passing his hands through my face. "Aren't you too young for this kind of thing?"

Oh, please! Wasn't he the one that kept calling me a spinster?

The stripper's hat was thrown wild, and pelted Rosemary in the chest. She managed to catch it, and then dropped it as if it were on fire. A few of the other women laughed at her reaction and then the attention was focused once again on the stripper, who had jumped onto a low coffee table in the middle of the room.

Several women screamed in appreciation while the coffee table groaned in protest. Eugene let out a squeak, but didn't take his eyes off the scene. Apparently the party had only gotten started.

When the stripper was coated with a greasy sweat, the coffee table was on its last legs, and the older women began clutching their chests in order to catch their breath, the party began to wind down. However, one didn't need a skimpily clad dancer for women to turn to alley cats fighting over some rather worthless men.

"At least you won't have a horrible father-in-law, Colby," one of the women said as she gathered up her purse.

Did she actually just intimate that Marcus' death was a blessing in disguise?

It probably was. But no one should be crude enough to admit it in public—and especially not to his widow and future daughter-in-law.

"Except for Angela, I won't have any. And she's only Evan's stepmother anyway. That doesn't really count, does it?" Colby responded.

"Who knows, Colby?" Angela said from behind her. "Maybe I really will become a mother to you. Things can change so quickly in relationships." She shot Susan a patronizing smile.

Jillian looked confused, while some of the other departing guests sent each other looks that clearly said, "I can't wait to get to the car and gossip about the implications of that statement." The thought of Angela ousting Susan and marrying Dean, thereby becoming Colby's stepmother, seemed too far-fetched, even if they were having an affair. And I still wasn't sure if Angela had managed to seduce Dean or not.

Colby looked both stunned and horrified at the same time, while Susan started to blubber about Angela being an excellent mother to Evan.

Even Magdalena looked disgusted at Angela's innuendo, shooting her a nasty look and patting Susan's arm in a slightly comforting manner.

Rosemary, who had been listening to the conversation while helping the maid pack up the presents turned around and bristled. "No one could ever believe you have any maternal feelings, Angela. And you could never take Susan's place in Colby's life."

Angela turned to Rosemary, a look of surprised delight on her face. "Ah, Rosemary. You're one to talk. You don't have any children, either. Or do you consider yourself maternal despite that? Perhaps you think there are some women born with a maternal instinct and some that are not? Or maybe you just start feeling maternal when you reach a—how do I say it?— mature age. " Angela purred.

The remainder of the guests, Jilly and I included, beat a hasty retreat, leaving the family to squabble amongst themselves.

Eugene was silent for most of the ride home. His posture screamed disapproval and his nose was raised a fraction higher than usual.

What did he expect would happen at a bridal shower/bachelorette party? Tea and a poetry reading?

"That was the chilliest bridal shower I have ever been to. And I'm not talking about Colby's behavior toward us," Jillian remarked once we had left the quiet street and hit the expressway.

"I know. That family has some serious issues they need to work through. Worse than any issues my mother and I have."

"And that's saying something," Jillian joked. "But what is all the tension about? You must have some idea since you've been spending so much time with them lately. And don't tell me it's all due to the murder. No one there seemed particularly bothered by that man's death."

"Except for suspecting each other of killing Marcus Whittington, I doubt the murder would have anything to do with it. Susan is worried Angela is going to steal her husband. And Colby is extremely protective of her mother." And while I was not likely to win 'The Nicest Person of the Year Award' this time around, any uncharitable thoughts I had were definitely put to shame by that group of women.

"I get it now. Angela Whittington was implying that she was soon to be the new Mrs. Raines." Jilly said.

"Probably, but I doubt it would ever happen. If Dean Raines wants to be the next governor he is not about to dump his long-time wife for the young widow of a recently murdered man."

Jilly laughed. "That wouldn't be very good press, would it? But if that's the case, why did Angela even make those kind of comments? Surely everyone knows she's just blowing smoke?"

"I imagine Susan suspects her husband of at least having an affair. She's taken to drinking a lot and crying in bathrooms. I feel sorry for her. And not just because Colby is her daughter."

Jilly was silent for a moment. "I can't believe you hang around these people."

"Not willingly. The things one will do for money," I said half-jokingly.

Eugene groaned.

"Is Angela Whittington always like that?" Jilly asked. "It just seems out of character or something. Not that I know her at all really."

"She's not usually that mean. Maybe something happened between her and Susan or Colby that annoyed her." Or maybe Dean had finally succumbed to her charms (or her blackmail).

"Well, at least that ordeal is finished. Now we just have to sit through the wedding, and then we will be free of any obligatory social contact with Colby for a very long time. Even your mother couldn't fault us," Jilly said cheerfully.

That was being too optimistic. "My mother could find fault with Mother Theresa."

Jillian just shook her head. "She's not that bad. You are too hard on her."

"You only say that because she isn't your mother," I argued. "But you are probably right. I am just so tired of people harping on how I'm still single and how I should give my parents grandkids. And trying to set me up with any man they can find." I gave Jilly a pointed look. She had also been guilty of that last part lately.

"Could you imagine having Susan Raines for a mother?" she asked, still thinking about the party "I am so glad I had my mom."

"True. My mother isn't really so bad either."

"And even your mother wouldn't have looked as if the apocalypse were upon her if she saw a stripper enter her living room."

"That's true." I laughed. The picture of my mother entertaining a stripper was rather funny. "She would probably have offered him tea and suggestions on how best to keep his costume clean." Or she would ask if he were single and try to foist him on me. From the phone call I received from her last night, in which she extolled the virtues of the local trash collector, it had become apparent that I had reached the age where a man's occupation should not be a deterrent in beginning a relationship.

"Do you suppose your mom keeps wads of cash handy for just such an occasion?" Jilly asked. "She does say that she is prepared for any occasion or emergency."

"You women scare me," Eugene wailed.

When Jilly dropped Eugene and I off at my apartment with a promise to call later that evening with some gossip about her own mother-in-law, Eugene waylaid me before I could open my door.

Actually, I probably could have opened my door, but I was still squeamish about sticking my arm through his body in order to grab the door knob.

"While you and the other women were making asses of yourselves with that lothario, I was actually doing something productive," Eugene scolded.

"Oh, yeah?" Who did he think he was? The queen wasn't this self-righteous! "Do you remember that photo we saw in Evan's room?"

I nodded. "I think so. The one of Colby?"

"Yes. No. That's just it. It isn't Colby; it's a much younger Rosemary Tate."

"Rosemary? Are you sure?" That didn't make sense. What could Evan possibly want with a picture of Rosemary?

"I'm positive. I don't make those kinds of mistakes. I have an eye for faces," he said arrogantly. "And besides, I compared it to those photos of Colby, which are fairly recent. This photo is a good twenty years old."

It didn't make sense.

"But Jezebel had that photo. Who knows which room it actually came from?"

Chapter Twenty-Five

Ghosts are not beneficial to one's mental health.

I was suddenly receiving calls from men claiming that my phone number had dialed their cell phones (amazingly enough they were all in the restaurant business). My mother was stopping by every day because she was concerned about me. Apparently a friend of hers had seen me sitting alone on a bench in a dog park. I'm not sure if my mother was more concerned that I was sitting alone or that I was in a dog park when I didn't own a dog. But concerned she was. The fact that I had started renting four or five movies a week from the red box also bothered her. It was bad enough that I was still single, but the fact that I was wasting my life watching old movies was too much for her to take. I was soon to be disowned, my father would hear about this behavior, and what would Aunt Maude say when she visited next month?

Since Aunt Maude had made dire predictions about my future my entire life, I was certain she would be ecstatic. It would probably make her year.

Unfortunately, my mother was of the opinion that any graduate of The Sylvia Pearson School (For Blueblooded Belles) could not end up with a less than spectacular life. It was her duty to see that I was properly set up in the world, and she would double her efforts if necessary.

So she did.

I spent the next week attending a stream of boring dinners with the country club set, while Eugene, who had realized after only two dinners that there was no real entertainment to be had at these functions, stayed home watching Humphrey Bogart films and training Jezebel to move a ball across the floor with her nose.

I spent an excruciating amount of time at the Raines'

house, seeing to last minute preparations and visiting with Magdalena, who had purchased several paranormal journals off of the Internet.

Each time I saw her she would have an article about ghostly hauntings in Kansas, Massachusetts or England that involved bloodthirsty beings scaring people while they slept. Her latest idea was to contact the Capuchin monks in Italy because they had catacombs decorated (literally) with bones of past dead monks. I emphatically vetoed that idea and Eugene, for once, agreed with me. He didn't want any playing with his bones, and I didn't blame him. Magdalena's assertions that she simply wanted their spiritual expertise didn't fool either of us. She would probably love to exhume a body.

Still, the worst part of this time had to be the hours spent with Colby and Susan, going over every wedding detail a dozen times until I could have screamed in frustration. It was obvious that I was the only one of the three of us that knew what needed to happen, but you couldn't say that to a client. Instead, I had to listen to them tell me what was wrong with every other wedding that had ever occurred.

And if that weren't bad enough, Angela would suddenly appear, sending both Susan and Colby into dark moods that bordered on manic. Every day Susan's drinking would start a little earlier, and Colby's temper would flare a little sooner. And Angela would laugh and chirp like a pretty bird, fluttering here and there before snapping her beak over some unsuspecting worm (usually Susan).

I had just returned home from an exhausting day in which I had to visit the paper before rushing over to the Raines' home and helping unload far too many cages of swans and doves, overseeing the placement of tables, chairs and tents, and checking the progress of the caterers, bakery, and church by phone.

My back hurt, my neck was stiff, and there were fuzzy bright spots hindering my vision. The only thing I wanted was to lie down and not get up until morning.

But when do I ever get what I want?

Eugene, standing in my bedroom, was pointing at my closet door and demanding that I open it immediately.

"Why? You have your own closet, and you don't need me to open doors for you anyway."

"I know, but you are always so annoying about my barging into your closet when I haven't been invited. I am trying to respect your privacy," he said frostily.

"But I haven't invited you into my closet," I protested.

"That's not the point."

I might have been tired, but even I could see that that was exactly the point.

"The wedding is practically upon us," Eugene continued, "and you haven't decided on a dress. As a matter of fact, you haven't even told me who your date is."

"Dress? I don't know. One of them should do."

"You aren't going to wait until the last minute to decide, are you? What about that pale blue one you just bought? Or the pale yellow one? Both of those would work."

Boy, was he getting annoying. He sounded more and more like my mother. I wondered if she left a message along similar lines, and he erased it?

I threw off my shoes and lay down on my bed. An hour's nap and I would be my old self. "You pick one, Eugene. You know how I look in all my dresses at this point."

"Fine, but I think you should put your hair in rollers tonight, and you can't expect my help with that," he added peevishly.

I didn't respond, already half-asleep, when the phone rang. "I don't suppose you could get that?" I asked Eugene.

"Even if I could pick it up they wouldn't be able to hear me," Eugene said.

True. I suppose that meant I had to get it.

"Hello," I said into the receiver, hoping it was a wrong number.

"Hope, you have to get over to the restaurant right now," Jilly demanded.

Her voice was urgent and I sat up, clutching the phone with both hands.

"Why? What's wrong? Has something happened to Martin?" A vision of Martin lying in a hospital bed with a tear-laden Jilly holding his hand popped into my head.

"No. Martin's fine. It's about Colby," she reassured me.

"Colby? Don't tell me she has gone and killed Angela?"

Eugene, suddenly finding the phone conversation more interesting than my closet, walked over and stood next to me, his ear so close to mine that I turned the phone out slightly just so that his head wouldn't go through me.

"Not that I know of. It's about her rehearsal dinner. They're holding it here at The Bon Vivant?"

The image of Colby behind bars, which was rather pleasing, also faded from my mind, to be replaced once again by those fuzzy lights. "I thought they were holding it somewhere in the city?"

"They were. Mrs. Raines was quite clear on that point in particular. As a matter of fact, they were having it at that restaurant you went to with the mafia guy. Somehow their reservations were lost, which they discovered when they called to confirm, and the restaurant didn't have any tables for a party that size. So now it's here," Jilly proclaimed, with just a touch of triumph. She was probably happier about the inconvenience to Colby's rehearsal dinner than about the business for her restaurant.

"And they chose your restaurant?" This was too bizarre! Colby was too snobbish to settle for anything less than the most expensive restaurant in the city. But then again, the idea of Jilly having to wait on her might be quite appealing to Colby.

"Well, don't make it sound like my restaurant is a cheap burger joint. My restaurant is not cheap and it is always getting great reviews."

Except that one from Eugene.

"I didn't mean it like that. It's just that I thought Colby would rather die than have to ask you for a favor."

"But she didn't ask. Her mother did," Jilly said matter-of-factly. "But that is besides the point. You need to come over here right now."

"I do?"

"Of course. I'm going to need your support. And besides, this way you can point everyone out to me and tell me which one you think is the murderer."

"It will be just like a Poirot episode," Eugene chimed in. "All the suspects will be in the same room together, making little slip-ups that give the murderer away."

"Not all the suspects will be there," I said to Eugene, though Jilly thought I was addressing her. Then again, who else would she think I was addressing?

"Well, no. But most of them. I know both families will be there, and the Tates, because they were in the restaurant when Evan and Mrs. Raines came in to check the place out. They were invited on the spot. Maybe they thought the more people invited the more palatable the idea would be to Colby."

"I wonder if they even told Colby ahead of time. I would hate to see the scene she would make if she wasn't consulted first."

"That's even more of a reason for you to come," Jilly argued.

"I don't know. Seeing Colby in a bad temper hasn't exactly been a novel experience for me lately." It was more of a daily--no, hourly--experience.

"Then come for my sake. You can hide in the kitchen the entire time."

Eugene was nodding his head and beseeching me with his eyes.

"All right. Let me take some aspirin and I will be over in about an hour. Is that enough time?"

Jilly gurgled with happiness. "Yes. They aren't scheduled to arrive for another hour and a half. This is going to be so much fun."

Eugene seemed to share that sentiment, though I wasn't sure what about it was supposed to be fun.

I hung up the phone and pulled out the first dress I saw. Eugene made no comment on my choice and I realized that he was even more excited than I had thought.

I hope he doesn't intend to try his hand at knocking

glasses into people's laps.

"Your friend should really thank me since it was all due to my ingenuity," Eugene declared smugly.

"You?" I choked out in horror.

"Mm-hmm. I erased their reservations when we were out with that thug."

"You erased their reservations? How could you do something like that?"

"With the pencil that was sitting on the host's podium. It was really quite simple. All I did was use the eraser and rub out the name. And not to worry, no one noticed a floating pencil. I know how you get about that sort of thing, so I made sure no one was looking," Eugene clarified.

"That is not what I meant and you know it. What possessed you to erase their name?"

"You know, Pip, you are extremely hard to please. I thought you would find the situation amusing. Can you imagine how they felt when they realized that their name had been forgotten? And then when there were no more tables?" he asked me. "It turned out even better than I could imagine."

"Eugene!" I bellowed.

He looked at me, surprised at my vehemence. "What?"

"You can't just go around doing those sort of things to people, no matter how much you dislike them."

"You're just upset because you didn't think of it first," he declared.

"No. I'm upset because it's wrong." Where was he raised—a barn? "What is the matter with you, Eugene? You didn't do this kind of thing before you died." At least not that I was aware of.

Eugene looked thoughtful. "For one thing, I didn't have the time when I was alive. And for another, I would have been caught. It's very liberating to be able to get away with things you only always wanted to do before. And don't tell me every person on this planet doesn't, on occasion, want to play a little joke on someone else. If you were stuck on earth without a thing to do, you would probably have set Colby's house on fire."

"Arson is a crime," I reminded him. "And can be extremely dangerous." I was suddenly worried I might be harboring a closet fire bug.

"Okay, I didn't mean that literally. But I wouldn't be surprised if you switched her toothpaste with hair gel. And you would probably find some chains to rattle in her attic. Don't deny it."

I wasn't going to deny it. He was probably right. But I reminded myself that it still wasn't really an excuse for his behavior. "I just hope I never find out if that *is* how I would behave."

"For your sake, I hope not, too. Now get dressed," he ordered. "We don't want to be late."

His fear of being late was completely unwarranted, and we walked into The Bon Vivant a few minutes before promised.

Jilly was waiting for me with a Cobb salad in one hand and a pina colada in the other. "I thought that if you were going to keep me company, the least I could do was feed you."

Eugene rolled his eyes. "She couldn't come up with something better than that?"

"It's perfect," I said, just to annoy Eugene.

"My paralyzed grandmother could make something better than that," Eugene retorted.

Jilly escorted me into the restaurant's kitchen, which was large and roomy, although it was decidedly warm. Several large stovetops and ovens were crowded with a half-dozen sous chefs and her lead chef, a short, stocky man named Cal.

As I was eating my meal and watching Jilly work with her employees, Eugene was wandering the kitchen examining the quality of the food and the precision of the chopping. He must not have found anything to complain about because he was extraordinarily silent.

It didn't take long for the wedding party to arrive, and they made their presence known immediately upon entering the doors.

Jilly, called out to the dining room by a server wearing all black with a pristine white apron, told me she would be back soon to describe the unfolding drama. Eugene, deciding that watching me eat was not as entertaining as watching the bickering wedding party, and left with her.

Unfortunately, she didn't come back soon, and neither did Eugene.

Sweat was beginning to drip down my arms from the warmth of the ovens, and my dress was getting clingy and uncomfortable. This was the last time I sat in a kitchen just so that my live-in ghost could listen in on a roomful of murder suspects. The fact that Jilly had the same bright idea rankled. What was she thinking, leaving me here alone with her surly chef?

Well, maybe 'surly' wasn't the word for it. 'Taciturn' probably described him better. When he talked it wasn't necessarily in an unpleasant manner. He just never talked. Ever.

Jilly said that was his best quality.

Then again, Jilly claimed that my best qualities were my convenient memory and my selective hearing, which oddly enough, were the very same qualities I most disliked in my mother.

Jillian and Eugene returned about the time I was debating whether or not to head to the outdoor patio to cool off.

"What a bunch of schmucks," Eugene spat at me. "Where do you find these people?"

Me? What was he talking about? He was the one that wanted to come here in the first place.

"You should hear them, Hope," Jillian started, "they are such a bunch of posers. Nothing would do but they have the best wine, order the most expensive meals, and talk about Mr. Raines' campaign as if he had already won and was now well on his way to being president."

"She's exaggerating, they didn't order the most expensive items. At least not all of them did. And the wine isn't that fancy here, so saying they ordered the best wine wasn't saying much," Eugene declared, while Jilly was still trying to talk.

"And when I commiserated on Mr. Whittington's death, everyone looked at me like I had mushrooms growing out of my head," Jilly continued.

"That's true," Eugene agreed, "they did look at her like

that."

"And I'll be honest, Hope, I wouldn't put murder past any of them, not even some of those silly bridesmaids I met the other day. Look how they got over some stripper. I thought they would actually start beating each other up over him."

I laughed. "Too bad they aren't suspects, Jilly."

"Jillian is right, Hope. Their behavior with the stripper was abominable. I thought I saw some fists flying, myself," Eugene cut in.

"And even Evan seems capable of murder when you hear how he is throwing around money."

"She's exaggerating again," Eugene said. "He isn't throwing around money. He is simply talking about investments. There is a difference."

Jilly continued to take apart the characters of the diners, while Eugene rudely interrupted every other comment to assure me that Jilly was exaggerating yet again or that she was indeed correct and I should see it myself.

After a few minutes of this I decided that I had had enough of the conversation, and excused myself.

I stepped into the dining room and looked at the large party Jilly had seated at the back table. The wine was flowing freely and the conversation quite gregarious. Evan was talking to Rosemary while Allan listened in before turning to Magdalena and whispering into her ear. Colby was addressing Susan and Dean in a low tone, shaking her head and nodding her head in rapid succession. Several of the bridesmaids were flirting outrageously with both John and Vincent and the best man, whose name I could never remember. Angela was flirting with two youngish men seated on each side of her, occasionally sending Dean languishing glances, which he missed entirely as he was absorbed in a discussion with his wife and daughter.

"What did I tell you? If there is a sensitive soul in the entire lot I haven't seen it," Eugene said from directly behind me.

I didn't respond, but headed out to the patio, where a nice breeze was cooling the air. The tables were empty, as were the benches, and the flagstone wall was cool to the touch.

I was there for only a few moments before Magdalena came out onto the patio, her arms waving in delight. "Oh, my dear. I saw you walk out here and I decided to join you right away. The others are in such strange moods tonight. Everyone is being so nice it makes me ill."

"I would think that being nice is a good thing."

"Only if it's sincere. Instead, it just feels as if everyone is playing some sort of game with everyone else. And God only knows what prize the winner gets. A knife in the neck probably."

"Do you really believe that one of them wants to murder someone else?"

"I suppose not. But it isn't as if any of them are sorry about the murder. As a matter of fact, it is the one thing no one dares to talk about tonight, even though it has been on all their tongues since it happened."

"Maybe they just want the wedding to take precedence over everything else tonight." It sounded reasonable.

And maybe all men, everywhere, will remember to put the toilet seat down. Or better yet, clean the toilet every few days.

"No, they just didn't care about Marcus that much. Not that I did either. But if they think talking about elections and weddings and the latest in stocks is going to make it go away, they are very wrong.

"And they seated me between Allan and John again, which is absolutely dreadful," she continued. "I think Susan does it on purpose. The two of them talk nothing but politics, and are always talking across me. Susan knows how I hate it. I have complained about it more than once. But perhaps Susan doesn't realize; she has been a little spacey lately. If it weren't for Rosemary being willing to switch seats all the time, I would probably start knifing people myself."

"Hope, ask her about the dinner," Eugene said with a hint of excitement in his voice. "This could be the information we need to close the case."

Police closed cases. I simply wanted off of the list of

suspects.

"Were you seated next to Allan and John at the fund-raiser?" I asked, enunciating every word so that my meaning couldn't be misconstrued.

"What? Yes. I remembered quite clearly just the other night. I was sitting in between Allan and John, although Rosemary kindly switched with Allan towards the end of the meal. Politics are so boring sometimes."

"Did you tell the police that you remembered?" I asked nonchalantly.

"Yes. I called up that nice policeman and told him so as soon as I remembered. He didn't even mind the late hour. I was hoping he would stop by to take a written statement, but he said he didn't need to." She sounded terribly disappointed and I wondered if it was the excitement of an investigation or the company of another person she wanted most.

"He will probably have to stop by sometime," I reassured her.

She smiled gratefully. "Is Eugene here?"

I nodded. It felt more and more like he was my shadow.

"Oh, good. Have you made any progress in finding out Why He Is Here?" The way she said the words made it sound like Eugene was bigger than Jesus in her book.

"No, but we're working on it," I replied, lowering my voice to match hers.

"Hah! Not much of that. You are too busy doing other things to be thinking about poor old me," Eugene argued.

Didn't he know I had to work to keep a roof over his head?

"Have you had any more luck in your research?" I asked Magdalena, hoping to get Eugene off my back.

"No. Since you won't consult the Capuchin Monks I have been researching other religious groups, but most of them seem like devil-worshipers, and I know that isn't what we want." She sighed dispiritedly.

"At least she has realized that," Eugene said, obviously grateful for small miracles.

Vincent stepped out onto the patio and Eugene groaned.

"Oh, great! Here comes Mr. Suave to annoy us."

"Hello, ladies. Enjoying the fresh air?" Vincent asked.

Magdalena smiled and clasped her hands in front of her. "I saw Hope and had to join her. Another minute in there and I would have killed someone," she said coquettishly. That is, if you can talk about murder while being coquettish.

"I know the feeling. I keep getting disapproving stares from Mrs. Tate, and those silly bridesmaids are beginning to simper. If I were a murdering sort of person, they would be the first to go," Vincent joked.

Magdalena laughed, and I gave a small smile, but Eugene just harrumphed.

"What kind of person jokes about murder?" he asked petulantly.

"I came out for a cigarette, but I seem to be out. I believe I have a pack in my car. Do either of you ladies wish to accompany me to the parking lot. I could use some protection from the other women," he said in a melodramatic voice.

I laughed, but shook my head.

"I don't smoke, dear, and parking lots are not my style," Magdalena said. "But you can accompany me back to the dining room on your way."

"With pleasure," Vincent said, taking Magdalena's arm and leading her back inside.

"I hope he doesn't come back any time soon," Eugene said pettishly. "We have important matters to discuss here. This might be our last chance at learning who the killer is."

I was really going to have to cancel my cable before Eugene started insisting we open up a detective agency.

The door to the patio opened yet again, and I was disappointed that Jilly had not joined me. How she could stand the heat of the kitchen was beyond me.

"Are you alone, Hope? I thought Mr. Torrelli had joined you," Rosemary said casually, although she appeared to be searching for him

"Mr. Torrelli has gone out to his car for a cigarette," I said. "Were you looking for him?"

"No. I needed some cool air and there is something about him that bothers me. Maybe it's just that I can't seem to like men that smoke frequently," she confided. "It shows a real disregard for personal wellbeing."

I nodded noncommittally.

"Not many people smoke anymore, but a few still do. The worst are the ones that smoke cigars. I've caught Allan smoking one once or twice with John or Marcus." She shuddered slightly. "I just don't understand it. It kills people. You would think grown men would know better."

"Hope, here's our chance. Find out what she knows about the cigar. You can be subtle, I know it!" Eugene insisted.

Great! Did Eugene really expect me to trap a murderer? I was no Sherlock Holmes. My brain just didn't work that way. I wasn't even in Nancy Drew's league.

"I didn't know Marcus smoked cigars," I said.

Not the greatest question ever asked, but it was subtle. That should satisfy Eugene, I thought wearily.

Rosemary nodded. "Marcus gave up smoking cigars a few months ago. Angela told me she was the one who insisted on it. But Marcus still liked to put unlit cigars in his mouth. He did it until the day he died. I guess some habits are hard to break." She cringed with revulsion. " And it was a disgusting habit even when the cigar wasn't lit," Rosemary said.

Eugene gasped and then clapped his hands. "She did it, Hope. She's the killer. How else would she know that he was smoking a cigar?"

It occurred to me that she could have seen him with it, and still not killed him. But Eugene was extremely determined to resolve the murder before the wedding, since he wouldn't have much of a chance to do so afterwards.

A loud cheer erupted from the dining room. "The mood seems to be rather festive. Don't you want to go join them?"

Rosemary looked thoughtfully toward the dining room. "I suppose so. Evan needs a lot of support. I hope Colby is going to be good for him."

Her blue eyes turned back to me, a sorrowful look filling them, and I knew Eugene had actually been onto something.

"You're Evan's mother, aren't you? That's why he has a photo of you in his room," I stammered. "I didn't realize it until I saw you two sitting next to each other just now. You have the same eyes."

"I knew it," Eugene declared triumphantly. "She's even going to admit it."

Rosemary started to tear and nodded. "Photo? Oh, I know the one. He found that picture among Marcus' stuff years ago and when he told Evan it was of his mother Evan kept it. He didn't recognize me, but there really wasn't any reason he should. I was so much younger then." She paused and look at me, her eyes pleading with mine. "You won't tell anyone, will you?"

"No. Though it won't be long before the police find that out. You should tell them. If you don't, they might start to suspect you. Does anyone else know?" I asked sympathetically. She had always been nice to me and I hated to see her so upset.

Rosemary nodded pathetically. "Allan knows, but no one else knows except Evan. And maybe Angela. She seems to learn people's secrets with surprising ease." She paused, her eyes taking on a far away look. "Evan found out the night Marcus was murdered, purely by accident. He overheard me talking to Marcus, who had never wanted me to have anything to do with Evan. I suppose he thought I would be a bad influence on him. You should have seen how he reacted when I moved back to Everton a couple of years ago." Rosemary laughed hysterically.

"I don't understand why you continue to keep it a secret. Or why you kept it a secret for so long. Why would anyone care that you are Evan's mother?"

"I didn't want Evan to know that when he was born I gave him up. Marcus' father hated me. I wasn't in their class, I guess. It wasn't long before he turned Marcus against me. That is, if he ever had any real feelings for me anyway. Marcus and I hadn't been married when I got pregnant, you know. And after I found out, well, I was broke and confused and so I took money from Marcus' family to stay away. I actually took money to abandon my own son. Can you imagine how ashamed I am?"

I shook my head. It seemed to me that Evan was willing to forgive the past, so no one else should have any right to hold her past actions against her. But I said nothing. She wasn't listening anyway.

"And now he is grown up. All those years wasted. All those years that Marcus wouldn't let me see him. Telling me that he would tell Evan horrible things about me if I even tried to tell him the truth." She cried even harder. She seemed so pathetic that I squeezed her hand in support.

Eugene was staring at her in horror. "You can't actually feel sorry for her, Hope? She abandoned her own child for money. That is despicable."

But I did feel sorry for her. Everyone made mistakes. And worse, everyone usually ended up paying for those mistakes.

"Do you promise that you won't say anything, Hope?"

I nodded.

"Thank you." She looked back into the dining room and took a deep breath. "I should probably go wash my face and get back to the party."

She left before I could respond, and no sooner had the door closed on her than Eugene turned on me. "You didn't ask her about the murder. Why didn't you ask her what she knew-- or even if she was the murderer? She was probably that woman we heard in the office with Whittington. I bet she did it, and you didn't even ask. And Magdalena said she sat next to her at dinner. She could easily have taken that knife. You're letting her get away with murder."

"I am not. We have no real proof she did it, and I doubt she would just admit it even if we did."

"You're going to tell the police who she is, aren't you?" Eugene demanded, not at all mollified.

"The police probably already know. They aren't dumb."

"That didn't answer my question. Are you going to tell them or not?"

"I don't know."

Thankfully, Jilly entered before Eugene could give me a

speech on the duties of every law-abiding citizen, which I could tell he was prepared to do.

"Sorry it took so long to get away," she apologized.

"No problem. I've been entertained by Magdalena, Vincent Torrelli, and Rosemary Tate in the last few minutes. I almost feel as if I have been invited to the rehearsal dinner."

Jilly laughed. "Now I really am sorry."

"Don't be. That was the reason I came, right?"

"What was the reason you came?" Allan Tate said, walking out of the dining room.

"To be entertained," I said lightly.

Eugene harrumphed again.

"By whom? Your friend here, or the mangy lot inside?" Allan asked.

It amazed me that none of the people dining together inside seemed to like each other at all. Didn't any of them have anything nice to say about one another?

"Both," I admitted.

Allan nodded. "You aren't the only one. The entire dining room seems to be entertained by the party. Of course I heard a few whispers about Marcus' murder when I came out here, so I suppose their interest is only natural."

"I hope no one has bothered your group," Jilly said solicitously.

If she hadn't said that merely to keep the topic of murder open I would eat my pants. (Okay, so I wasn't wearing pants. The next time I was wearing pants I would eat them.)

"Not at all. As a matter of fact, just when I was getting up one of those dumb bridesmaids brought up the subject, too. She had the bad taste to say that she had never eaten at a table with a murderer before."

Jilly gasped, although I could sense a little laugh there as well.

Eugene just rolled his eyes.

"She obviously hasn't been reading your column, Hope, or she would know what a faux pas that was."

"Actually, I don't think I've ever addressed that particular issue. Maybe that should be the topic of my next column. Something along the lines of 'Things Not to Say When Dining with Murder Suspects.' It might be a big hit with my editor."

Jilly wasn't about to be sidetracked. My pants were safe from future consumption.

"You really think someone at the table murdered him?" she asked.

Allan shrugged his shoulders. "It's possible. And the police certainly seem to think so."

"But why? Isn't everyone a friend or family member?"

Didn't Jilly read the newspapers or watch television at all? Stuff like this happened all the time.

"She's kidding, right?" Eugene asked. We were definitely in accord on that subject.

"I'm not surprised he was murdered," Allan said. "He used to lord his money over everyone. I doubt Evan did it, but I wouldn't put it past Angela or that Torrelli fellow. Maybe even John."

"Really? I would have thought John would be too smart to kill Marcus. He must know that he would eventually get caught and any future in politics for Dean would be over."

Allan just shrugged. "Maybe it was a crime of passion. Maybe Marcus threatened him or tried to pay him off and he just struck out."

"I don't know. The police think it must have been somewhat premeditated. Otherwise the murderer would have used the lamp or the clock or something, rather than a knife that had to have been taken at dinner."

Allan looked thoughtful. "Maybe the murderer found the knife lying around. Maybe Marcus took it to use as a letter opener and the murderer just saw it there on the desk."

"A letter opener? Wouldn't he already have one?"

Allan shrugged. "I don't know. Probably. I'm just trying to play devil's advocate here."

I laughed. "Maybe you should stick to playing devil's advocate in political discussions. A man taking a knife from his dining room table during dinner to use as a letter opener later on just seems like grasping at straws."

"You're probably right. I suppose we will just have to wait for the police to catch the guy. Not that I think they will have much luck. Apparently there aren't any fingerprints or DNA samples to go by, not even a copy of the last check Marcus wrote."

"Last check?" Eugene asked, backing up a few steps. "Be careful, Hope. He couldn't have known about the last check unless he was the murderer. Everyone assumes the last check Whittington wrote was to you."

"You're right," I said sadly. "Even though its obvious that the murderer wiped down the knife, picked up the torn pieces of the check, and raced out of the room before anyone could see him, without fingerprints or DNA evidence the police will never find him."

Allan nodded. "Yeah. It's too bad. But who knows? Maybe the police will get lucky."

"See, Hope. He just accepted what you said about the torn check. He obviously knew about it," Eugene said, echoing my thoughts.

Could Allan really be the murderer?

"Maybe," I responded.

"I wouldn't worry about it," Jilly said staunchly. "Peter's a good detective. I'm sure the man will be caught."

Allan looked over at me and smiled at Jilly's implicit faith in the police. I couldn't seem to return the smile.

"Have you seen Rosemary?" Allan asked. "She's the reason I came out here in the first place. She's about to miss the toasts and dessert." He laughed. "I know she'll be upset if she misses dessert."

"She went to the ladies' room." I answered rather glumly.

This night was not turning out as I had hoped.

And then it got worse.

Chapter Twenty-Six

"I told you I would call him," I responded to Eugene's question for what had to be the hundredth time. "But it's late. I can call him first thing in the morning. We might be completely wrong anyway."

"No. You should call Peter now. He needs to know what we know."

"But that's just it. We really don't know anything. I don't want to point a finger at someone who could be totally innocent. Allan has always been a nice person," I argued.

"It's the job of the police to find out if he did it or not. It's our job to give them a helping hand by reporting what we know."

"I know. And we will, first thing in the morning. He can hardly go arrest a man tonight based on our word. My word."

"You're just embarrassed to call Detective Sergeant Jameson."

"Why would I be embarrassed to call him?"

"You tell me," Eugene challenged.

"Fine. We'll call him." I would do anything to shut Eugene up at this point.

I located my phone book and dialed the number I had listed. When there was no answer and Peter's voice could be heard asking for me to leave a name and phone number I hung up. "He's not answering his cell phone. He's probably asleep."

"Call his office."

Eugene was really bossy tonight.

"Fine." But Peter wasn't there either and I declined to leave a message for him.

"How hard is it to say, 'Hi, it's Hope. Call me back'?" Eugene asked from the sofa where he was sitting with his arms folded across his chest, a mulish look on his face.

"Can I go to bed now?" I asked. "We can call first thing in the morning. I promise."

"Not good enough. Call your mother. She will probably have his home phone number."

"No. Didn't he give us his card? It has to be here somewhere. Maybe it has an emergency number or something." But it wasn't to be found in the drawer with my address book, the drawer with the phone book, or the drawer where the car keys were kept. It wasn't on top of my desk, in my desk, in the kitchen, or in my purse.

"This wouldn't be a problem if a certain ghost didn't try to play practical jokes all the time and move around my papers."

"Don't blame me if you're careless enough to lose things," Eugene grumbled. "You'll have to call your mother now. And you just wasted twenty minutes. If you thought she would be annoyed before, imagine how annoyed she will be now."

He was obviously imagining it, and with great pleasure.

But he was right. If Allan was a murderer then the police should be told. And if that meant waking up my mother, so be it.

The phone rang three times before my father picked up.

"Hello," he said, coming awake.

"Hi, Dad. Is mom up?" As if it mattered if she wasn't.

"Hold on." I could hear him speaking to her in the background before my mother picked up.

"Hope, are you all right? Is something wrong?"

"No, Mom. I know it's late, but I need to get a home phone number from you."

"Oh. You woke me up for that. Couldn't it have waited until the morning?"

"No. It's really important." Did she think I would have woken her up if it weren't? I had lived with her for years. I knew how she valued her beauty sleep.

She sighed. "Okay. Whose?"

"Peter Jameson."

"Oh?" she said excitedly.

I could read her thoughts as if she had been standing in front of me. They went something like this: 'Hope has finally come to her senses and decided to call a *nice* man for a change. Thank God for this miracle. My prayers for grandchildren haven't been completely wasted.'

"Let me go find the number. I am certain I have it." I could hear her tell my father to go back to sleep while she got up and started moving around.

"What do you need to speak to Peter about? Have you finally decided to give him a chance?"

I had to depress any of her expectations before I found myself gagged and bound and on the road to the altar. "No. I need to speak to him about a police matter. That's all."

"Really?" Unfortunately, that prospect only held slightly less interest for her. "Is it about the murder?"

"Yes."

"Oh?" she responded, almost completely successful in keeping the curiosity out of her voice.

"But I'm not going to say anything right now. I need to talk to Peter first."

"I completely understand, darling."

Sure she did. And I was going to lead the next Macy's Thanksgiving Day Parade.

"I'll tell you all about it after I speak with Peter. Tomorrow." Sometimes extra clarification was necessary with my mother. She might actually wait up for me to call her back.

"I found the number. Do you have a pencil and paper?"

"Yes. Go ahead."

She gave me the number, making me repeat it back to her three times before being reasonably certain that I did actually write it down correctly. "Now don't stay up too late. You'll need your beauty sleep if you're going to have to see the police tomorrow."

"Yes, Mom. Good night."

"Good night, Hope. Sleep well. Call me tomorrow."

I agreed and hung up. That had gone far better than I expected. She didn't even mention the fact that I had probably woken the visiting Aunt Maude, who felt strongly about single women that kept late hours.

"Don't just stand there, call him!" Eugene instructed me.

"I'm calling now. Be patient."

I dialed Peter's home phone and he answered on the second ring. "Hello?"

"Hi, Peter. It's Hope. I'm sorry to bother you so late, but you said to let you know if I learned anything."

"It's no problem. What did you learn?" he asked quickly.

"It's about the check you told me about. Well, tonight Allan Tate mentioned that the police didn't even know to whom Marcus' last check had been written. I remembered that you said no one knew about the check, and I just thought you should know." That sounded lame even to my ears.

"Tell him about Rosemary being Evan's mother," Eugene urged. "In for a penny in for a pound."

God I hated that expression!

"That's interesting," Peter said noncommittally. "Is there anything else?"

"Actually, Rosemary Tate just told me she was Evan's real mother. I don't know if that information helps at all." I felt like a huge tattle tail and a fool.

"We had already learned that, but thanks for telling me." I could hear him moving something around in the background for a moment before speaking to me again. "Can I come get your statement tonight? We already had enough evidence on Allan Tate to arrest him, but this will help too."

"Okay. What evidence?"

"Evidence?" Eugene exclaimed.

"Some fibers on the deceased's coat matched ones from Tate's. It isn't a lot, but we are still looking for more evidence."

"That doesn't seem like much to me," Eugene grumbled.

"I'll be over later with my lieutenant. You'll still be up?"

"Yes."

He hung up and I turned to Eugene, who was gloating. "See? It was important that you called tonight?"

"Was it?" The only thing I was certain of was that I would have a late night and probably feel and look like crap for the wedding tomorrow. Oh, and that Eugene would probably be crowing for months about how he single-handedly caught a killer.

I was tempted to get ready for bed despite the upcoming visitors but the thought of my mother learning that I received police officers (one of which she considered a possible marriage prospect of mine) while wearing a bathrobe was too much to take. And to be honest, it wasn't very classy. Look at Angela talking to the police in her robe. So what if hers was practically see-through and mine was fluffy terry cloth? The principle was the same.

I decided that washing my face and brushing my teeth would not be in bad taste, especially since Eugene had been complaining about my garlic breath all evening. The truth was, not only had I not eaten any garlic all day, Eugene couldn't even smell it if I had. Still, if he were not complaining about my perfectly fine breath he would probably start pretending that I had dandruff or chin hair. I didn't need to develop any complexes, after all. If brushing my teeth three or four times a day kept him happy, who was I to make a fuss.

About a half hour after I had hung up the phone with Peter, and ten minutes into an argument with Eugene about which toothpaste was the most effective, there was a knock on the door.

"Peter's here," I said as I walked to the door. "Let's get this over with. I have a long day ahead of me tomorrow."

"Aren't you going to ask who it is?"

"Who else would call this late but Peter? And the only other time I have had an unexpected late night visitor here was when you showed up. And I asked who it was then, and you still came in." And I was still regretting that night.

"What are you doing? Let me stick my head through the door before you—"

It was too late. I had opened the door, not to Peter, but to Allan Tate. Eugene was right again. I hated it when that happened!

"I knew it. He's come to murder you," Eugene moaned.

I *really* hoped that wasn't true.

"Hi, Hope. Sorry to bother you so late. Can I come in and talk?"

"Hell no," Eugene declared, trying to step in front of me and shield me from Allan.

Okay, play it safe, Hope. The man is a killer! You don't want to piss him off. "I don't know Allan. It's awfully late and I was in bed." Since I was still fully dressed I figured that not even Eugene's blind grandmother would believe me. And this was yet another reason to curse the fact that I was brought up with manners. No one else would put off changing their clothes just because of a few policemen.

"I know. I'm sorry. It's just that Rosemary told me about the discussion you two had, and I wanted to speak with you about it." Allan didn't sound threatening, just a little weary. Maybe he didn't realize that I knew he was the killer.

What should I do? I didn't want to let a killer into my house, but not letting him in might tip him off.

"I'm expecting someone. Can we make it fast?" I didn't move aside, and he was left standing in my doorway.

I suddenly wondered what my mother would have done in my place. I bet she would have let him in, never dreaming to keep someone standing on the porch, not even a murderer. She probably assumed that no one would kill her because to do so was in bad taste.

"It's just that I know you figured out who Rosemary was, and I was hoping you would keep it to yourself. It wouldn't do anyone any good if it got out. The police know. Evan confirmed that, but I think they will keep it quiet."

I nodded. "Is there anything else?" I asked, eager for him to leave.

"There you are, Allan. I knew you would come here after I told you about Hope," Rosemary said from the porch entrance. "I followed you."

"Rosemary, you shouldn't be here. I told you to stay home," Allan said severely.

I could see tears beginning to form in Rosemary's eyes. This wasn't going to be pretty.

"I know, but I didn't want you to upset Hope. I know she won't tell anyone."

Too late for that.

"This is bad, Hope. You should slam the door in their faces and then lock it," Eugene decided.

"I know, but it might not even matter now," Allan declared. "Evan has already told the police. I just spoke with him a few minutes ago. He told them he heard you and Marcus arguing and found out about who you really were. I think Colby convinced him he had to say something in order to save himself from a murder charge," he said disparagingly. "It also seems he discovered Marcus' body before anyone else and then left the scene for someone else to find. He admitted that too, at Colby's insistence." Allan looked as if Evan had disappointed him personally. "But the police believe him, so he isn't a suspect anymore. There is nothing for you to worry about. And maybe no one else will need to know about your past."

Rosemary started crying and edged her way past me and into the apartment, looking for a Kleenex.

"Evan told them?" she said in shock. "But he said he wouldn't. He knew it would make me look like I had a motive."

Apparently I wasn't the only one to break my word to poor Rosemary.

She seemed as if her mind had stopped functioning, and simply stared into space for a few moments. Allan approached her and she seemed to focus on him. "Do the police suspect me now?" she sobbed, sounding more than a little paranoid.

From her behavior one would think the walls had ears.

"There is no reason why they should. Is there, Hope?"

If he was looking to me for reassurance, he had asked the wrong person. My living room had just been taken over by a murderer and his hysterical wife, and I was no longer feeling hospitable. I just wanted them gone.

"I don't know," I answered as honestly as I could, still trying to maintain a semblance of courtesy despite my rising temper.

"It hardly matters that Evan is my son. That doesn't make me a murderer," Rosemary said to Allan before turning to me. "I mean, they would have just as much reason to suspect you as me, Hope, right?"

Was she joking?

Eugene laughed. "She needs a dose of common sense. Or a slap in the face."

"No one said you were a murderer," Allan assured her. "Everyone knows you're not capable of murder."

And I am? Enough was enough. First they barge into my home, and now they are practically hinting that I am a viable suspect in Marcus' murder. This was too much! They obviously didn't read the rule that stated you should never accuse your host or hostess of murder.

No more Miss Nice Girl. "Except I had no motive, whereas you did. I heard you arguing with Marcus that night," I told Rosemary in a dispassionate voice. "And Magdalena said you sat next to her for part of the dinner. You could easily have taken the knife that killed Marcus, though I don't think you killed him," I added as an afterthought. There was no need to have her hysterical on my floor if it could be helped.

"Of course she didn't kill him," Allan protested. "How could you even hint that she would?"

Rosemary looked at me, her expression suddenly intense and angry. "I intended to kill him," she said eerily. "At least I think I did. I don't know. I was so angry. He had been threatening to disinherit Evan. I heard him." Her voice cracked and she looked at Allan. "I took the knife from the dinner table along with a napkin and kept them in my coat pocket. And then I saw Marcus later on the porch, holding that horrible cigar, and I confronted him. And do you know what he did? He just laughed and said that I had sealed Evan's fate."

She started sobbing now, and I went over to her and offered her the entire box of Kleenex.

"Are you insane, Hope? Get them out of here. Do you want Peter to think you keep company with criminals? He probably won't ask you out again after this," Eugene declared stoutly.

I was now fairly certain that Eugene's mind was as demented as my mother's.

Rosemary continued talking, Allan watching her in concern. "I threatened him with the knife and he just walked away into his office. He laughed at me. And then he said he was going to write me another check to disappear. Just like last time." She started dabbing the Kleenex at her eyes and Allan came up and put his arm around her.

"Marcus deserved to die," Allan said to me. "He wanted to ruin Rosemary's life, and Evan's. He didn't have an ounce of compassion."

"And so you killed him," I responded matter-of-factly. "How else would you know about the torn check? You slipped up in the restaurant earlier. No one else knew about it. I only knew because the detective mentioned it to me."

Eugene gasped. "Now you've done it, Hope. You're supposed to wait for the police. I just pray he doesn't kill you to keep you quiet."

Eugene had watched way too many films at this point. Allan wasn't likely to kill me in front of Rosemary. And the police would be here at any moment.

"What is she talking about?" Rosemary asked Allan. Her eyes were widening and she took a step forward, clutching at Allan's sleeve. "You didn't kill him. You were in the living room. You said so. I saw you there."

Suddenly the entire scene appeared in my mind. "No he wasn't. Not the whole time," I corrected her. In for a penny in for a pound, I guess. "I thought I would have heard someone cross the foyer when I was in the dining room, but that wasn't true. All a person had to do was take his shoes off. When we came into the living room Allan's shoelace was untied. He took his shoes off, crossed the foyer and into the office, and stabbed Marcus with the knife you took," I told Rosemary.

"Good thinking, Pip, but really dumb of you to say," Eugene groaned.

Allan looked at me gravely. I could see his mind working quickly, trying to come up with plausible excuses. But we both knew there were none.

"Did he tear up the check he had written to Rosemary, or did you?" I asked him, feeling as if I were watching the scene from an outsider's perspective.

When he didn't answer I informed him of the conversation I had with Peter less than an hour before. "The police know it was you. They have evidence and a warrant. And they will be here soon to take my statement. You might as well admit it."

"Say you didn't to it, Allan. Tell her. The police are wrong. You're wrong, Hope," Rosemary pleaded.

A look of despair settled over Allan's face. He clutched Rosemary against him, and she started wheezing into his coat. "Marcus tore up the check," Allan finally admitted. "He threw it in my face right after he said that he intended to tell Evan what a stupid whore his mother was and how she deserted him for money. And then he planned to disinherit Evan. He told me he had already cut off Dean Raines campaign money because of some shady stock market deals and that he was now cutting off the rest of the leeches. He was going to tell everyone about Rosemary's past, and I knew it would destroy her. She had worked so long to forget the hell that bastard put her through when they were together. He never paid for the abuse he heaped out. It took Rosemary years before she trusted another man. And we came back to Everton so she could form a relationship with Evan, even if she never got the opportunity to tell him who she really was. What kind of bastard tells his son that the boy's mother is dead?"

"This is worse than those soap operas," Eugene proclaimed, fascinated by the drama unfolding around him.

I hope he doesn't take to watching soap operas and film noir. The combination was likely to be lethal.

"He was an evil son-of-a-bitch," Allan continued, addressing Rosemary now. "He sat down at his desk after tearing up that insulting check and told me not to slam the door on my way out. Before I knew what had happened I had picked up the knife that was lying on his desk and stabbed him. When I realized what I had done I saw the napkin and thought to rub down the knife. I knew you had taken it, and I didn't want either of our prints to be found. And then I left as quietly as I could. I had already taken my shoes off because I hadn't wanted anyone, especially you, to hear me approach Marcus. I wanted to protect you from him. I didn't intend to kill him. It just happened."

"Don't worry, Hope," Eugene said gallantly, "I won't let him kill you because you know the truth."

I looked at Eugene in disbelief. Now I knew the truth. He had *already* started watching those ridiculous soap operas.

Jezebel, who had been watching the scene from the living room sofa with bored eyes, jumped up at Eugene's vehement words and started barking ferociously.

Eugene stepped boldly between Allan and I, and I wondered yet again what he was thinking. Allan was so intent on comforting Rosemary that I doubt he even remembered my presence; and even if he did, and intended to kill me, Eugene wasn't much of a buffer. Allan would simply walk right through him. But it's the thought that counts, and I was grateful to Eugene for his overblown heroics.

"Sic him, Jezebel," Eugene ordered the frantic dog.

And she did—right in the nuts. At least that is where it would have been if Jezebel hadn't passed right through Allan and ended up skidding to a halt at the edge of the porch.

"Good girl," Eugene praised her. "Now try again."

Actually, I probably would have laughed at the ridiculous scene if I hadn't been staring at a confessed murderer.

Fortunately, any further heroics from Eugene and Jezebel were unnecessary. Peter and his boss, Lieutenant Arthur Stand, arrived at that moment, realized who was occupying my living room and took charge of the situation.

"Finally," Eugene sighed. "I thought they would never come."

While Allan was being read his rights and Rosemary was sobbing on the floor, Peter approached me. "Are you all right, Hope? What are they doing here?"

"Allan came to ask me not to mention Rosemary's past to anyone. And Rosemary followed him." I smiled gratefully. "I'm glad you came when you did. Allan had just admitted to Rosemary and I that he had killed Marcus, and I wasn't certain what I was supposed to do next."

"Make a citizen's arrest, of course," Peter said smiling.

Was that a joke? I really hoped it was. The thought of me tackling Allan and holding him down until the police arrived was laughable.

"Exactly, Hope," Eugene declared with fervor. "Maybe you should start lifting weights or something. That way the next time we come across a criminal you can make a citizen's arrest and be able to keep the perp under control."

Chapter Twenty-Seven

I sincerely hope that Colby's wedding day was not the happiest day of her life. I say that without the least bit of malice because I sincerely hope that a wedding day is not the happiest day of anyone's life. What is a wedding but a large party, attended primarily by people you hoped wouldn't accept, full of stressful details, bickering relatives, and a distinct lack of perfection?

Perfection just doesn't exist, and if it did, it would not be likely to show up at a wedding where there are too many uncontrollable variables. If perfection exists at all, it is in those brief moments of complete fulfillment that are so quickly gone. It is a sort of timelessness that disregards the future and exists only for the now. There will always be more laundry and dirty dishes to come, and for most of us, not enough money or a bleak future at a boring job. But in perfect moments, those things don't matter. They are temporarily forgotten because the now could not be any better. It is as if time is suspended for a second and one is completely happy, even knowing that the happiness won't last. The details of our life vanish for an instant, replaced only by a feeling.

The problem with weddings is that the details don't vanish leaving feelings of anxiety, strain, and quite often nausea. And that's just for the groom. The bride is beset with even more problems. No one will convince me that brides are so ecstatic they don't care how they appear in front of all the guests and that the colors of the bouquets, the quality of the food and wine, and the amount of alcohol consumed by the wedding party aren't paramount in her mind.

When the bride is up on the altar saying her vows she is rarely thinking of how she adores the groom. No, she is instead wondering if her hair is falling down, if she looks like a fat meringue in her dress, and if her make-up is overdone and will make her look dreadful in the wedding photos. She is also probably wondering if her mother is crying, if she is going to break down into tears herself, and whether that feeling of nausea in her stomach means she is about to be sick, or if she can control it and simply pass out instead. A few of the lucky brides are so concerned that they will burst into nervous laughter, that all other thoughts vanish under the strain. But the really lucky brides are the ones that watch in horror as the groom faints, thereby giving their own thoughts a different outlet.

Even Colby must have realized within the first ten minutes of the wedding ceremony that her "dream wedding" was not going to be idyllic. To begin with, the church was really too small to accommodate the large number of guests that accepted, and was therefore hot and stuffy, a slight scent of body odor permeating the floral air. Maybe Colby didn't notice, but the guests did.

I was pretty certain that Eugene and I didn't smell, and neither did my date, but I wasn't so certain about the large gentleman next to me, who introduced himself as a cousin of Colby's from New York. I wasn't surprised. Except for his fair hair, he looked like a big New York Strip Steak--but in the nicest sense. His wife, a petite blond, must have also suspected he was one of the guilty guests, and had scooted a little closer to the gentleman on the other side of her, who her husband claimed was an uncle on Colby's mother's side.

My parents were seated on the other side of my date, and were conversing with him in the most amiable manner while Eugene was forced to constantly dodge my date's extravagant hand gestures.

Jilly and Martin were seated behind me, and Jilly took the opportunity to poke the back of my head while my parents and my date were enthusiastically discussing the latest tennis match.

"Hope, I can't believe you didn't tell me you were going to the wedding with him," Jilly whispered, gesturing at my date with her neck and head.

Oh, God! Here it comes!

"You should have told me last night!"

"You didn't ask, and if you recall, there were other things going on that distracted me." I found apprehending a murderer a distraction, even if Jilly didn't.

"But still. How could you have failed to mention who your date was?" she continued to whisper, while Martin shot her reproving glances.

I cleared my throat as the music started up and turned back around, once again facing the altar. What difference did it make who my date was? Wasn't one man almost as good as another for these kind of occasions?

Magdalena, wearing a bright fuchsia dress with a sheer purple shawl, strolled down the aisle unconcerned as to whether or not her leisurely walk delayed the procession. She winked when she saw me, sent a questioning look at my date, and then moved on, winking at a handsome man on the groom's side who laughed and then winked back. When she approached Angela, who was wearing a white suit and was seated in the first pew on the groom's side, Magdalena gave a slight nod of her head that would have made the queen proud.

As Father Martinez and an extremely tall best man (whose name I still couldn't recall) entered the chancel with Evan, the audience turned to the church doors in expectation of the bridal party. And what a bridal party it was! First Susan, with John holding her arm, entered the church and took their seats, Susan already crying into a snowy white handkerchief. The two ushers then walked down the aisle, quickly moving to the groom's side, followed by a procession of six bridesmaids, each walking four paces apart in tune to the music (sadly, I was required to tell them the appropriate distance), before stepping up to the bride's side of the chancel. The bridesmaids all wore full-length rose pink taffeta, and carried pink and white bouquets of roses, and when they stood side by side, looked like a wall of Pepto Bismal vomit. (That's not to say they weren't attractive individually, or most of them anyway).

Vincent, from the other side of the church, caught my eye, and I knew he was also amused by the abundance of pink.

As a matter of fact, there was so much pink in the church, I was surprised all the men weren't shifting uncomfortably in their seats, wondering how soon they could leave this bastion of feminine fantasy.

Following the bridesmaids was the maid of honor, wearing a slightly darker pink dress than the others, and carrying a slightly larger bouquet. Two flower girls, scattering white and pink rose petals as they went, practically skipped down the aisle to Susan's horror. At least I think it was to her horror since she started crying even harder. A ring bearer, a charming boy of about five, walked solemnly down the aisle, the white satin pillow in his arms tipping alarmingly as he walked. I was just grateful Colby hadn't decided on a pink satin pillow.

And finally, the moment everyone had been waiting for—the bride.

"She looks more like a deflated pillow than a meringue," Eugene said rather loudly.

It didn't matter that I was the only one who could hear him. It was still tactless. Didn't he know that one was not supposed to verbally insult the bride's appearance until after the reception?

Not that he wasn't correct. While her hair and make-up were done expertly and showed her face to advantage, the dress was a mistake. The underskirt of the dress was somewhere between a tutu and a crinoline, fluffing out on all sides, but not enough to form a circle. Rather, the skirt looked like it had been intentionally flattened in the front and back, which caused the sides to expand. Of course, that might not have been so noticeable if it weren't apparent that Dean Raines was having a hard time standing next to Colby without being pushed out of the way by her dress.

The top of the dress was held stiff by a built-in corset, allowing for very limited movement, and which flattened her breasts rather than pushed them up. She did indeed look like a white satin pillow, albeit a pretty one.

"Do you suppose she can breath?" Eugene asked.

Did he think she would still be walking down the aisle if

she were truly lacking oxygen?

But then again, Colby might not require air; I was pretty certain she melted when it rained.

As she and Dean walked up to the chancel and the service began, Susan's crying grew even louder. John murmured something in her ear and she nodded before pitifully trying to hold back the tears.

"Her mascara's going to run," Eugene pointed out, though it was apparent he was no longer addressing me, but was simply speaking his thoughts aloud. "And isn't it bad luck for the mother of the bride to cry? They have already had a murder in the family, they don't need any more back luck."

I doubted anyone present thought that Marcus' murder was bad luck for Evan and Colby. Just the opposite, in fact.

By the time the priest reached the part of the service that called for the vows, Eugene was fake snoring, my date seemed to be truly snoring, and I could hear Martin shifting in place behind me, causing his pew to squeak mercilessly. My mother, who loved weddings above all things, turned sharply around and gave Martin a severe glance, which froze him in his place.

Colby had insisted that she and Evan write their own declaratory vows and memorize them. I could have told her that would be a mistake. Anyone who knew Evan could have told her it was a mistake. The boy who worked at the gas station could have told Colby it was a mistake. Evan couldn't remember a three-item shopping list, let alone a paragraph of vows.

So, Evan being Evan, and Colby being Colby, disaster was bound to occur.

And it started with the vows.

Traditionally, the bridegroom recites his declaratory vows first. That is, if he can remember them.

Evan managed to successfully remember the first sentence of his vow, and even managed to say it with great fervor. It was simply every sentence after that which lacked coherence.

"Whom I love more than..." he paused, groping for the words Colby had given him. (No one in the audience believed that she would let him write his own). Unfortunately, rather than make something up off the top of his head, he continued to try and remember the original vow. "Whom I love more than...."

A few people started to titter in the back of the church, and primarily on the groom's side.

"Whom I love more than..."

Colby was beginning to look annoyed and embarrassed, and Father Martinez was patting Evan on the arm and whispering to him.

Evan nodded and gulped, "Whom I love more than anyone in the world. She is my..." He gulped.

"Not again," Eugene mumbled. "He should just give up while he's ahead."

A few other people started to chuckle as Evan's pause grew in length.

"She is my....life," he finished lamely.

He seemed about to take a deep breath and continue when Colby, to the obvious relief of the entire bridal party, interrupted him to hurriedly recite her vows.

When she was finished the audience let out a collective sigh of relief and Eugene muttered, "It's about damn time. What's the matter with Catholics, anyway? I'd swear we've been here an hour at least."

My date, who had ceased his light snoring but continued to keep his eyes closed, shifted slightly, causing Eugene to hurriedly move away and slide partway into me. We both shuddered and he stood. "I am going to stand at the back of the church, away from this..." he looked at my date and continued slightingly, "loafer."

By the time the rings had been exchanged (Evan only dropping Colby's ring once) and the contractual vows spoken, Colby was red from embarrassment and the audience was red from heat. And did I mention the smell?

The recessional took a few minutes, which I spent gathering my belongings and speaking a few words to Jilly, who was in a surprisingly good humor considering the fact that my mother was lecturing Martin on inappropriate behavior at weddings. Since I saw my father nod off once or twice, I figured she was saving his lecture for the car ride over to the reception.

And the reception was even more entertaining than the wedding. I even found myself enjoying it, despite the disposition of my date.

As soon as I had deposited my date at a bar set up under the canopies, I sought out Jilly and Martin, eager to exchange views on the ceremony. Eugene, having no desire to stay with my date, accompanied me with a sulk.

"What are you doing here with *him*?" Jilly asked without preamble. "Go away Martin, so Hope and I can talk privately," she said to her husband, who had started to sit down at a shaded table.

Martin smiled at me in a preoccupied way and moved off toward some men that he had known since he was a child, occasionally stopping to chat with an old neighbor or acquaintance.

"Well? Are you going to answer me?" Jilly demanded.

"I didn't have a choice. A few weeks ago my mother saw him at a party, found out that he didn't have a date for the wedding—which is no surprise—and told him I would love to go with him."

Jilly looked flabbergasted. "Your mother? Even she wouldn't be that bad."

My eyebrow rose a fraction of an inch before I answered. "Wouldn't she? Aunt Maude just got into town."

Jilly nodded in understanding. "And heaven forbid you don't have a date when Aunt Maude is here. But still, you could have found your own date. She must have known you would hate going anywhere with that guy."

I laughed. "I don't think she was overly concerned. When I found out what she had done she insisted that it was too late and that he was counting on me."

"You are too nice, Hope. I would have called him up and refused to go."

I sighed. That was exactly what I had wanted to do. "I know. But when I called him, he went on and on about how excited he was before I could get a word in."

"So excited that he fell asleep right away?" Jilly questioned.

"It's probably penance for all my horrible thoughts lately."

"Your thoughts are probably a lot better than most people's. I'll say it again. You are too nice."

"There's no such thing as too nice. And if there were, I wouldn't be in the running."

"Just let me know the next time you are forced on a date with Sinister Sinclair. I'll bring a machete along to protect you."

"I don't think Colby's cousin is as aggressive—or as passive aggressive—as she is. He really isn't that bad, considering he's related to Colby."

"You'd do better to go alone and just bring a book or an iPod. I'll probably be bored to death by the time the food arrives," Eugene said sulkily.

Did he think I intended to save him an empty chair?

"I don't think a machete is necessary. He seems to have lost any philandering tendencies and replaced them with alcoholic tendencies. Oh, and possibly narcolepsy as well." Sinclair had spent his college years doing little but picking up anything that wore a skirt. After college his family expected him to get a job, and the disappointment of it crushed him. He seemed to find work distasteful, and became a bit of a loafer, which made those women suddenly find him somewhat distasteful. But he wasn't a bad guy, really. He just seemed somewhat crushed by real life.

Jilly still looked annoyed. I had seen the seating chart, too. She and Martin were seated right next to Sinclair and I. It was going to be a long afternoon.

If the sight of masses of pink roses, pink lanterns, pink candles, and pink tablecloths was enough to put one off of one's appetite, the food made up for all that. It was excellent, and interested Sinclair enough that he barely said more than a few words to me between bites. And that was exactly how I liked it.

After the cake and toasts, Vincent appeared at my elbow, sent a quizzical look at my date, and drew me aside. "I heard about last night. I can't even believe it. I see you are quite recovered from those rather traumatic events, though. You are looking very lovely today, Hope."

"Thank you. As you recall, I recover from those sort of things quite rapidly."

"About that flower pot incident—it worried me that someone might want to hurt you, so I looked into it. I was right. Someone did try to kill you." Vincent said smugly.

I just stared at him. "Well, who?"

He smiled broadly. "Can't you guess? Susan."

"Susan? Why?"

"She thought you were Angela, with that dumb hat on. Apparently Colby knew that Susan had knocked over the pot too, but didn't say anything for fear her mom would end up in jail. And Colby thought you were Angela, too, so she wasn't that upset about it at first. To give them some credit, they were both rather horrified at the thought they might have killed you instead of Angela." Vincent smiled wickedly, and then winked at me. "At least Susan was."

"How did you find this out?"

Vincent gloated. "Your policeman friend isn't the only one who can ask pertinent questions. Do you remember that conversation I overheard between John and Angela?"

"The one where he was telling her to keep quiet about what she knew? The one that made you think John was the murderer?"

"Hey, everyone makes mistakes," Vincent protested. "But that is the one, yes.. It turns out Angela saw Susan push the flower pot, knew it was intended for her, and decided to try and blackmail the family."

I looked surprised. If I knew someone wanted me dead I probably wouldn't laugh about it and then try my hand at blackmail.

Vincent looked delighted at being able to tell me the story. "First, she tried to get Dean to have an affair with her-- and you should be pleased to know that he refused--and then she tried to go after John. I wouldn't try to blackmail John. He's a vicious player. I still say he could easily have killed Marcus Whittington without a second thought."

"You might be right, but hopefully we will never have to find out what he is capable of."

He nodded in agreement. "So who is that man you are with?" he asked curiously.

"Sinclair Raines. Colby's cousin."

Vincent choked on his drink. "You're kidding, right?"

"I wish. Actually, he's not that bad," I said kindly.

"You mean he doesn't say much."

"At least Mr. Suave here has some sense, Hope. You'd have been better to have brought him as a date," Eugene said glumly. Apparently weddings weren't a boost to his ghostly spirit; he was far more animated at funerals.

"True. Are you staying in town much longer?" I asked Vincent, changing the subject. He didn't need to know that my mother had found me my date.

"No. I'm leaving tomorrow. Evan and I have made some plans for that real estate deal based on my suggestions. This time it should work. I'm certain of it."

"In that case, good luck!"

"Thanks. The next time I'm in town I'll expect you to have dinner with me," Vincent said matter-of-factly.

I smiled. Could I even get out of it if I wanted to?

"Can't you find a decent date? Am I going to have to step in and help?" Eugene asked me after Vincent had moved away to speak to some other guests.

"Definitely not."

"You mean you definitely can't find a decent date or you definitely don't want my help?" Eugene asked belligerently.

I didn't answer for two reasons: One, I wasn't going to dignify his question with a response; and two, Magdalena was bearing down on me with her arms clapping together and a smile of anticipation on her face.

"Hope, I have it. The very idea we need. Is Eugene here?"

"Yes. Right here," I said and pointed to my left.

"Oh, excellent. It's lovely to see you again, Eugene. You know what I mean. Obviously I can't see you and it's only a figure of speech, but I am glad you are here. Perhaps you could find a picture of Eugene for me, Hope. Or maybe you can draw one. Do you draw?"

"She's batty," Eugene declared.

"What's your idea?" I asked before Magdalena could digress any further.

"A séance. It's perfect. I was reading one of those journals last night while trying to fall asleep." She leaned in closer. "I could hardly sleep with all the excitement about Allan, but you must have had the same problem. To think he was the murderer. It makes one's blood run cold. He was always so charming."

One can never trust a person described as 'charming'. There is something about that word that implies an inherent dishonesty or lack of character. If one is charming, one has the ability to make people like one despite one's behavior. Hitler was said to be charming. And look at Snow White's Prince Charming—or was it Cinderella's?—who fell in love based solely on looks and a kiss. Did he even attempt to get to know the woman? No, he most certainly did not.

"But that isn't what I came to talk about," Magdalena continued. "I want to talk about a séance. We must have one. I am certain that is the way to send Eugene to the spirit world. I can't think why I didn't try it with Roger."

"A séance? With people linking hands and floating tables?" I asked. I didn't even bother to hide the disbelief in my voice.

"Yes. What else? I'm not sure about the floating tables, though. That probably isn't a requirement, although I believe the linked hands are."

"Tell me you are not seriously considering this, Hope," Eugene asked seriously.

I thought about it for a moment.

Why not? It probably wouldn't hurt.

"We should try it." I addressed Eugene. "You said that you wanted to get to heaven or wherever it is you are supposed to go. This might be the answer."

"You're doing this to spite me, aren't you? I have no intention of participating in such a farce, and without me it would be pointless to continue." Eugene sounded stiff and angry.

"Why not? Don't you want to get off the earth?"

He didn't answer, and I searched his face for some sign that would let me know what he was thinking. And then I saw it clearly in his eyes.

"You're scared?"

"No, I'm not," he denied.

"Scared?" Magdalena chimed in. "Oh no, don't be scared. Nothing bad will happen. We won't try to send you back if you don't want to. We'll just try and contact a spirit that has already made it over and ask what you need to do," she reassured him.

Eugene looked thoughtful and then he turned to me. "You promise not to try and send me anywhere? I don't want to end up burning in the flames of hell because some amateurs tried to send me somewhere and got the wording wrong."

"I promise. We will do just as Magdalena said."

"Fine," Eugene agreed begrudgingly.

I nodded at Magdalena and she beamed. "This is wonderful. I'm sure it will give us the answers we need. Now, I believe you mentioned you know a psychic. We will need her assistance to get things started. Do you have her number?"

I nodded hesitantly while Eugene groaned.

"I shall start preparations immediately," Magdalena said excitedly.

I watched Magdalena as she gaily chatted on about everything she would need to do while Eugene harrumphed around kicking at the lawn with his immaculate shoes.

If I had known a few months ago that I would soon be helping to organize a séance so that a ghost and his dog, both living with me, could maneuver their way into the spirit world, I would have had myself committed then, as a preventative measure. Now it was too late. My life had altered dramatically, and it didn't look to be quieting down any time soon.

But these rather discouraging thoughts were soon interrupted by the events unfolding at the reception and Eugene's burgeoning good humor.

Poor Colby! There were times when I truly felt sorry for

her. Okay, I admit that what I was really sorry for was the fact that her character was so pretentious and intractable the littlest of incidents caused her embarrassment. That still constituted a form of pity though, no matter where it was really directed.

And when I compared this wedding to some of the others I had attended, this one really wasn't that bad.

So what if one guest was hit by small bird dropping when the doves flew off, much to the delight of the other guests? It wasn't that bad when the guest uttered an alarmingly loud exclamation of horror and disgust, and then listened patronizingly while her neighbor assured her that such things were good luck in Italy and that she shouldn't be so distressed. To the further delight of the guests, she firmly declared that this was Pennsylvania and not Italy, screamed that the concerned gentleman was a 'gibbering fool' and swept off with what little dignity she had remaining—which wasn't much.

The swans might have attacked two children who had been trying to chase them down, which Eugene felt the children deserved despite their cherubic countenances. But that didn't constitute a disaster. And the fact that only child ended up in the pond was really quite remarkable. Four of the guests had to be taken indoors due to severe attacks of hay fever, but only one guest toppled onto the dancing floor after Sinclair had spilled one of his drinks. Susan, kept on a tight leash by Dean and John, remained sober, though that did not stop her crying through the entire reception. If anyone thought her sobbing during the toasts was annoying, her sobbing and hiccuping during the father-daughter dance was dreadful. And when Angela, flirting with a handsome blond gentleman the entire day, accidentally spilled champagne all over Susan's suit, no one said a word in anger. Overall, the reception was a mild success.

Apparently John Raines thought so as well.

"So, Hope. All's well that ends well, right? With the murder no longer hanging over us and the wedding over with, life seems to be back where it should be," he said gaily.

Did he really expect me to answer that? A man was dead, another man in prison, and a woman heartbroken. What had ended so well?

"Wonderful wedding. And it is all thanks to you!" John continued, oblivious to my silence. He caught sight of a possible financial donor for his brother and decided he had best make his move and pounce. "I'll see you around. And don't forget to vote for Dean in November," her urged me.

"I don't care if you have to change parties, Hope. If you vote for Dean Raines for governor I am leaving," Eugene declared.

Well, that decided it. I was *definitely* voting for Dean Raines.

Chapter Twenty-Eight

Eugene and I entered Magdalena's cottage in a state of trepidation. Neither of us had ever attended a séance, and we weren't certain what to expect. And in Eugene's case, he wasn't certain where he might end up. And I'd better not end up with another ghost haunting me and rearranging my kitchen utensils because of it.

Yes, I had fears of acquiring yet another houseguest.

Jezebel, who accompanied us, was wagging her tail at the new adventure, and trying to sniff everything in sight. If Eugene had lost his sense of smell, wouldn't she have also? I supposed it could have been instinct, but I wasn't sure. The only thing Jezebel seemed to have an instinct for was causing me trouble.

Magdalena, attired in bright purple and green, greeted us enthusiastically, going so far as to try and hug Eugene, who shied back when she went right through his chest.

"Isn't this wonderful," she declared exuberantly as we walked farther into the lit room. "I wasn't sure there would be enough people, so I invited the Herberts."

I looked farther into the interior, which was dim from the closed curtains and lack of electricity. The only light came from a dozen candles placed randomly around the living room. I doubted that a dark room and hazardous candles (and they were obviously hazardous because Magdalena had placed them on tables with no metal or glass plates supporting them) were necessary for a séance, but I hadn't exactly researched the subject, so I refrained from commenting on the décor.

When I finally did spot the Herberts, who were unknown to me, I saw an elderly couple with balding heads (yes, both of them) and drab clothes. They looked to be about a hundred, and I wasn't even certain they were awake.

"I sometimes visit the retirement home in Wakefield, and the Herberts are a couple I regularly visit. They are both around ninety, and it is such a treat for them to get out. But I must have them back by four for their baths. And don't worry about them revealing your secret, because I'm not sure they will even remember coming. Actually, Jack keeps calling me Sarah, which I believe was his sister, and Ruth can never remember me from one visit to the next. Usually I take them to the movies, but I thought this would be just as entertaining," Magdalena explained.

Eugene gave me a sardonic smile and I pretended not to notice. This was Magdalena's show and she could arrange it however she pleased.

A closer inspection of the room showed another figure sitting at a table full of odd items. There was a crystal ball that I thought might just be plastic, some unlit candles, tarot cards, and what looked like "The Dummies Guide to Seances". And slouched in the chair was Madame Muscovy.

She rose slightly in greeting and asked where that ghost and his dog were, and if they were indeed serious about contacting the spirit world.

Eugene assured her that he was, and when she continued to look at me blankly I told her that not only was Eugene serious, that he was more excited than he had ever been in his life.

Eugene told me to can it, and I laughed and approached the table from which Madame Muscovy and Magdalena were hastily removing the aforementioned items. The crystal ball was left in place, and Magdalena urged the Herberts to sit down.

The Herberts, quite ambulatory, did as they were told without protest. They seated themselves to the right of Magdalena, which left me the seat to the left of Madame Muscovy.

For the occasion Madame Muscovy had donned a brightly-colored, filmy skirt and a black top. She had attempted to pull her hair back into a ponytail, but only succeeded in making it look even more greasy and unkempt. Like Magdalena, Madame Muscovy had several bangles on her wrist; however, where Magdalena's were real, Madame Muscovy's were either neon colored plastic or sparkly metal.

"Be silent," Madame Muscovy said. "Focus your minds on the crystal ball. Focus your thoughts on the poor departed spirits of..."

She hesitated and then stared at me until I realized she couldn't remember their names.

"Eugene and Jezebel," I supplied, before Eugene took it as an insult.

"Yes—the poor departed spirits of Eugene and Jezebel. Breathe deeply and allow your mind to think of nothing but them. Imagine them as lights surrounding you. Allow their lights to grow brighter, holding you in their glow."

Eugene, who was leaning against my chair, laughed loudly. The ridiculous atmosphere overcame me, and I gave a little twitter as well.

"Silence," Madame Muscovy said to me.

Magdalena gave me a reproving glance, and I hastily apologized.

"I said quiet. Maybe it would be best if we took hands and closed our eyes. That way our minds can meditate without distraction."

The Herberts, looking around them blankly, followed the suggestion immediately, and I was certain that Jack Herbert was so quickly in a meditative state that he managed to let out a soft snore or two.

If anyone other than myself noticed, no one said any-thing—at least for a few minutes.

By the time Madame Muscovy had explained how to make one's mind blank and how to recapture the lights of Eugene and Jezebel, Jack Herbert was well on his way to a good snooze.

"Wait a second. He's asleep," Eugene said irritably. "If I am going to participate in this farce, the least you do is keep everyone awake for it."

I opened my eyes and shook my head at Eugene. I didn't want to break the chain of concentration Madame Muscovy had weaved around the group. Or maybe I just didn't want her to yell at me again and make me feel like a wayward child.

"Fine. He is probably concentrating more like this, any-way."

I thought the same thing. Maybe if Mrs. Herbert fell asleep we there would be a slim chance of making this success-ful.

"Do you hear us, spirits? We are calling to you!" Mad-ame Muscovy sang out. "Spirits, we need your help. Eugene and Jezebel need your help."

"I don't hear anything," Eugene grumbled.

Jezebel decided to start howling.

"Sprits, do you hear us?" Madame Muscovy continued. "Come to us, Spirits. Come!"

I don't know what I expected to happen (okay, I ex-pected *nothing* to happen) but it wasn't Madame Muscovy jumping out of her chair, yanking my arm in the process and booming in a deep voice, "I am come."

Eugene rubbed his hands through his hair. "Oh, please!"

"You called me. I am come," Madame Muscovy contin-ued in that low voice. She raised her arms and bent her upper body slightly, before raising it again. After she had repeated the process a few times, she moved her arms in front of her. "I am come. Who calls me?"

"Who are you?" Magdalena asked, staring wide-eyed at the bizarre woman before her.

"I am the spirit Chara. I know many things. I am able to visit the world of flesh. Who calls me?" the low voice boomed out, sounding rather arrogant.

"Chara? Couldn't she come up with a better name than that?" Eugene asked.

I secretly agreed. What kind of respectable spirit went around with the name of Chara? For that matter, what kind of respectable spirit would choose to haunt Madame Muscovy? The act was so unconvincing I wanted to laugh. Strangely enough, Magdalena seemed quite intrigued by the new Madame Musco-vy.

"Eugene and Jezebel call you. They seek answers," Magdalena said hesitantly.

"Yes. I sense their presence," the greasy spirit answered.

That wasn't surprising. She could hardly claim that she sensed nothing.

"Ask me what you will," Madame Muscovy said, her eyes wide and unblinking.

It was really rather unnerving in away. I realized that a seance would be an excellent birthday gift for Jilly. She would love the drama of it all.

Madame Muscovy, holding herself erect, walked directly to Eugene, who had moved to stand behind Jack Herbert and thus get a better view. "What do you wish to know from Chara?"

Okay, so that was a little creepy. How did she know where he was? Was she a really good guesser?

Eugene looked momentarily surprised before be smiled smugly. "Don't you know what my question is?"

"You wish to enter the spirit world. You wish to leave earth. You wish to know how this can be done."

Hardly a trick question. Madame Muscovy was well aware of our intentions in holding the séance.

"Well," Eugene said impatiently.

The spirit Chara didn't answer, but stared at Eugene for several moments. "I can not answer until the question has been asked."

"How does Eugene get to the spirit world?" I asked impatiently.

Eugene looked exasperated. "Hope, *I* was going to ask her. I want to prove her a fraud!"

"Sorry," I apologized. "Go ahead and ask her."

Jezebel was again inspired to start howling, only this time she addressed her howls to the bird cage that was soon to adorn her closet room.

Eugene watched her for a moment before turning back to Chara. "It's a little late, but fine. How do I get to the spirit world, if that is where I want to go?"

Madame Muscovy, or Chara, or whoever she was at the moment, didn't immediately answer. When she did, it was not what anyone wanted to hear, least of all Eugene.

"You must follow the path that has been chosen for you. The only answers that matter are the ones you believe." She turned away from Eugene and headed back to her seat.

"That's not an answer. I was expecting something a little more specific like, 'Turn left at the bridge and right at the railroad tracks.' This has to be the worst séance ever. Can't you come up with something better than that," Eugene demanded.

For a moment I experienced déjà vu. Hadn't I already played out this scene?

"Your anger is justified. The answers you will find in time. But you must believe. The path you walk will lead you to great things if you believe." Chara responded, eerily enough seeming to answer Eugene directly. "Great things. The Starman knows."

"I don't want great things. I want out of here," Eugene whined. "And Starman is a movie, not a person. And she is just saying that claptrap to try and convince us she isn't a phony."

But Chara/Madame Muscovy had already sat down. For an instant she remained erect, looking at Magdalena and I in turn, ignoring the Herberts completely, and then she slumped over and onto the table.

Magdalena gasped and jumped up, trying to shake Madame Muscovy awake.

Eugene just laughed.

I really hope he hasn't suddenly gone over the deep end, I thought. If he has, he's going home with Madame Muscovy.

Within seconds Madame Muscovy was sitting up and rubbing at her eyes. "What happened?" she croaked.

"You put on the worst performance of all time," Eugene said nastily.

Since I was the only one who could hear him he immediately fell silent.

"You were in a trance," Magdalena said to Madame Muscovy. "It was amazing."

"Really? I don't remember anything," she replied.

Yeah right! And I'm the Santa Claus! Despite the fact that she appeared to have heard Eugene, I couldn't quite find it within myself to believe her. What can I say? I might have two ghosts living with me, but I was still a skeptic.

The séance was broken up immediately after that, Madame Muscovy claiming that she was too exhausted to continue and Magdalena unable to get the Herberts to wake up from their naps and try again.

Madame Muscovy told us that she was going to be generous and not charge us for the day's effort, and that she would continue her research and call me with any new information.

Eugene just sulked.

Maybe he had put more hope in the séance than he had let on.

It was time we tried other methods of learning about how spirits move on. "Magdalena," I said firmly, "you need to tell Eugene and I about Roger. And you need to tell us everything."

Eugene stood up and moved closer, awaiting Magdalena's response.

"I know. I'm not sure it will help you, but it might." She picked up a teacup and took a sip. When she set it down she looked over at the Herberts, who were still asleep at the table, and lowered her voice slightly.

"Don't hate me when I tell you this, but I cheated on Roger."

Magdalena paused to see if I would renounce her friendship. When she saw that I was surprised, but not condemning, she continued in a slightly louder voice. "Roger was quite a bit older than I and gone so often on business. I guess I got lonely. And that was when I met Sam. We didn't last long. The truth was I only ever loved Roger and I think I wanted to get back at him for leaving me alone so often."

Eugene frowned at Magdalena, but remained silent. It occurred to me that Eugene's father might have cheated on his mother before abandoning her.

"The day Roger found out about the affair was the day he died," Magdalena said on a sigh.

"If she tells me she murdered him, I am leaving," Eugene told me in a horrified voice.

"Be quiet, Eugene, and let Magdalena finish her story."

"I'm sorry if you're disappointed in me, Eugene," Magdalena said to a wall (literally), "but I want you to know the truth."

Eugene did his famous 'harrumph' and started to pick some imaginary lint off his suit, but remained silent.

"Roger had stayed home to do some work on the house, despite the fact that we had gardeners and handymen. It wasn't this house, but the original one that was torn down just after Roger died. He had decided to clean the gutters, or maybe it was retile the roof, I just can't remember.

"Sam came over unexpectedly. I had already ended our relationship at this point, and he wanted to return something. And Roger saw him. It didn't take long for him to realize what relationship Sam and I had had. Roger and Sam got into such a fight. They were shouting and Sam tried to hit Roger but missed. Roger just laughed. And then Roger called me by some horrible names. I was so upset. I thought I had lost him and I couldn't forgive myself for my stupidity," she said, not holding back the tears that had slowly been building.

"Roger started climbing the ladder again, so angry with me he couldn't even look at me. I remember crying and calling his name. Sam hit the ladder with his fist and walked away."

She shuddered violently and I put my arm around her shoulders. "Go on."

Magdalena looked at me with a sorrowful glance and then continued, her voice breaking after every few words. "When Sam hit the ladder it swayed a little at first, but didn't tip over. I thought everything was fine, but then Roger, who had nearly reached the top, lost his balance and a foot slipped off. The ladder was stable again, but I think he reached for the next step up and his hand slipped. I just remember that he suddenly fell. It was the most horrible thing I had ever seen. He broke his neck. I could tell he was dead.

"I ran away. I couldn't bear to see his dead body. I didn't know what to do. I went for help but no one was home. It didn't occur to me to call anyone. By the time I returned to his body, he had been found by a gardener."

"And then he came and haunted you. You told us before that he showed up at your bedside."

"Yes. He came two nights later." She looked at where she suspected Eugene was sitting. "Hope saw you leave your body. I didn't get to see Roger leave his. But he came to me. I don't know if he thought I would be able to see him or he just hoped I would. Or maybe he was still angry with me and wanted to punish me. Roger wasn't usually vindictive, but he had been so angry."

"What did he do?" I asked.

"He woke me up. And I looked at him and screamed. He was so happy that I could see him. And we talked and talked, and he never really left my side again. At least not for several years. Not until he left for good."

Eugene jumped up. "This is what we want to know about, Hope. Don't let her fob you off again."

"You need to tell Eugene and I why he left for good. Or how. Whatever you know could be important." I didn't know who wanted this information more, Eugene or I.

"But that's just it. I really don't know. I can only suppose he finally forgave me. He always told me he had, but sometimes he would argue and he would bring it up. And then one day he just told me how much he loved me and had enjoyed the extra years he was given and he sauntered off somewhere and, well, disappeared. I think so, anyway, since I never saw him again. And I looked everywhere. I thought that he had really forgiven me then, and God let him go where he needed to be."

"The problem is, this doesn't help us," Eugene said morosely. "You never did anything to me."

"You were in the street because of me," I said helpfully, while offering Magdalena my napkin to dry her eyes.

"So? I would have remembered my lunch and gone back anyway. And I could have had you bring the bag to me. Then you might have been hit instead," Eugene replied. "If there was anything to forgive, which there isn't, I forgave you a long time ago. It has to be something else."

"I agree." I turned back to the petite woman next to me.

"Magdalena, Eugene and I don't think that he is here because he needs to forgive me. Could there be something else? Something you forgot? Maybe there was something that happened that you just didn't think was important at the time."

Magdalena looked thoughtful, but finally shook her head. "I don't think so. I'm sorry. I can only guess that every ghost's reason for remaining behind on earth is different. Chara must be right. You have to follow the path laid out for you, Eugene, and not question it."

Eugene looked depressed. "Easy for her to say. She isn't stuck on earth as a ghost. How does she know my path isn't to find a way to..." he paused, "well, to where ever it is everyone else goes?"

I sighed. I wasn't sure who I agreed with. Magdalena might be right in that Eugene had to accept the fact that he was here, and probably for a reason that would eventually be revealed. But Eugene might be right in that the reason might not be revealed unless Eugene actively tried to find it.

"Let's go home," I said to Eugene. "It's been a hard day on all of us."

"Must you go now?" Magdalena asked, obviously not wanting to be left alone with the rather boring Herberts. I doubt they ever discussed anything as interesting as ghosts and murders. Actually, I doubted that they ever spoke.

"We'll visit later in the week," I said to her. "I promise. But right now Eugene looks like he needs to go home and take a nap."

The fact that he didn't even respond made me think that he probably did indeed need a nap.

As Eugene and I walked back to the car, Jezebel at our heels, Eugene turned to me and said, "Maybe I need to find out who killed me. Maybe that is my path."

I had suspected that might come up.

"Maybe," I said.

"We were pretty good about discovering who killed Whittington. I bet we could easily find out who killed me," Eugene continued, getting back some of his zest for living. Or being dead, depending on how you looked at it.

"Eugene, the police are doing their best."

"I bet we could do better. Come on. You know you want to."

Did I? I wasn't so sure. The only thing I was sure about was that Eugene needed to get to heaven (sooner rather than later) and it was obviously my destiny to help him.

"I suppose I could call that detective again. What was his name—Collins? Maybe he has some new information."

Eugene glanced at me, a sly look coming over his face. "If you lost the number, you could always call Peter to get it. He's a nice guy, after all."

"Eugene, stop. You are so much like my mother sometimes it scares me."

"I'm just looking out for you. Your life was so boring before I moved in, that when I'm gone, I'm worried you will go into a decline or something. You're going to need someone in your life. Someone besides Nutter Butter."

"I can find my own someone."

"Yeah, but I don't trust your taste in men. And you aren't really looking hard enough. You need me to help you. Admit it." He bent over and patted Jezebel before continuing. "And finding you a decent man would be small repayment for you taking me in. And what else am I going to do with my time?"

"Take a class." I looked at Eugene, practically skipping to the car. Or maybe it was more floating. He wasn't so bad, I supposed.

"Hurry up, Pip-Squeak. You aren't getting any younger. And I think I want you to make Beef Wellington today."

I sighed for what must have been the hundredth time that day. Any charitable thoughts I was having quickly vanishing. "If we need to find out who killed you in order to get you out of my hair, that is exactly what we will do." Eugene would likely cause me to lose all my hair by the time I got rid of him.

He stopped and turned back to me. "This could be the beginning of a beautiful friendship, Pip," Eugene said, rather dramatically.

"Oh shut up, Eugene" I responded.

That was it. The television was definitely going.

www.ingramcontent.com/pod-product-compliance
Lightning Source LLC
Chambersburg PA
CBHW070746120726
47910CB00001B/180